THE
GOLD
COUNTER

A Mystical Fantasy About
Adventure, Companionship, Magic & Love

ANDREW P. WILD

Bobbie,
Thank you for all of
your wonderful energy.
Your output is incredible
and contagious!

Andy.

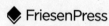 FriesenPress

One Printers Way
Altona, MB
Canada

www.friesenpress.com

Edited by Katherine Wild

ISBN
978-1-5255-8034-5 (Hardcover)
978-1-5255-8035-2 (Paperback)
978-1-5255-8036-9 (eBook)

1. FICTION, FANTASY, EPIC

Distributed to the trade by The Ingram Book Company

For Nan,
And for all the times we sat together,
watching our favourite shows and eating takeout.

You will be forever remembered.

ACKNOWLEDGEMENTS

For my sister, Amanda; mother, Kathie;
father, Paul; and my grandmother, Sonja.
Thank you for always believing in me.

For my mother especially:
Thank you for taking the time to go through my book,
page-by-page, just to review my work and
bless me with your magical editing skills.

••• I •••

"Twenty-two, twenty-three, twenty-four . . ."

The man continued to count. On one side of the desk was a large mess of gold coins; some had even spilled over onto his ancient, oak flooring. On the other side sat an abundance of neat piles of varying heights.

"Twenty-five," he said out loud as he moved the completed pile to the tidy side of his desk next to the other coin towers. Turning back to the messy side, he paused. The count had been going on for hours. When had the tallying begun? Shortly after sunup? That was thirteen or fourteen hours ago. At that moment, he was exhausted and the sun had already begun to set. His 87-year-old fingers were stiff and sore from the endless counting that had taken place that day. The sharp, tingling sensations made them feel as if they could snap at any second.

After a moment, he attempted to continue with his work. However, the elderly soul realized he could do no more. What had been done was substantial and no more could be done that eve. In fact, the old man had been at it for days.

One thousand two hundred and ninety-one finger-numbing, painfully tedious days, to be exact.

He glanced up at the cobweb-covered window. The sun wasn't shining anymore. It had begun its descent without him even noticing. With a sigh, he sat there staring out the window. It was the best time of day. A mirage of colours had been painted across the sky. Innocent clouds sat perfectly still against a backdrop of fuchsia and violet. Soon, the night sky would come creeping in. Though the heavens were showing their truest beauty, they were no comparison to the exquisiteness of the pureberry tree standing proudly just beyond the old man's window.

His office had always been his most cherished room and the tree seemed to breathe life into the room, from beyond the glass. The berries glowed a deep shade of crimson wine and so they should have! They were used to make bottle after bottle, with a delightful flavour.

The flavour of each pureberry was something akin to the combined flavours of a cherry and an orchard apple. Each pureberry dangling from the branches was nurtured by the gentle winds blowing across the meadow. And what's more, the flawless berries were pit-free, providing a well-deserving farmer with perfection.

The tree had been there longer than the man could remember and longer than the memory of his father! At some point, many thousands of moons ago, the seed of a tree had fallen and taken root. It was a flawless creation, the meadow's finest gift. For it wasn't just pleasing to the eye, it was the gift of food, of life.

Beyond that tree, lay rolling hills, scattered with endless pureberry trees. Some areas had one or two trees, at random, atop gentle hills, while others had many trees, clustered together. All of the trees grew divine, untouched fruit, waiting to be harvested by any passerby or lucky critter.

In fact, it was rare to find any other sort of vegetation, making the land entirely unique. For every hundred pureberry trees there would be only one tri-arch tree, its yew-like limbs standing slightly higher than the rest, never producing a single fruit, but instead, an enormous display of emerald leaves.

This landscape was tranquil. The gods had blessed it. Aside from the occasional wolf, there was nothing but trees, the odd bush, some ferns, and the abundant population of content little critters, mostly squirrels and rabbits who enjoyed their free roam.

For as far as anyone could ever remember, this particular vista had provided an unspoiled way of living for those lucky enough to find it in their journeys. Very few had stumbled upon this land, as it had been a hefty distance from the great nation's prominent trade route. Not many had reason to travel this far north though it had only been a one-week journey by horseback. It was, however, a great enough distance to keep the old man separated from society. And alive.

The Great Trade Route of Varroth had always been unpredictable. The farther a caravan traveled between cities, the more likely it was to encounter unlawful happenings. Due to the vast reaches of land, Varroth had been deemed to have areas of safety but it had its risky areas as well. The north-eastern paths were well known for snowstorms, especially in the mountains. The paths to the south became targets for bandits. The farther west you traveled the closer you came to the highlands and barren region. But then there was the eastern route. Though promising with the hopes of immaculate gems and magical underground essences, the paths to the east were far rockier and incredibly dangerous, more dangerous than any other route. At its final reach of the eastern route was Koraivindahl, Varroth's port-side capital and home to the land's so-called "gracious" royals.

The Great Trade Route connected the lands busiest cities and grand merchant trading venues. Dotted with villages and townships along the way, the route was used primarily by three groups: travelers, traders, and thieves.

With the sun setting, it was time for the old man to begin to his evening habits. Though he was far from completion, he still had a few days to meet his deadline. On a good day, he could count, stack, wrap and secure 2,400 individual packages, each consisting of exactly twenty-five coins. On a great day, or on a day when he was rushed to meet a deadline, the old man could stack 2,600 towers or more! On this particular day, he had only completed 1,800 stacks.

Rising slowly from the table, he was reminded of his father's rule from ages ago: there was a time for work and time for drink. Drink always came after the other, but never before. That was the time for drink.

He made his way out of his office, through a short hallway into the parlour. The house wasn't large at all; in fact, it had barely been big enough for both him and his wife. Upon entering the parlour, he passed the cookery, making his way toward a wicker chair that sat in the center of the tiny room. In front of his favorite chair was the fireplace, its brickwork more than a century old. It sat deep enough into the wall to hold a fair-sized cauldron for boiling stews and water for tea. The room itself also contained three cabinets, a small table for dining, some knit rugs and an eclectic collection of antiques.

Some of the time the house brought memories of his father, but more so of his own wife. It was kept clean for the most part. How could it not? The old man didn't have much, and that was fine. The furniture and items he possessed were functional. It was all he needed, aside from the odd glimmer of hope.

Hope that one day, he would see his wife again.

He worked his way across the small parlour to a cabinet with a broken lock. Inside were vials of important potions procured by his wife, a couple bottles of pureberry wine and mead, a bottle of potato vodka, a bottle of foxfire whiskey and a small bottle of ginger liqueur. The potions stood dusty, without labels. It had been so long since his wife had made the concoctions that he had forgotten their names, and kept them more as a reminder of her.

Throughout the years, his wife had crafted potions of an infinite variety. It was her ultimate art. He, himself, had never had the patience to study the art of fine alchemy and transformation. Since his wife was a little girl, she had made potions that cured diseases or caused them, depending on the need. Some potions allowed you to breathe underwater, while others made it impossible to breathe at all. Some made you wiser, stronger, more handsome. Some even made you appear younger. But these were only a few of the examples. After decades of work, his wife could create almost any potion imaginable, so long as she was given enough time and the right ingredients.

Alchemy was by far one of the toughest skills to master. It wasn't just a frog leg here, and an eye of bovine there. It required the concentration, willpower and diligence of only the smartest. One could study and practice alchemy for fifty years, but without the right level of perseverance and intellect, the only thing to show for it would be a lifetime of wasted energy. It was as if the right person was spiritually linked with the creation of such potions. After all, alchemy was dependent on a certain communication with the spiritual world and the magic contained within a human being. These essentials made the craft very rare, hence the lofty price.

❈ ❈ ❈

One day, a scout, sent by order of Varroth's Royal King, was exploring the bountiful land in search of fine resources when he had stumbled across the old couple's humble abode. Never before had they received visitors and so they invited him in. It didn't take long for the scout to realize that the old man's wife was an alchemist. His stay was short. He enjoyed a cup of tea and was quickly on his way.

A season later, twelve of the king's men rode up to the old man's home. Upon entry they expressed a desire to make a deal, one that would change the old couple's lives indefinitely. The king had need of a personal alchemist, a potion-maker who could brew important concoctions to aid those in battle. This request came as a result of a terrible vision that the king had of a war, brought to the gates and port of the Royal City that lined the Eastern Sea border.

In return for keeping his elderly wife safe while working within the palace, the old man received a promise that their land would remain a secret, untouched and secure.

Considering the location, it would be many years before anyone would find the meadow and settle down. The couple agreed, thinking only about living out their days in peace together. They agreed to the conditions, knowing that the old man's wife would be returned to him after a single year. It was either that or risk murder by the king's guard.

Since that day, three years had passed until finally, a single soldier returned holding an important letter:

My dear old soul,

Never in my life have I seen such talent in the hands of a single person. This woman's gift is truly something of the gods - I am completely astonished. It is because of this; however, that I bring unfortunate news.

Due to her exceptional powers, we have further need of her skills. It has not become clear to me when this war will take place, for I have not had any further visions of such an event, and for that uncertainty - I apologize. I am unsure of when or even if we can return her to you at all. I am not an unfair man and so I have a new proposal in mind.

Due to hard times in our kingdom, my counter has run off with a large sum of gold coins. It was supposed to be payment for my soldiers, and it is unlikely that I will be ready to trust another to take his place within the Royal City for some time. Here is my proposition: I wish for you to become my new coin counter - a cure for your everlasting longing and no doubt boredom.

If you would be willing to count my payroll for me, I can promise you that your wife will be returned to you safely. I cannot say when, but I can say it is my highest priority that she will be returned home as soon as her role here is complete.

Should you choose to agree to these conditions, I will put the wheels in motion, and send you instructions in the coming days.

I highly recommend that you consider this option.

At the bottom was the king's bold signature, scrawled in ink that appeared blacker than the Void itself.

Removing the whiskey and his only crystal glass from the cabinet, the old man slumped down into his chair. The cushioning moulded around his body perfectly. Sixty-three years of sitting in the same place will do that to a chair. Next to him, sat his wife's chair, identical in tightly woven wicker yet the shape pressed into its cushions was that of a petite figure. Her blanket was draped neatly over the back.

The old man took a moment to gaze at her chair. They had always been together out here, the two of them, happily confined to this tiny cottage in the golden meadows.

His father's father had built this cottage. That same man, once upon a time, had been a merchant who had followed the trade route to the south. It wasn't until a squad of bandits had run him off the road that he had came upon the meadow, exhausted. It was here in which the man made it his life's goal to erect a house and live in it with his wife.

Shedding a tear of sadness for his father, the old man turned back to the fireplace. Stroking his unkempt, whitened beard, he stabbed at the logs with a poker, reawakening the fire he had started earlier. As the flames warmed the room, he poured himself a glass of whiskey. At the bottom of his side table was a rickety shelf where he kept a pipe and a small linen cloth. It was wrapped tightly around a bundle of dried goreath thistle, his favourite smoking herb.

Once his pipe bowl was packed, he lit it with a twig from the embers. The full-bodied, earthy smoke filled his lungs, confirming that it was indeed the end of the day. Most men did not inhale this smoke without suffering nausea, but he was used to it and part of him didn't care anyway. What pleasures in life did he have left? After all, his wife was gone.

Was she alive?

What would happen to her?

Where was she?

The first sip of whiskey caused the man to sink further into his chair. Eighty-seven years ago, he was born into this house. His mother had passed during his birth and his father was the one who raised him. He was a good man of average height but heavier build, who spent many a day chopping wood for the warmth of his hearth.

When he wasn't woodcutting, he spent his time with his son: raising him, feeding him and teaching him everything he knew. One day, he left for the trade route with two crates of pureberry wine and a bundle of wool strapped to his horse.

He never returned.

Since that moment, the young boy feared the trade route. He was even terrified of traveling beyond the vicinity of his home. Over time, he taught himself to survive off the land by raising livestock and harvesting the pureberry bounty of the meadows. Sometimes, the hardest things to accomplish were the smallest, such as making rabbit traps and starting fires with flint.

Eventually, he overcame his fear and began traveling toward the trade route himself. By coincidence, traveling within one of the caravans heading west, was his future wife.

···2···

Thowmp! THOWMP!

The old man opened his eyes suddenly at the sound of his front door being hammered upon. For a second, he thought only of his wife. Then he realized that he had fallen into a whiskey-induced sleep. His pipe's seed long out, just like the ashes of his fireplace.

Thowmp! Thowmp! THOWMP! The noises increased in volume.

"Open up! King's Brigade!"

Shooting up out of his chair and stumbling as he did, the old man was forced into alertness. His aimed to reach the door before the men had a chance to smash through it. At his age, constructing a new front door would not be an easy task, or an enjoyable one at that.

"You have three second—"

The guard was cut off just as the old man swung the door open.

"We are here for the gold!"

How was it possible? The Counter had only been given seven moons to tally the rolls when it should have been fourteen!

"This cannot be! You haven't given me enough time!" choked the old man, his voice the sound of weathered parchment, scraping in the wind.

"Not my concern," snapped the lead guard, standing boldly in front of the two others, his uniform slightly dusty from days of travel.

His breeches ended in black leather boots fixed with copper buckles. His shirt, beige as it were, was adorned with a red cross sewn above his heart. Straps covered his torso. A sheathed dagger was strapped to his front and a sword hung from his belt. On his hands, he wore gloves that stretched tightly over his fingers but loosened along his forearms.

The other two men wore similar outfits, yet theirs were slightly more tattered and appeared to be in relatively inferior condition.

"With the war looming, the king has employed more soldiers that have already begun training." Lucky, as they were to serve the king, they too would be paid. "You will be counting the same amount as before, but now we will be here to collect it every seven moons."

Originally, the old man had agreed to count coins for the king every fourteen moons. As part of the agreement, a group of soldiers visited his house on a regular to ensure that he didn't escape with the gold.

"Impossible!" the elderly Counter cried out.

The argument was brief. The chance of him making any headway in the conversation soon became unlikely. There was no use in arguing; the old man gave in.

"Fair enough. I will see to it that the count is complete before your seven precious moons," he hissed, slamming the door in the guard's face. Immediately after, his feelings changed quickly from anger to anxiety as he waited for the captain and his men to remove themselves from his porch.

As the day wore on, the old man spent his time nervously pacing around his house, occasionally sipping a goblet of rum and puffing from his pipe. In an effort to calm down, he attempted to stack the coins, but failed. His focus was just not there.

How long until his time would be reduced to five moons? Three moons?

He peered out the window only to find the three men making themselves comfortable by the pureberry tree that stood at the front of his cottage. They chatted amongst themselves, periodically sucking back the liquor they kept in their hip flasks and chomping away on fallen berries. The scene continued for a while, until almost sundown before the captain raised his voice. He then jumped up and struck one of the men upside the head, causing him to stumble over a patch of rubble.

"You dare speak of my wife that way?! Do it again and you'll be chewing on these stones!"

Startled, the man clambered to his feet, anger brimming in his eyes. He was clearly older than the rest; his skin had been darkened by many years of harsh sun exposure. The valleys of his face told tales of constant alcohol consumption. The other man, in his forties, just like the captain, stood bravely in the foreground of the discussion.

The captain went on, "The next word you speak to me, should be of the utmost respect, I warn you. Furthermore, if you have any dream of being paid once we return, you can start by pouring me another," he said to the older fellow, as he handed him a branded flask, motioning towards the keg-horse.

Without another word, the older guard made his way to the barrel, obeying the order. Afterwards, the men remained silent. Periodically, they would stroll into the meadow, returning with the carcass of a rabbit caught in their traps. Eventually, the crew built a pyramid of kindling and lit it with a few strikes of flint. It didn't take long for the fire to reach its fullest as it had been fuelled with hay. Relaxation and the intoxication of drink had begun to set in as the men started roasting the rabbits upon skewers that they had fetched from their saddlebags.

For the old man within his home, boredom soon became his primary state of mind, taking over from anxiety. He was too nervous to sleep and too edgy to relax. He stared at the men from his window until evening brought with it a hollow darkness. The men were too busy drinking to notice the man watching.

Eventually, fatigue set in. The old man silently locked his door, and headed to his bed that was big enough for two, but at the moment only slept one. An undying loneliness had set in the night his wife was taken, much like that of a festering wound. Although he lay there for many hours, sleep had still not been on his side. As the night went on, an irregular stream of shouting and hearty laughter from the drunken soldiers within his front yard constantly disturbed him. He stared into the rafters of his cozy sleeping chamber.

He had to leave.

He had to search for his wife.

There was nothing but memories here.

It was at that moment his memory seemed to serve him well as he recalled that his wife had been working on a potion she called her "Elixir of Youth."

She tested it on their farm animals, pouring it into the wooden drinking troughs for their cows and pigs. She even sampled some of it herself. Though she tried variations of ingredients, none seemed to work reliably. Some vials contained enough magical essence to slow the speed at which the animals aged, some seemed to contain the opposite. Some vials killed the animals and some didn't. Of course, at the time, the sample she tested on herself had been deemed safe by her way of testing.

Through tiresome years, trial after trial, the Elixir of Youth underwent hundreds of tests. The potion itself changed in colour, vibrancy and viscosity. At one point, the old man remembered, it shined with a kind of fiery, clear pink light that seemed to glow, even in the darkest of night. The next day, after she had finished altering the recipe, it changed to a forest green that looked so rejuvenating, not even a glass of pureberry wine stood to compete. Her infamous potion changed from green, to cobalt, to hazel, to tan, and sometimes even to a deep, royal purple on a daily basis.

Shortly before her unexpected departure, she felt she had almost solved the problem. The Elixir of Youth was nearing completion. It stood, in all its glory, in a single test vial, a strain of formula that was the purest color of liquid gold ever seen by the eye of man. Its beauty alone made it nearly impossible to resist. Even more remarkable, the contents would decrease the drinker's age *by three quarters of their original years!*

But with the age reduction, came a great consequence, as the potion had never been perfected. Once the person's age had been reduced, the speed at which the person subsequently grew older increased. This served as a cruel punishment for consuming the formula during its incomplete phase, meaning that a person could age a single year in just three and a half days. The Elixir of Youth worked, but it was madness. Suicidal, as any wise man would agree.

It was the old man's only option if he wished to embark on a journey to save his wife.

The man protected that vial from possible intruders by hiding it in the back of the upper shelf in the liquor cabinet, behind the other liquor and fine wines. It had faded from its perfect golden yellow to a dull, cloudy, greyish liquid. The contents of the vial were not recorded on the outside. Though his knowledge of his wife's alchemy was limited, the old man did retain some idea of its valuable limitations. Some elements lost their effectiveness in potions nearly immediately after being mixed, whereas some remained true and correctly functioning for years, perhaps forever.

He had to find out the ingredients in the Elixir of Youth. Then he would have the information he needed before consuming such a substance. The old man bounded out of his warm bed and made his way to his wife's laboratory.

※ ※ ※

Alchemy and botany are frequently connected, likely due to the commonality of their ingredients. More often than not, a new surprise would be waiting when the old man entered the laboratory. Depending on the season, the lab was home to an infinite variation of vibrant plants and ingredients, some of which included a collection of wild animals and gruesome insects. They were great for performing tests on, but more importantly they were harvested for their parts. It was surprising what one could create with a chicken brain or perhaps the squelchy innards of a silver river eel.

But alas, the past three years had left the lab in a state of decay and sadness. It was the one room where the old man chose never to wander. Wiping aside his mounting tears, he pushed open the door and walked over to the desk, which stood proudly in the center of the room. The area was stuffed with books, papers, dead plants, lanterns, vials, and everything else one could imagine in the laboratory of a true alchemist.

Despite the fact that the guards were out front getting as twisted as the desert winds, the old man knew he had to work quickly as their drunkenness was moving them along a path of unpredictability. At any moment, one of them could come bursting through the front door. The old man blocked out the noise of the outdoor events and began searching the clutter for the recipes pertaining to the Elixir of Youth.

Some moments passed and to his surprise, he found the recipe rather quickly in the second drawer he looked in. Come to think of it, it was rather odd the king's men did not pillage the lab for all its worth when they came for his wife in the first place.

The light from the fireplace in the main room was not bright enough to read, so he lit his lantern, pulling it close as he unrolled the recipe.

ANDREW P. WILD

THE ELIXIR OF YOUTH

For best results, use 2 standard boiling flasks and 1 standard mixing flask paired with an alchemy table with fixation magic. The qualities of all items listed should be in their purest essence form and original origin. Regarding the order in which to mix, consult the Tomes {Tri-Form Witchcraft, Black Magic, and Alchemy}.

Failure to follow any of the instructions may result in death or serious suffering.

- 1 full dropper of blood belonging to that of a baby prairie snake
- ½ vial of moonglow mushroom husk (pre-roasted and ground into dust)
- 2 spoons of prairie bee honey
- ⅛ of an imp pouch of fine emerald dust
- 4 spoons of goat milk (pre-treated with "suftweed" to avoid expiry)
- The juice of 1 adult pureberry – must be juiced at night.

Upon use of proper ingredients, correct time of day, ritual, and precise power of imbuing, the ingredients thus far shall be entirely united but not finalized until proper flame boil. Once bubbling has occurred, reduce the temperature before removing from flame.

Place in direct sunlight for at least an entire afternoon.

As far as my research is concerned, this recipe requires one more ingredient until 100% finalization and publication of this private concoction. Until then, this is a draft – not to be tampered with, or used by any other.

Each ingredient seemed long-lasting to the old man - all of them except for the juice of one adult pureberry. Even the healthiest of pureberries only really lasted thirteen moons before turning into a discoloured mess of mouldy mush. Then again, it was just a pureberry. How much of an impact could it really have? He certainly wasn't drinking the Elixir for flavour either.

So, it was decided. He would drink the Elixir of Youth. It was his only chance to save his one true love, and escape this empty life of loneliness.

He extinguished the lantern's flame quickly, and left the laboratory, shutting the door behind him. As he made his way to the liquor cabinet, a loud shout erupted from the front yard.

"EMPTY? How in the Devil's Chariot can we be empty?"

The disturbing yell came from the head guard, causing the old man to make his way to the liquor cabinet at a much quicker pace.

"Nonsense!" exclaimed one of the others, "We brought two kegs!"

"Then how is it that I return from the keg-horse bearing witness to only one?"

"It was him!" the third guard piped up, "He drank the rest of that keg and dumped the barrel along the way!"

"Bullshit! You prick! You should know better than to report on those you seek to be like!" the oldest of the three spoke with a great slur in his voice.

"This much must be true! Upon departure, the king granted us loads of gear. Some of it unnecessary sure, but by the Divine's way, I would never forget that we were given two

kegs!" proclaimed the captain, animosity strongly building within. "You drunk old fool! You couldn't keep your damn hands off. You bloody well knew we were in this; the three of us, deserving of our shares, but you just couldn't resist!"

A sudden, loud clatter of equipment and debris erupted. Obviously, a brawl had broken out, presumably amongst the oldest and the captain. For the old man, time was running out. He planned on grabbing the Elixir of Youth, drinking it, and returning to bed before one of the guards came busting through the front door in search of more liquor.

Pop!

He pulled the cork from the vial.

A strange aroma, reeking of mold, filled the air. It was indeed the stink of a pureberry that had long since seen its last day. Nonetheless, it was time to drink.

He raised the cylindrical vial to his weathered lips.

And that's when the chaos began.

··· 3 ···

The front door burst open with the force of ten men. The quietest of the three guards stood panting in the doorway; he was just as drunk as the rest. A fire that burned in the voices of the other guards also showed vigorously in the young man's eyes. It took mere seconds for him to make his way towards the old man and his liquor cabinet when he then realized the elder had been holding the vial to his lips.

"Whattya got there?" questioned the guard loudly and with suspicion.

"As if an old dog can't have a calming drink, especially with such drunkards ripping my property to pieces!" the old man covered the invaluable elixir with his hand.

"A drink?" fired the guard, motioning to the vial in the man's shaky hand. "Drinks do not come in vials. That which comes in such a vial must have a magical property. And what's more, if you were to kill yourself now or transform into some kind of rash wizardry, we would surely be sunk by His Majesty!"

It was at that moment or never. The moment that defined the future of the old man was upon him. He dumped the

Elixir of Youth down his throat, the essence of mold only hampering him slightly.

"Bastard!" shouted the guard.

As if moved by the wind itself, the guards swooped over the old man, grabbing him by the scruff of his neck, as one would a cat, knocking his glasses to the wooden floor. The guard raised his boot and deliberately smashed the old spectacles. His hand struck the old man across the face. Tears began to well in his ancient eyes.

"What you just drank will soon be covering the floor of your kitchen!" roared the guard drunkenly, punching the old man directly in the heart of his belly.

The pain was immense, and yet another blow sent the old man farther into the tunnel of pain, nausea building quickly. *"Stop!"* wheezed the old man, the single word barely passing through his lips.

"You will stop!" The captain appeared in the doorway, just as the old man belched up a mouthful of liquid onto the floor.

"What is this!?" roared the captain. "You idiot! If you kill this man, you can forget your job, never mind your pay! I'll discipline the *shit* out of you here and now!"

The frantic guard looked from the old man to the smashed vial and then to the captain, "He was trying to poison himself! I came up to grab some whiskey from 'im, an' he was holding a vial of poison! I been' trying to jostle it out of him, he may as well be dead right now! I just—"

"Enough!"

Then all was quiet. Clearly something had happened to the oldest guard as he was nowhere to be seen. The attacker and the old man stared intently at the captain just as a gentle breeze brought the scent of honey blossom and delicate pureberry through the front door. A smell that one would associate with a pretty girl, accustomed to a lifestyle of wealth and pleasantry.

"This is true?" asked the captain.

"I . . . no . . . of course not!" answered the old man.

The breeze settled, and the cabin, once again filled with the strong scent of liquor-filled men.

"Well?" the captain again.

"It is my wife's potion! I use it to sleep. Sometimes I am caught pondering a world of thought and horror, and I take it to settle my nerves. This time however, it has been because of three damn fools. Might I remind you that I am tasked with counting your—"

"Shut up!" yelled the captain, stepping forward, his boots making heavy, threatening sounds that rattled the heart. He pushed the guard out of the way.

"I'll take a whiskey," ordered the captain, his hands already in the liquor cabinet.

"Take what you will."

And with that, the captain and his guard grabbed four of the largest bottles and headed out the front door. The night was long, but it was about to be longer with such a substantial amount alcoholic ammunition.

Pain was still lingering in the old man's body. He stood, leaning against his dining room table. It was a wonder he was able to stand. His thoughts were ever changing. Had he thrown it all up? What remained in his system, coursing through his veins? What if the elixir had failed?

Fear soon became the driver. His old chair by the fireplace beckoned to him to seek its refuge. However... sleep? Not likely.

Violence and turmoil aside, it took only a few moments of lighting, puffing and repacking his pipe to send the old man into a state of unconsciousness as he slumped into his lounge. His poor decrepit body ached, his muscles burned, especially those lining his tired torso and belly. Age had required more time to heal wounds, but perhaps, not for much longer . . .

Pristine.

Such a word could only describe the scene. The old man stood upon a sheet of ice, floating through a series of enormous, aquamarine glaciers. The sun, bright, as it lit the surrounding, motionless icebergs like pillars of massive diamonds. The sheet of ice itself, on which he stood, floated freely upon the surface of the black abyss of water below. Drifting effortlessly into a direction of nothingness. It was . . . blissful.

The water, dark and with limitless depth, carried the old man. Above, in the sky, a raven floated languidly - its colour not quite normal.

Not black, no.

Not black at all.

It was more like cyan and periwinkle, as seen on maps depicting an array of luscious, blue valleys.

Where was he?

He should have been worried, but he felt nothing but serenity. No one mattered, nothing to care for. Was this . . . death? But this atmosphere seemed like magic, warmed by the sun, yet not melting. This place brought feelings of relaxation and purity. The old man was truly calm.

Turning his attention from the frost raven floating around the beaming, midday sun, to the crystal-clear water on the horizon, he noticed something. Directly in the middle of two glaciers, a fin appeared. Was it prehistoric? It seemed to swim without direction, zigging and zagging as if without a goal.

Suddenly, it turned, and started heading towards the man. Had it seen him? This beast?

Before long, it had built up a ferocious speed. Albeit far away, it was like staring across a town square at an unknown animal that continued to close its distance, gaining speed. As it did, the fin became clearer, rising out of the water with gashes and lacerations. Seconds passed before it had covered half of the span, its body beginning to rise. The beast was an enormous predator of sorts. It was charging with full steam through the water, causing rapids of spray to shoot out left and right.

Then the nose burst out of the water, followed by the gaping mouth, with its rows of razor teeth. The old man began to scramble.

Death was coming for him. Screaming at him.

The jaws of the beast opened wide as it engulfed the man and the entire platform upon which he stood. It consumed him - whole. The blades on its teeth ripped, scored and slit open every inch and morsel of the old man as he smashed violently around his prison of razors and spear tipped teeth.

"*Gaaaaaah—*"

His cry was severed, just as his head was from his very torso.

The abruptness of his dream caused his eyelids to fly open. The old man jolted out of the chair and came crashing to the floor.

He gasped and choked as he convulsed on the floor, grasping the leg of the table. The dream, as vivid as it was, also the most horrific vision he had ever experienced.

While calming himself down from his panic, he sat up slowly and peered out the open front door.

The guards lay still, poisoned by the liquor. They were fast asleep in a whiskey-induced slumber. The oldest of the three was lying closest to the fire, or what was left of it. He was covered in bruises. The captain and other guard lay propped up against each another.

As the old man rose, a surge of energy and fortitude bloomed, taking over his body. A reminder of his youth, his spirit was stretching its beautifully crafted and ever giving wings ready to take flight. Glancing at his reflection in the mirror, it had become clear that the Elixir of Youth had worked . . . with flawless perfection.

The impossible had become real.

The world suddenly seemed under-qualified for his level of ability and strength. The body of an ancient soul suddenly flared with the unstoppable flow of raw energy. His hands, smooth and masculine, were no longer tainted with liver spots. His skin was tightly wrapped around his muscles and his chest beamed with confidence and hardy iron.

Age was of a lesser problem, but for only so long. From this moment forward, he would have to be quick if he were planning on saving his wife. He could only remain this way for so long and the aging process had already activated. Though no signs had begun to show in the few short moments lit by candlelight, it was only a matter of days.

The first obstacle was the guards out front. Escaping would only lead to further trouble. They could come after him. It wouldn't be hard, even without any tracking experience.

After the investment of time and speculation, it became clear that this would be the beginning of his journey. They were corrupt men. The words and actions in their drunken speech had summoned up images of their evil spirit, especially when it came to the tales of their so-called "wives" and other peasants within their stories of travel. To think of it – one would be senseless not to punish these fools. Who could possibly walk up on an old man, badger him, threaten him, and beat him only to carry on with a simple night of drinking? No, these men had earned punishment. Iniquity and destructive ruling through false promise had been their way . . . but no longer.

Bounding silently to the door with newfound energy, he peered out. With time on his side, every decision was made immediately. Without further ado, he spun around to the kitchen returning momentarily to the door with his meat cleaver, sharpened only days before, for he certainly didn't have a sword.

The drums beat from within his chest as he approached the men. A heartbeat this strong would have killed his older, former self. With the fire extinguished, the guards were lit with the bountiful white light that shone from the Moonstone and the Divines above. They stood watch supremely above, but with some approval for what the boy was about to do.

"Quickly," he told himself. "Quickly with this weighted blade, and so begins my journey."

He approached the captain whom was slumped next the young guard and stood directly over him, blocking out the moon. The Gold Counter's eyes fixated on the captain's awkwardly stretched neck which displayed a bold, beating vein.

Raise the cleaver. Strike.

It was so simple, yet impossible. Eighty-four years later and his only 'murders' consisted of his farms animals, the worst being his cattle, and all for the greater good of survival, of course. But this was not of bovine matter. Besides, this choice was for his wife. The time was right.

The boy held his breath, and began counting. At five, he would bring the blade through the guard's neck and with such savagery, begin his adventure.

One . . .

Two . . .

The meadow wind swept gently across his face.

Three . . .

Four . . .

And—

This was a bad plan. He lowered the cleaver. It would only be days before more guards came to check on the ones that didn't return. If he could hide and then administer a quick, clean death then his chances would be better.

The captain burped noisily and shifted his position.

The boy thought of the elements of poison and paralysis that were scattered around his wife's laboratory, but he knew he could not press these guards into consuming them. Perhaps if he were still old and with previous resemblance, he could have brought them out a bottle of whiskey, infused with castor root - a bitter tasting, poisonous plant that lay shrivelled atop her desk.

No. He had done this all wrong. He could not escape. He needed to get the guards down to the pond behind his house. It was big enough, and with the depth of the sewer well, it could consume their bodies without sign of ever being there. No one would look for them there and the fish would eventually feed on their weighted bodies. At that point, all he had to do was make it look like a robbery; He had to pack most of the coins in his office, somehow strapping them onto the militia horses.

That plan was better. It had a way out. The only problem was getting the guards to the water in order to drown them, but how? Had they slept enough to sober up? Would they wake only to a simple movement? One guard would have been no match for this newfound strength of his, but three men provided a much greater challenge.

The moon continued to shine, but only then with a hint of departure.

···4···
AGE: 24

One would be quite surprised by the number of compounds found within the workshop of an alchemist. It was common even in a lab belonging to a purely virtuous conjurer to find harsh ingredients. For example, the most common potion used for curing those contaminated with minor plague symptoms during the Black Span, consisted of pufferfish bile (that of the river, *not* the ocean) and doomshade, a plant that thrives in musty, filthy conditions such as the sewers in most cities. When properly mixed and imbued by the right hand, the potion worked to mend the internal wounds of countless numbers of innocent peasants. It was the combining procedure that made it key.

Another example of such a compound: the innards of a spoon slug. Most commonly found in marshy overgrowth, the blood of a spoon slug was known to paralyze any who came in contact with it. Though the paralysis is not lethal, it does take a short while to kick in, depending on which section of the victim's body becomes infected. It is written that if the innards come in close contact with an individual's heart, the victim will become paralyzed at a much quicker rate than those who become infected through the hand or the foot.

The most commonly found of these slugs was the "sydra" spoon slug. The Gold Counter's wife would go in search of these during her multiple day journeys in her younger years. But out here in the meadows, one had to walk at least half a day before finding the right marsh; home to the sludgy sacks of immobility.

Perhaps he could poison a blade and impale the guards, one by one, just enough to cause paralysis. Surely his wife had kept a slug under preservation somewhere within her lab.

He entered his wife's domain once again, and searched the darker recesses of the tiny room for a jarred slug or two. With luck, it took but minutes for the boy to source out a glass container of sydra specimens.

The preservation jelly was the same texture as what one would spread over a piece of bread, and cutting into the long-dead slug was like butter. Its olive-green body, speckled with flecks of black and salmon, was nearly the size of man's hand. The slug split gracefully when the boy applied his sturdy meat knife. Its innards, purple.

Carefully, without managing to cover his fingers in this slightly sting-inducing form of liquid matter, he slathered the end of the blade generously and wiped the remaining innards into an empty jar nearby. For the full effect, he was going to have to re-coat the knife before each gouging.

The guards, still dozing, were unaware of their fates.

The boy approached the captain. For whatever reason, the thought of taking him out first was oddly satisfying.

This was a process of agility and speed. And this time, there was no waiting. He was just going to go through with it: first the captain, then his supporter, followed by the old drunk. The boy tipped the blade downward, in an effort to get the full amount of the poison to coat it. With a quick movement, he nicked the captain directly across his heart.

"Awwugh!" The shouting was immediate and accompanied by a full-body jolt to the reaction. The captain peered down at his chest, just as the Gold Counter retracted his knife and prepared to attack the next guard.

"What the hell are you doing!?" blasted the guard with a deafening volume, clambering for his sword, which lay on a boulder behind him.

Before the next guard knew what was happening, reality had set in for him. The boy ran his blade across the guard's chest just as he had the last. At this point, the first guard was on his feet brandishing his short sword. He lashed out and missed the Gold Coutner's neck by inches; the boy dodged the blade with an impressive pace.

"I don't know who you think you are, *boy,* but you've welcomed the void's hand now!"

By the luck of the gods, the eldest, still very drunk, stumbled over a rocky out jut, sending himself crashing forward which presented the boy with the opportune moment. He slashed through the guard's uniform, and into his leathery skin, sending several trajectories of blood squirting from his back.

What had been a night of misfortune soon became a batted eye of hope. The guard jumped back up to his original stance and spun vigorously, expecting a sword or two to come hurling his way. Alas, he was incorrect. The venom of his spoon slug had begun to take affect. The captain and his partner were in much different positions, laying upon the grass. The only movement they could make was with their eyes. Like an ant to tree sap, they were stuck, both in physical and mental realms.

The Gold Counter turned back to the drunk, who was attempting to get up - he too failed. As a result of his gashes, the serum of paralysis was seeping into his veins. He came crashing down to the earthy floor.

··· 5 ···

Proud and shocked, the boy stood amongst the three bodies. Twenty seconds of fortitude had brought this gift to him. The paralysis had an unknown working time, sending him straight to work in the business of "bodies-to-pond." As the modest body of water behind his house was not visible from the front yard, it would no doubt provide an excellent hiding spot.

He made quick-like, as the worst was over. One by one, he dragged the immobilized guards down to the water's edge, made prayer to the individuals, and prepared to conduct the unspeakable. It was barbaric, yes, but it had to be done for him to achieve his one true goal.

Their bodies fit perfectly, after some rearranging, into the monstrous chest he had removed from his office. What had once held the king's gold earlier that evening, held the king's men.

He dumped the chest in the water and quickly dove in after it. With extensive pushing and shoving, and consistent breaks to return to the surface for air, the boy managed to finally position the chest at the deepest part of the pond. Out of sight, but most certainly not out of mind. Eventually, the bodies themselves would begin to dissipate, leaving only the pearliest of skeletons crammed in a box.

The darkness of the night sky had long since been diminished. The moon had set, and the florescent phases of rose, tangerine and plum had begun to touch the eastern vault of the heavens. Birds woke and chirped with the freedom of a new day, its welcoming glory.

Once inside, the preparation for his quest had been simple. The mental note he had made of the required items for his quest, short. It was based on the contents of his home.

- 3 loaves of bread
- ½ a wheel of pressed goat cheese
- 2 bottles of red wine
- the remaining half of a pureberry pie
- 1 hand-sized flint rock
- 2 bundles of venison jerky
- 1 bundle of fine kindling wrapped in a cloth
- 1 preserved spoon slug
- 1 additional vial of (*presumably*) the Elixir of Youth
- the captain's short sword embossed with a crescent moon

And last but certainly most important:

- a handsome sum of the king's gold coins, to be packed into the empty liquor keg atop of the guard's packhorse

Granted, he would be a year older within the next three and a half days his journey ahead was to be of top speed. He was about to start moving toward the first village along his path: Faulkstead. At least then he could rest, have something to eat and regather vigor.

It wasn't long before the boy had packed the horse with the thousands of coins, tightly wrapped in dried "finger" leaves provided by the Red Hand, making it easier to transport the coins from house to horse. Weight was the key aspect to bear in mind when going on an adventure, or quest in this case. Not too much so as to weigh down the horse or horses, which in itself could cause a multitude of problems, but enough to get from place to place.

The coins wrapped, sealed, and deposited in the keg, he made quick work of the rest of his jobs. Luckily, the trade route, with the weight of his items would take only three days at a steady pace. Taking into consideration, of course, that traveling at night was much more dangerous.

He packed his travel bag and attached it to the saddle of the lead stallion. Orist had always been his strongest horse, capable of enduring any climate and terrain within reason. He made acquaintance with the other horses, totalling four in all. Each of the guards' horses looked as though they had seen better days.

Saddled and set, the tide of time pulled out, grasping at the young boy's newfound intellect and soul. He returned to the site of the skirmish in his front yard and surveyed it. It felt like searching a fully stocked baker's pantry for the remnants of mouse droppings. Without clean perfection, surely a king's man of keen eye would notice something askew upon return. Should that be the case, the next move would be searching for the bodies of the missing men.

Not a drop of blood or twig was left to give away the event that had happened at the heart of the evening. A feeling of cleverness and wit was given as self-praise when he had moved from the site, downwind toward the pond. Nothing. And that was how it should have been. No one would have noticed the drag marks in the grass. That said, he spent extra time re-smoothing grass blades in one area, and trampling them in the next to even out the field. To settle his paranoia, he released his herd of sheep amongst the grasses from their confinement. Surely, their hoof marks and continuous hunger would cover what he hadn't.

He returned to the front door of his house, and then to his office. This time, his house felt different, smaller, and increasingly mournful. The melancholy energy of the counting room filled him with despair. He cursed the room, both at it and in it, but then, he realized it would be that room he would probably miss the most. For it had not always been "the counting room". It was his space and it always would be until whoever came upon it. Eighty-four years, and he had not only watched his father live within that room, it had been handed down to him. The room had truly matured him from boy, to man, to elder. It bore witness to the remarkable return of time. The four walls made him who he was, and he was to leave it all behind. To think the room would one day embrace him again was as foolish as a thought could be.

He slid his desk aside along the hard planks and centred it against the wall, covering the area where the chest had been. The room was an absolute jumble of incessant clutter. Papers, coins, quills, inkpots, hardwood surfaces, empty wooden boxes, full wooden boxes, lamp blubber, lamps, empty wine bottles, leather satchels, wooden plates, tin goblets. All of which had been kept in their place because this was his way of "organization".

It was the coin that mattered at that moment. There must have been another sixty thousand or so gold shillings within the confines of his soon to be abandoned headquarters. Sixty thousand!

The idea that his return was possible left him conflicted about abandoning the money. Should he hide it? Where?

Sixty thousand gold shillings was enough to provide incredible opportunities. One could build a massive house on an extraordinary plot of land, more than enough for himself, his wife and their three children for their entire lives. It would put the children through any college; provide them with homes, a lifetime of food, and then some!

No, such an enormous amount of coin could not be abandoned. He had to hide it.

With the bed vertical against the wall and the floorboards pried up, he dug the money pit. Even the thought of uncovering such a mass of gold was spine-rattling. He moved every bit of gold into the bedroom until it lay heaped in mountains next to him.

With his trusty shovel he dug and hollowed, the clay of the earth resting upon his bed sheets. Amused, he plopped every last coin into the pit. The sound of the shillings colliding represented the ultimate revenge.

He filled the pit and levelled the clay once again, stomped on it to ensure a flat surface and dragged the rest of the earth, wrapped in sheets, out back to the pond. He dumped the contents into water, and returned with the dirty sheet. He packed the floorboards back together, ensuring they looked exactly the same as before. Finally, he made the bed with his ancient blanket and made sure the bedroom still had a "forever untouched" homey feel of trinkets and odd furniture.

Bags packed, dirty blanket secured and gold sealed, the time had come to venture forth. This newborn life, destined to be short-lived. The grapes of eternity had been juiced of their forgiveness, and this was his time to travel.

The boy climbed atop his favoured Orist and set forth southbound toward the trade route. Accompanied by the other three horses, the party of five had begun their journey. The path ahead lay sparsely traveled upon, touched by only rabbits' feet and the occasional guard that would no longer find the lad within his residence.

Upon nearing the peak of his first effortless summit he looked back upon his home that stood within the meadow. Peace laid claim to his mind.

The chimney stood dormant, as did the pureberry trees undone by the sweet breezes of the west. The sheep had finished their meal behind his home, and soon began to work their way into the forest. Everything was tranquil. Its blissfulness awaited the works of nature to take its toll.

···6···
AGE: 25

It was the eve of the second day into his travels. One more and he would arrive at the grand route. The journey had started out most calm.

Hard as it was to believe, the boy, formally the old man, had never been to any city beyond the reaches of the pureberry meadows. He did, however, have the knowledge of all of the main cities, as well as their interior parameters. Though he and his wife kept to themselves in the northern meadows, the tomes of knowledge stored within their attic, product of occasional trade route visits, held a great deal of information and vast histories. The boy had made sure to keep his wife up to date with the happenings upon the travel route. The caravans transported all sorts of goods as they traveled every five days or so.

This world, once populated by the simplest of nature's creatures, had long since developed into one of trade and prosperity. In doing so, this Royal Trade Route became established, and had existed for many eras.

It had started with the early settlers who had arrived via ships on the eastern coast formerly known as Varroth, or "The Royal City". At that very moment, this city belonged to the king, and was labeled royal. In doing so, the city was granted the name "The Royal City". Its correct name: Koraivindahl, Sea City of the East, pronounced for the first time nearly five hundred years ago. After the first settler to "make it so," Merek Sidanthis of Ravenshire (a city from the Eastern World,) had found its ever giving reaches. He had begun construction immediately. His unending leadership abilities enabled him to bring the area into the age of the Gold Era. With swiftness, each wall of The Royal City rose out of the sand, the grass, and the dirt. Named after Merek's only love: Rose Koraivindahl of Ravenshire, the name was really quite a mouthful. Over the years, "The Royal City" had become a more commonly coined title.

Years passed, and multiple towns began to dot the ever-growing lands, which eventually developed into this, the Magnificent Kingdom of Varroth. Some of them turned to cities, whilst some kept the sleepiness of small villages. Regardless of size, the desire for literally everything imaginable became apparent, and the Royal Varroth Trade Route was born. What started out as the odd caravan with the contents of cured meats, mead, and fortified wine, exploded into the provisions from the four corners of the world. Weapons, horses, and building materials were among the earlier trades, then came jewelry, art, and fine foods. Soon enough, the area was spilling at the brim. There was trade of magic scripture, potions, foreign plant life, domesticated pets, pottery, silver, art of various clay and tile forms, even humans.

As a frequent visitor of the route, the boy had traveled along it often, and in doing so acquired a collective knowledge of the existing kingdom. It was not uncommon to see a member of the land ride up to the convoys of shipments, so long as they were checked first by the guards that accompanied them. Security was always tight and extra fortified. Though shipments had been robbed several times in the past century along the route, one could travel relatively safely between cities with the caravans, for a price of course.

The boy had made a point in his previous lifetime, of acquiring a book or two on various subjects when he visited the route. Usually, he would wait beside the road, in somewhat of a bushy area, in hopes of trading for something to make his life easier – such as flint, new blades, and clothing. At others times, he was sent by his wife to happily and hopefully collect new ingredients from the traveling potionists to aid in her alchemy concoction at the time. But regardless of his journey for such specifics, the boy had always made sure to bring home more knowledge. Living in such a perfect area was nice, but throughout his entire life he had lusted for more knowledge about the Kingdom of Varroth.

One could ask of him "How many people lived in the town of Iron Creek?" and 108 would be his answer. Another could ask, "How would you describe the differences in monarchy between the Eastern and Western ruling families of this Holy Nation?" His answer would provide insight and names of every individual from within the kingdom.

So, it could be easy to mistake the boy, or in the previous case, the old man, for nothing more than a farmhand. But those who met him along Varroth's cross-country trail were surprisingly mistaken!

He sipped from a bottle of pureberry wine. With all the deliciousness that flooded his mouth, he only wished he had brought a goblet. Drinking from the neck of a wine bottle was so . . . primitive? Besides, the aroma and flavour were all the more enjoyable when sipped from a chalice.

He rested, propped up on his side by his elbow, peering into the campfire he had built. Somewhere along the way he had attracted the attention of a spirit. Unbeknownst to him, it had accompanied him to the fire. Most likely just looking for the warmth of human comfort, it sat two feet above a log next to him. It had no face, nor did it have a body, or even a voice for that matter. It was just a faint, pale glowing ball of powdery blue.

The ghost was friendly. It meant no harm, human spirit indeed, but not angry. Every now and then in his home, north of where he currently was, a random ghost would visit. Each time, it was a different one. They were just spirits travelling along their own journeys. To see a spirit with a face was extremely unlikely, as it was usually related to a lifetime of previous frustration. The boy was more accustomed to the orb-form of spirits.

It was easy to disassociate from the spirits. Most were respectful and understanding. When requested to leave, a spirit in these meadows, would simply do so.

So, it was nice. Sometimes the journey to the route was boring and the occasional silent company was welcome.

"It is a fine evening for travel!" proclaimed the boy.

The spirit remained the same. In hopes to get some reaction, the boy spoke up once again.

"Are you from these parts, spirit?"

Again, the ghost had just remained, bobbing ever so gently in place. Was it sleeping? Can spirits sleep? The ghost had accompanied him along his way for the better part of the evening, as soon as the sun began to set. The notion of silence and also serenity was strong between the two. The boy decided to change his focus to his wine, and the loaf of bread he had drawn from his bag. The wine was a nice blend and as he munched on his bread, he remembered the goat cheese.

Unfolding the cloth that surrounded it, he pulled chunks of the magnificent cheese from the half wheel. Ah . . . such a divine taste could have only been a product produced purely by the heavens themselves.

Fulfillment became the central feeling. The relaxation of the evening was reward for all that had happened. The boy dined on his meal of dairy and wheat. The horses dined on the untouched grasses of the meadow and the ghost dined on the company of the boy and the horses.

··· 7 ···

The piercing cry of a jester hawk brought life to the meadow the next morning. With a jolt, the boy awakened, startled by the unexpected shriek. He lay on his back, clutching his bag partially for the safety of it, and partially for its warmth. Dawn had brought fresh sunshine, blanketing all that was in its wake with just the right amount of morning heat.

Again - the jester hawk cried out, this time even louder than before.

"How annoying," thought the boy. This bird's name was certainly perfect for such an animal. The primary motive for the hawk was the same as all living creatures: eat, breed, sleep, repeat. However, the jester hawk, which was found in various regions across the kingdom, was well known for waking up travelers and any other sleeping beings. Furthermore, it was worse than the average raven when it came to stealing food, sometimes right out of journeymen's bags! To the jester hawk, it was enjoyable. There was no other reason for it. It just being one big game, hence the name "jester." Silly as it was, the gods had put all beings in this world for a reason, although the boy never could understand the purpose of the jester hawk.

The ghost was gone, and the fire had died out. It was time to set forth, another half day and he would arrive at the route.

Horses unhitched from the nearby poplar tree, he packed what was left of his wine and began to wake his mind. Tea would most certainly have been another nice item to have. Nevertheless, he was well prepared.

Perhaps the day would bring more peace than the hawk. The boy was looking forward to the next pond. It was time for his lips to taste pure aqua and the horses definitely deserved as much. Funny how thirst became such a focus when one was between destinations of great distance. Perhaps it was boredom. He hadn't had a drink of pure water since leaving his residence. It had been mostly wine and whiskey. But travel offered a different train of thought.

Over the years, the caravan train had never betrayed him with its endless parade of interesting items. "Something for everyone," his father would say. Right he was. The shimmer of various trinkets, jewelry and the myriad useful household items made for a truly rewarding day's journey. But that to which that could never be compared to was the endless varieties of both local and foreign cooking.

Oh, the food . . .

The food was truly astonishing. Once discovered, the taste buds would be enraptured with:

- Endless species of cooked fish
- Unending bundles of deliciously cured meats
- Salted crab legs that grew to be the size of a chair leg

- Fruits of exotic places and distant lands
- Perfectly mixed dairy butters combined with an array of seasonings
- Tiger tenderloin
- Lemon brisket
- Terimol's mixed nuts
- Treats of mouth-watering sweetness
- White rum
- Dark rum
- Even darker rum
- Whiskey
- Pine nuts
- Hammer seeds
- Roasted coconut
- Literally the ABC's of Varroth's perpetual cheese list, from any animal that produced milk
- *Even* the nearly extinct: Mammoth steak. (And for enough coin, they would happily cook them for you as well.)

Perhaps not every shipment would have *all* of these items, but one only had to stand near to that particular part of the beaten path long enough and eventually anything would pass by.

Suddenly a new thought interrupted his contemplations of feasting. It was not so appetizing . . .

Upon contact with a caravan, all travelers were subject to a search. In previous times, the boy had mingled with the guards as well as the merchants for short treks, but never did he travel for long. Trading was a definitive part of the caravans whilst traveling; the merchants were always excited to meet those along the road.

But joining a caravan was a different story and it went as such: meet the scout guard heading the convoy, state the business of trade or travel, become subject to search, pay the bill of protection, and join up. At any other time, it would be fine to do this. However, this interaction could be the moment that would make or break his grand crusade. Should the guard discover the keg containing the 6,000 gold pieces, it would produce more than just questions.

One traveler alone never carried so much fortune. This amount of money was far too much, especially at his 'young age'. It would no doubt lead to many questions. And he would have no answers. If he did tell the guards he was en route to a new homestead, they would then search his pack only to find food and no real belongings. That would lead to further questioning.

No, he needed a plan once again.

Or . . .

Maybe he didn't?

Often, a journeyman would stop for drink. Clearly, on a road that stretches to what seemed like mind's end, surely a man couldn't be expected to make one bottle last between refillable locations?

Perhaps it wasn't so suspicious after all? When asked, he could reply, "Ah yes, this is yet another batch of pureberry wine, from my orchard in the northern meadows."

Undeniably, the guard would then ask for a drink, because why the hell not? (They are all self-righteous, crooked bastards anyway.) But instead of offering the "wine" from the keg, the boy would then pour from the bottle, as it had a "better" flavour than the current batch.

Perfect. Or at least as close as he could get to perfection with the sub-par improvising. What other option did he have? Dump the money?

No, not 6,000 coins. He wasn't that stupid.

Okay, Plan A then. And with that he set off. By the time he was to reach the road, the sun would be at its highest, perfect for the circumstance, assuming the caravan would be there today.

···8···

The voices of the sky spoke only of promise. With the day ahead, the clouds had made way for the rays that touched all with the introduction of daily rebirth. Could the future be as fine as this moment?

Varroth's Royal Trade route was only a half breeze away; the boy eyed it with hope, but also with worry. What was about to happen was based on the even flip of well-versed conversation. The words that were to be exchanged wrote the next part of what was to occur within his journey.

He rode up to the route and peered westward, down the path. With luck, his first encounter would be a caravan heading east. With misfortune, it would be heading west. For if he were to run into a shipment heading west toward the desert towns, he would be searched. The less attention from the guard, regardless of direction was obviously preferred.

While on the journey from his homestead, he ran across some clover, which the horses seemed to love. The fact of the matter was it was difficult to keep them on track when the tasty aroma of the four-leafed plants sidetracked the lovely animals, especially Orist. It was funny to think that those with hearts and brains other than humans, had favourites. Orist had always favoured clover.

Since the first part of his journey had gone swimmingly, he presented Orist with a bundle of finely packed clovers he had collected shortly after leaving the camp. Three other sets of eyes gawked intently as Orist wolfed down the treat, leaving the boy with the feeling of unfairness.

Did horses like venison jerky?

No, obviously not. They are herbivores . . .

He reached farther into his bag. What about bread?

He tore some pieces and presented them to the rest of the horses.

The bread was tasty.

The horses were happy, the boy had a full stomach. All was good.

It was then that a figure appeared on the path, clearly on horseback. Gods pray that it would be the scout. The boy would take him over a band of scar-ridden bandits any day. Eyes narrowed, he surveyed intently, his attention no longer on the horses.

As the horseback figure approached, additional figures appeared on the horizon. It was indeed the caravan. Of which, all of the merchant carts and horseback guards were moving at the same speed.

The distance soon closed, and the first figure to fully appear was definitely the guard. With fingers wrapped nervously tight around Orist's reins, the boy stood next to the route rather than on horseback, in hopes of showing a sign of respect.

"You there!" the man called out through a steel helmet, as he finalized his short distance. "State your business!"

"I wish to travel with the caravan," requested the boy urgently. "I have the gold to pay for safe travel."

"What weapons do you possess?" questioned the guard, coming to a complete halt and staring down into the eyes of the boy.

His uniform was the same as the surrounding guards. Various straps and buckles surrounded his torso, hips, and upper thighs. His tunic was painted also with the crescent moon of the king's infantry. It was tough to say if he wore anything beneath it. If not, he certainly was a large man and so he should be, charged with the protection of the Royal Trade Route. But what stood out the most was his incredibly shiny, cavalier jackboots with heels of monstrous size.

"I have only a simple blade for protection, sir!" claimed the boy, "I intend never to use it, unless my life or my horses' lives are in danger."

"Let me see it," the guard retorted, removing his helmet.

The boy pulled the sword from the sheath.

Damn.

It had been branded with the royal crescent moon.

"Boy, show me the blade," his right hand was on his sheathed weapon, clearly concerned.

He had flipped the handle, only to find that it had the crest on both sides. Time was up; he had to hand it to the guard.

The guard took the blade.

"This is a sword of the Red Hand. Why do you possess this?"

"I . . ." stammered the boy. "This . . . I bought this from a man when I had last visited Talramor." (A nearby town to the east.)

"It's contraband."

"I had no idea, please take it! I only wish to ride alongside until we reach Faulkstead."

With the heat of the moment rising, the conversation carried on.

"Your bag, empty it."

The boy did as such, only to reveal what was left of the food and as planned, the near-full bottle of wine.

"What's in the keg?" the guard asked, eyeing the half-sized barrel.

"My own famous brew. It is the pureberry wine of my meadow residence . . . Would you care for a taste?"

"No, I am a whiskey man. But my friend, Rall will." He turned to look over his shoulder.

All of a sudden and out of thin air, two more guards came riding up. The tenseness of the situation had robbed the boy of his awareness of the surroundings. The energy had shifted, and the boy was at the mercy of the guard.

"Is that a barrel of liquor I spy?" the other guard inquired.

"A taste of its contents will be necessary," said the third guard.

Members of the army were never known for their politeness. Their actions were mostly executed without explanation. The Route protectors never had patience, and they were always thirsty.

"If you wish to taste my finest wine. I urge you to drink from the bottle!" exclaimed the boy producing the violet infusion, glowing in the sunshine.

Rall snatched the bottle from the boy and pulled out the cork with his yellow teeth. He glugged back a rather large mouthful and turned to the other man.

"Now this is something. A bit sweet for my liking, more your type."

"Piss off, you mangy rat," countered the third guard, taking a swig from the bottle.

The guards continued to debate over the wine, analyzing its sweetness and vibrancy as if they were kings. It wasn't until they had nearly polished off the bottle that the original guard cut in.

"Oye! You bastards! Give the poor boy his wine."

They did, and the boy eyed the wine with distaste as he peered down at the last two mouthfuls, suddenly infected with more backwash than a swine's drinking trough.

"Why do you have four horses?" continued the original guard.

"Alas, my mother has died, and I wish to start a new beginning in the east."

It felt right to leave the "eastern location" open-ended in case the guard further questioned him.

"I am sorry for your loss," the guard said, this time with sympathy. "Travel as you wish. We will take care of you and your horses while en route to Faulkstead. You will be responsible for the care of your horses, though they will be tied to one of the caravans. You may wish to ride atop the travelers' wagon for extra coin. Any wrongdoing and you will be charged with aggravation. Any violent crimes, and you could be charged and punished by death. Do I make myself clear?"

"Yes! Perfectly! How much can I—" The boy was cut off.

"Eight gold bits for each of the horses, plus an extra twelve for you. Eighteen if you wish to ride with the luxury of the travelers' cart."

With that, the boy opened his money pouch, which was attached to his waist belt, and pulled out the payment. He made sure to pay extra for the cart, as riding horseback for the next set of days days was bound to feel dreadful. The guards waited with the boy as the caravan neared. It wasn't long before the horses were tied and he was escorted to the "wagon of luxuries."

··· 9 ···

The caravan consisted of multiple units, none of which came to a complete stop between each town. Should an adventurer wish to travel or trade, he had to do so at the speed of the caravan. Of course, there was money to be made at any point along the route, but the shipments stopped for nothing. Not even death itself.

One could never truly tell what was held within each wagon. The goods were sealed in behind wooden planks equipped with hatch doors for easy access or shrouded beneath giant woolen blankets. It was important to keep the goods protected and stowed without any hint of the contents. Apart from the endless scents of fresh baking and recently roasted meats, the visuals of the goods, or that lack thereof, kept any suspecting road bandits from getting too close – most of the time.

Of course, like anyone, the bandits of the route got hungry, too. Who wouldn't after days of thieving from the innocent? Not everyone traveled with the protection of the caravan. Some didn't have the coin; others reckoned they could do it themselves, which had never been the smartest choice.

Regardless, the ideal spot to hit on the caravan was the cart of jewelry, money, fine gems, and valuable metals. Some aimed for the cart that held weapons, tools, and blacksmithing items. Nevertheless, keeping everything wrapped and out of sight was a good way to keep the guessing game afloat should a takeover be attempted.

This particular lot had seven carts, all sizeable enough to contain a profitable number of goods. Some carts were towed by two horses, some by four. The seventh held some packages in the lower carriage, probably from multiple couriers with the paying customers sitting atop the "luxury" deck.

The platform was not luxurious. Lower than the height of the other vessels, it had no roof. The rains of previous times had left the dense pinewood still slightly damp. Nothing about the setting was enjoyable, to say the least. In fact, the seating brought to mind an idea of riding uncomfortably upon horseback. This particular wagon held a handful of eclectic individuals:

- A mother and son, both in tattered clothing
- An old man, wearing only a robe, the colour of the glaciers he had dreamt of days before
- A . . . woman? Dressed in a black, skin-tight suit, seated furthest up toward the front, opposite the rear entrance of the cart. Black hood up, it was hard to tell the gender, but the boy guessed it was a female
- A beastly looking man, muscles and all. Tattoos of various styles and a shoulder mount made entirely of wolf skin. Its pristine white hairs, tarnished over time,

resembled a tufted, shabby shoulder piece. This one was definitely a barbarian of sorts

- And finally, a tiny man, his body child-like, shorter than the boy's.

None of the clan seemed happy, and no one spoke. Not in the short time the boy had boarded anyhow. A few had acknowledged him with a nod. They gave the impression that the fatigue of travel was obvious.

Midday had passed, and though the seating was damp and rough on the ass, the boy felt good knowing he was traveling with the easy navigation of the caravan. The only thought that interrupted his calmness was the keg of gold atop one of his newly claimed horses. The "luxury" cart was the last in the line of wagons, but it had clear view over the horses that were tied evenly behind it. Two guards flanked the corners, but they had been getting their booze from somewhere else up the line.

Be that as it may, the sheer beauty of the countryside lowered feelings of stress. Much like his property, the meadows, cut in half by the Trade Route, provided a man with serenity and security; the open area provided little fear of robbery. For a trip through the meadow, especially during daylight, was different in comparison to the mountain and desert portions of the road. With the current protection from the guards and the warmth of the sun, this was the place to be.

After hopping aboard and taking a seat next to the tiny man, he studied the characteristics of his fellow travelers. If something were to go wrong, it would most obviously start with the barbarian, who had been drinking a sort of strong mix from his tankard. Clearly, his capacity to care for others was impaired by his lack of morals, and his knee space took nearly all of that side of the cart. *Almost inhuman,* thought the boy as he looked at the giant.

The child that sat alongside his mother was closely studying a dragonfly that he had captured inside of a small jam jar. His mother sat with her arm around the little boy. The cloaked figure, which he realized was indeed a woman, stared off into the distance, as did the older fellow.

Judging by the length of his beard, the old man could have easily been a wizard out of a fictitious story. Any wizards caught studying, using, or obtaining destructive magic were to be sent to a swift death. This included spells in which fire, ice, lightning, growth, rebirth, and any other arcane types of magic would cause immense damage to anybody and anything. That said, this old man merely looked the part of a fairy-tale wizard, just an old man on the road.

Strictly enforced, the only types of magic allowed in this time, were those involving alchemic powers. Even then, those who practiced it had to keep a keen eye on things, to avoid catastrophic problems.

"Fancy a drink?" The barbarian's heavy voice directed toward the boy.

"What are you drinking?" asked the boy, as he noticed the giant offering him a goblet in one hand, and an unlabeled bottle in the other.

"Rum of the Old Monk," he beamed. "The brew o' my brothers and myself. Got a still in the mountains. My father, 'e was the one *believin'* in all the meditation voodoo. Since his passin' eight years ago now, we brew this in his honour and warm the vast hearts of Varroth."

Thowp!

The barbarian pulled the cork from the oversized, rectangular bottle. The glass was dark with the hue of a tarnished oak, with edges that had been squared off at the corners. He proceeded to pour some of the rum. The liquid was so dark it reminded the boy of the black marsh water, east of his homestead.

The boy accepted the goblet; what else was he going to do? He took a swig, expecting nothing more than a sharp bite from the barbarian's reserve. At first, the rum tasted like any other, but was soon followed by an overpowering clobber of intense fire!

The strength of the drink nearly knocked his soul from his body. It sent him hacking uncontrollably! Caught by surprise, the boy was overcome with embarrassment and felt as though he had just been poisoned. All eyes were on him as he grasped the back of the caravan bench from where he sat.

"Yar. It's a bit strong, but nothin' you can't handle if yer raised Ironhold style," retorted the barbarian, knocking back what was left in his chalice.

Finally, the boy was able to regain his composure. He attempted to reply; his voice completely decimated, "Is that where you're from?" his words barely squeaking from burning his lips.

"Yar. Been up there my whole life. Thirty-odd years . . ." guessed the giant. "Wait, no. Forty years . . . fifty . . .?"

The lot of the travelers fixed their eyes on the barbarian as he attempted to figure out his own age.

"I don't know anymore. Somewhere around those numbers," laughed the man, as he poured himself yet another drink.

It clearly was a shock to everybody. Both the tolerance the barbarian had to such a drink and the lack of clarity he had with regards to his own age. His size, scars, and overall mentality made it hard to judge even which decade of life he was in.

For the rest of the day, the boy and the barbarian exchanged life stories across the cart, leaving out the finer, more illegal details. Numerous times, he turned down the offer of additional "Old Monk." Somehow, he did manage to finish the single goblet of drink before the sun had reached the horizon.

Oddly, nobody mentioned any names. It was as if the comfort of the road would have been disrupted should somebody ask such a question. No, it seemed right to continue the journey with conversation, but with a degree of anonymity.

Toward the later evening, the tiny man joined the conversation. Then the old man joined in, as well. Perhaps it was the drink that gave him enough courage to participate. Following that, the mother spoke, and soon all but the cloaked traveler had joined in the dialogue as the sun set.

They spoke of the pearlescent colours that filled the sky, and the journeys they had made from the west. Daft life stories and odd events were the next topics. At one point, the barbarian commented on the size of the man-child, leaving the tiny traveler raving in an angered state. He had risen in threat to knock the giant off his seat but was soon quieted when the giant said, in his bellowing laughter, "Sit down, little man!"

The camaraderie grew, just as the darkening sky did. Even the cloaked girl drank from a glass of her own. Heavens only knew what she had brought to drink, but still she remained silent. The boy felt as if he had joined a new family for the time being. Flooded with the warmth of acceptance, he played into the dialogue just as everyone else did. It was the banter of authenticity and honest truths. His nerves relaxed but still his eyes kept sneaking away to glance at his keg-horse. Although the night had gone much smoother than expected, he longed for the attention of the girl who was near the party, yet alone in her own sense. It had been a lean sixty or so years since he was last this age. Alas, he was a devoted husband and for that he was eternally grateful. Not a single piece of temptation could turn him away from loyalty to his wife, yet he did look and admire from afar.

It was that moment that she rose to her feet.

··· IO ···

The scenery was different, not by much however. The once-flat meadows had become dimpled hills, dotted here and there with extra tufts of shrubbery and tree life. What's more, the rolling hills had, scattered amongst themselves, abrupt knolls and small rocky outcroppings. The last pureberry tree the boy had witnessed was back on his property, long before the route. Suddenly there were poplars, pines, and willow trees.

Boulders were sprinkled about, new objects to keep the mind entertained whilst peering over the side of the traveling wagon. The crust of the landscape had also provided new areas of shade and slight mysteriousness. The thought of treasure, or the entrance to a cave was easy to summon to mind, but it was obvious that no such venture existed this far from any busy comings and goings of town life.

Or was it?

Standing, clad in tightly wrapping, leather boots, the woman spoke.

"As I wish you all no harm, the time is now that I will seize the bounties of this caravan. Agree to my demands, and you shall remain the same, but if you defy me, I cannot promise your safety."

The man-child who had merrily played his wooden flute stopped abruptly mid-song. The conversation, so rudely interrupted, dissipated at the presumptuous demand of the silent young woman.

The horseback guards rode in sixes alongside the caravan, dressed in full armour, from head to toe. Two in the rear, two front, two middle. Clearly, there were two sets of protectors. The day and the night had somehow switched shifts without drawing attention. On horseback for the daylight hours, the first crew lay sleeping somewhere ahead in a wagon of the convoy, thus the night guard had taken up the task. This new demand, belted from the lips of the black-clad female, had left unjust confusion in the air.

The suspicion of a joke or a farce flooded the energy surrounding the wagon. The new happened had been that of humour. It had to be. A single woman could not rob this shipment and disappear with such riches alone.

"Sit down lass, your humour is that o' the rats!" bellowed the barbarian above the brim of yet another drink.

Without hesitation, she produced an ebony-shaded scimitar from behind her back. From where it was hidden was simply unknown; perhaps she had it secured beneath her cloak as such a location would have been overlooked by the guards prior to the journey. In the same movement, the appalling became reality, as she lunged forward, gouging the tip of the sword directly into the stalky neck of the barbarian.

With a roar loud enough to shake trees, the giant man screamed in agony as he clutched his neck and fell to the floor of the cart, shaking the entire wagon.

"Bastard! What have you done to me?" he screamed, writhing in pain and clutching his neck.

The woman motioned for the passengers to look over the sides of the cart. The men guarding the caravan throughout the evening were not the guards of the Red Hand. No, helmets removed, the scar-tattered faces of the five men and another woman revealed their true identities: thieves – posing as protection. What a perfect setting for a robbery, amidst the giant boulders of the transitional landscape.

The perception of security disappeared with all hope. It was no longer the men of the king that played fear in the mind of the boy, but the thieves of the Trade Route. He took it upon himself to lean backward over the rear of the bench where he sat, surveying the line of carts. Sure enough, three of the thieves had bows drawn and lined up directly with a cart farther in the line. The nature of the situation had become purely barbaric. With the day guards hostage in the wagon ahead, the remaining thieves were able to do as they pleased. Furthermore, the blood of the injured barbarian had begun to pool among the feet of the travelers.

What had once been lively entertainment and fun drink had become an evil sideshow of trickery and horror. The scene was a lake of evil, flooded with hungry piranhas darting in the direction of fresh meat. The gang was driven more by the plunders of valuables than human life itself.

"Untie the horses!" the cloaked woman shouted. Clearly, she was the leader of this gang. The three thieves at the foot of the convoy did as directed.

The boy watched with a stare of soul-crushing trepidation as they untied the keg-horse along with several other horses belonging to the travelers. Just like that, all but the eighteen gold coins he possessed from within his traveler's bags, disappeared. All 6,000 or so shillings.

"Search the carts for jewellery and round up the merchants," ordered the woman, sending the next in command down the line.

The merchants, who previously had the comfort of riding in their own carts, with cozy areas to lie down and sleep in, were rounded up and grouped next to the horses. The majority of them were older. One of them began barking at the imposter as the thief grabbed the man by the underarm and shoved him forcefully in the direction of the others.

"You dare touch my pendants and I will slaughter you well and truly!" yelled the jewellery merchant receiving a backhand that sent him to flying to the dusty gravel. The jeweller attempted to retaliate. He got up and lurched forward, fists readied to strike back. His actions were soon undone by the bandit, as he plunged his blade upward through the old man's neck, sending the jeweller to his gruesome death.

"Fool!" yelled the woman, "It is bad enough I had to kill this barbarian; we needn't have any more bloodshed!"

Angered, the murderer removed his sword and made his way toward the next cart, leaving behind the lifeless body of the old jeweller. The child began to cry, as did his mother. Tears were flowing amongst the travelers, all but the old man, who remained perfectly still with eyes shut. How could one meditate in such a moment?! Or perhaps he was praying—

Suddenly, an orb light beamed from the clasped hands of the ancient soul. Eyes open, the old man revealed his true secret; he was in fact a wizard. He had to be! The secret wish of the boy had come true from the beginning, but what had he just done? The orb soon fizzled out, leaving a trail of smoke drifting through the night air.

"What have you done?" questioned the lady, lifting the old wizard to his feet by a fistful of his beard.

He remained motionless. Even his eyes were stone. Deadpan with an icy emptiness, the wizard stared defiantly back into the eyes of the woman. Time stood still as the two scrutinized each other's souls. Getting nowhere, the woman cast aside the wizard and turned back to monitor the thieving of the jeweller's cart. The boy cast his view toward the barbarian, who grunted under his breath. Whatever the wizard had done, was of aid to the barbarian, for his neck wound had magically healed, leaving only a wretched, burn-like scar.

Distracted, the leader of the thieves had been too busy to notice that the barbarian had recovered. His massive arm reached down and grabbed the woman's ankle, pulling her from her feet. Confusion flooded her mind as she fell, striking her head on the wooden planks of the bench. Without time to think, he then clutched her by her throat and rose to his feet.

The man certainly was a giant. He was the size of a watchtower, as portrayed in the books the boy had read in his previous life. Built by the stones of Ironhold, the gargantuan stood taller than eight feet high. He blocked out the moonlight with just his stance alone.

This commotion caught the attention of the rest of the thieves. In an effort to further conduct the robbery, the leader had done right in attempting an execution on the barbarian. At that moment, her very soul was at his mercy. All he had to do was squeeze his fist, and she would pop like a starfruit of the Jalhabi desert.

"You will release these merchants unharmed, girl!" demanded the giant.

The thieves, realizing their fate had been swapped with those of the travelers, hastily motioned for the merchants to rejoin the convoy.

"Your stolen goods will be deposited where you found them, and horses left where they stand!"

The woman was choking; clawing at the barbarian's straight-arm as blood seeped from her nails while they tore vigorously into his skin. Her feeble attempts to make words were matched with her inability to draw breath. Each of the real guards rose from their temporary prisons within the carts, no longer under threat of attack. They joined the commotion. At that moment, the bandits had banded together, clustering with fear and anxious whisper. Then, as if the enemy clan had all shared the same mind, they mounted the nearby horses, one of which being the keg-horse that held the Gold Counter's stash of wealth.

"STOP!" commanded the giant, throwing the cloaked woman to the floor of the wagon with force.

He leapt down to the dusty ground in a single bound and chased the bandits on foot. His heavy boots shaking the ground. Each of the fleeing bandits whipped at the horses while the fear of death fuelled their escape. With the gargantuan man behind them, it was a simple matter of life and death. The last thief unknowingly rode atop the keg-horse which had begun to lag behind severely behind due to the weight of the hidden gold.

All sets of eyes were on the cowards. The man-child was shouting curse words of various degrees all while the cloaked woman remained on her back. The guards of the Red Hand shot arrows at the escaping thieves, but to their dismay, missed.

Finally, the brute caught up with the keg-horse. He reached out and grabbed the top groove of the keg, causing the horse to slow, thief on its back. Just then, the barrel ripped free of its straps and came crashing to the ground, bursting open in a shower of golden riches. Both the giant and the criminal stopped abruptly and gawked at what they saw. But, with nerves at the ready for anything, the barbarian spun around to the man and grabbed him by the back of his armour, tossing him to the ground.

The man's attempt to speak was brief, as the thief was cut off when the giant picked up his body as if it were a child's toy, and flung it towards a nearby boulder. Instantly, the thief's skull split against the boulder's sharp protrusion, crumbling him into a lifeless, bloody mass.

··· II ···

One would describe the events that had just taken place as both good and bad luck. The thieving wolves, disguised as simple sheep, had made their way to their vast hidey-holes northward. Whereas the 'cat' that existed in the keg, was suddenly 'out of the bag', so to speak, on display for everyone else aboard the convoy.

Regardless of their role, each guard, traveler and merchant were dumbstruck; frozen in place with the shock of seeing the merciless violence and exposure to such a grand amount of coin. Even the young child had ended his tears. Nothing was said. In fact, the only audible noise that filled the air was the gentle whisking of the tall grasses on the nearby hilltops.

The people of the caravan had certainly never seen this much wealth all in one place. It was likely that the majority of the crowd had never possessed more than a few hundred coins at a single time, if ever.

With the menace of sudden thievery no longer an issue, the day guard, more awake than ever, had this new information to ponder. Furthermore, they began to branch off, all six of them, away from the convoy in the direction of the bloody-fisted barbarian.

The captain, or so he had appointed himself, spoke in the moonlight: "What is the meaning of this? Whose coin is this and how was I not made of aware of such wealth?"

Ownership of course, belonged to the boy, who at that moment was still in his own state of shock. He said nothing.

The captain again: "To travel with such coin is ridiculous!" He stared at the travelers, then to the merchants.

"How can I know this was not the reason for the ambush? I demand to know the name of the person to whom these shillings belong!"

Again, the blades of grass whispered their secrets. No one dared to intrude on this scenario, as the first to speak would most likely be the one to face consequences. The passing of time reminded the boy of his aging, though it had not been all that long of a passage. If he somehow saw his way through this mess, he vowed to travel a less risky path if possible.

"So be it." The captain finally spoke. "The gold is now mine to share with my guards." His baiting attitude reminded the boy of the jester hawk from the previous awakening.

With that, the captain began strutting towards the gold, the giant, and the bloody mess, his boots kicking up dust as he treaded.

To the boy, it felt just as bad as losing the gold to criminals. In fact, ironically enough, he was about to watch it pour into the hands of the men for whom it was actually intended from the beginning – just in lesser amount. Why did he bring so much gold to begin with? Perhaps it was the time to forfeit? The idea seemed enticing, but the more the boy thought of parting ways with his self-proclaimed fortune, the more he resisted following that train of thought. Greed really had imprisoned him. But never mind that, managing the rest of this journey to the Royal City would be seemingly impossible with just eighteen coins . . .

Bearing that in mind, he decided to speak up.

"The gold is mine!" shouted the boy, causing the guard to spin in a swift pivot.

For a moment, the guard eyed the boy without speaking.

"How can a boy of your stature have this amount of coin?"

It was too much. Between the robbery, and this questioning, his brain was on the verge of explosion. "The gold belonged to my father!" lied the boy, "He was good at saving coin and owned a farm to the west. This gold, combined with that of my grandfather's now belongs to me, as was written in their wills."

"And how can you prove this?" responded the guard.

"I cannot."

"Well, then I cannot be sure that you are not some kind of thief, can I?" questioned the captain.

Damn. He had him there. The boy should have come up with a different story. Granted, the Gold Counter was slightly pleased with himself as he was able to summon such a myth without stumbling over his own words too much.

The man of the Red Hand, turned back toward the gold, which had literally spilled into a massive area around the giant. The olive and chestnut shades of earth were illuminated by the gleam of thousands of shillings, beaming their proud radiance of glowing prosperity in the moonlight.

"Regardless of the matter, I have to take it upon myself to confiscate this treasure as it was not declared at the time of the search. I doubt you'll miss this gold, as you said, it was your father's and your life will continue on just as it did before you acquired it. If that is in fact your real story." The captain's words were forceful with a purposely-aggravating tone. "Dorison! Fetch me an empty crate!"

He turned and walked to the pile of treasure.

"No!" yelled the barbarian in his abominable voice.

"You deserve nothing! This ere' gold belongs to the boy. What of it do ye deserve? You an' your little men did nothing for us poor folk while we were bein' robbed of our goods n' all!" His voice was like thunder, ripping through the night sky. Even the torches on the exteriors of the caravan seemed to bend when the barbarian raised his voice.

At this point, the captain had realized that perhaps that was not a battle worth fighting, regardless of the fortune at hand. The cascade of guilt felt by him and his men was far too great.

"You might as well get back in yer little sleepin' holes and head off to dreamland where you're nice and safe!" barked the barbarian.

Frozen, all six of the members of the king's army stood numbly. The five around the cart just stood and watched in disbelief as their 'captain' was knocked off his proverbial pedestal.

The giant made his way over to the guard whom had returned carrying an empty keg. He claimed the barrel for himself and trotted over to the gold. It wasn't long before he tipped the barrel on its side and shovelled the gold into it with his brawny arms. With that, he popped the lid back onto the barrel and knocked it in with a single pound of his fist. Then he hoisted the container of riches onto his shoulder and brought it back to the wagon with relative ease!

Climbing into the back of the "luxury cart" he dumped the keg in front of the boy with a harsh drop. The noise had made everyone jump, except the unconscious lady lying face down on the floor. It was unclear if she too had died by the hand of the giant, or if she had been rendered senseless once she had hit the floor of the wagon.

"Give me two hundred coins," demanded the barbarian.

Without question, the boy slipped his fingers under the barrels lid and yanked it open, shuffling his hand amongst his reclaimed gold. The giant held his massive hand out, making it easier for the boy to count as he handed over the coins.

Once the task was completed, the giant then handed the sum of money to the old wizard, who still sat with wide eyes.

"I cannot—" the wizard was cut off.

"Take the money."

At this point, no one was foolish enough to dare argue with the beastly man. It was not an offer. It was an order.

The wizard did what he was told by opening a well-worn leather travel bag, into which the barbarian dropped the money.

Back in his old spot, the giant relaxed once again. Nothing had happened, so said his appearance. From out of nowhere, he produced a brand-new bottle of "Old Monk" and poured himself a drink.

"Well!?" he belted out, several moments later. "Are we ever going to get this damned cart moving again?"

And with that, the convoy recommenced its journey, guards back in their original stations beside the turning wheels.

No one spoke. The noise of the squeaky wagon wheels was all that was heard. The music of the flute had long since stopped, and no one drank except the barbarian. This silence went on for miles. No one could sleep, though a majority of the cart's occupants very much wanted to.

Occasionally, the odd rock would throw the balance from one side of the caravan to the other, though it was never enough to spark up new conversation. As the night wore on, so did the need to rest. One by one, the cart folk began to sink into a well-deserved sleep. Finally, the only two awake were the boy, straddling his keg of gold, and the giant.

The barbarian looked down at the Gold Counter.

"I'm Thul," he said, holding out his hand.

···12···

AGE: 28

The rest of the journey carried out quite nicely. The cloaked woman did in fact wake from her disoriented state, only to find herself in custody on the guard's horseback. After the travesty of the attempted theft, the occupants soon returned to their original selves. Banter and laughter became an ongoing routine once again, as the distance between the travelers and the town of Faulkstead shortened. In fact, in some way or another, the mess of such events, had only ensured added strength amongst the crew.

As the night watch crew no longer existed, it took the caravan longer than expected to reach Faulkstead. The captain and his men took watch as they traveled during the day but they decided to stop and sleep at night, with the exception of one alternating guard who took the job of "lookout," each evening. The blazing sun had made it hopeless to sleep during the light hours.

Prior to reaching the riverside town, the boy had decided to tip the guards one hundred gold pieces each. That was more than two seasons of pay per soldier. The reason being, he had hoped that they would not pursue him farther on his journey. That, and the fact that they would have seized his gold if the barbarian hadn't sided with him. Convincing as his story was, it was not enough to deter the corruption of the king's men. Surely, they would have taken it upon themselves to greedily call that gold their own had the opportune moment arisen.

As the first segment of his journey closed, he had begun to bond with his gargantuan new friend, Thul. They shared stories that took place in Ironhold as well as those of the pureberry meadows, rather than touching on serious personal matters, as they had only just met days ago.

As long and pleasant as the remainder of the trip was, the boy's signs of aging had already begun to show. This was his primary concern. His fears were proven when he knelt by a pond to drink the earth's revitalizing nectar only to find that his facial features had begun to change, ever-so-slightly. In the days he had been traveling, the mirror of growth had already started to reflect its true self. Although nobody had commented on his appearance, or even noticed for that matter, it did nothing to diminish his stress over his changing appearance. The Gold Counter looked to be within his late twenties. Although the thoughts were in the forefront of mind, the sunny appearance of Faulkstead brought a welcoming relief.

What was once a dense pine forest, divided by a rushing river, painted with shades of sapphire and crystal turquoise, was at that moment a full-fledged town. Faulkstead or "The River Town of the East" as it was more commonly known. Although the town was not "big" enough to be surrounded by gates or a fortified wall, its ever-lasting beauty was enough to calm the mind of any weary traveler.

The river that flowed directly through the centre of the town provided the folk and fair travelers with plenty of fish, especially salmon of various species. The fresh mountain water that flowed from the north meant that the taste was pure, without contamination from algae or other parasites.

The majority of the business were home-based and situated within the lush town. Some of the main shops, which received shipments from the caravans, were those belonging to the blacksmith, clothier, and alchemist. Other parcels were claimed by the owners of the general store, trading company, jewellery stand, brewery, and the town inn, formerly known as "The Goblin's Rest", which also doubled as the primary drinking hole. Most of the inns that dotted Varroth were known for their sales of spirits and their heart-warming, lute-strung melodies.

The warm, daytime temperature of Faulkstead was enough to tempt anyone into dipping their toes within the refreshing river. With the rays of glowing sunshine seeping through the branches of the great pines, one could only imagine that the heavens were not much different. Rarely did it snow in this town, though the evenings were cold with the icy heart of the north and the majority of the homeowners spent their nights indoors either at The Goblin's Rest or in their residences.

The only danger in the town was the occasional griffon that floated high above the forested area, hence the roofing on the buildings. No such creature dared damage any structure in hopes of finding a human snack, but one had to be careful when walking alone along the wilderness paths.

As the caravan unpacked, the boy made his way to his horses. He had kept Orist, along with the other horses, in good health along the trip. The road that lay behind him had offered many snacks of clover patches and fresh grass, with the occasional drink from a creek or small body of water.

He decided outright to donate two of the horses to the other guards in an effort to further make amends. The captain, in return, gave a look of appreciation but then one of uncertainty. It was enough for the boy to feel at least somewhat satisfied, before heading back to the wagon, only to ponder the next question: what was he to do with his barrel of gold?

Sure, the cloaked woman was finally jailed somewhere in Faulkstead but his fear of losing the gold remained the same. Only those who traveled with the caravan truly knew what riches exsisted within his oak barrel, but it wasn't long before word would spread.

"Go inside. Find yerself a room with two beds. I'll look after the gol . . . I mean the barrel o' ale," said Thul, proceeding to sip from another bottle of Old Monk.

"Two beds?" questioned the boy.

"Of course, boy. Where else am I going to sleep?"

※ ※ ※

The boy made his way to the door of the inn. Just like that, his privacy had been zapped from existence. He had no choice. With one swift move, he could end up like the thief who became one with the boulder. On the other hand, there was no way he could keep the keg safe, especially not on his own. He had to sleep sometime and even if someone did make a

THE GOLD COUNTER

move on it, at least he could tuck away some of the coins into his travel bag and stash that elsewhere. Besides, he then had a pact with the barbarian, one that was strong against the Red Hand.

A friendly, elderly, white-haired male introduced himself as Esbern, the Innkeeper. Upon entering the quaint tavern, he had offered the boy an assortment of rooms. None of which had two beds of course, but one did come with extra pillows and additional blankets, perfect for a makeshift bed on the floor. Furthermore, by spending the extra coin, he was granted with a key to lock the door. Finding an inn with such amenities in this time was uncommon, and he considered it a stroke of luck. The boy took the offer, paid the six gold pieces for the evening and went back to collect Thul.

Once he and the giant, along with their belongings, had become situated in the room, they decided to part ways for the afternoon. The boy didn't exactly feel like drinking all day with his new friend. He had done enough of that on the caravan, and was beginning to build up a tolerance to the Old Monk, which worried him.

The Gold Counter set off on the dirt road that led through Faulkstead. The majority of the shops and stands, flooded with wares, were positioned down this main patch that led through town. As he placed one foot in front of the other at a casual pace, his mind began to ponder the rest of his overall journey. Perhaps traveling by caravan was no longer a smart idea. With Thul on his side, perhaps the two of them could travel together. Unfortunately, he had not yet spoken with the barbarian about his destination along the Trade Route of Varroth.

The tall pines, robust with a thickness of pure wildlife felt rejuvenating to be around. They were the gatekeepers of the sky; allowing clear lines of daylight through their passages of evergreen branches. It was a perfect setting for a town - No wonder Faulkstead was one of the most popular areas to settle in.

A shimmer of ruby caught his eye. With just the right amount of sunlight, the gem in the jeweller's signage came into view. Clearly an establishment of wealth and design - he decided to pay a visit and explore the beauty of gold and refined treasures.

As he entered, a rather young fellow, with an odd haircut, greeted him. It was as if someone had placed a bowl on his head and cut around it, leaving a sort of mushroom shape on the top of his skull.

"Planning on buying some jewellery on your travels?" the mushroom cut asked.

"Perhaps. More so just browsing at the moment," replied the boy. "How could you tell I am a traveler?"

"Please. I can tell a traveler before he walks through that door!" he smiled back. "By the way, I am Vasha. If you find anything you'd like me to show you, please let me know."

The boy stepped in and browsed the jeweled finery displayed upon the back wall of the store, behind the shop keep counter. For such a growing town, clearly there was much to be had. Upon the wall dangled an unimaginable amount of worth, entwined in twists of gold and rare stones.

There were jewels, bracelets, and brooches made of gold and silver, necklaces, ornaments, and tiaras. Everything, at one point or another, had required a great deal of patience and talent to create. One medallion, in particular, grabbed his attention.

"Have you made all of these yourself?" questioned the boy.

"Nay." Vasha drank from a goblet, its trim encrusted with rubies surrounded with an amber coloured metal. "Some I have, though most come in on the caravans. With the Eastern border being so close, I get second or third pick from the treasures of Koraivindahl."

The medallion hung on the end of what appeared to be a silver chain. Though unlike the rest, the centre was a jade carving, in the shape of a vial. It reminded him of his wife and he thought about how, time and time again, she longed for his opinion when it came to new concoctions. Most often, the questions were, "How do you like the colour of this one?" or "Is this smell too off-putting?" She asked her questions when handing the various vials to him for inspection and approval.

"Let me see that necklace. The one with the alchemic vial," requested the boy.

Vasha brought the medallion down for further inspection.

"You have an eye for beauty!" and so began the sales pitch. "This here medallion has always differed from the rest. For years, I have had this. To create such a design would have taken a great deal of time. In all honesty, I cannot remember where I acquired this one, but it did not come from a caravan."

Just then, the medallion morphed, changing in shape from a vial to that of a human skull! It caused the boy to drop the piece of merchandise carelessly atop a set of bangles that Vasha had been constructing upon the boy's arrival.

"Did you see that?" the boy's nerves stung as if hit with the electric shock of a sorcerer.

"Aye. It's the one magical piece that I currently own." The jeweller nonchalantly sipped from his goblet again without any change in expression. "My father always tells me to get rid of it - throw it in the river, or have Hadvar, our blacksmith, properly destroy it. He says it's the work of a Necromancer. Every now and them it will morph, changing from vial to skull and then back again."

A jade skull looked back up at the boy, as if it were peering into his soul, ultimately creepy and definitely the work of some dark magic. Perhaps it was treasure deep from within a mighty dungeon, one of great evil and life-threatening traps. Or maybe, it was a power-granting prize, for a dark mage to harness evil power. Whatever the reason, it was a risky purchase. In all of his readings, never had he come across a materialistic property of fine stone that appeared to change its own features. Although his conscience told him it was a bad idea... he had to have it.

"Name your price," he offered courageously.

Vasha returned, "Are you sure this is what you want? I must tell you; I once sold this amulet to a traveler much like yourself, only she was a tad older. It was but five days after she started out on her journey when she returned and literally threw it at me. For whatever reason, she didn't even want her coin back. Instead, she just left after parting with it. Not a word to be said."

The jeweller's warnings were as clear as the Faulkstead River.

"Though I wouldn't be against selling you this, are you sure this is something you are interested in? Perhaps, you'd be more interested in a different kind of gem. We have many amulets that aid in both mental and physical healing. Depending on your preference in stone, I have had many imbued with the hea–" he was cut off.

The boy reached down, touching its immaculately shaped skull. Within seconds, a flash of pure blackness clouded both his vision and his thoughts. A blaze of evil had disconnected him from reality completely. Some threshold of evil, like a portal to the nothingness beyond the end, opened from within him. It was a feeling he had never before experienced. He wished for nothing else in the entire world, but to have the amulet as his own.

"I want that amulet!" barked the boy, his voice with that of a shout, as he grabbed the medallion. What was he doing? His actions were of some great corruption. Something had taken hold of his spirit, moulding it and shaping it to its own liking.

In the heat of the moment, Vasha lashed out abruptly, striking the boy's forearm with one of his formation hammers. It was an unexpected move, which sent the young man reeling backward from the counter, seized with pain.

"How? I . . . you . . ." his thoughts were caught between his inexcusable actions, and the pain that shot down his arm. His attempt to speak once again failed.

The funny-haired jeweller proceeded to call for assistance. It was only a matter of time before one of the few Faulkstead guards showed up. Unaware of how protected the riverside town was, the boy found it in his best interest to apologize hastily and withdraw himself.

He stumbled backward through the door of the studio and crashed onto the dirt of the main roadway. Vasha had seemingly teleported from behind his counter to the front door of his shop within a brief moment. With a warning to never return, accompanied with a foul name calling, the jeweler's door slammed shut, sending a thickly wooded boom thundering down the street.

All street eyes were at his mercy. He felt embarrassed and agitated, engulfed in misery and confusion. What had just happened was something of great evil. In all his nearly ninety years, he had never felt this way. Some chaotic monarch of evil had descended in there, taking over his mind. His body. Like some mind control spell used in the dark books of hopeless fairy tales and woes.

One could describe the moment as the worst nightmare ever. For that matter, his recollection of the event was not fully clear but for a brief moment, the image of the multi-faceted amulet was burned into his mind.

Gods only know what had happened to its previous victim – the female traveler who had once purchased it. She must not have been aware of its corruptive nature or destruction when she had purchased it. But how? The boy had been at the jeweler's but a few short moments and in that time, he had succumbed to a complete alteration.

···13···

The act of getting up in the street was painful, thanks to the power of the jeweller's hammer. In an attempt to stand, the boy braced himself with his right arm, only to be reminded of such pain. It had been a moment of awkwardness as onlookers whispered quietly to each other as they watched him attempt to stand.

Once upright, his first thought was to disappear from sight. He did so by going through a gap in the forest to the wilderness beyond the residences of Faulkstead. With the momentum of a fox, he bounded through some bushes and past a few clusters of homes until Faulkstead was a window behind him amongst the pines.

Some moments of time were needed before a feeling a calmness and serenity returned to the boy. His first excursion in a new place - a failure, as one would think. He brushed his hand against some overgrown moss, attached to the fallen tree upon which he rested.

Some length up the log, there was a large pumpkin snail with a shell the size of a grown-man's fist. It was much larger than he had read about. Its sluggish, mucus-covered body was sliding along, first in one direction, and then the next. Such a simple-celled mollusk, it reminded him of the crimes he had committed not one season ago. The idea of drowning the guards had come back to him, infuriating him only more. His next action was one of hostility as he picked up the pumpkin snail by its stone-like shell, and hurled it far into the forest. It was this action that took him back a notch, changing his feelings of anger to sharp regret, as his little snail victim had done nothing to deserve such pointless aggression. Surely, with a shell as strong as an iron ingot, the pumpkin snail was bound to be perfectly fine after such a throw; it was the thought of committing the act that saddened the boy.

That was when it hit him. His journey seemed impossible. He was in a town full of people who appeared to dislike him and whom may try to steal his gold. Nobody wanted him; he was nothing more than a seemingly "violent" trespasser on a journey with no end. Aging faster than any man alive, he was a victim of his own crimes. A gravedigger whom had dug far too deep and suddenly felt too hopeless to climb out with a broken shovel.

Tears rolled down his face and onto his clasped hands. Giving up felt as though it was the only option. He had failed, and was destined to be a meal for any ferocious beast in this relentless wilderness. He remained like this for some time, draining his being of all its pessimism and unfavourable weaknesses.

Eventually, shades of the setting sun began to set through the holes in the pine trees. Hunger had taken over his body, and he was thirsty.

✖ ✖ ✖

As he neared The Goblin's Rest, he noticed that the merry sounds of the lute could not be heard. This was a magical time of day, in which travelers took a drink at a leisurely pace, or picked away at their suppers. Lute music was a lovely part of the evening.

As he neared the inn's thick oak door studded with bronzed rivets, he heard a shout from within. It was one of panic, not of gambling or merriment. Thoughts of turning back entered his mind, but since he was of a curious nature, he decided to investigate further.

He pulled discreetly at the door, allowing only a single eye to peep through. The Goblin's Rest had been turned upside down and a live skeleton was standing amongst the rubble. Bones, yellowed with signs of rot and malnourishment, were holding together a soldier from beyond the void. In one skeletal hand he held a fierce flail, equipped with three, dangling spheres of ridged, razor spines evidently capable of mass damage.

"The gold . . . all of it . . ." rasped a voice from within him.

"I haven't any more! You must leave this place! There is nothing more for you." It was Esbern, keeper of The Goblin's Rest. "You have my gold; you've killed my barkeep. I have nothing left to offer you. I beg you to leave!" his voice, old yet shrill with terror.

"You know very well, there is more gold here. I can sense it, as can my pet."

If this was true, his abilities to sense treasure had surely picked up on the barrel full of coin that the Gold Counter had stashed within his quarters. Undoubtedly, Esbern would have received such knowledge from some sniffer or guard aboard the caravan and the boy suspected that more towns-folk had been made well aware of his riches. What else was there to talk about in Faulkstead? If his fellow innkeeper did in fact have this piece of private knowledge, he was doing very well to keep it so.

In an attempt to gather more about what was happening, he pulled open the door slightly farther. The skeleton, or "pet" of the necromancer, failed to notice the door opening. Thul was positioned at the bar, alongside many other folk of various ages and sizes. His eyes met with the boy's. Then the boy noticed a hooded figure, dressed in dark robes the colour of night, with shiny symbols embroidered into the openings.

"The gold, innkeeper!" roared the necromancer, blue flames sparking from his shoulders beneath the shawl. "Or you too will become one with the Void."

From his peripheral vision, an empty wine bottle of ama-ranthine shading caught the boy's attention from behind a cluster of ferns outside the inn. This could serve as a poten-tial weapon, as the boy had nothing threatening but his bare hands.

Quickly, he moved to grab the weapon from behind the greenery. Every second was of priority, and he had only a sliver of time to think. Perhaps if he could smash the bottle upon the back of the necromancer's skull, a moment of freedom would open up, allowing Thul to seize the skeleton.

This action of brutality came with infinite consequences should it go wrong, but his choices were limited. What else was there to do?

Once again, he pulled open the door of The Goblin's Rest. Without a moment to think, he instantaneously swung his wine bottle with such ferocity even Thul, with all of his strength, was stunned by such vigour. However, he failed to notice that yet another skeleton stood on the right side of the necromancer. His actions caught the necromancer's attention, but before he had time to spin around, the bottle smashed his foe's skull with enormous force. Millions of tiny glass shards, both from the empty wine vessel and from the black wanderer exploded in the room.

To everyone's surprise, both of the skeletons had become unsummoned and crashed to the floor in a clatter of disorganized bones. No one had realized that by destroying this new evil comer, its evil skeletons were doomed to perish as well.

If calmness and beauty were to be sought, Faulkstead's Inn was not the place for it at that moment. Before each traveler and settler, lay the remains not only of the skeletons but also their diseased master. The dead barkeep was the inn-keeper's son.

All but one of the customers stood up, in admiration of the lion-like courage but also in shock of the tragic nature of what had just happened. Silence was cast among each of the members except one, a woman, who ran to the barkeep.

Her bawling and shrieking, that of pure misery. It became apparent to the boy that she was in fact the mother of the dead barkeep; the innkeeper's wife. Esbern went to comfort her. Eventually he made his way to the boy, and thanked him for his grand efforts of defeating the sorcerer of dark magic, with such elementary use of a wine bottle. He knelt and in his distraught state and began absentmindedly picking up each piece of coin that the necromancer had attempted to steal in an effort to repay the boy for his heroism.

But the boy graciously turned down Esbern's offer of the recovered coin, leaving the innkeeper stunned momentarily. To take gold from someone who had just lost a son was simply unthinkable. Furthermore, the amount of gold he had was still far too much to spend in his time anyhow.

Esbern seemed a type of man who could never accept "no" as an answer. With promise of repayment, regardless of the form, he graciously thanked the boy for preventing any further chaos from happening within the inn.

One by one, each of the bodies, or sets of bones in some cases, were removed from The Goblin's Rest by the Faulkstead guards. The body belonging to that of Esbern's son was handled with utmost care. The same could not be said for the others. Some talk was made with Esbern on a funeral to come.

Eventually, both Esbern and his wife left the inn. One of his friends would take over the management of the inn for the time being. It would have been impossible to have Esbern return to his duties so quickly after such tragedy.

The boy took up a seat next to the barbarian. Gradually, each of them delved into a conversation on more personal matters. Perhaps it was time speak of the boy's true story.

···14···

Both Thul and the boy chatted late beyond the middle eve. Stained with such drama from earlier; a sort of refurbished truth-bringing evolved in their steady conversation.

The boy went on to speak of his story: his wife, her alchemy, her "kidnapping" and so forth, leading into her Elixir of Youth. Each reaction from the barbarian during the story brought about a variety of responses. At one point, Thul had laughed incredulously once he had heard that the boy had "simply" let his wife leave in the first place. To which followed his dialogue that went something of the nature: "Well, I would've jus' bashed them buggers' brains in!"

How uncomplicated had the Ironhold mind reproduced a modified version of stories, more suited to that of each northern individual. Perhaps an idea that involved letting your loved one vanish right before your eyes, regardless of such a threat of political injustice, was incomprehensible to his new friend.

And so, it became apparent to Thul that the boy had limited time remaining to reach his true love and there were many miles to go, with unforeseen obstacles. Secretly, the boy hoped that Thul would be willing to go with him.

"That there is a real heartbreaker, if I've ever eard' one myself," Thul spoke, as the boy reached the end of his story. "What've ya done with all that king man's gold?"

"That's the part I was getting to next," retorted the boy.

Both of the friends went on to sip their mead, rum, and other various alcohols as the boy continued to tell the barbarian of how he had stashed some 60,000 or so coins in his home. His plan had never been to return to collect the coin, but rather leave it for someone truly deserving of it, someone good-natured and true. Thul was becoming this envisioned person.

"Sixty thousand coins?" Thul said again, "You must be mad! Aye, if that were me, I'd ave taken off to the palms o' that there desert oasis in the far south!"

The boy went on to inform the giant that he would happily draw a map of the location of the gold, as it was clear that Thul was a man who lived for coin. Thul's entire vocation was to travel to Varroth, selling the Old Monk at every town. A man on a mission such as this would be keen on raising his profits by another 60,000. He had mentioned earlier that evening, that he had only four crates of Old Monk left, each of which would hopefully sell for 150 bits of gold each, permitting he didn't drink them all first.

"So, yer tellin' me as of this moment, you'd draw me a map o' that giant gold stash if I help ya find yer lady friend? What's the point? She's so old. Why don't you just find yerself a nice young lass?"

He wasn't really getting the point. But the boy's mission had already proven to be beyond the difficulty that he had anticipated.

So, an evening of sadness turned into hope. This became clear to the barbarian as the sun began rise. Everyone in the bar had gone to sleep, including the temporary barkeep.

Before sleep demanded the closed eyes of the adventurers, it was decided that Thul and the boy would venture forth to Koraivindahl, The Royal City of the East, and re-capture his wife.

A new beginning awaited the travelers upon their next awakening.

··· 15 ···

Thul was more of a careless, impulsive person. He wasn't a sharp man by any means, but what he lacked in smarts was made up for entirely by his purely jubilant energy levels. Hours of sleep meant nothing to him, nor did the quantity of drinks in an evening (albeit, more was always better). No, he did what he wanted, when he wanted. For this was likely one of the reasons for why the two had slept into the early afternoon.

His backstory was quite plain – he was born in the mountains and destined to die in the mountains. He had gained just as much knowledge as he had lost over the years, especially due to the drink. Old Monk was clearly his favourite, probably because it was his own. Though he was always one to delve into whatever was offered to him. An assassin could just as easily offer him an instantly, death-invoking chalice of venomous serpent blood disguised as mead and he would have it polished off before you could skip a stone across a shallow stream.

His strength was impressive. Anyone could see that. Scars told tales of his past, and made it clear that he truly lived up to his barbaric heritage. Thul's father, an exaggerated black-smith and heavy drinker of the mountains, hadn't always been the most forthright, hence the personal development of Thul over the years. A love/hate relationship between the two had offered Thul knowledge and a fortified barricade of mental resistance.

The giant woke before the boy, startling him as Thul's bed creaked heavily upon his rising. They made their way back to their drinking spots from the night before, this time ordering some food.

Breakfast had passed, but lunch was at the ready: rabbit stew. Wonderful for those who enjoyed a thick, creamy broth packed with an enormous amount of protein. This dish, in particular, was one the boy had enjoyed for decades in the pureberry meadows.

A meal such as this was necessary after an evening of so much physical exertion and prolonged drink. The hangover didn't affect Thul in the slightest, but it did dangle its ten-tacles of headache and muscle ache over the boy. The stew, paired with a cup of Faulkstead's cold, clear, river water was most desirable.

They spoke of what was to come, not what was in the past. The path to The Royal City had changed over time and the boy had not been aware of this. The original road to the East was blocked by the plagued city of Crease. Once a bountiful, thriving capital of Varroth, Crease used to be home to tens of thousands of folk, much like Koraivindahl, but it was struck by a dastardly plague. This came as a surprise to the boy when Esbern spoke of the diseased city.

"I'm surprised you haven't the knowledge, being an avid traveler and all," Esbern spoke quietly beneath a sad-eyed expression.

"Everybody knows that . . ." added Thul.

The boy replied, half embarrassed, "I'll admit I haven't traveled much in my youthful days. Please speak more of Crease."

Esbern sipped from a steamy tankard of strong brew coffee. "Crease fell to the poison forty odd years ago. To this day, no one knows what caused the plague, yet everyone who ventures there leaves with a sickness in their veins; a skin-changing disease. This plague is one that will change your appearance within days. A man as youthful as you would turn into a sack of withered skin and bone. You would probably survive, but your life would surely be diminished by many years."

Disbelief overcame the boy.

"And what's more," Esbern spoke, "you best believe you will be turned away from anywhere else after a visit to Crease. I've seen it in their yellowed eyes. Swashbucklers returning from The Plagued City have been destroyed on site in efforts to prevent the plague from spreading outward through the Kingdom of Varroth."

The idea of Crease infecting those who traveled through it left the boy with an unsettling sickness that had put him off his breakfast.

"What options do we have? There is limited time before I am due in The Royal City."

Esbern shook his head as he wiped the bar top. "The quickest way is to follow the Trade Route north. The path that once ran through Crease, now veers north through Rosenthal, Orchid, and Nomad's Hemlock."

It was out of the question.

"How long would it take to reach Koraivindahl in that time?" asked the boy.

"Knowing that the caravan stops in each city for a full day and night, you would probably arrive in 100 to 110 days."

Upon hearing this, the boy's mouth fell open.

"Sounds 'bout right," agreed Thul.

Such travel time would find the boy in his mid-sixties, maybe even his seventies, taking into account the Elixir's speed. At that point, he would be too old to save his wife.

A lack of hope began to fill his thoughts again. There was no way he would make it in time. The idea of failure was too great. His wife may have even died already from old age herself.

"Of course," the innkeeper interrupted his thought process, "You could just travel through Crease and hope for the best. If you don't have a choice—"

"And traveling around the outside of Crease? The perimeter? Is that not possible?"

Esbern burst out laughing, much louder than obviously needed. Clearly, the man had been affected by both the loss of his son and the lack of sleep.

"Crease is surrounded by cliffs. Unless under spell of levitation, your only way through, is the centre of the city. Then the route leads north, bypassing all of the mountainous ledges, through a thick, dense forest."

Just then, a fourth voice spoke, "Perhaps I can be of some assistance."

At the end of the bar sat an ancient soul, hunched over a goblet of drink. The elderly man wore a pointed hat and a fluffy shawl, both of which were the colour of crimson, dotted with spirals, stars and other various shapes. Next to him, sat the old wizard from the convoy, still in his pale blue clothes.

The boy's conversation with Thul and Esbern, had left him unaware that these two had been eavesdropping. The boy turned to look at the two wizards.

One spoke, "I am Opus. Though I am not much with knowledge of travel, I specialize in the alchemic factors of Faulkstead."

Both the boy and Thul stared blankly at the speaker. The banter of conversation continued in the background, as did the clatter of dishes and goblets on tabletops.

The blue wizard nudged the red. He looked as though he was in his hundreds. Behind round spectacles was a face of endless wrinkles and enlarged liver spots. His rigid nose was home to the largest boil the boy had ever seen on a person. "Perhaps there is something I can sell you . . . to keep the plague at bay."

The boy and Thul waited, watching Opus who stared absently at his drink. Was he okay? Although his mind was riddled with negativity, the boy fought the urge to laugh at the old alchemist. Comedic as his trance-like gaze was, Opus could provide some other way of reaching The Royal City in less than a lifetime. Turning back to Esbern, expecting to be made fun of again, he repeated, "How long would it take to reach The Royal City if we passed through Crease?"

This time, the innkeeper kept himself collected, "If you don't travel with the caravan, you might make it in as few as sixty days." He replied with confidence.

Sixty days.

That was perfect.

Sixty days . . .

He did the math in his head.

Sixty days would leave him youthful *enough* to fight and climb if need be.

"You can meet me at my laboratory once I have finished my lunch," stated the crimson alchemist.

Thul looked down upon the empty space that lay before Opus. Not a drop of drink was left within his brass goblet nor had a plate even existed.

"You have no food, old man," laughed Thul.

Opus was taken aback in amazement and his eyes widened. "Well then! I guess we can head there now!"

Time had always been the unstoppable force. More so for the boy than anyone else who lived in Varroth. Time decided everything. Blessed were the Divines, for it was they who had cast time upon the world. It was the truest aspect of all. Those who could correctly harness the power of utilizing it chose a path of security and happiness. For money . . . was not everything.

※　※　※

He who is most accepting of time must take
extra care in relinquishing his daily burdens.
For he who surrenders such endeavours,
allowing for the deliberate ponder of life's
eternal rose, its endless refinements and
all, is truly the man to find fulfillment.

···16···

The outskirts of town revealed a small, perfectly rounded house. The cedar plank that swung from an iron beam above that door was illustrated with two potions in front of a multi-pointed star. Evidently, this was the shop of Faulkstead's alchemist, as the wizard had indicated.

Memories of his wife flooded his mind, as the boy made his way to the door. Upon entering, the emporium appeared to be much different than what he had anticipated. Cyan and violet smoke filled the modest shop from multiple sticks of incense, surely those of a magical property. Various potions were proudly displayed on top of brass and iron structures, sealed with different sized corks. Bookshelves held tomes of assorted volumes and thicknesses, their information to the average reader mere jabber without specific knowledge of advanced potion craft.

"Greetings! Welcome to the Toadstool!" came the voice of another ancient soul.

An additional wizard met the boy. The trifecta was complete, as this shorter of the three, wore an outfit of malachite green, dotted with countless, flaxen-shaded squiggles and magical runes just like the other two.

The green-clad wizard set aside his book, titled *The Diamond and The Chef*. It was a true classic, and one of his wife's favourite books, pertaining to that of thievery and mischief. The story tells of a young couple of thieves who stole a diamond the size of an apple. In turn, they run into an older lady, one with a mind filled with knowledge of both magic and foolery. She goes on to use her alchemic power to brew a potion, which causes the consumer to be granted temporary invisibility. In promise with some shavings of the diamond, for future mixtures, she offers to trade her elixir of disappearance. One thing then leads to another, when she goes to prove that the potion did actually work. As soon as she indeed becomes silent to the human eye, she makes off with the diamond.

The story was one of intrigue, indeed. But not nearly as intriguing at what lay before him, completing the atmosphere of the entire laboratory altogether. It was a display case, exploding at its seams with endless ingredients. The glass-covered unit was home to a surplus of living, dead, materialistic, liquid, and gaseous items. Three individual shelves were overstuffed and jammed well over the desired weight of its walnut veneer.

One single book had been opened purposely and lay on the counter, evidently a price book. It was opened to page 63, though the book had probably close to three hundred pages, if not more. How the organization of such prices worked with the chaotic array of the items on each shelf left the boy in a state of bewilderment. He glanced at the page:

Wings of a Luna Moth (x2) .... 80 Silver

Grotto Fish Scales (small sack) .... 76 Silver

Phosphorescent Nettle .... 40 Silver

Blue Valley Pufferfish Venom (1 vial) .... 2 Gold

Death Root .... 1 Gold 30 Silver

Bear Fangs (x2) .... 1 Gold

Northern Foxglove Petals (dried) .... 65 Silver

Northern Foxglove Petals .... 2 Gold

Blood of Crypt Toad (1 vial) .... 2 Gold 25 Silver

Silver Valley Mushrooms .... 90 Silver

Rose Petals .... 40 Silver

Earthworms (1 small container – live) .... 18 Silver

Mountainside Toadstools (Randomly picked – dried) .... 65 Silver

Imp Blood (1/8 vial) .... 8 Gold

Yew Wood Ash .... 32 Silver

Standard Mold (1 capsule) .... 55 Silver

Distilled Croftwood Vines .... 75 Silver

Essence of Wraith (demonoid) .... Please Ask

Essence of Wraith (humanoid) .... Discontinued

Raspberries (dried) .... 40 Silver

Finzbay Grapes (fresh – 1 single cluster) .... 85 Silver

Carndale Cavern's "Green Gel" .... 6 Gold

Bonemeal (Bovine) .... 40 Silver

Quail Egg .... 90 Silver

Weeping Tree Sap (1/2 Vial) .... 2 Gold 20 Silver

Clover (1 bunch) .... 10 silver

East Sea Barnacles (preserved) .... 85 Silver

Surely, not every ingredient of this entire book can be inside the case at this current time, thought the boy.

"Opus! What can we offer these folks? They seem of lesser knowledge with our craft." The green alchemist had spoken in the direction of the old wizard.

"Ah yes! We have a cure for your stiff leg right here!" cheered Opus.

Blind stares.

"You'll have to excuse him," started the malachite wizard. "His memory is not what it used to be, though he is ten times more capable than I when it comes to performing flawless potion craft."

"Oh yes! Crease! I remember now!" Opus piped up again, prattling on from where he left off. "The Plague City! Yes. Well . . . You've come to the right place. Together, Vlodus and I can prepare you a potion of anything you wish – for lots of gold of course. You have gold, right?"

"Don't be rude! Of course they have gold, why else would they be here?" the malachite wizard snapped, apparently named Vlodus.

Somehow Vlodus wasn't a very fitting name for that of an old man dressed in green. Either way, the boy was more consumed with his building frustration as the two elders bickered back and forth, only to be joined by the third.

"He has gold, you idiots. I saw it on the caravan ride we took together."

Vlodus waved his new guests around his store. Squeezing past a nearby octagon table, covered in tattered books and dog-eared scrolls was not a problem for the boy, but as Thul proceeded to move past, he knocked the surface several times, sending the majority of the contents to the floor.

"Oye!" Vlodus exclaimed, irritated, "Be careful! I don't have time to play clean-up after some oaf!"

He turned back; his gaze fixated on a massive chest that could not be seen from the front lobby of the shop. A few moments later, Vlodus succeeded in removing five iron locks, each with its own key, from their homes in front of the chest.

Upon opening, a bottomless passage revealed itself. Gently, the malachite wizard made his way into his chest, and down a flight of spiraling stairs. Before he had reached the halfway mark, he reversed up a few steps, popping his head up from the mysterious strongbox.

"On second thought, the big man can stay up here! Don't touch anything!" He commanded Thul. Vlodus spun himself down the rest of the spiral.

The boy, with hesitation at first, disregarded his fears and began to descend as well. For a moment, a nagging thought of fear tainted his mind. What if these wizards had lured him here only to harvest him for human ingredients? Each human body was known to produce an immeasurable number of reinvigorating elements, perfect for various potions.

Upon reaching a dirt floor, Vlodus's basement revealed home to an entire colony of different species of plant life growing among individual rectangular boxes filled with soil. Bursting with amazing colour, each seedling, shrub, mushroom and flower showed a multitude of endless vibrancy and consistency. The room was double in size compared to the room from which he had just come, stretching into a lengthy corridor.

Opus joined the two, making his way down towards a table of mixology, much like the boy's wife's laboratory, which stood at the end of the botanist's hall. On the table was a mortar and pestle paired with a cook stand, test tubes, various glass decanters for heating, and a myriad of differently shaped vials and bottles, all of which were currently holding some form of coloured liquid.

"If you plan on traveling through Crease, and I must add that it is highly unsafe - you will need something to keep the plague at bay, boy. A once beautiful city, now home to sickness in this time. It is also full of unsavoury characters."

"If Crease has become such a disaster, then why do people still live there?" questioned the boy, pondering a mental image of what remained of the city compared to the illustrations he had seen in his younger days.

"Because, my boy, those who venture to Crease, choose a life of no return. Once you have contracted the sickness, your appearance will show it. You will grow withered with bagged eyes, white hair and disease-like blotchiness. Those who are unlucky enough to become sick, live for only thirty years; less for those who are already as ancient as I."

Clearly, Vlodus was the brighter of the two. It seemed these brothers in alchemy chose to brew potions of all kinds, though none of them added to a strong memory.

The malachite wizard continued, "If you truly wish to travel the path of Crease, and come out alive on the other side, you must act wisely. Opus and I can craft you an elixir of plague countermeasure. The concoction will be foolproof, and you must drink a single vial every day you are within the city. A double vial each day will be required for your oaf of a friend up there."

"You know he means well," replied the boy, this time showing that offence had indeed been taken.

"So be it, good or bad, I can have the elixir prepared for you by tomorrow morning."

Thul called down, wondering what was taking so long. The boy was perplexed by the collection of such botany. In the past, he had read of underground plant life, but this was of much different measure. As he listened to every word Vlodus had to say, his energy changed into an uplifted aura, like that of a grand crusader coming across a long search for treasure.

How could he know this elixir ensured safe passage? Was the babble of this old man just an attempt to acquire some of the boy's large wealth? It was a comfort to know that he still possessed a sum, far greater, under his bed at home. A sum he knew would go to Thul, should they succeed in their quest. The idea of handing over the large amount came easier and easier as the friends' relationship built itself up, hand over brick.

"Is today not a good day to make the preparation?" asked the boy.

"Hah!" Vlodus laughed noisily. "I'm building you a potion of plague resistance! The Plague of Grand Crease at that! I'm not brewing you a drink of simple water breathing. Listen, my boy, if you wish this to be a concoction of flawlessness, you'll give Opus and myself the time we need."

Such knowledge of prolonged preparation surprised the boy. Time had been his greatest enemy, but it was a matter of acceptance for yet another eve. Thul probably wouldn't mind, as his boredom was being quenched with an ever-flowing river of liquor.

"What is the price?"

"The price will depend entirely on what is used."

"Which is what exactly?"

Both Vlodus and the boy set their gazes towards Opus. He had been sitting on a tiny, thatch stool, propped against another fully stacked bookshelf. Somehow, he had fallen asleep, eating a brittle chunk of blue cheddar. How exactly was this alchemy to be finished, when one of its primary potionists could barely keep awake?

The malachite wizard spoke for Opus, "Never you mind that, for now. So long as you have the coin, I'll keep us on track. See us at high sun tomorrow, and we will have the elixir finished."

The boy agreed, cautiously, shaking hands with Vlodus. It was time for him to leave. Without a declared price, it was obvious that the coin for such trade was going to be an enormous amount. Though hopefully not too extreme, a promise was made to the barbarian that he too would receive a splendid amount. The boy made a prayer for both luck and good fortune as he climbed the spiral passage back into reality.

··· 17 ···

A night of restlessness was upon the boy's state of mind. He drifted in and out of sleep, only to dream of hostility. Each subconscious image was of war and death. He also dreamed of the amulet from the jeweller's wares. Images of the skull and vial clouded his dreams.

For each time he woke, fatigue would wear him back down into a stage of sleep, only to bear witness to the horrible images once again. It was as if a dark power had entered his mind.

Suddenly, it was day, signalled by the call of a proud rooster, waking the sleepy riverside town. The night call of the owl had been severed and soon a mighty sun rose once again in the east.

That time, the boy awoke at the same time as Thul. A few steady glugs of leftover red wine was enough to wake the barbarian, but the boy had a craving for a taste of coffee.

Breakfast was a couple bowls of cabbage and turnip soup, paired with a loaf of crusty rye. Not ideal for a meal with the rising sun, but it would have to do. Their next tasks prepared them for the journey ahead.

For the better part of their day, Thul and the boy took the time to visit a variety of shops, building a fully stocked, yet lightweight inventory of food for their dangerous journey ahead.

With some effort, Thul was finally convinced to part with his remaining crates of Old Monk. He did, however, insist on keeping eight bottles for himself. For some folks, a bottle of water brimming with vitality would be number one on the list when it came to travel, but not for Thul. In fact, he hadn't consumed a single drop of water since arriving in Faulkstead. The more the boy thought about it, the more he searched his brain for instances in which Thul drank water. None came to mind.

With aid from Faulkstead's general store, the two were able to track down a fairly comfortable set of traveling packs large enough to hold a bear cub in each.

Smoke rose from a pipe the boy had smoked, sold to him from the same store. It's riverside tobacco, fresh with an organic flavour to it.

"Okay, Thul. We have tracked down a couple bottles for river water, a couple bottles of red wine, a wheel of lamb's cheese, a few bundles of dried grapes, four loaves of rye, four pieces of salted steak, eight dried salmon, six apples, a few of Esbern's croissants, and a bag of riverseed. . . I've never had riverseed, though folk from The Goblin's Rest recommended it. What do you we left on your list?"

The barbarian pulled a completely rumpled, half-torn sheet of yellow paper from his pocket and presented it:

1. Rum
2. Meeet
3. Gold – becoz its payment
4. Mor Rum
5. Dezert
6. Rabbit

"And the rest I'll catch with me 'ands," he added with a quick, but confident head bow.

It was a wonder Thul had made it this far in life with his lack of literacy.

"Very well. Good list." The boy nodded in approval, mostly just so that his friend's list seemed acceptable. "Let's make our way to over to the wizards."

Once again, the mystical laboratory was full of unbearably strong incense. Opus was asleep at his front desk, causing the two travelers to wonder if the elixir had even been started.

"Oh!" He awoke to noise of the front door slamming shut. "What can I help you with?"

The boy reminded Opus of their conversation the day before.

"Ah yes! The elixir! I know you! Come with me, my boy!"

Again, the boy was led down into the garden of secret undertakings. A small table, which had not been there before, held twenty-four vials, each of which contained a glowing, emerald green nectar. His eyes, having seen many concoctions in the past, had never before seen such a shade of brilliance. Somehow, in only one evening, the alchemists had succeeded in crafting his request.

"They look . . . incredible!" He paused. "But what of the taste?"

"Perhaps not first-rate to the taste buds in a human mouth. A tad sour, in all honesty, but nothing a drink of wine can't wash away. Please make sure to drink one vial for each day you spend in the troubles of Crease; two vials will be necessary for your friend."

His advice was duly noted. Next came the question of straightforwardness.

"And the price?"

Vlodus twiddled his thumbs beneath his flowing sleeves.

"Well . . . we had to use a number of expensive elements. Some of which even came from outside Varroth." He paused to gauge the boy's reaction, to which he said nothing. It had become a bit of game, to see how much a plague resistance truly cost.

"Between the blood of an icy deep-sea octopus, hawk eggs, nectar of the ultimately rare Salix growth, ten vials of oasis leech saliva, seven capsules of—"

"Never mind," the boy interjected. "Just tell me the price."

"Ah! Ummm . . ."

Opus cleared his throat before Vlodus spoke once again.

"Well, uh. Eight hundred pieces of gold."

"What?!" stammered the boy, almost hysterical. One would think an alchemist of such knowledge might attempt to levy such a high price, but this was ridiculous! It was clearly an overinflated sum. Eight hundred pieces of gold was the value of three-quarters of Faulkstead's entire real estate.

A conversation of serious haggling ensued for quite some time, during which the boy even speculated trading his horse alongside the gold to keep the cost down. But he feared these alchemists would harvest poor Orist for his parts.

Eventually, they agreed on an even 475 gold pieces. After paying with coin, which he had extracted from a stash well within the depths of his new travel bag, goodbyes were exchanged. His next stop was The Goblin's Rest, one last time. He had made up his mind. Through a deep cycle of saddening thought and decision, the boy had decided to give Esbern, the innkeeper, his most cherished friend and stallion of pure devotion. For present-day Crease was no place for a horse like Orist.

··· 18 ···

The departure from Faulkstead was one of heartache. Despite his unforeseen run-in with the town's jeweller, his stay in the riverside community had been one of both stimulating activity and generous hospitality. Though the necromancer and his conjurations had caused a violent and ultimately tragic scene, the boy chose to remember Faulkstead for its better qualities.

Hard enough as it was to leave the town, the worst part was leaving Orist, such a gentle being; truly a horse of utmost loyalty. Albeit not a word had been communicated in full between the two, both the boy and his horse had built an entire relationship on love and care. Years had passed since Orist had entered this world as a small colt. At that moment he was sturdier than ever, he had proven himself ultimately dutiful and most affectionate. He was an animal that not a single 4-legged being in the world could compare to. When it came down to it, regardless of shape, size, nature, race, or variation of species, the one true universal language that had been spoken since time itself had first begun, was one of acceptance.

An image of Orist's magnificent figure, his mane of flaxen, gold perfection, would remain in the boy's memory forever - next to that of his wife.

A moment of true sorrow, and one of prolonged endearment, the boy finished his goodbye by giving Orist a handful of fresh garden carrots. Orist returned the affection with a gentle, yet lengthy embrace of his elongated nose. It was clear that Orist too had sensed this was their final goodbye.

When the time came, the boy, alongside Thul, parted ways and headed down the town path, leading eastward. Glances of love and unmitigated despair were exchanged between Orist and the boy until his impeccable steed vanished from sight, to be left in the earnest care of old Esbern.

⠿　⠿　⠿

Ahead of the two companions, lay a path of the unknown. The better part of the day was spent traveling the path of the Trade Route that cut evenly through a forest of thick wood. Mighty with towering height, each tree provided a great shade from the grand sphere of circulating solar flame. It was the season in which the sun released its greatest heat over the entirety of Varroth.

After nearly four hours of travel, they stopped for a spell to feast, and regain their energy under a large, black walnut tree. Upon reaching its mighty base, the sac-like pouches surrounding their nutty treasures had revealed themselves to be in midgrowth; not yet ripe enough to eat. Nevertheless, surrounding the fallen trees, the moss, and various shade-induced overgrowths made way for numerous clusters of earthy morels. The last time the boy had tasted morel mush-rooms was so long ago, but their taste - so uniquely delicious, it was impossible to forget.

Thul, reluctant at first, eventually joined in on eating the brain-like mushrooms alongside his smaller companion.

"These ain't alf' bad," he proclaimed as he tasted his first bite.

"It's best you eat them with something else, so you don't overdo it and get sick! Perhaps some bread?" the boy offered. He was right; too many morels would leave any man on the verge of nausea, regardless of his size. Such richness in a fungus had proven its problems in human stomachs time and time again.

"Fair enough," Thul accepted the boy's offer, munching away on a chunk of crusty rye.

Intervals of silence fell over them as they refuelled, occa-sionally kicking back to admire their surroundings. Each mouthful of mushrooms and bread went down quite nicely with a splash of wine from their goblets.

Occasionally, a sparrow would fly down to a nearby perch to investigate the travelers. It was hard to tell if anyone in existence had ever laid foot in that particular location, off the main path.

Thul was the one to break the silence.

"You know, boy," he started with a note of slight discern-ment, "Come to think of it, ye' be lookin' a wee bit older now."

"Alas," answered the smaller of the two, "I do know this. I have seen it when I look at the glassy surface of still water."

The barbarian sat there simply staring back.

The boy spoke, "I fear we won't make it. I'll become too old to save her in time. The potion... with all of its defects... I fear it will ruin me with its curse of aging. The life I lived as an old man has revealed more than just acquired knowledge. I've learned that once you get to a certain age your body just ... breaks down ... It's awful!"

He paused – figuring a way to spin the conversation into that of a more positive manner.

"My friend! I'll admit from when I first saw you, I was worried that you were a violent man!"

"Bah!" quipped the barbarian. "A violent man indeed, but only when needed. All who know right, leave me be when I'm drinkin', to me happy thoughts o' course! Then there won't be no problems. But ye best believe, in everyone's interests, I'll be givin' ya a good smashin' should ye' be botherin' me and mine."

A once blossoming friendship had evolved into a fortified structure of trust and brotherhood. Yes, Thul was in it for the money, but the two went on chatting for quite some time, exchanging compliments with one another, revealing that the barbarian was indeed a true friend – perhaps even one with a bit of a soft spot way, way down.

"That reminds me!" off-guard, the boy sprouted with energy, "I have yet to draw you a map to my home!" This led him to bring forth an empty quill and inkpot, which he had purchased from Faulkstead's General Store.

Since the place where the boy originally joined up with Varroth's Trade Route was familiar only to his eye, the ability to draw a map to his residence amongst the pureberry meadows was a difficult task. Surely, with enough detail, Thul would come across the house, should he follow the directions closely enough. The barbarian had already provided such great service in helping the boy through a handful of very risky and dangerous episodes; he deserved the best map possible.

By the time he had finished his navigational drawing, the shade from the tree had shifted its position, as had the sun. The boy had succeeded in drawing what he felt confident to be a "proper" map with various landmarks as noted by a variety of asterisks and other such symbols.

"Remember Thul, once you get there, it might be in shambles. The king's men will likely decide to overturn everything. But I am confident in knowing that the gold will still remain under the floorboards in my bedroom."

"All sixty thousand, right?"

"That's right," replied the boy, watching the eyes of his giant friend as they glowed in excitement along with his greedy smile. It was clear that the barbarian was at a stage in which he trusted the boy undoubtedly.

He handed the map to Thul, who was clearly thinking of all the things such amounts of coin could buy him. To the boy, such a feeling was best described as the generosity of a saint – as if a beggar had been granted free pass to a castle equipped with infinite amenities, extreme wealth and endless pleasures.

"Never ave' I met a boy like you!" beamed the barbarian, positivity radiating from his core. "Thank you! Thank you for this! I am yours til' we find yur' lady friend. Through bloodshed an' through tears. You might think this'll be a hard job but ye' never fought' longside me. Bah! It'll be an easy quest. Even if ye' get too old, I'll carry ya' over me' shoulder!

So, it was done. Financial business out of the way, and a couple bundles of fresh morels to boot, it was time to yet again set foot on their way back to the trail. Nightfall was still some hours away, but nevertheless gaining on their heels.

···19···
AGE: 33

Varroth had always been home to one of the most adverse terrains in existence. The surrounding lands shared somewhat similar qualities when it came to such various groupings of distinct biomes, though none had ever matched the eclectic realms that existed within the great land.

Bordered by two of the great seas, Varroth, in all of its grand, colossal fashion had always been a bountiful land of endless possibility. Perfect for adventurers and treasure-seekers, it remained home to dangerous, yet unknown territory. Its ever-stretching borders to the north and south joined with distant nations. Varroth appealed to all kinds of living beings as it offered more than anywhere else.

It was as if the kingdom had been crafted by every divine nature from all four corners of the world: deserts of unliveable, scorching heat, monumental mountains of never-ending snowfall, thickly treed woodlands exotic with undiscovered species and tundra of eternal barrenness. Literally every imaginable, habitable ecosystem existed here, all except the terrains of a rainforest. Those were found further south where the hemisphere's areas permitted a much greater humidity. This landscape was positively filled with the extremes of both horrors and miracles.

At one point, on the fifth day of their new travel, the adventurers reached a fork in the road, between which stood a grouping of signs. One post had two signs indicating the paths that led to Rosenthal and to Crease. Farther along the path to Crease stood another sign reading:

Entry denied.

The path ahead is closed.

Ahead lies only a deadly plague.

Those who neglect this sign will be condemned
to Crease's fallen city for all eternity.

You will not be warned again.

Turn back now, or continue north to Rosenthal.

According to their log, they were nearing the end of their seventh day of travel upon their new journey. In this time, the remaining features of the boy's youthful presence had begun to elude him further. A once younger face was slowly being replaced by that of someone older. This face, still far from being traced with the lines of future advancement, showed evidence of true maturation. His cheekbones, forehead, and brow had become slightly more prominent with full adulthood. Muscles of stockiness and endurance held together his body, with the skin leathery, yet still somewhat soft. Even his build had morphed. Thul was no longer calling him 'boy'.

Not all of the changes were visible. He felt the ache of ongoing travel in his knees and lower back. Despite having the strength of an ox, time was making itself known, for his agile bloom was making way for new bodily discoveries, not all of which were good – yet still minor in change.

Since the beginning, the aging Gold Counter had wondered how the Elixir of Youth really affected a single person. He remembered feeling curious about how it would age him both mentally and physically. On one level, a feeling of greater intelligence came over the traveler, but perhaps that was just his mind adapting to all his new experiences. The physical aging of his body was definitely far too real.

For some reason, the hair on his body, including his head and facial features continued to grow at the same rate as an average human, as did his nails. Such peculiars must have had something to do with the ingredients used in the crafting of the potion.

❊   ❊   ❊

The days of travel brought a world of change in both climate and terrain. The lush greenery of the forest stood far behind them at that point. For a spell, they hiked through an area of trees that were alive, dead, and somewhere in-between.

They soon walked through a land far from what one would call "lively."

Their trek into the badlands of plague had brought them to a land of rotting, sloshy terrain, home to a seemingly endless amount of skinny birch trees that had long since died. Every sinking, squelching, muddy footstep brought them more and more emptiness. Shrouded in fog, thicker than the foam of a freshly poured stout of dark, frothy ale, lay a landscape of colours ranging from rotting plum and dark indigo, to utter blackness.

The ground, which held various sizes of puddles filled with rotting algae, stretched indefinitely through the smoggy lands. It made new growth impossible, for the only life it contained was one of crooked death.

As the adventurer and his giant friend made their way cautiously through the swampy lands, the cry of a blood raven broke their silence. Since entering the dreadfully lonely land, the light had faded from the sky, as the fog only granted them ten or so feet of visibility. A feeling of discomfort washed over the younger of the two, as it had become apparent to him that he had forgotten to pack a blanket, or some sort of material to sleep on in wet, cold conditions.

"Perhaps we should rest for the night," he suggested to Thul, motioning to the sky, which provided notice that the daylight hours had come to an end.

The barbarian agreed, and they began searching for the driest possible area near enough the path. It was dreadful. Everywhere they surveyed was covered with differing intensities of black water and sludge. The area was suddenly more liquid than it was mud.

"To hell with this! I refuse to sleep in mud!" roared Thul, full of obvious frustration. He grabbed the skinny trunk of a nearby birch, snapped it free and broke it in half. With minimal effort, he made the task look easy. He then continued on to break off more trees from their stumps, until he had snapped off twenty-odd treetops, which he laid together on top of the unforgiving marsh.

"There!" he exclaimed, a twist of confident tone to his voice. "We shall lay on these. It won't be comfortable, but at least we'll be dry."

His ways had always impressed the Gold Counter as he had once taken the barbarian for someone of fewer brains. Had he traveled alone, the idea to sleep on piles of branches would have never crossed his mind. Further to that, the Gold Counter's strength would not have allowed him to snap off the treetops anyways.

The two of them went on to build a small fire toward the centre of their temporary swamp raft. With multiple rough, downward slashes, the young man successfully lit a pre-wrapped bundle of tinder with the use of some flint and a piece of steel.

Then out came the three young rabbits they had caught earlier and a bottle of Old Monk. Oh, how the travelers had become bored with the taste of the long-eared critters, but they hadn't any other choice. Their dried edibles had to be saved for moments of dire need, most likely within the walls of Crease, where not a single living thing remained healthy enough to cook and consume.

Though the flames were not huge, they were enough to cook the meat. Secretly, he prayed to the gods, thanking them for the small bounty of meat that had been provided to them that day.

"I have ventured to many a place, but none like this mess," spoke Thul through a mouthful of dinner.

The young man swallowed before speaking, "I agree. These lands are truly horrible. Hopefully, we will reach the city soon."

Once again… silence.

Their position amongst the long, forgotten woods was lonely. Entirely quiet with the eerie sensation of something watching them, despite the thick, heavy vapor of the swampy smog. Far from any sort of civilization, the two travelers remained still with fearful anxiousness and unease. Even Thul, as barbaric and as fearless as he was, portrayed a subconscious appearance of subtle aghast.

Just then, another cry of the blood raven erupted from somewhere in the distance, its cry echoing through the foggy depths.

"It would be wise to start into our resistance potions. Perhaps we should have done that earlier when we first entered this place." the Gold Counter questioned.

"Best leave it. We've yet to come into contact with any lively creatures yet. I wouldn't worry 'bout it til' mornin'."

The young man's heart thumped like a war drum from within the caverns of his chest. "Do you really think we will run into something dubious in Crease?"

Thul paused before emptying his second goblet of Old Monk. He always drank four or five as much as the Counter. How his body processed such amounts of excess was a mystery.

"I think there'd be good chance brother. We must be ready. This is no mere camp of thievin' scum - more so bands of hungry, rotting fiends I'd imagine. This ere' is the city o' Plague. Not to be taken lightly... One wrong move, we might as well be ghoul dinner right then n' there."

The thought of ghastly teeth chewing through human flesh overwhelmed the young excursionist, putting him off his meal.

"Don't worry, brother. You stick with ol' Thul n' you be right as rain. You'd better believe my words!" laughed the barbarian, warm spirited with the fervour of nourishing meat and back-home rum.

Eventually, the two friends finished their evening snack, and began settling in, as best as they could, atop their make-shift beds in hopes of sweet dreams. Night became its darkest and the relentless fog remained heavy and dense. The far-off raven had too, turned in for the eve, as its calls were no longer. The small crackling of firewood soon turned to silence, as its warm flames flickered out of existence.

It was cold.

Cold with the icy emptiness of desolation...

And death.

Thul, naturally, had fallen asleep quickly. That was to be expected after polishing off a half bottle of home-brew rum. The Gold Counter, not-so-much, as he lay still, wide-eyed, beside his new friend.

The young man reached for the bottle of Old Monk. It certainly wasn't his drink of choice, though it was growing on him. After a day of travel, the dark nectar with its hard-liquored taste, appealed more to him at that moment than it did before. Besides, its warmth and intoxicating qualities was a necessity for sleep in such scary, unfair conditions.

He poured a solo goblet of rum and sipped from its brim. From beyond the bog, a wolf howled a great distance from their location, causing him to choke on his freshly sipped beverage.

"Easy, brother. You'll acquire its taste one day." Thul, evidently woken by the young man's struggle, chuckled with closed eyes.

Thul was a truly incredible man, capable of real feelings like love and compassion. Throughout their travels, he had exhibited a grand amount of authentic interest in the young man's mission to save his wife. Did Thul himself have a wife? Perhaps he did, yet the young man had never asked him this question. Half a chalice of the barbaric brew was enough to send any man into a trance of thoughtful reflection.

Finishing his contemplations, as he did his drink, the young adventurer readied himself for his departure to the land of dreams. His nerves calm, then was the time to rest. He pulled his travelers cloak around him, and curled around his sack of money and food. No doubt the Old Monk aided in his feelings of warmth and serenity in addition to taking his mind off his makeshift bed.

The calmness of his demeanour blocked out the lonely, empty surroundings just as a mother fox blocks out the coldness of winter once wrapped around her pups. After much thought, a feeling of pure tranquil bliss had finally been reached.

And that's when it happened.

The unjust darkness of Crease made its first horrid appearance.

···20···

A sudden creaking belonging to that of a rickety wagon wheel came squishing through the swampy mud, stealing away all peace of mind that had been so longed for.

From where the young man lay, he had a clear view of the trail they had traveled down. Out of the blackness, a soft glow of light appeared from within the dead trees. A flickering torch. Its flame, a florescent blue, like the heart of a sapphire, grew closer with the noise.

The feeling of tranquility all but vanished, as the young adventurer watched the traveler draw closer and closer. Surely, whatever it was would no doubt come across the sleepers, as they were not in the most secluded area.

Another light source then appeared, though it was not of a torch, nor was it of a peaceful nature. Its brightness was of a burning red, belonging to the eyes of whatever pulled the dreadful load.

As the foreign convoy drew nearer, a wagon revealed itself. The chest atop supported a hooded, incredibly hunched over, sickly looking individual. The rider's legs, wrapped completely in bandages, probably some sort of plague-resistant wrapping, dangled freely as they bounced against the face of the chest. Its head and torso were fully covered by a single, dark robe with a frayed hole around the face... or lack thereof. From what the young man could see, the shrouded figure did not have a face, but just a black emptiness, blacker than the Void itself.

To make matters worse, a nightmarish, horse-type creature of abnormal form, painted in blood with voodoo-like symbols had been pulling the convoy ahead of some loosely held, tattered leads. Its all-black body, a shade of darkened charcoal and ash, appeared desecrated with gaping scars. The horse's eyes glowed with a vivid, yet truly hateful shade of garnet red.

It was obvious that this dark passenger was not in any sort of hurry as the vehicle upon which he travelled moved deathly slow through the sludge of the wetland. The head belonging to the shrouded figure never moved. It was focused on the rotted fishing pole ahead that held some sort of a root vegetable in front the demon horse – a common motivational technique apparently regardless of the being of tow.

If there had ever been a time to pray to the gods, that moment would be it. It was probable that the ghastly figure would notice the two travelers.

With his heart beating like a war drum, the man watched as the rider neared.

Death, every man's greatest fear, suddenly thrived but feet away. Time, which had been so critically fast for the young confidant, had abruptly defined itself as nothing more than frozen and lethargic.

Finally, the caravan rode within its closest range. As it did, the Gold Counter's heart pounded so powerfully, he was worried that whatever rode atop the condemned wagon could hear its beating. However . . . it just... continued on. Its hooded banshee of a rider was still fixated just as intently on the suspended root vegetable as its horrific steed.

Praise to the gods.

The boy thought of waking Thul, but changed his mind. Doing so would probably cause a disruption – the last thing they needed at that moment.

He watched the caravan inch farther and farther into the darkness.

A feeling of calmness began its descent from within the boy's soul, only to be severed by the stopping of wheels. The caravan, only fifteen or so feet away, had come to a complete stop on the edge of the thick fog. War drums began thundering just as before.

Why now? thought the boy.

Why wouldn't this evil being just continue on its journey? What was stopping the caravan?

His stillness matched with that of the frozen air that surrounded them.

What had been a release to freedom, soon turned to horror as the hunching shadow leapt down from its post atop the convoy chest, landing carelessly in the mud. Slowly, it turned... and began treading towards the travelers. Though it held a blue torch in front, the facelessness of the rider's void still remained unseen.

As the gap closed, it became apparent to the young man that the nearing figure did not in fact have a face at all. It was a ghost, a wraith, one of sick, evil, destructive nature, something that would feast on the fresh innards of healthy travelers.

The sound of mud squishing underfoot grew louder and louder as it approached.

What was it searching for?

There was nowhere to run, but into the impending depths of the plague. He couldn't do that. The elixir of resistance was here. Thul was here. What constituted his entire life - was right here!

Suddenly, the figure stood above them.

The young man watched as the figure, whatever it was, gazed down upon the supposedly sleeping companions. To say what it was thinking, or perhaps mentally conjuring was impossible. With no obvious objective, the spectral figure stood motionless, casting its deathly vision upon them.

It was at that moment that the young man's fight instinct kicked into gear. In one swift movement he jumped to his feet and shouted, "Get away! Get away!" his voice bouncing off the trunks of dead birch trees in the vicinity. "Thul! Get up! Wake up!"

Thul rose immediately, clearly taking assertive action to being so rudely awakened. It took less than a second before he, too, realized what horror lurked in front of them.

"Bastard!" Thul's voiced boomed through the empty vastness as he swung his giant left fist at the wild banshee. It was unclear if his brute force made contact with the specter, but somehow, he knocked the torch from its grasp, sending it to a hasty end in a muddy splash.

"Get away, foul spirit!" he yelled with such a fright, even mountain lions would seek refuge. Thus continued his frantic swinging and shouting before eventually calming.

"What in bloody hell!? Where did it go?"

Only the glow of the garnet red light could be seen, emitting from the demon horse down the path. Surely the banshee still lurked nearby, though it was out of sight. Nothing could be seen, as the darkness enveloped them, just as a bucket of water ends a luminous campfire.

Finally, the creature spoke. Its voice was somewhat ghostly, each word followed by echo as if coming out of a tunnel.

"You will forgive me, humans. I had assumed you were dead!"

Suddenly, a ray of light beamed from the direction of the ghastly words. Blue flame, the same as before, flashed into existence from an opening within the dead trees.

Poof!

Such energy - clearly that of magical essence.

Bewildered, the two adventurers stared at the faceless banshee, once again manipulating the magical torch.

"I bid you no harm. It caught me by surprise to find you still alive!"

A feeling of nervousness was in the young man's lifeblood; though the same could not be said for Thul. His blood ran thick with vengeance, anger, and hostility.

"You! Why in god's ways are you sneakin' up on us? You will not dine on us tonight, foul being!"

Its voice picked up again, "I truly bid you no harm. You see, I take pleasure in harvesting souls. I like to—"

The young man piped up, cutting off the spirit, knowing that Thul would back him up no matter what happened next.

"You will not take ours!"

"Please!" the ghost tried again, "I cannot do harm to any human! My touch, my flame, even my magic is from a different realm, a realm of the dead, a realm of the plague, the other side. Even if I wanted to kill you, I couldn't."

Silence again.

"Sure, I could make my way into your dreams every night, and give you nothing but sleepless horror for the rest of your life. Yet I do not wish to do that. I merely want your souls."

"What? Then why the bloody hell come over here, ya' fiend? State your name! Your business! Or I'll have your head!"

The voice that answered was actually quite calm.

"Your efforts in doing so are pointless. As for my name . . . I go by many names, as does my kind. You can call me Edgar. I was once a happy citizen of Crease, before the disease that is. This much is true. What I can tell you, is that I perished from the evil sickness that struck our poor city. I, along with many other unlucky folk, met the likes of death. But . . ."

Something in his voice changed. Something . . . sad?

"But what you do not know is that dying by the plague means . . . well . . . it means to never be fully released. One is . . . stuck. Stuck here in this world, in this city, an endless eternity of wallowing around these forsaken lands. Completely the opposite of the blissful heavens . . . Entry denied to the Kingdom of Gods. In other words, to die with the plague guarantees a life of infinite wandering and thirst."

"Of thirst?" questioned the young man.

"Yes. That is why I had hoped you were dead. To die with the plague, curses your empty soul with an undying thirst for just that. More souls. Just as all humans thirst for water, we plagued apparitions thirst for the souls of the recently deceased. There is pleasure in knowing that by having your soul consumed by my type, you can be reincarnated. Much better than the alternative around here, which is to be condemned to spectral thirst forever."

Thul looked to the young man for some answer, but he in turn had none. He then pivoted to the ghost.

"So, spirit what yur sayin' is yur wantin' our souls cause ye be thirsty? Well ye can't have 'em!"

Fury took hold once again. Thul, swung at the ghost, again knocking the torch to the ground, extinguishing the flame.

"Will you *pleeeease* stop doing that! Do you have any idea how much energy it takes our kind to rekindle a light source like this?!"

The young man turned to his barbarian companion. "Thul, ease up a bit."

"Thank you! *Sheesh* . . . Just because I have an eternity, doesn't mean I have all night!"

The torch sparked to life once again, somehow back within grasp of the wraith.

"I feel as though I am answering all of your questions, though I have yet to ask my own," claimed Edgar, further consumed with curiosity. "Tell me your story. What brought you to this place of ultimate sickness? Don't you know you could have contracted this disease the second you entered The Forest of Ill?"

The Forest of Ill. What a name . . .

The abrupt appearance of the ghost, paired with the surrounding forest left little patience in the young man. His thoughts were of either sleep or travel, yet he was unsure of when either of these would occur. He owed no explanation to this ghost, nor did he plan on telling him where they were headed. He reached for his bag and pulled from it the first set of resistance vials. Before any other action took place, his impulse took over. He slurped back the first vial, just as he handed Thul his required "double" dose.

Its nectar had such sourness to it. Like fresh lemon drops, only exceedingly amplified. The tartness invoked a feeling of fresh nausea. Whatever the alchemists had brewed into these potions, they clearly had a most acidic base to their ingredients.

"No offence intended, but my partner and I here are on a quest, which we do not speak about to others. I feel as though such information is private. If you do not have any other business with us, or our 'souls' for that matter, would you please leave us to our own ways?"

As much as he was willing to admit it, this was his quest of non-forgiveness. Someone was bound to die, be it them or the enemy. The countless days he spent fireside, awaiting his wife's arrival, day in and day out would all be for naught if he were to fail. At one point, the king had made a promise, an oath even, only to break it. No, this was a quest of perseverance in the name of true love, and any who stood in the way would be struck down. That said, he fully intended on laying his own soul to rest, better that than to be devoured by some torment.

"Health is clearly on your side. This much is true. You have taken preventative measures to bring with you some elixir to aid you against the disease."

Edgar's guess was correct.

"As for the reason you travel to Crease . . . I do not know. What do you seek among the poisonous ruins?"

Could he be asking out of sheer curiosity, or was there more to it than his simple questioning? The conversation was beginning to get frustrating.

"Never you mind!" boomed Thul.

The young man shot his barbarian friend a quick look of 'quiet down.'

"We are passing through Crease, en route to Koraivindahl. We do not wish to stay," said the young man, immediately regretting his words.

"Ah, so you wish not to remain here. Smart choice. For better reasons than I can think of, I don't know why you didn't just travel north, following the Trade Route through the mountains. You do know that imminent danger awaits you amongst the ruins to come, don't you?"

As the conversation went on, so did the hours of the night. Not a wink of sleep was to be had as the two travelers listened to Edgar speak of Crease's endless villains. One thing they had not thought of, was the fact that such a plagued area was still home to various beings both living and dead. Those who bring death with all of their so-called "traps" and "weaponry of generous toxicity."

To be caught in Crease as an untainted human, was like throwing a house mouse into a room of hungry felines. With such danger, having Thul as close company was something surely to be thankful for.

Eventually, after many warnings of the shattered souls to come, followed by a few tales of personal woe, Edgar offered to accompany them on their travels between the city gates. Still, his intentions remained unknown. His words did indeed provide helpful warning of what dangers lay ahead, though his offer to guide the two was declined. Such soul-harvesting torment could just as easily lead them into a trap.

The banter went on for some time before coming to a close. The ghost had clearly wanted something from the two, yet he never spoke of it.

"So be it," said Edgar, "then I bid you all the best. You are going to need it."

And that was it.

The conversation between Edgar, and the two companions ceased.

Before long, he had returned to his post atop the travelers' wagon, only to ride off towards Crease, in the direction of his dangling vegetable.

Some talk was generated between the two, followed by some goblets of Old Monk to ease their spirits. Before long, Thul had fallen back into his unconscious state soon after for the Gold Counter to do the same. Worries of The Ruined City flooded his mind, but they held no match against the copious amount of barbarian rum.

··· 21 ···

"*Craawh!*"

The morning sun had come with the spine-tingling screech of a blood raven sitting on a high branch amidst the tops of the dead birches. Such a noise was enough to wake even the most hungover of men, as its voice was that of a demon.

"*Craawh! Craawh!*"

For centuries, ravens and vultures alike had been the undertakers of Varroth. Many a time had lost folk become one with the landscapes, only to be picked apart postmortem. Though they usually preyed upon smaller vermin, a dead body was better than nothing. Usually, the blood-raven could be found in areas of many deaths as there was more to feed on. Perhaps that had been one of those situations.

Thul peered up at the onyx-clad bird watching them from above.

"Be gone! *Shoo!*" he yelled.

Rather than fleeing, the raven remained perched, taunting his newfound potential victims.

Before long, the two had gathered themselves and were on the road again. Strangely enough, the tracks of Edgar's cart were nowhere to be seen. Dark magic had been recently among them.

The two traveled on, walking through the unforgiving sludge. How they longed for drier conditions, and drier moccasins. Such footwear was to be worn upon dry city cobblestone, not the depths of a swamp.

Not much was said, except a conversation they had pertaining to Edgar. To follow him into Crease last night would have been a bad idea, or so they had decided. Furthermore, the lack of sleep would have done neither of them any good. Eager to gain energy, they ate a well-deserved feast of crisp, ruby apples and what was left of Esbern's croissants. The once flakey pastry had become soft and soggy, yet such a savory snack, mixed with some lamb's cheese was enough to brighten anyone's spirits. There was something to be said for old Esbern and his baking.

With a bottle of red wine to wash it all down, their food was nearly enough to make the travelers forget the poor conditions of the travel route. One by one, a larger number of black ravens joined in on their travel. They had been stalking them since they rose, shrieking at and taunting them with every movement. From moment to moment, birch trunks blocked out their view of the adventurers, causing them to swoop ahead to other branches. Their bodies were far bigger than an average raven - close to that of a small cauldron.

Nuisance was not all that they brought. For their gathering appearance could give away the travelers' position amongst the birch trees to any further lurkers within the foreign landscape. A gathering of ravens was usually a sign that they were following something or someone. In this case, these "someones" were of perfectly good health; an excellent snack for any prospective ghouls.

Though thoughts of death worried the young man, it was Edgar and his type that frightened him the most. The more he thought about it, the more he feared the loss of his potential afterlife.

"Thul, do you believe in reincarnation?" the young confidant spoke, breaking silence.

"Re-in what?"

"You know? Reincarnation! What dies now will live again. Just as something else."

In a sense, the idea of reincarnation was fascinating, yet being reincarnated into something of a less fortunate nature, such as an earthworm or a housefly was frightful.

"Ah yes! Reincarnation!" What he lacked in vocabulary, he made up for in brawn. "Sure. Well, reincarnation clearly ain't real. Once ya die, your soul heads on up to the Great Sky Anvil."

Such belief was culture-based amongst those from the Northern Mountain Belt. Years of constant mining and blacksmithing had evidently worked different sacred rituals to their fullest, leaving behind a religion of craft speculation.

"But I'll tell ya! If it was real, and I did some of this reincarnation, there ain't no doubt I'd be coming back as one of them cave grizzlies!" His tone was rich with boastful confidence.

"Makes sense to me. You definitely have the stature and thickness to show!"

"Oye!" Thul continued, jokingly taking his companion's statement as an insult. "You callin' me wide in the thighs?"

"Of course not! You—"

The young man's sentence stopped mid-speech. To the left, beyond some of the birches stood a tree far different from the other dead ones in the vicinity. Its lush pearlescent green leaves burst through all else, putting everything in sight to shame. Such a sight caused the companions to be speechless.

"Do you see that?" the Counter's voice was set with such a mood of amazement and wonder.

They made their way through a thicket of brambles, directing themselves towards the flawless beauty of the tree. Upon further venture, its age gave way, as its bark was withering with flakes. But still it rose with a mighty strength. Atop its branches, grew a glory of perfectly untouched leaves, each one literally glowing a greenish-turquoise from its tiny veins within.

The area around the surrounding branches was crystal clear. An endless marshy fog that remained had simply vanished within closeness of the tree.

From where its massive roots grew, a tiny stream flowed from the ground. Its source was unknown. Could it have been a spring in the ground? How odd.

Of all the dead, grey, gloomy parched land on which they had journeyed the last while, this was truly an incredibly breathtaking sight. There was no doubt that some magical essence was coming from that tree. For even its trunk glowed with various arteries of the same turquoise vibrancy. Suddenly, a whirring chime grew louder from an enclosed proximity.

Absolutely out of place, it just stood there. The tree's massive limbs grew much taller than all neighbouring birches. Such a tower of limitless beauty could not have simply grown here alone . . .

Could it?

The young man reached out to touch its trunk. Upon doing so, he discovered its surface to be warm similar to that of a cup of tea. Not so hot as to burn, just enough to grant such warming energy.

"Thul! Come up here! You have to feel this!"

The barbarian did as he was told. Upon wrapping his arms around the stocky base, he too felt the warmth. Perhaps such botany was the work of a wizard. If so, had its nature been one of sweetness or corruption?

Why here?

What was its purpose?

Embracing the tree and all its warmth imparted a positive energy increasing over time, and their loitering cling continued. For all the travelers knew, it could have been a tree of great evil; one to draw voyagers off their trail.

"Lookie here, brother! A sign!"

Thul motioned to a large boulder in the mud. Its surface was smooth, as if someone, or something, had cut it in half. Upon the surface was an engraved message, in perfect, bold writing.

You view upon the

NEXUS LENS OF VITALITY INVOCATION

Its roots tunnel deep
Far beneath the crust of Land
In connection with an undisturbed well
Of invigorative healing properties

Those who drink from the stream
Will be granted prosperous
Vitality and Mental Fortification

Picking the Leaves of Vibrancy
Or harming the Nexus in any way
Is Forbidden

Consequences will Prevail

Below the scripture was an engraving of a scythe assuredly associated with the likes of Death. Could the water itself be linked to annihilation? Was it really just meant to warn of the deliberate damage that the magical tree would invoke?

Though the tree had seemingly stood here for far longer than Crease and its surrounding lands had been contaminated, the real question was . . . why?

Its purpose eluded the young man, as it did Thul.

Evidently, the barbarian himself could not read, so he had it read to him. After hearing the message, they made their way back to the tree only to find two empty wooden cups. They appeared to have an oaky veneer, though their touch revealed something of a slightly . . . furry . . . feel. It was as if the cups were covered in exceptionally tiny, velvety hairs. What's odder was the fact that neither adventurer could remember the cups being there prior to reading about the "Nexus."

"Should we drink from the stream?" asked Thul, pending his friend's approval.

"I—" the young man started, pausing midsentence to think. "I'm . . . not sure."

The odd texture of the cups suggested a rather daunting nature.

For the first time since the two had met, Thul attempted to drink some water. Upon dipping his hands into the stream, something of an unexplainable magic happened. The water itself literally dodged out of the way of his hands. Regardless of where he moved his hands in the shallow bed of the trickling stream, the water simply evaded him, creating a pocket of air around his hands.

The young confidant tried his luck only to experience the same result. The water continued to evade them just as olive oil pushes back from the simple acidic nature of vinegar.

Evidently, its magic was of an extreme measure. Such a liquid probably should not be consumed by humans. On the other hand, for a tree of such beauty to grow among such dead lands implied something different. If the water veered away from the touch of a human, gods only knew what it did to one's insides.

Alternatively, such water could perhaps be acquired with the right instrument – such as the odd, velvety cups. Against better judgement, but still curious about the mysterious power, the two tried their luck with the magical cups, only to find that the water could indeed be held within them.

Of course, both the adventurers were hesitant, more so the young man, though Thul also showed signs of doubt. Neither of them said that they would drink such a mysterious liquid, yet secretly they both wanted to. Perhaps though, if they did decide to do it, it would be best for one to try first. The other could simply observe what happened. The idea was communicated between the two, and settled on the flip of a gold coin. With heads being chosen by the young man, it was up to him to drink first.

Without further ado, he knocked back his half-cup of enchanted, sparkling aqua. Its taste, though similar to that of average stream water, had left his pallet, as he swallowed, with a hint of earthy but somehow succulent sweetness. A sweetness, similar to the honey-glow blossom that grew in the gentle forest near the pureberry meadows of his home.

"Well? Do ya' feel healthy?" The barbarian's curiosity was eating away at him. It was almost as if he had been holding a mug of Old Monk, yet he was not allowed to drink it.

"I feel . . ." he paused for a brief moment. "I feel the same."

It was true. No such epiphany of health or vitality struck him in any way, just the rejuvenating quench of utterly fresh water. How nice it was to sip something from such a clean source, especially since their travels had begun in the badlands. He went to dip his cup for more water as Thul knocked back his first cup.

It seemed a good time to rest. Each cup was more inviting than the last. With breakfast out of the way, the rejuvenating water source, combined with multiple comfortable, mossy perches to sit upon made for an excellent spot. In a sense, it felt like a positive omen. It was time to replenish hydration within the body. The likelihood of another clean water source was slim.

It was at that moment, five minutes into their rest, that the two of them were hit with a reaction to the magical water. As the sands of time dwindled at that very moment, a sharp increase in vitality took place within the travelers. A feel of instant energy and strength coursed through their bodies

"Thul! Do you feel that?"

Such a feeling was almost indescribable. The young man had gone from one of minor energy, to that of a strong warrior, waking up after a night of undisturbed rest, full of energy.

"I feel—" Thul spoke, rising to his feet with an exaggerated speed.

"I feel..."

"I feel!"

"I feel like I have all the strength in the world! Like I am a king! A ruler! I feel like I can climb any wall, destroy any army, lift the weight of ten anvils! I feel more alive than I ever have!" He shouted exuberantly at the top of his lungs.

Such excitement was far too much to contain. The energy that coursed through their veins was one of immeasurable volume. Something so strong, so unbelievably exhilarating, it felt as though the young man had no control over himself, yet somehow at the same time he still had control.

"Let's drink more!" his excitement rang from the bottom of his lungs.

"Yes! Yes!" Thul went from madly clapping his hands, to filling another cup only to knock back the liquid of everlasting intensity.

This went on for some time. Cup after cup, they consumed, bringing more and more energy and mental fortification. It was as if the water had made their inner energy so extreme that it was impossible to control, but their heightened mentality allowed perfect discipline of both conscious and unconscious action.

"This calls for a splash of rum!" Thul's overflow of excitement was equal to that of his partner's, and so the Old Monk was opened.

A quick pour for his young friend was made, followed by Thul swigging directly from the neck of the rectangular bottle of his favoured mountain brew. One swig led to another, and somehow, within moments, he had nearly finished the entire bottle of rum.

Sure, the young man had witnessed his friend consume a single bottle, if not more of the Old Monk in a single evening, yet he had never seen Thul drink an entire bottle in mere seconds. Perhaps drinking the water in the first place was a bad idea for it opened some sort of mental door for Thul, as such a copious amount of alcohol was enough to put his friend over the edge. Suddenly, instantly drunk, how was the rest of the day going to go?

"I wish you hadn't done that! What now? What happens if we come across something or someone? You're clearly drunk!" the young man pointed out with fear in his voice.

"Relax, brother!" yelled Thul, his answer came drunkenly apathetic. "I feel great! A bottle never hurt no one! I can do anything I want! I feel great!"

To see such a giant man instantly lose control to intoxication was frightening. For the first time in their journey together, the young man felt scared about what might come next. He filled another velvet cup of stream water, handing it to his partner in the hopes that it might calm him down.

He felt like an idiot.

What had he done?

And why?

Why midday?

The barbarian did not notice that his friend was trying to help him. Carelessly, he hurled the empty glass bottle at the tree in a fit of sloshed excitement, smashing it with such force that it sent dozens of tiny fragments scattering amongst the surrounding area.

"Oh yeah! This is it, brother! The feeling all men could only wish for!" his voice, so loud, it was as if all of Varroth could hear him.

ANDREW P. WILD

"You fool! Stop! Calm yourself before you kill us both with your drunken carelessness," the young man spoke.

He looked at the spot upon the tree's withered bark where the bottle had smashed. Its hardy, yet wrinkled texture had been damaged by the strike, showing a gash in the bark, its innards a mixture of greener and white membrane. The one thing that the stone-carved scripture had specifically warned not to have happen.

**"...Or harming the Nexus in any way
Is Forbidden**

Consequences will Prevail"

"Thul!" the young confidant desperately attempted to gain his giant friend's attention, yet Thul was much too busy stomping around, dancing like the fool that he was. It was no use.

Bwam

A noise, so loud it was as if an entire city had fallen to rubble, echoed from somewhere far within the badlands' relentless fog.

BWAM-BWAM-BWAM-BWAM-BWAM ...

Another crashing sound blasted through the swamp.

Finally, Thul gathered himself, staring off into the deathly mists.

Silence fell between them.

Nothing was said. No wind to rustle any Nexus leaves. No ravens. Nothing.

The only noise was the slight trickling of the tiny stream.

Thul looked to his "brother" for answers, with an expression of guilt. His face suggested an instantly apologetic nature, as regret had taken over. The young man just stared back, anger in his eyes. In a sense, he was not so mad at Thul. He was infuriated with the energy that the water had given them, leading up to such carelessness.

"Thul, the message. It specifically said not to damage this tree in any way!"

The giant just stood there, speechless. It was funny how a man of such strength could appear so weak,

The silence broke.

From far off, the sound of steady "booming" was heard. Something . . . large?

Yes. Something very large was... running?

Yes. Running...

Towards them - with great speed.

The constant boom grew louder, rumbling the ground with every thunder. Miniature quakes were thundering through the earth. Something was coming . . and it was did not sound happy. These were the footfalls of something extremely large; a beast of substantial size.

Then came a horrible, hair-rising noise of cracking timber. Birch trees. It had to be. The sound of trees cracking, bursting, exploding, as they were getting smashed and thrown out of the way by whatever was sprinting through the deceased forest. It was truly a thunder of some ungodly manner, bringing with it promises of anger, death and bloodshed.

"Run! Run! Get out of here!" the young man shouted to Thul, who apparently had already begun to flee, suddenly

ANDREW P. WILD

ahead of the Gold Counter. He pivoted, breaking into a full-on sprint, unable to collect their bags in time.

The two ran beside each other, but the impending stomp of Hell was faster. It was getting loud and louder. There was simply no escape. Nowhere left to hide but mud and dead trees. Tears of disbelief flowed steadily from the Gold Counter's eyes and down his cheeks as he bounded frantically through the trees. A quick glance at Thul revealed that he too, was truly scared. His luck, and steps were not as efficient as his younger companion's, as his tipsy mind tripped him up with his own feet. He fell straight into a puddle of dirty water.

"Get up! Get up!"

The young singleton halted, turning to encourage his friend.

BWAM! BWAM! BWAM!

Finally, what had been pursing them burst through the birch trees within only mere steps from where they stood. With one single swipe, the brittle trees were smashed and ripped from their stumps only to be thrown far above all the rest.

Suddenly, right in front of their eyes, towered the most gargantuan, godless, scar-wrapped beast the boy had ever seen.

···22···

Such a hellish being could only be described simply as the most horrific creature ever released from the Void. Towering over forty feet in height, the gargantuan, rugged, hairy beast stood in front of them, its massive chest pumping widely as it panted in the murky air of the badlands. Its shape, though far larger, was similar to a human, yet its neck was non existent. Its head was somehow joined to its colossal chest, with a face of giant, amber-coloured eyes - its rectangular pupils, similar to those of a goat. Its mouth, lined with razor-sharp triangular teeth, capable of tearing apart the mightiest of warriors in a single bite.

Whatever this monstrosity of a hellhound was, surely it had something to do with guarding the Nexus. "Consequences will prevail," and so they most definitely had. If they had known the results of their actions, the two would have obviously avoided the tree to ensure its protection against the tiniest amount of damage.

All was about to be lost. Thul was at the monster's mercy. He clambered backwards frantically, too afraid to stand. Their bags, back at the tree that had brought them such great evil, contained their weapons, food, but most importantly their potions of resistance.

There was no time.

Next came the smashing of its enormous fist directly atop Thul's fallen being, mashing the barbarian's body into the mud as his bones distorted right in front of his partner's eyes.

"Ahhhh! My spine! You've broken my—"

All of a sudden, the other fist, blasting its way through the barbarian's robust skeletal system! Only a short yelp, similar to that of an injured dog, emitted from the barbarian and then . . . nothing. His body went limp, lifeless.

The beast just stood there, looking down upon his victim. Thul's eyes were closed.

"Thul!" his partner's name barely seeped from his mouth.

Nothing was left for the Gold Counter except for damnation.

Only the promise of death for the single remaining adventurer, just as it was for his partner.

Thul's body just lay there. His soul, seemingly resting, most likely to become one with those who endlessly walk amongst the marshes. He had failed the barbarian. He could have prevented all of this. A flashback of their talk about reincarnation passed through his woeful mind. Tears were streaming down his cheeks.

"You bastard! You killed him!" the young man lost it, in a fit of rage. He didn't care anymore.

"You killed my friend . . .! You killed Thul!"

The colossal demon reached down to Thul's body, carelessly picking it up with one swoop of its giant fist. Limbs of smashed bones revealed themselves as the barbarian's torso and arms dangled carelessly downward. His once muscular, mountainous body was nothing more than a fleshy bag of bloody innards.

The young singleton's flight or fight instinct then kicked in. His obvious choice was to flee, as the alternative would prove less than successful. He turned, once again breaking into an instant sprint.

What was he doing?

There was no aim, no purpose.

No chance!

But still he ran, his heart, his lungs, blasting with overexertion and horrible fatigue all at the same time. It was as if the power of ten men had gone to work on hammering away at him from the inside. He ran faster than he had ever thought he could.

After some time, the sound of the demonoid's thundering footsteps were no longer heard, though the traveler couldn't tell, as his sheer panic had sent him fleeing at what felt like an ungodly speed.

Just then, the vision of a moldy, old, run-down shack came into his view from beyond the withered birches. For some reason, it beckoned him. Though such feeble walls could never protect him from such danger, something about it struck a vein in his mind. Maybe there was something in there - anything that could help him.

Without hesitation, he sprinted towards the hovel, finding the door facing him. He smashed through the rotting passage; it gave way instantly, sending him crashing to the floor. However, the floor too gave way as he made contact with it, propelling him further downward, this time onto multiple sets of strategically placed spikes.

His speed and impact caused parts of his body to become impaled upon sharpened points of strategically placed wooden spears. It was a trap.

"Aurgh!"

The pain. It was so real, so horribly undeniable. His body lay limp, just as Thul's did, only he had spikes protruding through his gut and chest. There were probably five or six spears, impaling though his immobile figure, limiting his ability to evaluate his injuries.

With blood pouring out of his various injuries, there was no doubt he was dying. He would die - almost certainly within a matter of moments. From what he could tell, his heart had not been punctured. One of his lungs definitely was, as his breath had become so weak, it felt as though he were breathing through a river reed.

Every gasp of air brought pain. It was at that moment that that he wished for death. He wished so dearly to be dead. Prayed even. He wished that he had stayed with his friend, only to be crushed by the fists of the beast. At least then, his passing would have been quick.

His throat and mouth filled with the bitter taste of blood.

The end had come.

···23···
AGE: 34

It is written, in many forms and by numerous individuals, that Crease had once been a flourishing city before the touch of the plague. Since the day of the breakout, there have been multiple speculations on what caused the disease in the first place, though not a single person knew for sure what it was truly caused by.

Stories of a giant rat, disturbingly rotten with a festering contagion, were most commonly spoken of. It supposedly worked its way out of the sewer system and went on a rampage through the area, attacking people and infecting them left and right. Another well-spoken tale was the one of the sickened necromancer. Apparently, he had all but come down with the nastiest form of bone disease. In turn, he became angry with not only himself for he lost most of his mobility, but also with the Divines for cursing him with such a tragedy. He went about cursing the city folk with spells of corruption and internal weakness.

All of this has been spoken and written, although it is nothing more than guesses. However, the plague itself was very much real. It caused an undeniably slow, and agonizing death, accompanied with an infinite afterlife of endless wandering and thirst. Such a thing could never be wished upon any man, regardless his evil nature or crimes.

On average, humans and animals alike shared similar resistance levels against infestations. A singular primate such as the Amazonian gorilla, native to the Taanzig Rainforest of the Eastern Sea Islands, could come down with a common "Fey" or cold, just as easily as a human could. A prairie dog of the pureberry meadows could come down with a case of rat-bite fever just as easily as a nobleman's most cherished and pampered dog. Common colds and varying infectious diseases could be harmful and destructive to regular mammals, yet some beings or monsters thrive in such conditions.

Varroth was home to a landscape of glistening waterfalls, friendly townships, mystical forests, unending grasslands of flaxen perfection, emerald seas and amazing gold mines. The list of its beauty was almost endless. It doesn't mean that Varroth was without evil. And with evil, came great conditions such as hatred, pain and death.

An untreated area, especially one as giant as Crease and its surrounding so-called "badlands," became a cesspool of festering decrepitude, and in turn, powerful with sickness. Especially one race in particular: The Blight Goblin.

Blight Goblins, also known as "Ones of Afflicted Worm Children," were Crease's most common race. Just as one would picture a standard goblin, they were four or five feet tall, varying in shades of drab olive to a murky brown. Some Blight

Goblins lacked hair but had extra veiny, mole covered, liver-spotted skin, usually home to multiple boils and warts. Just by touching their skin, a swift infection could be contracted.

Once the plague began, Crease's population, both human and some mountain folk, (various larger men mixed with diverse dwarven beings) soon morphed into a population of Blight Goblins.

With such an increase of sickening folk, the Goblins took hold of Crease, consuming live humans along the way. Generally, they are found within the sewers of the larger cities and can create havoc when a city becomes overrun with them.

❌ ❌ ❌

There was nothing except a smell of ultra-mustiness filling the air, similar to the smell of a basement or some sort of cellar that was badly in need of a good scrub. It was a smell packed with layers of dust and mold and various degrees of filth.

The young man was in pain. Excruciating agony.

Was he dead?

Is that what death was like?

It was horrible. Still, he was able to breathe, which suggested that perhaps he was alive. The young man attempted to open his eyes. They were swollen, almost entirely shut. Where was he? Was he upright?

No.

He was strapped to a board of some sort, propped into a vertical position, his hands bound to either side of him.

Through narrow eyes, he was able to look at himself. In addition to feeling as if an entire army had trampled him, he noticed that his gaping wounds had been scorched shut; burned severely with such that only the Divines could know.

How long had it been?

At some point over the last stretch of time, somebody, or perhaps something, had taken barbaric efforts to keep him alive by cauterizing his wounds. Gaping holes in his naked body, the size of a goblet's circular rim, had been burned shut with an element of incredible heat.

His first attempt to shift his stature was matched with extreme pain and stiffness. His body was immobile, bound or not.

"Aaauughh!" his voice leapt beyond the decibels of the stale silence.

This is what is must be like for rat to be caught in a spring-loaded contraption.

Damn this. Damn everything!

Damn the Divines!

Regardless of his swollen eyes, tears had made their way from his soul. It all could have been avoided if he had just turned his friend in the other direction. But Thul had followed along willingly, due to loyalty and true friendship. He trusted the young confidant.

Thul's path had led him to nothing!

To death!

To everlasting thirst, beyond that of the Void!

An image of Thul came to mind. One of him laughing, holding a goblet of Old Monk and sitting beside Esbern, back before he had lost his son. Back when everything was in order . . . the way it was supposed to be. If he could just go back, unwind the time, and re-do it all from the very beginning from when the king's scout had first wandered through the purity of his meadows - all could have be saved. It was just a bloody mess, all because of him.

Ker-chunk

A door opened.

It was the sound of a passageway being unlocked.

Next came the sound of off-kilter footsteps.

Light entered the room and he saw his surroundings, bound to a board, strategically placed in the centre of the cluttered chamber. Various pieces of junk: broken dishes, smashed furniture, and ragged clothes were strewn about and piled in the corners.

To his left was a table covered with tools of mummification – various embalming devices, hooks, pincers, and clamps. Clearly, they had been used multiple times, as they were rusty, or bloody, and had not been cleaned over the years.

To his right was another table covered with food: carrots, potatoes, and rock salts, as if someone were in the middle of preparing a meal fit for a hungry family. Some of the items were, however, gruesome. There were bowls of opaque sludge, filled to the brim, roots of some sort of disgustingly slimy, maroon-coloured plant, bloody innards of some poor critter, probably a rabbit, and a jar filled with small eyeballs. Most disgusting, was the mid-sized tray of multi-coloured matter that looked like vomit.

Just then, the footsteps gave way to two exceedingly nasty abominations. Blight Goblins.

"Oooo! Lookey 'ere, Bozag! Our scrumptious human is awake!" prattled the first goblin, its voice creaky and oddly high-pitched.

161

Disgusting, both of them. They looked like they had just crawled out from under a horse that had died in the sun months ago. Then the smell hit him. They smelled of rotting fish and sewage. The goblins were alike in appearance. Their saggy skin like that of decaying pickles, both in colour and texture. They wore nothing but loincloths, exposing their decrepit upper bodies. Their droopy limbs hung from massively over-hunched spinal columns. Their bare breasts and nipples were asymmetrical with a flabby disproportion that hung over their plump bare bellies.

Bozag, the first goblin to enter, wore a red loincloth, while the other wore one that might had once resembled a shade of golden yellow. Both were stained with what one could only guess. The goblin in yellow differed in only one way. One eye had been completely removed from its socket. He wore a monocle that appeared to have been fused into his face, its lens glass smashed out at one point or another.

"Oooo! He looks so tasty! So plump! And yummy! And juicy! And crunchy!" continued the goblin with the busted monocle, his voice spiked with uncontrollable excitement. "I can't wait to eat his nice fat leg! So squishy and mushy and oh so yummy! Oh, it's going to be so nice! So nice! Yes! And with side of slug guts! Yes, yes! Let's eat him right now!"

The young man was in shock.

"No, no! We must wait, you fool! We are 'ere only makin' sure he's not muckin' about in some way. We otta' wait for Bonestink before we do anything. You know this! Or else we gonna be the ones for dinner!" Bozag spoke. "He's gonna be back soon, and you know he's gonna be real happy we caught this 'ere human."

"Oh, never you mind, Bozag! Gorx waits for no one. Why does ol' Brutm Bonestink have to be part of the plan, eh? Why is it always: "Oh Gorx, go get me more rat guts," and "Oh Gorx, go fetch us some mushroom caps for the stew," and "Oh Gorx, go get some bird eggs fur dinner? Ol' bastard never does any of that 'imself! He's just a useless ol tit!" Gorx spoke, his yellow loincloth hanging just low enough to avoid exposure of his groin.

Earlier, the young man had run for his life, but at that moment he wished for the end, just as he did atop the spears. One would not expect a Blight Goblin, let alone two, to keep a man alive just to kill him and feast. Perhaps the reason behind it all was that a recently dead adventurer was tastier; fresher than one that sat around rotting for a few days. Either way, the idea of death was both longed for and dreaded at the same time.

"You will not! You know we cannot touch him! It's ain't about the feast! Bonestink's got something else in mind fur' this one. You go perduddling around his kerfunzles - you'll be getting a kick to the head! Don't ya think I won't give ya one me self if I ave' to." Bozag, clearly the smarter of the two hissed through his amber, broken teeth. Clearly, his pointed teeth hadn't seen a day of proper hygiene in years.

Enough. The situation, the smells, the impending doom of . . . Divines only knew what. Never had there been a time in the young man's life in which he had been kept in such gnawing uncertainty. His frustration was erupting straight from a 'just-get-it-over-with' feeling.

"You fools!" the young man barked. "Bloody fools . . . Just . . . Get it over with . . .!"

Every word, a beyond painful mutter. It was as if another spike was being driven directly into the boy's body.

"That's it!" Gorx of the yellow loincloth had reached end of his patience. "The leg! That's all I want!"

With some jostle and a quick step, the shriveled figure kicked some sort of lever beside the board, rotating the entire contraption clockwise, leaving the young man atop, completely horizontal, facing the ceiling.

Something about the appearance of the brickwork brought a sense of peace to the young man. It was difficult to explain, but the ocean blue shade that was lit by the surrounding torches reminded him of the brick in his wife's laboratory back home.

Back home . . .

"Gorx! You bastard!" Bozag neared him.

Gorx was the impatient one. He was wielding a hacksaw, probably not meant for use on humans, though in this case that was its purpose.

"You never listen!" Bozag reached forth, striking his friend's upper back with a wooden bat, or perhaps it was the leg of a chair or table.

Splut

Something from behind Gorx splattered, sending juices in multiple directions, some of which landing on the young man's lips. Subconsciously and without intention, he licked his lips and then immediately felt regret in doing so. The liquid tasted like . . . oh gods . . . rotten tuna. It came from one of the being's massive boils.

Immediately he began heaving. Belching, spitting, anything it took to rid his mouth and system of any trace of the boil juice, all while the two Blight Goblins went at it in the background.

"I— haven't—" Gorx's speech was interrupted with every rumble of his fists, "eaten— in a week!"

The fighting had escalated. Gorx had dropped the bone saw and readied himself. Bozag swung wildly back with his leg of furniture. The two shoved each other, Gorx pummelling savagely with his stubby, weak arms during which time Bozag repeatedly smashed him atop the head.

One targeted strike on Gorx's skull was unsuccessful when he dodged left, sending Bozag's wooden bat thundering against the floor. Without time to react, Gorx whipped around behind his foe, giving him a blast to the rear of his skull with his skin-stretched knuckles. The heavy hit knocked Bozag down, landing him on the young man.

"Ya bastard!" yelled Bozag, from atop the young man. Every movement meant more pain for the Gold Counter.

"I'm going to bash your brains in!"

The Blight Goblin leveraged his elbows on the torture table, pressing himself into a standing position, only to receive yet another fistful of brutal deliverance, this time enough to send saliva bursting out of his mouth. His head flew back with such a hit, and he covered his mouth with both hands, freeing his grip of the wooden leg. The echo of it landed on the stone floor

"My...my tooth!" He yelled. "You've knocked my tooth out!"

Some wave of caring expression washed over Gorx's face as he realized what he had done to his ... brother? Friend? It didn't last long. With a snarling grin, he soon returned to his hostile stance.

"That's on you! You should've been in on it! We could've shared that tasty leg together! You idiot! Now ye be lookin' like Bonestink the rest o' your wretched life." His laughter was clearly over exaggerated in an effort to show the greatest amount of offence.

From where he lay, the young man could not see Bozag clutching his face, yet the goblin's actions suggested he had been seriously injured, both physically and emotionally. For a time, he just stood there.

His bloodied hand occasionally drifted to his loincloth to wipe fresh blood on it.

"Listen. Bozag," Gorx began.

"I'm really sorr—."

The wounded goblin had had enough. He bent down quickly and grabbed the chair leg with renewed, hell-bent energy. Gorx stared back at his partner, wide-eyed with fear.

"Aaarrrreeeiiiyah!" With the fury of ten men, he lunged forward with his bat rising in one hand, and brought it down upon Gorx's head.

It had been strike of devasting measure.

Gorx fell back instantly, landing in a pile of clutter as he walloped his head against the unforgiving cobblestone. The sound of his skull cracking against the stonework was horrific; it was as if someone had dropped a cannonball from a cliff only for it to land atop of a pile of boulders.

The reaction, as sinister as it was, was not enough to stop Bozag.

"Look what you did!" His scream was full of rage; loud enough to bring down the brick ceiling of the chamber. He then went on to raise his club one last time.

"Next time, you listen to Bozag!"

And then, with one last blow, he brought down his weapon, smashing Gorx straight across his face, rendering him unconscious.

Teeth.

Blood.

It was everywhere. Morbidly everywhere. Gorx was dead in the centre of it all, slumped to one side against a pile of rubble. His body, limp.

Was he in fact dead?

How could his brother do this to him?

What, in all the holy land, had just happened?

The sight of such a macabre scene was enough to put the young man over the edge. His broiling stomach forced him into a fit of grueling nausea. Since he was restricted upon his horizontal trap, he did what he could to project his own vomit.

Bozag spun around.

"No, no!" he exclaimed, caught off guard.

"Get it in the tray!" He fumbled for the pan of dried particles next to the table. It had indeed been vomit all along.

Just then, the sound of a door opening in the nearby hallway was heard. Bozag's facial expression changed instantly to that of panic. Something within him had been struck with a fear vigorous enough to morph his entire mood. Whatever had entered the room must have been of greater standing than the bloodied goblin and his deceased partner.

Bonestink.

··· 24 ···

H is name was as direct as his appearance.
Bonestink.

Brutm Bonestink.

A Blight Goblin, much larger than the average, he stood seven feet tall. He had earned his name due to his bulging figure and enormous, sagging belly. His outfit consisted of torn clothing. A pair of tattered pants covered most of his legs. He wore toeless boots, no doubt the result of many adventures. However, it was his intricate jewellery that set him apart from the others.

Various chains dangled across his chest. Some were copper, some silver, some too rusty to identify. Some of them held medallions and symbolic pendants. This made it clear in the young man's mind that Bonestink must be the head goblin.

"Bozag!" His voice was shrill and yet destroyed by many years of smoking. In his hand he held a burning ember of some sort of rank, smoking herb, lodged in a pipe of gnarled, twisted wood.

"My liege! I . . . I . . . !" the lesser goblin shook with fear.

Bonestink peered down at the lifeless body on the rubble.

"He wanted to eat the leg! I . . . I told him we couldn't! I said we had to wait for you, my liege! For you!"

The greater goblin continued to stare at Gorx's figure, then back at Bozag.

"Look here! I assembled everything! For you! For you! One side for embalming! One side for food! Just as you like! I did it for you, my liege! I know you li—"

Bonestink ended his sentence by smashing his gruesome mace on the "food" preparation table, sending its ingredients of putridness in a variety of directions. The rank smoke of his pipe filled the room.

"Bloody fool! Look at what you have done to your brother!"

The giant goblin lunged at Bozag and grabbed his throat. His next movement was one of singularly effortless action, as he tightened his death grip, raising the little goblin directly into the air, sending his feet into a kicking fit as he choked.

"What ave' you done to that filthy cheese rat? I need him just as I need your mangy, pathetic ass so that I can become this district's pacesetter! You know this!"

District?

Did he mean this particular district of Crease?

Bozag was struggling for breath and making violent kicks. His rotting hands clawed desperately at Bonestink's grasp in an effort to free himself.

"My . . . liege . . ." his voice barely squeaked out as his struggle for oxygen grew.

One would probably guess, just by looking at Bonestink that he had most likely eaten the majority of his catches. Crease, home to an infestation of irreversible plague, left nothing but creatures of sicknesses. As the young man had just arrived, his bill of health was perfectly clean. His thirty-year-old figure spoke of youth and vitality. The Nexus Lens had probably added to that. This human of proper health would probably be consumed wholeheartedly by Bonestink – skin, guts and blood.

Why the embalming tools?

"Now!" boomed Bonestink, as he glared at the young man after casually tossing his lesser companion to the ground, "What to do with you?!"

The foul stench of Bonestink grew intense as he neared the prisoner, looming over the table. He set his pipe down, leaning in closer, his face only inches away from the young man. The worst part - his breath.

"Your innards will make for a grand stew!" he barked, laughing with a voice of phlegmy coarseness.

He rested his boil-covered hand next to young confidant's head, stroking his face. His touch was slippery with an unidentifiable grossness.

"My . . . My liege . . ." Bozag interrupted, some of his voice recovered. "What . . . what about the king?"

"What about the king!?" the massive goblin spun around, gawking at the cowering goblin.

"The king, my liege . . . what about him . . . won't he want to see the man?"

Bonestink stood with an unusual stillness. Each one of his actions had been of an unpredictable nature. His temper, in combination with his strength, caused feelings of unease in the young man and the goblin. This went on for a moment before he spun back to the young man, ready to speak once again.

"Awwrrrugh!" he screamed, with a voice loud enough to move buildings.

"Damnit!" he yelled. "I was so looking forward to munching on this one's tasty bones!"

With that, he picked up a bottle of embalming liquid, its neck sealed with a cork. His medallions banged together as he raised the bottle above his head.

"We had so hoped to feast on you and use the leftovers to decorate our home. How great to enjoy a meal knowing that there would be a head left for a trophy. But I'll tell ya' boy, you'll wish you'd been eaten here rather than where you're going."

The young man's attempt to speak was not quick enough.

Before the two had anything else to say, Bonestink slammed the bottle down across the young man's skull, sending him back into a world of unconsciousness.

··· 25 ···

AGE: 35

In a world of endless possibility, there has always been good and bad. Everything has balance. Sometimes the good outweighs the bad, though in times of horror, the reverse happens.

Through sickness and good health, suffering and prosperity, Varroth, over the many, many years of its existence, had always maintained balance in all its neutrality.

So be it, regardless of any placement on this planet, human or animal, plant life, even the unliving inanimate objects that fortify this world and the next, everything serves a purpose. Without corruption, without evil, this land, just like every other, would be utterly destined for endless days of nothing but positive goodness. We need bad days. We all do. Because without bad days, we would never know which ones were good.

❌ ❌ ❌

For the second time since hitting the unforgiving landscape of cold-hearted Crease, the young man came to from his state of senselessness, only this time with an increased deficiency. For however long he had been here, he had been without a single particle of food or a single drop of water. His tongue burned within the walls of his mouth, which felt as though it was made out of sand and tiny fragments of glass shards.

A feeling of pure exhaustion paralyzed him from the inside out. One could only describe his entire being as a pathetic waste of organs, meagrely wrapped in a skin sack. His cauterized injuries still burned, though it was his spine that hurt the most. Lords only knew how far he had been dragged to his current location.

"Open your eyes."

The voice rang with angelic virtue, echoing with a belonging that suggested its speaker was a god. The Gold Counter's body was limp with an inert lack of energy. Even the raising of his eyelids was almost impossible, though he succeeded in doing as he was told.

From where he lay, a massive stone cavern opened above him. He attempted to blink, clearing his weary eyes, only to reveal that he lay a hundred feet or more deep within the earth's crust. The far-off ceilings reminded him of the interior of a cathedral.

The stone walls were dotted with burning torches. In front of him rose a towering tree, beaming with an emerald-green intensity. Its branches, confident with an ultra-thick fullness of healthy leaves, reached forth, blocking out a view of the far-off church. It was as if someone, or *something*, had removed its floor, and hollowed out a massive, circular-shaped tunnel.

The young man struggled to prop himself up upon his forearms to gain a better understanding of his setting, though his attempt failed.

"Drink," the angelic voice rang again.

From his right, came yet another goblin. Similar to Bozag and Gorx in appearance, yet this one wore a loincloth of amethyst colour and some torso armour, customized to fit his hunched figure. He knelt beside the confidant, carelessly pouring a bowl of icy water across his face and into his mouth.

Immediately, the young man spat it out.

"Drink. It will help."

The goblin scurried off, bowl in hand, only to return with yet another.

What was the use? Whether he drank or not, he was doomed. His legs, in particular his knees, screamed in agony once he had attempted to move them. They had been broken.

The boil-covered minion attempted to pour the water in the man's mouth once again, its icy temperature shocking, yet somehow relieving. This time, the young man was able to swallow a mouthful.

"This is water of the Nexus Lens," echoed the saintly voice. "No doubt you've heard of it."

A sudden hint of energy began inside. It was a miracle. The Nexus water had once again, granted him some strange, revitalizing feeling.

"More," he begged.

The goblin continued to pour the water into his mouth, while some of it cascaded down the sides of the Gold Counter's face and neck.

After a moment of stillness, the young man attempted to once again prop himself up.

Success.

What he saw had been entirely unexpected. The smooth, stony floor of the gargantuan cavern gave way to a series of pews, fronted by an altar of demonic appearance. A lush, ruby red carpet, lavishly stretched its way up the center of the underground church, embroidered with various symbols of gold and black. The farthest wall had been almost entirely blocked out by an enormous tree, its trunk and branches covered with clusters of various fungi. Its base stretched along various bookshelves crammed with tomes exploding with dog-eared pages. The gaping cavern had been made into an entire cathedral, all on its own - lit with the flames of hundreds upon hundreds of torches, some attached to the walls, some scattered amongst the pews and other surrounding areas.

The underground cathedral radiated with a feeling of wickedness. Its style and appearance invoked a feeling of evil practice. Nearly every open space was full of ghastly creatures. Blight goblins, upright skeletons and blackened, gaseous specters clustered about the rooms in numbers that totaled more than one hundred, perhaps even two. Many of the dark beings were clad in customized armour accompanied with sharpened spears of steel and bone that had been specifically fashioned into points of unsettling, crooked angles. Only the dark wisps floated without any armour or clothing.

The foulest creature within the cathedral stood upon eight colossal legs just behind the demonic altar. The being - half skeleton, half spider, was so huge it could crush a simple building in a matter of seconds. Its lower half was arachnid in nature. Giant voluptuous legs that could easily stretch up to twenty, even twenty-five feet, joined a hairy, tarantula-shaped body. From where the boy lay stretched, he could not see its behind, yet he expected the beast to have a massive stinger.

Where the spider segment of the body ended, a skeletal system of abnormally large proportions began. It resembled a human skeleton, though it was at least four times larger. Its massive, decrepit torso was covered with a set of armour, tinted in ebony darkness. The armour was inlaid with variously sized symbols of golden, swirling style that seemed to glow with an ominous promise. A torn, olive shade cloak draped down from its back, pierced at the shoulders with spikes. Its head was shaped and molded with an endlessness amount of swirling ebony fusion. Death spikes protruding from its bare skull had been fused together into a crown of pure gold, inlaid with three massive sapphires.

"Do you know where you are?" an angelic voice asked, seemingly belonging to that of the half spider, half human.

The young visitor attempted to speak - his vocals weak.

"I . . . I'm in Crease."

"You are in Crease." The skeletal beast confirmed. "In the very heart of it. For you are now in the Stillborn Church of Suffering and Disorder."

Just then a force of some sort came over the young traveler, a feeling as though jets of water were blasting up against his back. Some sort of magical sensation embraced his body, caressing him as it slowly lifted his body and tilted him into a vertical position. To his surprise, the movement had not caused him any pain whatsoever. Even his legs, both broken at the kneecaps, felt fine.

The force went on to bring him closer to the colossal figure of the necromantic arachnid, its eye sockets lit with a raging fusion of swirling red effervescence. A feeling of panic washed over the young man, though his immobile position within the magical force left him in a bizarre state of calmness. As he was pulled toward the altar, the shrine's grand structure revealed an opening within its upper surface.

Inside...

A body.

Thul's body.

His legs were completely disfigured; twisted and broken into a multitude of different angles. His stomach, chest, and the majority of his body lay there in a sunken mass of uselessness, as though his entire bone structure had been shattered. His face and eyes, though beaten, bruised, and smashed to an unforgiving unfairness, suggested a nature of peace somehow.

The sight of his friend's lifeless body, victim of the beating brought on by the massive protector of the Nexus Lens, fueled a fire from within the Gold Counter. It was a fire of eternal rage, one directed at himself, the massive arachnid before him, and the Blight Goblins. Everything.

Such an emotion of sheer rage could not be contained, and so he went on to blindly yell at the leader of darkness. His efforts proved to be invalid, as something in the force of the magic had hindered his ability to speak.

"Your friend is dead . . . and you will be too."

All that was heard was the quiet crackling of torches, accompanied by the clinking and clattering of armour as two members of the darkened army shifted in their positions.

ANDREW P. WILD

"I am Nailreign, Necromantic King of Fallen Crease, Consumer of the Unworthy."

It made sense that this unholy being possessed such enormous power. Nailreign's leadership could only prove to be extensive within the confines of harsh Crease.

"I am the one who created the plague in the very beginning to serve justice to those who have done wrong within these lands. In addition, my destruction of Crease, has been successful in providing Varroth's lesser minions with a suitable home."

A cheer burst out among the crowd, filling the hollow opening of the cathedral. The young man had always known of Varroth's less favourable species: goblins, wraiths, vampires. They were all frowned upon and avoided at all costs. But for good reason! They all shared evil, destructive, disgusting, and dishonourable ways. He had never thought that these creatures, despite their intentions, required a place to live; a place where they could develop their own sense of "normal."

No. It had to be wrong.

Or was it?

The Blight Goblin was one of this land's most terrifying creatures. They were known for thievery and were destined for nothing more than a swift death. Perhaps with fallen Crease, these beings had a place to live; somewhere that would not disrupt the good citizens of Varroth. These loathsome creatures still needed a place to reside, despite being different from the rest of the world.

"You need not worry." Nailreign spoke once again, its horrific features burning into the mind of the young adventurer with every word.

"If I wanted you dead, you would have been the moment you stepped foot in my badlands. You have been brought here so that we can discuss a matter that pertains to both of us."

The adventurer was unable to speak.

"I can hear your thoughts . . . Ease your struggle! Save yourself the anguish."

What is it you want with me?

The young man pressed on with his thoughts. Though he was unsure if the "king" could truly hear him, he focused all of his energy into his telepathic questioning.

What could you possibly want with me?

Nailreign adjusted his focus, directing his eyes of burning, crimson fusion to the young man's legs. He raised his arms in front himself, curling his skeletal fingers as if he were holding an invisible orb of sorts. Suddenly, a sphere of bright violet colour flashed into existence, seemingly from within the palm of his hand. It swirled, flickering about furiously, sending snippets of light beaming outward in all directions.

A spell.

Instantly - pain.

An intense pain. It came rippling up from his bare legs, right through the entirety of the young man's being.

Arghh! What are you doing? My legs!

And then. Nothing. Not a single ounce of pain.

It had all been abolished. Completely eliminated from his system.

The force that had been holding him began lowering him slowly and gently until his bare feet touched the floor. He was standing! Weak, yes. But standing! On his very own two feet.

ANDREW P. WILD

Whatever magic Nailreign had cast, had instantly fixed his legs, his kneecaps.

He stepped forward expecting to fall, yet he remained standing.

The minions, scattered randomly around the vicinity, watched with amazement. Even the skeletons showed signs of wonder as some of them tilted their heads, as if to show their undead interest.

"We have a common goal, young man." The Necromantic King stepped forward toward the young traveler, leaning down and extending his face until it was but a few feet away. His closeness, discomforting.

"You and I... We both seek what is in the Royal Castle of Prosperous Koraivindahl."

How could he know this? How could he possibly know of the trip to the Royal City? There is no way Thul could have told him. He had watched his friend die before his eyes. He never told his previous captors, there was no way that Gorx, Bozag, or Bonestink knew.

Nailreign went on to speak again. "I know everything, young traveler. I can read your mind, just as you can read a book. What you seek from within the walls of the Koraivindahl's Citadel is different from what I seek. What matters is that you desire access . . ."

He paused. The cavernous air was still with quietness.

"I cannot gain access to the citadel, but you can... And you will!"

"And what if I don't?" the words of young man passed through his lips, shocking him as his ability to speak had since returned to him.

"Then I will kill you. You are nothing here."

His words were true. What was he going to do?

Run? Where?

He was entirely surrounded by an army capable of devouring his entire being in mere moments. A feeling of embarrassment coursed through his body.

"Furthermore, you too, now have the plague." Nailreign's angelic voice echoed throughout the underground church.

The plague!

The resistance!

It hit him. He hadn't consumed the alchemist's concoction in days . . . oh gods. He had it. He was doomed! Infected. It was only a matter of time - even if he did live through this and somehow reached his wife... he was done for. He couldn't do anything. Soon he would be awash with the conditions of the sickness and white skin, only to be forced out of every place he traveled. Any town. Any inn.

Once again all had been lost. Without access to humanity, to food, he would surely perish! One could not live within current day Varroth without survival skills. He would have to grow food! Hunt for it. But he was dying anyways – if not by sickness, then by the curse of the failed elixir! And his wife? What about her? Surely, he would infect her upon first embrace.

"But I am here to help you . . . And also . . . your friend," Nailreign said.

"If you choose now, at this very moment, to venture forth for me and fetch me what I desire, then I will cure you. I will raise your friend Thul back from the dead to his old state of perfect health, just as he was before he left this world."

Thul, his only friend.

His journey had all been about one thing.

Salvation.

But he realized at that moment that he had lost so much: his wife, his trusted companion and loyal steed, Orist, and suddenly . . . Thul. He had failed his every companion in so many ways.

Whatever wishes that Nailreign desired, the Gold Counter promised he would do everything he could to meet the requirements brought forth from the King of Fallen Crease . . .

For Thul.

···26···
AGE: 36

The conversation between Nailreign and the young traveler ended just as soon as he had accepted the blackened
king's quest. With a promise to continue their conversation
and all its details in the morning, the young man could no
longer stand. He collapsed to the floor with a mighty fatigue.

An assembly of goblins and skeletons lifted his body above
their shoulders and carried him through a door and down a
series of tunnels. Eventually, they reached a long, dimly lit,
cobblestone hallway leading forward, up a flight of stairs only
to be met with a massive set of double oak doors. The style
of this hallway was so completely different than anything else
that existed in the cave.

The doors opened to a large room of excessive luxury. Parts
of the chamber were similar to the Gold Counter's room from
within The Goblin's Rest, Faulkstead's rustic inn, though it
was larger, and much more lavish. Every piece of furniture in
the room had been lined with an unending richness of gold
and scarlet-red velvet. From the moment the Gold Counter

was carried into the room, his eyes took in divans of extraordinarily plump cushioning, seated around a beautifully crafted mahogany table. Next came a massive bed, decorated with a seemingly endless amount of silky, dense blankets topped with a multitude of fluffy pillows. A canopy of light, nearly transparent cloth shrouded its surfaces.

Near to the bed were tables, decorated with beautiful settings and equipped with a bounty of perfectly prepared food. There were bowls of juicy blackberries, loaves of olive bread with accompanying dipping oils and vinegars, wheels of cheese from a variety of animals, croissants, whipped cream, grilled fish, apples, oranges, slices of watermelon, frog legs, bowls of walnuts, peanuts, almonds, cashews, crispy chicken breasts, grilled steaks of bovine, hog and elk, pickles, eggs, entire bricks of dense honeycomb, boiled crabs, and even fresh lobster!

The list went on and on.

The chamber held within it a scene that one could only dream of. It was reminiscent of the depictions within the grand tapestries hanging in great halls and museums. The room was lit by a fire that burned brightly in an ivory construct fireplace on the eastern wall of the room. Near to it, some embroidered single chairs paired with an extravagant coffee table. The entire room filled with the smells of delicious food, in particular, the strong, savoury, mouth-watering smells of the seasoned meat and seafood.

With the little energy he had, the young man began a crazy rampage of mindless feasting. At such a point, he could care less if the food had been poisoned or cursed. Many days had gone by, and he had been without food. He didn't care. It was a gourmet banquet begging to be devoured.

A second later, there was a knock on the door. He was too famished to notice the interruption and continued eating. There was no acknowledgement of the guest who tapped at the door.

"I'm coming in!" the voice had a sort of a wavery tone.

The double doors creaked open, revealing a figure covered in a cloak. The upper half of the cloak was light beige fading into a more of a seaweed green. The cloak that covered the figure's head had been torn open in the front, only to reveal a black, faceless void.

Edgar.

"Hello!" His ghostly tone was high-pitched with positivity.

"How are you my friend? It's been but a while!" he joked.

Or did he?

The adventurer paused his ferocious feeding, staring over to Edgar. A note of awkwardness hit him – he himself was still naked.

"Tell me! How have you been? . . . Not so well, I'm guessing . . . You know . . . now that you're here and all."

Edgar's tone, lit with cheerfulness. Something about him suggested he had accepted his fate of endless wandering, and it no longer bothered him. Simply, he was just a happy ghost. Who would have guessed such a thing existed? Angry ghosts, sure. Aimless. Depressed. Maybe even confused. But happy? Bah!

The young man covered himself with a blanket and went on to tell Edgar the happenings of his trip since they had last met. It was a short tale of sadness indeed. Maybe he should have listened to what Edgar had to say in the first place. Perhaps this all could have been avoided. On the other hand, Thul's reaction to Edgar's first appearance could not have been avoided. There was nothing he could have done to calm his friend, and so perhaps joining with Edgar in the beginning would not have been a bad idea. Who was to say?

Edgar's reaction had been noted when he covered his 'mouth'. He didn't actually have a face to show his emotion of course.

"Wow. Such courage. And yet such stupidity . . ."

The adventurer looked to Edgar, taken back by his comment.

Edgar went on. "You are crazy! How could you have let him damage the tree? The lens? Don't you know that such a thing is strictly forbidden? Didn't you see the sign? Sheesh!"

"Yes, yes," piped the traveler. "We saw the sign. But you've met him! Thul! He was an absolutely fantastic, caring soul! But he could be such a handful, so out of control. He could have been useful in times of need, times of danger. But he just got too wild after drinking that water!"

Edgar laughed for a time.

"How long has it been since we last spoke?" questioned the young man, obviously not sharing the same sense of humour as Edgar.

The cloaked apparition went on to inform him that it had been about seven or eight moons, enough time for the young confidant to age at least another two years, probably three. Something in his appearance, in particular his eyes, showed signs of further aging. If he wasn't his forties yet, he was close

His forties . . .

From the beginning of his journey, the sands of time had poured so quickly. He was once a vibrant soul, just past his teenage years. Such an idea brought up great anxiety. He had probably another forty years to reach his wife. Twenty of those years would provide him with some limitations of mobility, whereas the remainder would prove even more difficult. The idea that Nailreign had not killed him, but rather spared him for reasons unknown brought some peace to him, a segment of hope. For the first time, he felt as though there was a chance, a chance that he could indeed succeed in rescuing his beloved.

"You know—" Edgar's voice intruded on the Counter's thought process, which had now been glazed with a new-found fortitude of clarity. "They are bringing him back."

"Bringing who back?"

At first, his reaction was clueless. But he soon gathered his thoughts.

Thul.

"Yes! They are fixing him right now. Preparing him. I was shocked to hear the same thing. Most of those who pass through Crease meet a swift death by Nailreign's hand. That, or they become a tasty meal for our foul beings. For him to have been given life goes completely against the king's normal ways. Surely, he has something in store for you both, what with your friend's revival and this fine feast and royal setting!"

The Gold Counter couldn't believe it. How was it possible that Thul's life could be restored? He had bare witness to the crushing of his barbaric friend, brought upon him by the fists of that cruel beast from the forest. How could such a revival even be possible? Thul's body had been crushed...

bones broken and organs destroyed. Surely, such a feat could not be done...

For a time, the two went on to speak of Nailreign's request in retrieving a certain something from the Royal Castle of Koraivindahl. Though neither of them knew what it was that the Necro King truly desired, the conversation went on.

As the night passed, they went on to speak of various subjects and historical information, most of which pertaining to Crease before the dark days of the plague take over. Time had not exactly been of the essence, as the adventurer required relaxation and healing prior to his future endeavours. Though his lifespan had been stretched thin on account of the faulty elixir and the dastardly plague that swam through his veins, the young man's mood was calmer. Perhaps it was due to the delicious, fortifying food and the glow of the warm fire that burned next to his bed.

Eventually, the conversations dwindled and fizzled to a close. His belly, full of warm breads and meats, induced a state of pure fatigue. No longer able to keep his eyes open, he soon passed into a deep sleep, one of well-deserved healing and prolonged rest.

··· 27 ···

"Rise."

The command that came from an armour-clad goblin startled the young man into a foggy alertness. His body, still with an achy harshness, felt much better than when he last woke in Bonestink's dungeon.

"Collect yourself. King Nailreign has summoned you."

He propped himself up from beneath the lavish blankets. At first glance, a vision of his slightly pale skin caught him by surprise. The plague had evidently begun to affect him. No doubt his poor health over the past little while had contributed to a weak immune system. The injuries that he had most recently succumb to had all been completely removed from his body! The lacerations, areas of impalements, bruising, bleeding. Everything! Not a single inch of his being showed any sign of even the slightest harm! Discolouring from the plague, indeed, yet not a single cut nor nail clipping a strew!

The magic that Nailreign had used, whether it was the food or perhaps a spell cast overnight, had healed his body entirely! It was as if he hadn't been part of a single physical conflict in his life. Before he had any time to further inspect his body he was interrupted.

"We have garments for you to wear. Once dressed, we will take you to him. Hurry now! Hurry!"

Without any hesitation, He quickly dressed into a new set of clothes. A breezy linen shirt, white as fresh snow, fit perfectly across his chest. Covering that was a black tunic. The front had been embroidered with swirling, elegant, amethyst-coloured threads. For pants, he was given a set of sand-beige breeches that were cuffed just below the knee. He wore black boots, with straps and buckles for adjustable comfort.

Two goblins entered the room, carrying a large, rectangular mirror. The reflective glass gave way to an image of himself he had never before seen in his life. Never, in his one hundred years of living, had he seen himself in such a perfect reflection, let alone such impeccable, exquisite attire. He looked as though he had just stepped out of a castle of bountiful riches.

"Quickly now!"

It was apparent that time was of the essence and so the traveler left along with the gnarly goblin folk. Once again, the Gold Counter walked upon his own two feet. Nailreign's magic had not only restored the adventurer's health, it had somehow brought his legs and overall mobility back to perfect condition. How could such magic even exist amongst the realm?

The group made their way down the hall and into the labyrinth of random tunnels, each more twisted and confusing than the last. Eventually, they arrived at their destination, the underground cathedral.

Upon gazing upward to the far-away ceiling, beyond the surrounding ranks, altar and massive tree that grew from behind the shrine, the Gold Counter saw that the stained-glass windows of the church shone with glorious sunlight.

Morning.

It had to be morning.

Thul's body was nowhere to be seen.

"Your energy is far greater than before," boomed Nailreign's angelic voice. He was nowhere to be seen.

The young adventurer stood between the two wart-covered minions that had escorted him, his eyes searching the caverns for the Necro King. His whereabouts were unknown, although he was no doubt nearby.

Just then, the mighty branches of the colossal tree that rose from behind the altar began to shake back and forth with violent action, yet not a single leaf fell from its branches. Next came a set of noisy clicking sounds, followed by the appearance of Nailreign himself, bursting from within the top of the enormous tree. His tremendously large arachnid body was all the traveler could focus on. He was just as he had been the night before, half spider, half skeleton.

Within seconds Nailreign ever so gracefully, yet hastily, clambered down from within the tree's confines.

"Where is Thul?!" the young confidant shouted, an angry fire in his voice. He realized that Nailreign did in fact need him, hence his continued existence.

"I would have thought some gratitude would be in order."

In light of his recent healing, perhaps his impulsive greeting had not been the correct way to begin the interaction, as it was Nailreign himself who had magically unbroken his knees right before his eyes and saved his life altogether. No, perhaps it was a time for patience, but also of diligent conversation.

"I . . . apologize." The young man's voice had a dryness to it. "I should start by . . . thanking you. Without you, I would not be here right now."

Nailreign raised his skeletal hand, prodding at one of his eye sockets.

"I would have been dead. So... thank you. Thank you for your help, for healing me, for the food, for the rest, for everything." The words had a sense of honesty to them, yet they felt heavy with a false attempt. After all, could it have been Nailreign himself who had dug the pit within Bonestink's confines, filling it with the deadly spikes?

"You have to understand that I have been through what no man ever should."

Suddenly he was struck with great emotion and deep sadness, a longing for sympathy. Though he had never been one for accepting the compassion of others when it came to his personal shortcomings, for the first time since he could ever remember, he longed for sympathy - even if it came from a hulking, eight-legged monster.

As his vision fogged with the saltiness of uncontrollable tears, he launched into his story from the very beginning, when he had first received the letter marked by the king, continuing on to the abduction of his wife for her perfected alchemic skills. The speech proved his ultimate confusion and loss, just as it had been for him when he said goodbye to his dearest Orist, and later when he said farewell to Thul.

Esbern the innkeeper. Vlodus and Opus, the potionists of Faulkstead. The man-child aboard the caravan. The cloaked woman and her crew of thieves. The necromancer from within The Goblin's Rest. The three guards that he had drowned within his property's pond. The jeweller whom had possessed the amulet of great evil. The spirit that had met him alongside the pureberry meadows. Even Edgar! Everybody! It all came out, his entire story. His journey. He wanted to rescue his wife.

The more he talked, the more it became apparent to him that he had achieved so much more than he had anticipated. Sure, his losses were significant, however even with the setbacks he had done so very well. His story, still told with the vocal energy of deep internal pain, was impressive to both himself and Nailreign.

After leaving the greenery of Faulkstead, he went on to tell of the badlands and eventually the Nexus. He wished only for the king's sympathy. Could such an amount tenderness allow for his release? Perhaps without harm?

The air within the underground cathedral was dense with a musty stench, as if water had sat within the walls for ages. None of the hundreds of armour-clad horrors made a single noise. Not a single grunt, not one shift in armoured plating. The only sound was the soft crackle of the fire.

"You tell a compelling story." Nailreign shifted, setting his gaze farther into the mind of the weak-minded man.

"For the sake of our audience, and your normal ways, we will not communicate by psychic messages and rely on spoken words instead. Tell me land-walker, have you heard of Hrogarrot, the Great Mountain in the Northern Belt?"

Hrogarrot . . .

"Hrogarrot," began Nailreign, "A volcanic mountain. It existed within the Belt even before the mountains were formed, pouring a steady flow of heavy lava across the flatlands. In fact, through the ongoing rise of the mountainous belt, the ever-changing, every-rising plates contributed to Hrogarrot's towering height. Now, the land's most ancient volcano rises as Varroth's tallest peak."

What did this history lesson have to do with him?

The Gold Counter simply peered at the king.

"Hrogarrot had once been a place of great natural magic – innate essence – placed in that region, and that region alone by the Divines themselves, for only they knew the reason for its location and conjuring effects. The area had been a place of healing. Creatures of the forest, the mountains, and the flatlands that traveled to that particular area soon became transformed into a state of near immortality. Animals became resistant to death and sickness. They began to live for much, much longer than their usual lifespans. Rabbits went on to live for six hundred years. Some elk wandered the lands for more than two thousand.

It was a place of greatness . . . one that, of its own essence, offered life and perpetuity. Of this place came a fine pollen that coated the fields and had no origin. One that had just . . . been there. Always. It was ingested when passing through the area. It was a simple deviation in the creation of this world, yet one that gave promise to a life of great extension and flawless wellness."

The Gold Counter thought about taking a seat on one of the pews, but dismissed the thought. Perhaps it was best to continue standing on his renewed legs. It was not a time to invoke even the slightest sliver of discourtesy.

"Eventually, the volcano erupted, blanketing the land of seemingly infinite pollen with thick lava. That day ended the reign of eternal life and shaped the land as it should have been. The lava turned into obsidian and from within those formations came the Opal Geodes of Hrogarrot, sheltering what was left of the pollen. The powder of regrowth, the powder revitalization . . . of rejuvenation . . . the Gemsand of Life."

The Gemsand of Life.

Such a name evoked the idea eternal vitality.

Something the Gold Counter could no doubt benefit from. But how?

What had this all been about?

The story had a feeling of promise. One, that from even Nailreign himself, had a morsel of hope. The king was telling him this for a reason.

The emperor of the fallen city went on to adjust his stance before continuing.

"If you wish to achieve what you seek; to rescue your wife and bring back all that has been lost. And to breathe the unsullied freshness of green-fielded freedom once again . . .

He paused for a moment.

"Then you will bring me these Opal Geodes of Omni Gemsand."

··· 28 ···

After being led through a series of upward winding tunnels, the goblins pushed open a set of mighty, cast-iron cellar doors. The Gold Counter was hit with a horrific stench of rot that filled the open air. For the first time since falling on the spears of death inside of Bonestink's trap house, he was reunited with the open atmosphere of Crease. Only this time, he rose from within the central city.

The sky, though cascading with the rays of daylight was clouded with thick smog, a dense vapour, replete with an aura of disease as it belonged to the centre of Crease and all its ghastly misfortune.

The cellar doors gave way to the rear of the original monastery. Its windows, with their one-of-a-kind stained glass, were broken.

The stone walls had withstood hundreds of years of endless weathering. It was a structure designed for prayer to the Divines. But it just stood, covered in crusty old ivy, towering over a tremendous courtyard.

In the centre of the church courtyard, among the overgrown brambles existed a large circular pond, holding a great deal of murky water. Its former purpose was that of a fountain of sorts, though at that time it was reduced to a vessel containing cloudy water.

Thul!

His body, once again intact with sturdy limbs and renewed features, was laying upon an altar directly in the middle of the pond. Feelings of renewed hope and friendship washed over the Gold Counter upon viewing his fallen friend.

Prior to the their arrival, Nailreign had perched himself upon a mighty set of stone pillars near the pond. The courtyard was filled with an array of lesser minions, skeletons, wraiths, and Blight Goblins. The majority of the army was clad in hooded robes and ritualistic garments, the colour of faint tanzanite and amethyst, giving the atmosphere a sensation of heightened liturgy. Some of the crew wielded staffs of various types of twisted, magical wood.

"Come to me," beckoned the King of Fallen Crease.

The confidant did as he was told, making his way through the ranks as they parted, giving way to clear passage. As he moved forward, the grunting of some was audible.

Was this an atmosphere of welcoming or hatred?

As he approached the king, the eyes of Nailreign fell down upon him, glaring into his very soul. His self-confidence was quickly dwindling.

"Minions!"

The king's voice was no longer angelic sounding. It sounded as though it had ascended from the Void itself.

"We are gathered here today for the very reasons to flourish, heal, and prosper!" he yelled with a voice of radical volume, facing his audience.

The army of minions broke into an instant celebration of ground-shaking cheers catching the young man off guard.

"Today! Alongside our guides, we are sending these creatures forth to capture the Opal Geodes!"

The deafening howl of the audience grew even louder, paired with the stomping of boots against thick earth and stony brickwork surfaces.

"Today! We set them free so that they can bring us the Omni Gemsand!"

The crowd grew wilder, bashing their staves against the ground, jumping in unrestrained excitement. Nailreign was manifestly energizing the entire collection of ghouls with his words alone Their voices revealed great longing. Surely, at one point or another, they had been educated with this wisdom of the ever-giving pollen - the Omni Gemsand with is mighty properties of healing and change.

"The Gemsand of *Life!*" Nailreign's sudden demonically metallic voice so loud, it felt like the confidant's eardrums were being crushed.

The multitude of minions lost their minds. Without any sense of direction or care, they whooped, bawled and screamed as they flung themselves about wildly. Such a celebratory nature of barbaric energy had never before been seen through the eyes of the young man. Some of the Blight Goblins went on to uncontrollably swing at each other, whereas the others just smashed about, shoving each other frantically alongside skeletal figures that were doing just the same with open-jawed features. The wraiths of swirling blackened shadows danced wildly through the air, blasting through the brawl and zipping overhead.

Such a scene of calamitous excitement would invoke fear from any normal mortal, regardless of strength, stature, or confidence.

Nailreign watched the scene with a look of sadistic pleasure.

Eventually, after much cheering, the army's overall volume decreased, its members regaining control of themselves and wiping the blood from their noses and mouths. They fizzled to silence.

"Since you have chosen to embark inward towards the confines of The Royal Castle," the king began, his attention set back to that of the young man, "then you will fetch me the Opal Geodes while you are there."

It still didn't make sense. At first, he had imagined these Geodes to be part of the mountainous Belt, Hrogarrot in particular, but . . . the castle?

"Ever since the founding of Koraivindahl, the first king set forth groups of men to explore the lands. As they spread, they came across the various features within the grounds of Varroth: golden veins of ore, rare gems, and precious metals. They too, came across the Opal Geodes of Hrogarrot. Unlike what any man had ever seen, the Geodes were beyond captivating. They appeared to display a series of infinitely changing rainbows on their surfaces, much like the effect that oil has on a pool of water, only these shades were the most vibrant colours ever seen.

With an eagerness to obtain more of these newfound gems, the king ordered his men to mine the surface of Hrogarrot, completely stripping the mountain of the gems. The king never knew about the magical properties of the gems. To him and his men, they were the most beautiful stones they had ever seen.

"Now, to this day, those of the royal blood of Koraivindahl, along with its citizens, still hold no knowledge of the magical powers of the gems. However, upon mixing the right alchemic concoction with the Gemsand, a consumer will be granted an extended life of a thousand years or more!"

Nailreign paused for a moment.

"It truly is the ultimate potion, granted you can recover the Geodes… it is the making of the True Elixir of Eternal Life!"

An atmosphere of serenity filled the stench-infused air, one of unbroken silence that followed Nailreign's spoken philosophy.

Could such a material actually exist?

If so, could it really cure the aging of man, let alone grant immunity to disease and any other ailments? It was a lot to take in. No such element had ever prevailed this greatly in all the years of humanity; none that had ever been recorded anyhow. Not by any man at least and yet such a creation was exactly what his wife had been working on for so many years. It had been her life's goal!

The confidant was overcome with a sensation of bewilderment. Had such information ever been distributed amongst a town, a city, or even a group of individuals, there would no doubt be a collection of individuals whom would be unaffected by bindings of time.

He was lost. Disoriented in a realm of endless possibilities.

"What's more," Nailreign added, "this concoction could cure the ailment of the endless wandering that follows death from this plague. You know this now, as our dearest Edgar has so informed you."

He was right. Nailreign had used his psychic ability to tap into the mind of the young man, revealing what Edgar had told him. To die by the plague, guarantees an endless wandering upon this earth in an endless thirst for souls, an infinite prison of torment and hungering distress.

It all made sense, why Edgar was here . . . why he was all along. He too desired the results that the Gemsand could bring. It was possible to obtain, now that the young man had plans to infiltrate the Royal Castle.

Finally, he worked up the courage to question the king.

"How do you know all of this?"

It was a fair question.

"Because, dear traveler," Nailreign's voice assumed an angelic nature once again. "I was there. From the very beginning, I was there. I once tasted the pollens of the lands, before the Eruption of Hrogarrot. I was blessed with the greatness of prolonged life, and I wish it now amongst our kind here in Crease. My time is limited, and so is all of ours. You are our hope."

A slight chill touched the young man's skin as a small breeze graced the still air.

"My attempts to infiltrate the Royal Castle have all been for naught. I simply cannot enter the areas I seek, as I am too big. My wraiths are not strong enough for the wizardry of the king's sorcerers that guard the palace. We just don't have the muscle or the capacity to seek what we desire.

But you . . .

I can sense it.

You and your companion, combined with the guides of my hand, have a chance to succeed . . .

I can see it."

It is the man who takes up the quest, well-being and all, to aid those who cannot aid themselves, who is put atop the peak of natural selection. One who goes forth unwillingly, with all chance of fail, in greatest effort to seek what is right, and fight, without doubt, for what is asked of him. For it is he who will truly prevail in such longed-for success.

To achieve what is desired by the rest, is to be blessed.

"I will retrieve the Opal Geodes for you."

It had already been the young man's quest to venture forth to the Royal Castle, what could be more difficult than retrieving something else once there?

Besides...

It was either that - or death itself.

···29···

"Din rahma jah fohsuring sinjaah . . ."

The incantation was boldly put forth at equal measure by three of the dark mages that had just entered the courtyard through a series of double cathedral doors. Their figures, tainted with both the prolonged sands of time and an evident series of illnesses, gave way to a texture of warped and wrinkled skin. Each wizard of dark magic wore a hooded robe of raven-grim blackness paired with leather belts.

What stood out the most, at least to the young man - their amulets. Each of them wore the same amulet that he had seen within the jeweller's studio in Faulkstead. Their jade figures portrayed a skull upon a forest-green surface. It was an ever-changing piece of jewellery, one that both bewildered the young man and left him with a feeling of unease.

"Filthrosis ah munj keevla shrough nova . . ."

Their words were spoken with perfect timing. Each of the wizards stood knee-high in the pool of murky water surrounding Thul. His body, wrapped in white linen lay atop the altar of resurrection. Though their robes were drenched with a foul wetness that saturated the better part of their legs, not a single care had been notably given by any of the sorcerers as they conducted their witchcraft.

Nailreign descended from his perch above a cluster of broken pillars, and positioned himself between two of the mages, his two front legs of arachnid horror pressed against the surface of the stony altar from beneath the water's skin.

"Thul of Ironhold!" he shouted, his metallic voice once again that of a demon.

Three pillars rose from the water's edge, climbing to the height of a fair-sized birch tree, their exteriors covered with a glowing design of symbols. The display was enough to send the army of minions backwards towards the walls of the courtyard.

"Through body! Through mind! Through soul!"

The incantation of the mages continued while the king spoke.

"You are hereby summoned forth from the land of the dead and given a second chance of life. You will go forth alongside your companion, in efforts to bring home to Crease, the Opal Geodes of Hrogarrot."

Thul did not move. His body - dead.

"Bring forth, from the Void and the Heavens, both the darkest of lights and brightest of dim. Centre the focuses of resurrection upon this mortal of mountainous descent, and reawaken his spirit!"

An orb of immense brightness burst from thin air directly above Thul's still, lifeless body, with a blazing glow so strong the young man had to shield his eyes or risk permanent blindness.

Nailreign had reached the end of the resurrection and commanded with deafening volume:

"Awaken!"

Just then, a shockwave of pure energy burst open from the orb, releasing an explosion of fusion energy that rattled the city, tossing within it its every being, minus that of Nailreign and the three mages.

BWAM! – BWAM! – BWAM – BWAM – BWAM . . .

An immense noise of cosmic reaction continued to rattle the cursed ground of the city for an extended duration of time following the outburst. The stupefied confidant struggled to regain clarity. A vision of jumbled blurriness confirmed that he had indeed smashed his head against the unforgiving cobblestone during the process.

Next came a clattering of equipment, combined with a series of loud grunts as the rest of Nailreign's minions attempted to regain their sturdiness.

Once regained of his clear vision, the young man peered forth toward the altar.

There, in all his barbaric glory, stood Thul atop the altar, on his own two feet, his linen clothing blowing gently in the breeze.

The impossible was suddenly complete, as if it had been effortless.

"You . . . Wha—"

Thul attempted to comprehend what had happened and where he was. He then recognized his companion, sitting among the fallen minions, beaming back at him with a face of indescribable awe.

"How—"

The attempt to resurrect the barbarian had been a success although his skin had the noticeable, pale sickness of the plague. Nothing could have made the young confidant happier than to see his once brutally murdered adventure partner, standing tall in front of him. This moment, blessed with the perfection of being granted a second chance, brought a wide smile to his face, an expression of virtuous bliss, of hope and endless wishes combined. It was an expression of love.

Thul looked around at the goblins, skeletons, and wraiths alike, only to return to his companion. Clearly, he was lost in a world of confusion.

"Where are we?" he questioned, his voice both fearful and full of baffle.

"Where's the rum?"

Of course.

The young adventurer burst into laughter.

"Enough," Nailreign interrupted. "Now is the time to go forth."

Obviously, Nailreign did not share their sense of humour.

"Bring us now, the beasts of safe travel," he commanded towards one the of resurrection mages closest to him.

✳ ✳ ✳

Upon exiting the courtyard into the street through a side gate, the reunited travelers were met with a scene of unpredictability: three enormous elephants, though not like any on earth. Each had sooty grey skin and a pair of eyes that glowed red with sinful promise.

The travelers looked up at the beasts - they had been conjured forth from some hellish ritual. Their size was much larger than the average mammoth, and their tusks alone were enormous. They were each equipped with a saddle of wicker and leather straps.

A man was sitting atop one of the creatures. His hazel-tinted hair was white in areas, showing his age alongside a fair-sized bald patch in the centre of his skull. His skin had been whitened by the plague, and his bloodshot eyes gave the impression of weakness. Gazing down upon his companions, he smiled and scratched its head.

Nailreign waved his hand, motioning for the two friends to climb on the remaining empty seats of the elephants. They did so as the massive mammals knelt to help them climb up.

"The items you came with are waiting for you at the guards' tower that borders Crease from the Highlands. There you will continue your journey forth to Koraivindahl."

The city of despair was becoming busy with various minions as they entered the streets, stepping forth from their homes and run-down establishments. It was a scene of surprising revelation, as one would imagine such monsters to live in the sewers and crypts, yet here they roamed freely, managing a lifestyle very similar to humans. Each shop, in its own way, resembled run-down versions of food markets, blacksmiths, tanneries, and jewellers. There was even a shop where you could purchase small animals of sorts for pets.

"Remember, young hero." Nailreign's angelic voice was gentle but serious. "Remember what you have promised to gather for me . . . You are joined here with Vici Myrddin, son of Fachtna Myrddin of Koraivindahl. He will be your guide to, and within, the Royal Castle. You will also be joined with Edgar, whom you already know."

He swatted one of the elephant's rears with his boney hand, causing it to groan and begin its journey down the street; the other beasts following close behind in tow.

"You'll also find a gift of my gratitude in your belongings. Take care, Hero of the Meadows," the king bellowed as he retired to the confines of the cathedral's courtyard.

His goodbye was quick, leaving Thul and the young man to the next segment of their journey. Who was this person who rode alongside them? He looked entirely human yet greatly infected by the plague. Why would any man live here? For what purpose?

Furthermore, why the elephants?

The young hero looked around, each gathering of minions beaming up at him, licking their wide spread lips, and grinning mouthfuls of grotesquely, amber-tinged gnashers. Perhaps the reason for these beasts of safe travel was exactly that, their statuesque height provided a difficult obstacle for any worm-child to overcome, despite their origin of dark conjuring. If they could only understand that this adventuring party was en route to a goal that included the possibility of extended longevity for these foul beasts.

The young man turned to Vici and introduced himself. "Pardon me, but why would you want to live in a place like this? Aren't you a mortal?"

Vici, lit with an expression of cheerful response, suggested that he hadn't taken any offence.

"Oh, my friend. If only you knew. I never chose to come to this place, I can't see any man ever wanting to at all!" he chuckled, his laughter quickly overcome by a fit of violent coughing. One would guess such a man of palpable sickness had lived within the confines of the Fallen City for quite some time.

He adjusted his posture on the saddle before speaking again.

"I have been banished here . . . for reasons that were not even my own . . ." his mood had shifted from a joyful nature, to one of sadness.

"Yet! I finally get to leave this place for the first time since I've been here! How could any man not be brimming with feverish excitement!"

Banished?

Such a statement always originated from a serious event. What's to say this man wasn't going to kill off the young confidant and his companion, only to feast on their much healthier bodies? Something about this man seemed off, especially his mood. On the other hand, any man who had been banished to such a place would indeed exude a truthful expression of glee had he been given passage from within the grasps of the city walls.

"Banished? For what?" Thul's fearless voice joined in the conversation. It was so nice to hear it again, however, perhaps it had not been the time to catch up.

"Well . . ." began Vici with some hesitation. "My sentencing was for thievery. Funny that, as I have never stolen a morsel of anything in my life . . . well, except an extra slice of bread at the dinner table."

He patted his belly, skinny enough to reveal his frail ribcage, while at the same time, producing a bottle of red wine from a passenger's bag, causing Thul's eyes to light up. Uncorking the bottle, he continued.

"There was a time though, when ol' Vici here was your happy-go-lucky runner-up around the fine holdings of Koraivindahl, before I was fired from my horrible job, only to be sent here in chains. I didn't have any say in the matter! Such ridiculousness, as many a time had I been praised for my unrelenting efforts of haste and accuracy."

"Wait? So, you were sent here for stealing from your job? What occupation could be so important that you were sent to a place like this? Why not a simple prison?" asked the young man.

Vici chuckled again, glugging back a mouthful of wine before handing it to Thul.

"Why, I used to be a gold counter . . ."

He paused momentarily, the booming of the elephant footsteps on the deeply worn, earthy street, ruling the silence as they made their way eastward.

". . . Gold Counter to the King of Varroth, that is."

···30···

What the man lacked in hair on his head, he more than made up for in his personality and certain knowledge. Sure, he came across as one who was light-hearted, though beneath such a humorous persona, existed a mind of wondrous smarts. At first, it had crossed the two companions' minds that perhaps Vici had been one to spin a lie, but they realized that he was telling the truth as time went by. He maintained his conversation throughout their travels through ceaseless market places and bazaars belonging to the lesser folk of Grand Crease. His lengthy tales proved worthy, especially when it came to the subject of explicit honesty.

The evidence that the former counter spoke of, especially with such in-depth description, gave way to a story which any man would find hard to distrust. There was no doubt that the man, whose middle-aged characteristics most resembled that of an ordinary clergyman, had indeed been one of the king's recent Gold Counters. One that endlessly provided an honest number on each of the soldier's payrolls, let alone their superior commanders and other higher roles within the Royal walls.

For the longer the young man thought about it, the more it made sense that in some odd way, he had taken on the role of the royal Gold Counter soon after Vici had been "banished". It was, by chance, that since his wife had been taken from him long before the journey had even begun, that the confidant himself had been aimlessly appointed as the Gold Counter – as fate would have it. A position that drove him insane, and aided in the decision-making that prompted this adventure in the first place . . .

Yes.

It all made sense.

Since before he had set out and prior to a further letter providing him with the unforgiving knowledge that her return to him would be that of an unknown length of time, he had indeed been assigned the occupation of the Gold Counter. One that had been given to him to keep him busy granted his old age, at the time, in his remote location amongst the "Pureberry Meadows."

He was given the job as Gold Counter, due to that fact that Vici, the king's most recent bookkeeper, had "stolen" from the Royal Family's purse. He was, in fact, Vici's replacement.

"Surely, my newfound friend, you believe me, don't you? Isn't it obvious that such a man as I would never steal? Never once! Especially since the pay for being the king's most important accountant, had such a refined wage as it was."

Vici's well-versed questioning alongside the noise from the goblin-filled communities was evenly matched in volume. His story, rich with detail, made for an entertaining listen, yet its entirety was depressing; the actions that were used to punish him had been quite unorthodox.

ANDREW P. WILD

Generally, one would know better than to steal from the king. Nevertheless, as the man said, he was not the one who committed the crime. It was an autumn evening when it actually happened. The emperor's army had taken hold of yet another Dwarven city across the Eastern Sea, bringing back a massive chest full of rare treasures belonging to the young King Bezniel, son of the once lively Dwarven King, Grarrik Largebane. He had inherited the plunder of emerald-studded goblets, golden plates, and masses of diamond jewellery. Once his father had died, he passed this on to Bezniel on his deathbed.

It was not but a few days after that someone ransacked the king's fortune, searching for the treasures right beneath his nose. Every last piece of Young Bezniel's fortune was taken, leaving Vici to blame, as he was one of the few who possessed the keys to the treasure room. Whether it was someone from the opposing Dwarven armies, or someone within the kingdom's confines, no one ever found out who stole Bezniel's fortune. Yet whoever it was, had lifted the treasury key from Vici's person as he slept within the locked confines of his luxurious bedroom within the Royal Castle.

"Then why are ye' here in this filthy gods forsaken scene?" Thul questioned, while drinking Vici's nameless wine.

"The king is not the kind of man to obey the ways of the old. Rather, he is a man of his own, and so he decides the fate of others for them; a man who makes his own luck, disregarding others in the process. For murder and treason, sure, one is punished by death of rope hang. For pettier crimes such as violence, theft and the like, one is usually given prison time, or a fine of some sort. Though, because he thought it was . . ."

214

Vici stopped to clear his throat before continuing.

"Instead of going to prison in Koraivindahl, the king decided to send me here, to this place that hasn't exactly killed me, not yet anyways. It's a place of prolonged agony. A sickly placement, enough to drive any ordinary man mad. No mortal should ever be sentenced like this, no matter what the crime."

※　※　※

The travelers riding upon the massive war-elephants came to a halt at the base of the guards' tower. Shortly behind it, rose a hefty gateway that separated Crease from the Eastern Highlands. Its gaping archway opened onto a space where the riders stood. Such a sizeable opening suggested that beyond that of just guard towers, but actual walls composed of heavy stone layers, had once guarded the city from the East.

A cranky screeching of hinges caught their attention as a Blight Goblin burst from a door of one of the towers. He looked far different than the rest. His skin fluctuated in colour between an orangey hue to that of a solid red, closely resembling that of a lava flow. His figure was far thinner than any other goblin that the Gold Counter had seen before. He was at least a foot taller, placing him at the height of an average human. His eyes, too, had a fiery-ruby shade to them, at least from within the iris, yet what was most strange about this goblin in particular, was his nose. It was as long as a fully-grown carrot, protruding forth from his face quite a distance, before dropping downward toward the ground.

"Well? What?" he cackled with an evil, cranky voice. "What are you waiting for? Come in - get your stuff. Quickly now! Pup pup! So I can go back to sleep!"

Perhaps the city was not under the best of protection. Having said that though, perhaps the outside world needed protection from those within Crease. The flame-tinted goblin waved them inside. With haste, each of the clan members made their way into the small circular room, making sure not to get too close to the wart-covered skin on the odd-coloured minion.

Before them, laid out carefully, was their original gear, along with a trio of iron chest plates, each varying in size for the Gold Counter, Thul and Vici. Edgar, of ghostly being, required nothing of the physical world to travel. Yet for the physical comrades: some shirts, some pants, a few pairs of hardy boots, one pair much larger than the others as they belonged to Thul, as well as their travel bags, still *somehow,* containing their masses of gold coins.

The next table displayed an assortment of travel foods:

- Butter croissants
- Baked apple slices with cinnamon
- A thick cut of elk steak, heavily salted
- Several legs of cooked, dried, seasoned chicken drumsticks
- 6 pouches of dried cranberries
- 4 pouches of assorted nuts
- 12 bottles of clear liquid labelled "Fresh Water"
- 20 pastries – cheese and olive
- A loaf of rye

- 1 massive boar's leg, cured
- A sizeable stack of jerky, its source unknown
- 6 freshly caught salmon

Amazing. How had Nailreign had this all prepared so quickly?

The barbarian looked at the minion, and then back to the bags of gold. He picked up one bag and dumped it out on the table. He then began to count each of the coins, plopping them into the bag. There had to be a few hundred pieces spread across the table. Nothing was said, as no one dared to trifle with Thul's patience.

"Listen, boy! The king has left you something in that chest! Open it!" the goblin's vexing cackle continued.

The Gold Counter looked at a large chest that had been placed against the wall. Its algae-covered wood surface, ancient indeed. It looked as though it held a dark substance within... A trap? Perhaps?

The young traveler had ventured this far, what was the worst that could come of opening the chest? He was glad to have Thul by his side. How nice a feeling it was to have his mountainous friend with him again. No longer would he fear dealing with Varroth's more perilous challenges alone.

He made his way across the room, placing his pale hands upon the chest. There was no reason to postpone opening the chest as any hesitation would just provoke the carrot-nosed goblin. With a quick heave, he forced open the chest, swinging back the lid in such a way that it accidently struck the wall.

"Be careful with that, you fool!" snapped the goblin. His consideration of the moldy walls was quite amusing.

ANDREW P. WILD

"Damned human . . . damned human and his damned carelessness," he muttered.

The confidant peered into the depths of the chest. Its contents were wrapped in a silky woven cloth, decorated with the image of a golden sun. He reached down, cautiously wrapping his hands around what felt like a crystalline orb.

Slowly, ever so slowly, he proceeded to unwrap Nailreign's "gift" until finally he had reached the core of the tightly wound bundle, dropping the elegant fabric to the floor. He revealed what was in fact a crystalline orb of ultra-deep blueness, almost as if it were an enormous sapphire. From the very centre of the heavy, fist-sized gem flashed a continuous pulse of glimmering light.

"What is this?" asked the young man.

"It will keep the bad magic away from you! No need to know anything else about it. Now come! Off with you! Grab your swords and get outta' here!" barked the goblin.

Swords?

The confidant spun around to an incredibly diverse collection of weaponry propped against the wall. There were morning stars, maces, one-handed swords, two-handed swords, javelins, axes, spikes, even a war hammer equipped with a thickly, studded head of solid steel, fastened atop a broad, sturdy handle of some sort of hardy wood. Maplewood perchance?

He let out an expression of astonishment, which distracted Thul in his counting.

"Blimey! That there is one wall o' blades, if I've ever seen one!"

The barbarian casting aside his task of counting coins, brushed past his friends, making his way directly over to the monstrous war hammer. He picked it up and tossed it between his hands as if it were light as a feather, though it must have had weighed at least that of an average pig, if not more. Vici made his way to the wall, taking a morning star of substantially less authority, yet it came with an orb covered in dastardly razor points hanging from a link of short chain – a weapon that would no doubt make quick work of anyone standing in its way.

"Gather your belongings and leave now!"

The Goblin, immediately hostile, wished them gone, as did his actions. His irritation continued to grow.

"C'mon, Thul! You can count those later!" the last thing the Gold Counter wanted was a battle between the goblin and his large friend. Such an outburst would lead to further disruption in their journey, and he preferred a setting of peace for the beginning of their journey.

Surprisingly, the barbarian shoveled the rest of the coins into his travel sack, tossing it to his companion. It was possible that Crease had instilled a notion of fear in Thul's being, as his departure was one of great swiftness.

"Right! Let's get outta' this dump!" he boomed, spraying the goblin with his saliva.

The annoyed creature shoved Thul's chest, his response indicating he had taken the barbarian's closeness with poor measure. Instantly, Thul shoved him back, though his push was much stronger, sending the goblin flying backward into his thatch-work table.

"Guards! Guards!" yelled the goblin, scrambling to his feet from the rubble, his voice shrill with obvious, shaking nervousness.

Gathering up their clothes and food, the companions bounded out the door, leaving the young adventurer last. He looked briefly at the goblin who was clutching his back. It didn't have to come to that... The Gold Counter then went on to grab the orb, his "gift" from the Dark King, and a fair-sized blade from the weapons wall before leaving out the front door, making quick work of it all.

Upon re-entering the cityscape, the sky appeared a slightly darker grey than before. The smog had given way to a sun that had begun to set.

"Hey! We better get going!"

They hurried to the gateway that led into the darkening highlands. Edgar was perched atop a caravan pulled by a demonic, red-eyed horse, just like the one they had first encountered before entering Crease. Next to him was another horse and caravan.

"Quickly now! Before the rest show up! Whatever you did in there probably wasn't for the best!"

The clan climbed aboard the caravans, Edgar and Vici in one, Thul and his young companion in the other.

"Hyah!" Edgar hollered, snapping the reins against the foul mare.

Within seconds, both sets of caravans began a steady acceleration into the vast, empty Highlands. The young man prayed that his next return to Crease wouldn't be for yet another million years, if not beyond that. Not that such an amount of time was even possible... Or was it?

···31···
AGE: 40

For twelve days they journeyed onward toward The Royal City. The Highlands were just as their name described. There was meagre plant growth. Occasionally a rugged tree, most likely deciduous, would dot the landscape, just as a drop of red wine splashes a single white tablecloth. These ever so sparse trees were no taller than the adventurer himself, for they were stunted due to the harsh winds.

Despite the fact the landscape was quite barren, the confidant's heart was once again filled with both promise and hope. How nice it was to reconnect with Thul… to hear his stories.

Thul attempted to explain his experience of 'being dead.' He said that he had remembered waking upon a blanket of soft grass. Everything was white. There was an infinite space of emptiness except for a gentle hill that held a grand tree, a species he had never seen before. He made his way to the top of the hill where he was met by a woman whom had stepped out from behind this tree. Her naked skin was pale and mostly covered by her long, glowing, ruby hair. The vision was enough to make him forget his own purgatory.

From that story, he described many events. He lay with the woman and conjured forth a session of much-desired love-making. Yet his dream then snapped to a close, opening next to another series of dreams. He went on through every single dream, each one containing a promise of love, only to end in corruption and true evil.

Maybe it had been the plague, but whatever it was, this description of death was enough to put off both Vici and the Counter. Edgar, on the other hand, who had long since died and passed on into his state of gaseous wraith matter, had no say in it, as his recollection of what had happened after his death had all but long since been forgotten.

Just then, a sneeriff dashed across the path, vanishing into a small hole beneath a tuft of wispy, parched grass. Thul jumped to the ground from where he had been seated upon the rear of their tiny caravan, and made his way over to the opening, banging his huge hand over it. This odd method of hole slapping was enough to send other sneeriffs scurrying from their underground burrows to the open land above.

To any man, this would have looked quite odd, but since leaving Crease nearly 15 moons ago, their rations had all been consumed, even the jerky of unknown origin. A sneeriff, whose body is nearly as big as a groundhog, made for quite the meal, although their lightning-fast reflexes made them quite a challenge to capture.

A crowd of golden-bodied sneeriff's zipped from their holes, clearly startled by the hollow thumping of the bar-barian's hand, shooting off into various directions. With unexpected speed, Thul brought his hand down upon one of the feeble creatures, breaking its neck in a single motion. After persistent effort, he was able to catch two of them.

"All right!" he said, the essence of self-pride in his voice. "That'll be dinner tonight."

Luckily, Edgar did not require "regular food"; his entire being, plagued by thirst. He occasionally quenched his thirst by gulping from a jar he joked was his famous "cabbage stew." Its real contents probably that of some poor fool's soul.

Thul stuffed the creatures' bodies into the travel bag. At least one of them had it in them to hunt. How had Nailreign left them with only enough food to get them partially through the Highlands? His belief in his new clan was high. Any leader, evil or not, would have known the food to last only so many moons. So why had he given them such a meagre amount? Surely a supply of sneeriff's would provide sustenance – granting the party was able to keep their energy to seize them. But a belly without a variety of vitamins and minerals meant only the worst of nauseating pain, followed eventually by a passing of untold torture.

The Counter, upon his rider's perch, looked down at his hands. An observation he had become accustomed to. Pale skin that had once stretched across his knuckles, baring the markings of age, as it had begun to wrinkle. His entire physical being had matured even more. He looked as though he was within his forties; a man who had finally reached his peak health, only to be cursed with a chronic sickness. It was only sixty some-odd days since he had lived the life of a twenty-one-year-old tenderfoot, one with a youthful abundance of spirit and livelihood.

Such terms as "youthful" and "fresh" no longer described him. He was an aging warrior. One who, minus his scars and other battle marks, still looked as though he had a story to tell, which he certainly did. Though the sands of time had aged him hastily.

Once upon a time, the Gold Counter had lived a life of simplicity; his years were peaceful, watching over his farm in the meadows alongside his wife. Finally, with the granting of a second chance, he had gone beyond and exceeded his expectations of what could be put forth from his being. On the contrary, any mortal, for the most part, only recieved one chance. Or so it is said in the eye of the beholder, but there was great hope. And not a soul should have thought otherwise.

···32···
AGE: 41

Eventually came the end of their sixteenth day of travel. The flatlands had changed into rolling hills; dwindling elevations that dipped down in the direction they were headed - towards Koraivindahl. The horses, despite their demonic nature, did not like that. Not one bit. Though harnessed so that their carts bore no chance of running forth into their rears, the horses did not care for the downhill travel.

"We must walk now." Edgar proclaimed.

As the voyage unfolded, Edgar alternated between walking on his own two feet and floating. For him, floating required less energy than walking. Perhaps one of the perks of being a ghost. Although, when he did choose to walk, it was a conscious decision, and he did so to fit in with the rest, regardless of his ghostly form.

It was the first time that Vici had spoken that day. Actually, it was one of the few sentences the crew had spoken since the sun had risen earlier. At that moment, it was on its rosy exit, flooding their sky with a decorative display of beautiful colours: ruby, tangerine, amber, and sunflower gold alike, blasting through any remaining chunks of half-clouds. A breathtaking sight, it would have been more enjoyable if they had eaten. Alas, it had been a full day since they were graced with the final body of a sneeriff. Their longing of food was large; an internal pain, right in the pit of each of the mortal's stomachs. What of the hunger that had once been a tinge of unpleasantry, suddenly the tremendous roar of a white tiger.

"We must walk from here." Edgar reiterated.

"What will now happen to the horses?" the middle-aged Gold Counter posed such an appropriate question. Each word a sapping of whatever energy he had left from within his soul.

"It's fine," Edgar retaliated. "They will walk themselves home. These horses aren't your average."

Even Edgar was at a loss for vigour.

The clan dismounted their carriages, unloading their belongings as they did. One of the bags belonging to the adventurer and his barbaric companion primarily held gold and an assortment of clothes. The other, a leather bag, contained a collection of lesser bulky attire and the mysterious stone that had been gifted to him, its power still unknown. Though Vici had at one point expressed interest in the magical gem over the journey, his knowledge of the item had not yet been discussed.

Along the journey, they had a number of conversations. Some pertained to the reunion of Thul and his associate, others had to do with Vici and Edgar's stories. There had also been talk of Koraivindahl and the Royal Castle itself, as it painted images in the minds of the travelers of grand, medallion-yellow walls of massive stone, shrouded in ivy. Wonderful images but each traveler wondered what brutal forces it protected both inside and out.

The stories took place while they trekked. After stepping down from the caravans, the journeyers began putting on their iron chest plates, allowing for less cumbersome foot travel. They readied themselves for yet another six days of crossing – according to Vici's 'best guess."

They strapped the chest plates to their bodies whilst each of them battled a sensation of utter exhaustion. Thul, in particular, was having the worst time. Perhaps it was his size alone. Such a man of boastful confidence, yet at that moment, a cranky child. He had lost what strength he previously had.

"Horseshit!" he yelled; his voice pained as though he had been carrying an anvil strapped to his back the whole time.

"How can we do this? It's impossible! There ain't nothing to munch! Nothing 'cept one another! If I didn't need this 'ere leg, I'd have eaten it by now! This quest is bloody damned! Never mind the gold!"

The Counter paused for a moment, looking up at him.

"We can do this, Thul. We can!" he started, attempting to strike hope in his friend, even though he had very little of it at such a time.

"We will find food! All we—"

He was cut off.

"Damn you! Damn you an' your gold! Damn your wife! Damn this place! This godforsaken hill! Damn it all!"

He threw his war hammer, which nearly outweighed him during his violent swing, sending it sailing off into a nearby patch of greenery.

The rest of the crew halted their actions, blindly gawking at the barbarian in all his frustration. He was a mess; an entire jumble of chapped lips, frayed hair and pale skin. A dehydrated mass of hunched over muscle.

"An' damn you!" he yelled, twisting his rage toward Edgar.

"What? What have I—"

"Damn you an' your damn city! Your goddamn horses! Your bloody damn king!"

His emphasis on the word king was childish and feeble, implying a great deal of disrespect. "Damn you all! I don't need any of this. I don't even need this gold!"

He threw his pack to the dusty ground.

Without further ado, he picked up his war hammer and marched directly away from the rest of the clan, heading downhill toward an entirely different set of terrain. All that lay ahead of them at the bottom of their half-day descent was a series of monstrous boulders. A landscape, as if the Divines themselves had at one point smashed what was left of the surrounding hills, leaving only plains of scattered rock; a labyrinth of stones, some as giant as a two-story loft. How such an odd atmosphere could exist was beyond the Counter. How had these boulders, these seemingly infinite, detached boulders, all come to be gathered amongst these plains for as far as the eye could see?

"Thul!" cried the confidant, desperate not to lose his companion a second time.

There was no response. Each of the three members just watched. Their most prominent friend of sheer strength, departing from them, headstrong, toward the series of boulders that, in their own way, formed a city of their own; a city of scattered, rocky chaos.

It is sensible to note, that most do not know how well they have "it", until "it" decides to up and walk away from them. Overall, it would be wise to take account of everything that is good in life, at any given moment. For there will never be anyone to tell you when you are in the "good old days." You will only know of them once they have truly passed.

···33···

The new day brought rays of strong light, though it did not bring back their dear barbarian. Before sleeping, the clan of humans and their wraith had made their way down the hill in pursuit of Thul. Edgar sent the horses back to Crease. How they knew of the way, the weak-minded Gold Counter could never understand.

A modest sleep was had, to say the least, though it did not do much to help the travelers regain their energy. What they desperately needed - food. Any food. Even Edgar had begun to act ravenous, as his final jar of "cabbage stew," had been consumed a couple days earlier.

They rose, and started their journey through the maze of seemingly infinite boulders, each one blotting out the light of the sky. Such an odd landscape, yet the Gold Counter had no knowledge of this place, neither did Vici or Edgar. Still, they plodded forth until eventually all ground was met with the blocking structures of yet more grey stone.

At this point, their only option was to climb over the enormous boulders. They proceeded slowly, painstakingly climbing the first part of the nasty terrain.

It had taken them half the morning to reach flat land again. The barren area held zero evidence of plant life, just looming towers of unrelenting stone. Everything was grey, including their clothes and belongings after climbing through layers of rocky dust. It clung to them like sand on wet skin. Only the sky offered an escape from the dullness, with its cloudless, vibrant afternoon cyan.

The Counter had had it. His soul was crushed with the combination of foodless journey, blazing midday sun and the endless labyrinth of graphite. Who could say how long this forest of stone went on for? Even if he knew the way, the traveler's body had finally given up on him. Not a single step was left within him. His feet were burning and swollen. Vici felt the exact same way.

The once banished Counter finally spoke.

"It's . . . impossible." His words scraped through his parched lips.

They collapsed in a desert region, one fortified with solid sedimentary formations. Just then, the sound of a fair-sized stone clattering down a series of surfaces filled the air. Each clan member, startled, looked around. Their reactions were not very enthusiastic on account of starvation and exhaustion.

Although the area appeared desolate and lonely, it proved to be the opposite, when a giant feline prowled out from behind one of the limitless pillars of elephantine rubble. It was a mountain lion to be exact. How or why, it was there was a mystery. Perhaps there were other cougars in the area. The source of its hydration was unknown, though its body looked robust.

There it lurked with a coat of thick, short hair that radiated in the blazing sun. It snarled at the three, evidentially preparing a plan of attack. Their energy changed to that of fear. The confidant's mindset had been to die of complete dehydration, not as a meal to a hungry, territorial oversized 'mouser'.

Without any further notice, the cougar charged forth, directing its strike at Edgar! Luckily, since he was a ghost, the oversized feline pounced directly through him, fangs at the ready to sink into some tasty flesh. It landed on the other side of him in a state of confusion, giving Vici the opportune moment. The once-accountant swung his mace vigorously, catching the cougar's flank with a hard blow from the end of his dangling, spear-coated flail.

With a spine-tingling howl, the beast fell off balance, stumbling backward a couple of feet as a series of bloody streams began spilling from its ribcage. For a moment, it just stood there, reeling from the pain brought forth from Vici's ball and chain.

"Save yourselves! Get behind some cover!" he cried out frantically to his partners, though really it was only the adventurer himself that had to worry.

The feline braced itself once again. A single blow was not enough to deter its fleeing instinct, though its flank had been significantly injured. The cougar directed its focus to Vici, and leapt. In the blink of an eye, the mountain lion knocked him to his back only to follow-up by pouncing atop the pour soul. Luckily, Vici was able to defend himself by grabbing his mace and blocking the gap between his face and the psychotic snapping of the beast's unforgiving death jaws.

"Help! Help!" he screamed, now at the mercy of his foe.

The blade-like claws pierced a multitude of inch-deep holes inside of Vici's chest plate as the creature mercilessly attempted to rip him apart with its deadly gnashers.

A feeling of paralyzing fright fell over the warrior, sending him into shock; a complete daze as he watched helplessly while his friend underwent a horrific mauling. Though he held his sabre in hand, his state of panic had left him motionless. He could have made quick work of the cougar with his weapon, however at that moment, he was nothing more than an empty shell. A man riddled with unmitigated fear.

Edgar, on the other hand, went on to mutter a series of foreign words as he clasped his spectral hands together. A chain of wavering, black outlines began spinning around his fists, erupting into a cloudy orb of deep shadows.

" . . . *Fazjavith!*" he yelled, as he finished casting a spell of black magic.

With a speed as quick as a lightning strike, the orb burst forward from his hands, catching the mountain lion directly in the side of its skull, just as it had broken its way past Vici's mace.

The fierce cat went flying into a gigantic boulder. The force of Edgar's spell and the impact of the beast colliding with the stone was enough to incapacitate the cougar, causing it to lay there whimpering in a bloody mess.

"Now!" yelled Vici. "Kill it! Kill it while it's down!"

Suddenly, Thul appeared from behind a pillar of granite, his presence magically lighting the scene, next to where the mountain lion lay quivering. In a single movement, he lifted his grand war hammer above him, bringing it down upon the head of the beast, smashing its skull into a myriad of fragments.

"Now why would ya' boys be fightin' a mountain cat without me?" he joked as each of his clan members stared back at him in awe.

Each member of the clan rushed to Vici's side. Though his armour had been damaged upon the upper torso, he was still busy praising the Divines for protecting him from death. To climb out from under a mountain lion would require a strength that not even a barbarian had. As luck would have it, Edgar had rescued him just in time, saving his face from becoming a tasty repast.

Once again, the overwhelmed travelers had difficulty speaking in full sentences. Although nobody was shocked with Thul's brutal way of bringing justice to the cougar, they were surprised that he had decided to reconnect with his friends at all. Granted, to find a mountain lion attacking a party of your own, one would expect any friend to be of aid where he or she could.

They were no longer afraid of death by starvation. There was enough meat on the cougar to sustain all three of the mortals for some time.

"I told you!" barked the Counter, his anger geared towards Thul.

"I told you we were going to be fine! To have you going off on us just because you're frustrated would not help anyone! What were you going to do out there by yourself? I'll bet an individual meeting between you and a mountain lion would not prove well in your favour."

Thul's reaction showed complete understanding, bringing on a reserved stance as he apologized profusely. Something from within the minds of each of the pathfinders understood that their barbarian companion had made impulsive decisions at one time or another. It's just the way he was. And so, they came to accept that fact in their own ways, just as they accepted his apology. Furthermore, what were they going to do? Decline his sorry words? They were all in this together. Besides, the feelings and actions of negativity expend far more negative spirits than the notions of advantageousness.

Despite Vici's protective chest plate, the oversized cat had managed to pierce its way through its metallic surface, slightly gouging the poor traveler's chest. The Gold Counter ripped a couple sheets of cloth from his once-fancy shirt that had been gifted to him from Nailreign himself. He dabbed it upon Vici's chest wounds, discovering thankfully, that they were of minor injury.

Just then, an odd tone came from the Gold Counter's travel bag. It sounded like a church bell ringing from a great distance away, though it ceased to end its gentle, holy-like ringing.

"What is that?" Edgar asked.

Without further pondering, the confidant made his way over to the ringing bag. What would he pull from the bag that was making the noise?

Wait.

Perhaps . . . the stone?

The sapphire that had been so cordially gifted to the Gold Counter from Nailreign himself.

He reached into his bag and removed the massive gem, wrapped in its fancy cloth. He unraveled it only to reveal the beaming of its gently flashing rays. The sapphire core beat strongly within, spewing out an array of light through its confines.

"Bring it to me!" Vici demanded as he clutched his wound.

The confidant did as was told, rushing back over to his partner's side, placing the gem in one of his hands. Vici proceeded to place the flashing sapphire stone against his chest. As he did, the gem began flashing at a speed faster than any man's heart could beat. The scene was ultimately blissful, as the stone's ringing continued.

Suddenly, Vici's armour lit up and his lesions began to close. Whatever magic the stone held within was one of truly magnificent healing properties.

"Blessed the gods!" hollered Thul, his being overcome with amazement.

Each set of gouges sealed up simultaneously, their seams meeting together in a manner that revealed a perfect close. Suddenly, there wasn't even a sign injury of ever being there in the first place! Where Vici's wounds used to be, there was simply his flat, untainted chest. It was a miracle.

"How . . . You . . ." the confidant was taken back by the scene.

Vici rose to his feet, wiping the remaining sweat from his brow.

"From what I've learned, brother... King Nailreign grants positivity once he has decided a fate of liveliness over death."

He was right.

Upon reflection, the Gold Counter was sure that death had come for him from when he had awoken before the massive arachnid. At that moment, he was grateful for his presence on his journey, granted he still owed much to the King of the Fallen City.

The rest of the day was designated for recovery and rest. Not long after the incident, Thul brought them the knowledge of a nearby spring amidst the dusty ruins. As destiny had it for the travelers, the natural spring was filled with fresh drinking water. Though such a body of water was only the size of an average bathing tub, each member took turns drinking endlessly from its source near a large boulder. This was a sign of great luck, indeed. There was no doubt that the Divines had meant for this encounter with such a special hydrating source.

Once they had consumed to the point that made any further drinking impossible, they went on to the carving of their foe, which in turn led to a grand feast of well-deserved nutrition. It did not take long for the travelers to prepare the mountain lion, nor did it take them much time to build a fire from what they had of remaining cloth from within their bags. Given their lack of wood, the fire did not last long, so they were careful to keep the fire going to sear their own pieces of cougar flank. It wasn't exactly a meal of perfection on gold platters, but a filling snack indeed.

As luck would have it, Edgar's ability to produce flame had also become an asset to the group. Unfortunately, such a skill was not all that valuable at the time, as their ghostly companion's efforts at casting fire were limited from his own weakness as well.

Despite their regained energy, the clan decided to take the rest of the day to heal, both mentally and physically. With an endless supply of water, they made themselves comfortable after carving up the rest of their new supply of juicy cougar steaks, wrapped in pieces of cloth they had chosen not to burn for that reason. Though the night was not yet upon them, they drifted off into lands of individual dreaming with hopes of no further conflict between themselves and yet more cougars. As luck would have it, the rest of the evening rewarded each of the travelers with a rejuvenating, peaceful sleep.

··· 34 ···

AGE: 44

The rest of their travels through the fields of irregular
rubble were tasking but doable. Seeing as the Gold
Counter was cursed with the aging of a year for every three
and a half days, his journey was far more excruciating than the
rest. Still, his love for his cherished wife kept him going.

On their nineteenth day, they stumbled across some
unforeseen groups of the king's men, each clad in various
robes and turbans. Such attire was obviously worn to shelter
their skin from the relentless rays of the sun in the desert
conditions. Nevertheless, the majority of their outfits were
branded with the well-known half-crescent moon that sym-
bolized their loyalty to the Red Hand.

At first, they wondered why such large groups of soldiers
were out there. But after they strategically worked their way
through fields of stone and past the ranks without being seen,
it became apparent that the king's men had been blasting the
stone in their surroundings. Evidently, their use of dynamite
and various explosives was in the hopes of finding precious

239

metals and building materials for their empire. That explained why the land had become such a crumbling mess. For the amount of blasting they had conducted over the years, the size of the area that they had covered was absolutely commendable. Certainly the "explosion" aspect of the work cost the men little to no energy at all, though transporting the TNT and goods had no doubt tired them out. The poor shmucks among the lesser ranks had been forced to pound out smaller rock with sledgehammers and pick-axes.

There was one point during their stealthy expedition, when Thul had nearly blown the lot of them to a fine dust after he came across a bundle of finely wound explosives. For some reason, he grabbed the bundle when he saw it. When he realized it was connected to a group of wires leading back to a push-box, he immediately threw it into a nearby opening, avoiding the detonation of his own party. In a sense, he was foolish to pick up the package, but then again, had he not thrown it the distance he did, the chance that the party would have survived was questionable. Nevertheless, out of coincidence, the bundle was triggered almost simultaneously by one of the king's men. After which, had evolved a random search for suspicious behaviour, as the bomb had gone off in a different location than originally set, sending the companions dashing wildly through the rubble in a directionless manner.

Eventually, on paths guided by the sun and stars, they made their way through the fields of formidable stone, finally arriving on the other side of the massive labyrinth. A sight greeted them with something that none of them thought they would ever encounter again, not even Edgar.

Lit by the dawn of new daylight was a scene of purity and plenty. Fields were flourishing with an abundance of healthy species of plants and animals alike. It was similar to the Counter's homeland within pureberry meadows. The new landscape looked like paradise. Occasionally, a cluster of light, breezy poplar trees would dot the land, only to interrupt a smooth, gentle-rolling panorama of innocent hills. From where they stood, they could see a variety of fish swimming freely in a nearby pond.

It was their prize... their reward!

They had made it this far.

They chose to go on, knowing that they would probably encounter more that the land had to offer in terms of its most terrible manifestations. Perhaps, the worst was over for the time being. But more than likely, their mission would increase in difficulty once they reached the unforgiving interior of the Royal Castle. Could it really be as horrible as what they had just experienced? After all, the four were once again reunited and none of them, despite the complex, inconceivable obstacles, had died.

"*In Omnia Paratus!*" cried Vici, as he emerged into the blissful landscape.

Before any of them had a chance to ask their friend of his meaning, he had taken off with great speed, heading directly for an enormous pond, its proximity closer than the rest.

"Not before me!" yelled Thul, his complete enthusiasm showing through as he too began bounding down towards the body of water.

It wasn't long before the remaining members joined them, dashing madly after one another. They were followed by Edgar who gracefully, yet swiftly floated down towards the pond.

What was once a cluster of hardened veterans had eventually magically evolved into what looked like a gathering of happy ducklings, swooping and splashing about without a care in Varroth. It was a picturesque moment in time. One that was so genuinely deserved. It was sincere and delightful. Not even the God of Love and Friendship could recreate such a scene.

This went on for some time, and they couldn't help celebrating. Any man with skin as white as theirs would have been wise to keep covered from the sun, yet they hadn't given much thought to it on their journey. And for some reason, their sickly pale skin had maintained its hue. It did not show signs of sunburn. Perchance it had something to do with the magical stone and its healing abilities. However, if the magical gem did have the ability to heal their injuries, as well as any sun damage, it did not heal their plague. This thought crossed their minds, yet none of them chose to speak of a cure until that moment.

"Although I cannot feel the sweet embrace of refreshing water against my skin, I would be lying if I didn't mention the fact—" Edgar's words were enough to pause their celebratory splattering in the oasis.

They looked at one another before, finally, their Counter spoke.

"What do you mean?" he questioned.

"Well," returned the ghost. "Once we return the Opal Geodes to the king, he will be able to undo my curse, sending me on to the next life."

A moment of thought pertaining to "the next life" was on each of the travelers' minds and they looked curiously back at Edgar, expecting him to speak more of this topic.

"Yes . . . the Gemsand within those geodes is enough to cure anyone of Crease's blasphemous curse, human or spectral. Though for someone who is already dead, this means to leave this world. To be sent on to the next life, whatever that may be."

Thul chimed in. "Why would ya' do then? You should just be stayin' the way ya are!"

"I cannot," their ghostly companion retorted, the nature of his tone revealing an expression of true sadness. "I cannot deal with this thirst anymore! Regardless of the amount of mortal essence that I consume, I cannot fully quench this horrible lust for more. It truly is the most dreadful I have ever felt."

His words, so full of sadness, touched each member with deep emotion. It was indeed distressing to think that their friend was never going to make it once they had succeeded in their adventure. At same time, there was an understanding to it all. For any who had been touched by the feeling of deep thirst, a feeling of such prolonged dryness, they truly understood the pain of requiring water. For Edgar, it must have felt even worse. To imagine a lifetime of unending thirst was unequivocally horrible.

"But!" he interrupted their thoughts of dismay. "That does not mean to say that we are not having fish for dinner!" Just then he dove beneath the surface of the radiantly, clear water, leaving behind not even a splash or a ripple.

Seconds later, he reappeared followed by a school of fair-sized walleye and perch that floated to the surface, their basil and chartreuse scales gleaming in the sunshine as their motionless bodies floated on the nearly still waters.

"Thul! Gather us some wood! We will feast immediately!"

Without further delay, the barbarian made his way over to a group of healthy poplars and began swinging away with his grand hammer. There was no doubt that Edgar's story had unhinged his party's happy mentality for a moment or so. The traveler had already guessed as much since learning of the Gemsand's incredible power. However, it was not the time for sad thoughts. It was the time for feasting and righteous celebration.

··· 35 ···

Finally, after a day and a half of travel, they arrived at Koraivindahl, the Royal City constructed on the shores of the Great Sea. It was otherwise known as the "City of Towers" as its superior height had far out-climbed that of every other city.

There, right before their eyes, rose the colossal city that they had been so desperate to seek out. It was built strategically on a mountain of its own so that if there were any possibility of attackers, the city's watchmen could spot them instantly due to the openness of the surrounding area. That way, the kingdom could prepare for lockdown and defence. Unlike most of Varroth's major cities, Koraivindahl also had the added protection of being constructed from walls of mighty density. Of course, once within the city, any traveler and homebody alike were graced with a presence of gentle, warming streets, lined with fountains and expensive emporiums.

There were few entries into the kingdom, at least for citizens of the law-abiding variety. The majority chose to gain entry through the Northern and Southern Gates, each of which reached by passing over a fortified bridge, leviathan in size and constructed entirely out of immense slabs of pure limestone. In fact, as it is noted in the tomes and scriptures pertaining to the history of The Royal City, it took the builders of Koraivindahl three years to construct each of the entry bridges.

The other method of access was through the city's massive port that had been strategically created along its eastern shoreline. One could enter by sea after paying the entry toll, and hiking up many of The Royal City's massive steps. All travelers were subject to an entry fee and a full inspection upon arrival. The party would no doubt be denied access, even if The Gold Counter had appeared younger than he had originally been from within the Pureberry Meadows.

They stood there in a clearing of fresh daisies, gazing up at the towering city in all its grand, massive stonework. The elegant design was glowing with shades of garnet and amethyst due to the special tile laid atop the roofs. It was the largest empire within thousands of miles of either direction of the Great Sea. What had once been a city of gracious limestone became covered in wild ivy, which only added to its magnificent beauty. A traveler standing within the mighty walls of Koraivindahl would encounter an abundant growth of varying botany. For in this kingdom, which some would say was as old as time, there were gardens filled with blossoming flower beds and fortified groves, in which one could find every species of plant in the realm of herbal beauty. To be exact, Varroth's first ever city had always been one of expensive taste, and an even pricier maintenance. But this is what made it such a place of desire... of status.

"City o' Towers? Hah!" Thul chuckled pitilessly. "More like City o' rich arseholes!"

His words held truth.

"So then, how do we get in? Look at us!"

Obviously, to cross over into Koraivindahl's interior through the ways of any of average travel would be begging for an imminent death. Not to mention that the confidant gradually looked much like his older self. His body, at that moment, appeared to be mid-forties or so, but the disease had aged his complexion to something of his mid-fifties, maybe even sixties. The plague not only aged one's skin, it brought on an aching sort of pain that filled the muscles and bones of its victims. Regardless, it was his vigour that kept him youthful in step. His energy and enthusiasm grew with each second as his wife's presence called louder and louder to him.

In addition to that, the group journeyed alongside a ghost. For Edgar to enter any city but Crease would be impossible, especially since the guard force of the Red Hand had battalions of sword-wielding soldiers and deadly sorcerers alike. The occupation amongst the king's ranks of "wizardry sentinel" brought in quite a handful of coin, making it an attractive position for those who had legally studied the art of destructive magic. Most of the time, the sorcerers decided that this position was better than death, as the grand lot of them had once been criminals themselves. The party's access would have to go unnoticed; it would be difficult. This brought to question exactly how they would gain entry.

Vici wiped his face. It was impossible to tell if he was covered with droplets of sweat or mist from the ocean, granted their closeness to the water.

"We must swim," he spoke, looking at The Counter and then Edgar.

How the party envied Edgar during many moments on the course of their journey. Granted he was tainted with a limitless thirst, at least he did not feel simple mortal fears such as physical pain and drowning.

Vici continued on, "Yes swim. Not by sea, but through the sewers. It's not the best, nor the cleanest, but if we take the way I remember, we can skip the city and gain immediate access to the castle cellar."

Perchance it was the only plan they had left.

Without giving any more thought to it, they followed Vici as he set off through the daises, nearing a blackish, modest lake. It was full of run-off from the city's sewers. There was comfort in mind, knowing that the somewhat stagnant water came from Koraivindahl's fountains and refined streams. As they had learned from Vici himself, most of the sewer's actual sewage was discharged into the ocean.

Rising from the lake was a gentle breeze that mixed with the mist from the cascading waterfalls. Just then, a massive hawk flew out from a point within the wall. Its species belonged to that of the Brass Walsh chain, a type of bird that was one of Varroth's more prevailing aviary species. It not only fed on rodents, but also winged creatures. Sometimes even in flight. Worst of all, was its natural instinct to seek out the jugular of any foe, even human, if an unwise traveler chose to sleep alone in an open area. It was widely believed that if such a Walsh flew over someone they would be cursed with poor luck, a myth that had its place amongst bar-talk.

Perhaps not every member of their clan had heard of its hapless sign, yet each had their focus set to it. Only then did The Gold Counter realize that the city walls had not just been for safe-keeping, but its structure provided homes to many citizens that lived within its confines. Their windows were staring out across the land.

"Are those . . . homes?" he asked.

"Actually, yes," Vici answered, "homes to city folk who are willing to pay the coin to be blessed with such a view of the lands and springtime daisy fields."

Far from where they were standing, a figure leaned out from an opening in the wall. It was a man smoking a pipe, or so his far-off appearance had revealed as he exhaled a large cloud of blueish smoke.

"Oye!" he called out, waving his hand down at the clan. "What're you doing down there?"

Of the party, not a single member felt a need to respond. His calling had come across as rude, not to mention that their business had nothing to do with his likes.

One by one, more citizens began to poke their heads through the windows that dotted Koraivindahl's mighty walls.

"Oye! You down there!" another cried out.

Had they not realized that Edgar was a ghost? Such a finding would surely trigger an alarm or panic of sorts.

"You'll be surely screwed ya filth! Serves ya right for comin' to Koraivindahl without the coin!"

Apparently, their wandering had been mistaken as homelessness. To look upon those loitering about the outer walls with such proximity suggested an aura of impoverishment, especially for those who wish to travel without an actual convoy. Had the yellers only known that the travelers were in fact the opposite.

It was Thul to come back first. "What is the matter with you?" he yelled out, his voice with frustration and verbal retaliation.

"Don't you know that the gates have been shut? Nobody is to leave his or her residence! You'll be dead in minutes!"

Minutes? How could this glorious day come with such daft talk of death?

What was the meaning of it all?

Finally, another voice, this one with an answer to it all.

"The war! It's happening!"

"Run now! You may just save your heads!"

···36···

Their panic was real... but was the war? If it really was the war, was it the same war that the Gold Counter's wife had been seized for?

There was no time. They had to move.

Vici went first, diving headlong into the run-off lake. In hopes that Thul knew how to swim, the confidant went next, frantically splashing into the water behind the first warrior. Vici headed for a waterfall that came cascading out from the wall before diving under it. The Gold Counter and Thul, who could in fact swim, did the same. Edgar, gently gliding above the currents, followed them.

Upon surfacing on the other side of the pounding waterfall, they encountered a substantial iron gate.

"Thul! Open this!"

He did as he was told, and began heaving on its rusty railings, the water splashing around his feet.

"It no use! I cannot get 'er to budge!"

Edgar began preparing a spell; smoky symbols waving back and forth.

Ker-chunk!

The heavy grate split free of its foundations, falling outward into the foamy waters.

Incredible!

What else was he capable of doing?

"Lucet conlustro!" their phantom partner cried out, sending forth an orb of bright cyan light from his clutched hands. It beamed forth and then waited for them within the midst of the tunnel. A light source! Useful, as there were no other forms of luminescence within the sewers of dank despair. Perhaps the idea of darkness was wise, as it would deter underground travel for thieves and other unsightly characters.

They entered the tunnel, their path lit with Edgar's orb. At first, it was nothing but a steady, knee-high flow of constant water paired with an overgrowth of drippy algae that lined the spherical tunnel surrounding them.

Suddenly, images of piranha, mouths full of sharp teeth invaded The Gold Counter's mind. Could such things exist down here? It was possible. He began searching the nearby water for any signs of the fish. There was enough rotten matter feed an entire school of them.

At last, they arrived at a splitting between tunnels. They climbed onto a platform above the rushing stream. Ahead was a sturdy oak door, held together by enormous iron bolts and bars. Though strong, it was no match for Thul's shoulder as he went bursting through the hatchway without any discussion.

The adventurers raced down the corridor of eternal blackness, only to enter a chamber, its gargantuan size revealed as Edgar's orb passed into it, illuminating its spaciousness. A multi-leveled room was filled with rotating cogs, stairwells and yet more flowing waterfalls of various speeds. Evidently, this was a chamber that controlled a portion of Koraivindahl's fountains and various aqua flows.

To have completed the upstream journey alongside his companions made The Gold Counter feel impressed with himself. He had been through enough to gain considerable strength and a newfound confidence in himself. Such qualities had not been among his stronger attributes in the past. Though his body had begun to show signs of his older self, his reflection on life the second time through made him feel immensely proud.

The platform made for an acceptable rest spot. It was not long before each of them had finished devouring what was left of the walleye and perch strips that the party had been carrying within their soaked, dwindling sacks.

"How is it that you know the way we seek?" asked the Gold Counter.

Was it possible for Vici to memorize such a system of tunnels?

How did he know of such a path in the first place?

One would imagine an accountant to be finely drab in a mantle of luxurious fabrics, working at a desk of elegant carpentry... not plundering about sewers. There had been little sense to it all.

"Many a night have I spent down here prior to my duties of being The Counter."

It was a lie...

It had to be.

The idea that any man would rise from a beggar to the official Gold Counter was practically impossible. Evidently, for what wealth fueled this city's grand hearth of circular economy, there had been little tolerance for any of the homeless kind.

Only for a moment's rest could the clan members regain their strength. For the remaining passages were unknown by all but Vici. For the confidant, it pressed a cold stone on his mindset of uncertainty. At any point he could ask their guide what distance was left, but the answer might lessen his spirits. Perhaps it was best to continue forth without knowing how much was left. Though exhausting, their mission had become one of excitement, rather than that of the constant worry of death.

Each traveler developed a mindset to explore the tunnels rather than to dread them. They continued on through the distorted shafts. Over time, some had crumbled, causing the group to travel through different passages. It wasn't until they reached a fair-sized chamber, stocked with old candles of which they chose to light in order to evaluate their setting.

Upon entering the chamber, the images of unholy symbols painted across the sewer walls came to light. The chamber was probably a place of foul rituals. The symbols were displayed with a darkened ruby hue, most likely blood.

"What's all this then?" asked Thul, clearly not bothered by the eerie scene that they had just stumbled upon.

"It's a place of ritual," Vici's knowledge of the room was surprising. Anyone could learn of these symbols if they were willing to take the time to research them.

"It likely belongs to a group of worshippers who praised words for Ragasp the Carver."

Ragasp was the name that belonged to one of the darker Divines. It was she who chose the fate of those who were killed without reason. For the most part, her role was to send forth the spirits of any men who had gone insane. It was written: any who choose to spend time learning her ways, in addition to a lifetime of constant prayer, could expect an afterlife of enhanced abilities within the Void. In a sense, it was a way of creating a sort of insurance should one decide to live a life of dedicatedly evil nature. Though it was also told that even those who follow Ragasp the Carver, down to the very last detail, were still not guaranteed a passing of fortified authority within the underworld. Such an idea was enough to deter a worshipper from further ritual, or increase the practice, depending on his or her mindset.

A feeling of numbing fear fell over the Gold Counter as he looked around at the macabre smears of sadistic ceremony. It forced the question: how many people, or *living* things, had been slaughtered here? Beneath their feet was a brick floor that had been coated in many layers of blood. Although the orb's light was enough to fill the recesses of the chamber, revealing that it had only contained the travelers within, it still felt as though they were not alone.

It was as if the walls were watching them; multiple pairs of eyes, each with invisible pupils. There was, of course, only stone behind the painted walls. Only the darkest souls could exist here to praise any Divine of blackened nature. It was a place for those who had lost their sanity, their way... or both. Their spirits haunted the chamber.

The travelers were filled with horror. They felt it in their very bones. But the eyes of the walls...

Real.

They were there.

Very much in existence as they watched the clan in perfect silence.

···37···

Eventually, the clan had made their way through the rest of the internal sewer system after following their guide: Vici. As luck would have it, they hadn't run into any evil worshippers or dangerous creatures. To run into a dweller from beneath this city of "fancies" would not have been uncommon, and so their group had been blessed with a way of fortuitous destiny. Granted, their progress led them through yet more rooms of prayer and musty, moss-filled shafts, they finally came to a dense hatchway atop a rather shifty ladder system.

Knowing that the horizontal doorway would lead them to a seldom-used storage corridor within the inner confines of the King's Royal Castle, Vici climbed the ladder first in order to press up against the barricade. His efforts were futile, yet luckily Thul was once again able to break through.

One by one, like rats in a system of pipes, the tribe of adventurers climbed the rickety arrangement of broken ladders until they found themselves within a snug, empty chamber. At first, it struck the Gold Counter as odd that the hatch had not been sealed with a lock. It was difficult to open due to the fact that the hinges and bordering rims had long since sealed themselves shut with an abundance of sticky wet algae. Such an entrance to the most royal structure in the land should have had at least a lock or some sort of protective measure installed. Any dweller, thief, or delusional worshipper could have easily made their way into the cellar with a little elbow grease.

As they stopped to rest, a simple quietness surrounded them. The acoustics of their intimate chamber providing a seemingly muffled environment on account of the tarnished tapestries, moldy rugs and mossy build-up. The boggy plant life here was significantly lesser than within the sewers they had just passed through.

"This is it," Vici started in. "We are in. This is the Royal Castle."

Thul went on to pull a handful of small, meadow apples from his bag, handing them out to each of the physical clan members.

Vici took a modest bite before continuing.

"This is where we cannot be mistaken in our actions. Although every one of us here is skilled in the art of weaponry and combat, it would take only one faulty error to end our lives."

Perhaps it was strange to be jealous of Edgar's standing amongst the world at that moment. For it was his being that could withstand any amount of physical damage. Surely, a spell of phantasmal magic could affect him in some deterring manner, but regardless of its force, it could not kill him. It was all part of his adversity, credited to his situation of being plagued. Though he could not be destroyed, which oddly enough was all he wished, there was no doubt that he could somehow be captured through the ways of further magic.

Such a demise could not even be fathomed, as a prisoner of endless thirst would have its own place amongst the ways of dastardly torture.

"We act as one, not as individuals. For this is not the place to split off and seek out curiosities of our own. What's more, if there really is some sort of a war, then we will be faced with much more than just readied guards at each corridor."

From somewhere beyond the only door in the room came a rumbling of frenzied footsteps and shouting from multiple men. It was far off, yet something in their nature was alarming. They were in a rush, which suggested that something had definitely gone wrong. If there really was a war that had just begun, the travelers' missions were about to become far more difficult than originally anticipated.

"Follow me," Vici shouted. "First, we will make our way to the treasury chamber within the vaults of the castle's underground crypts. Then, once we have obtained the Geodes, we will locate your wife. If she has been taken for her potion crafting abilities like you said, then she will most likely be in the Alchemy quarters."

"Where is that?" blurted the Gold Counter, his excitement growing.

"Well, that's where it may get a little tricky."

The clan looked at their friend and then back to Vici.

"The Alchemy quarters are in one of the highest apexes of the palace: a tower... one that for many years could only be reached by crossing a connecting bridge. If you—"

Thul cut him off midsentence. "Wait, so yur' tellin' us we outta be climbin' through these rooms o' wizards and potion boys in order to get to 'is lady? The place is gonna be crawlin' with hordes o' these scum!"

"Essentially . . . yes," replied Vici, finishing off. "But we have no choice. We are here for the Geodes and this man's wife – as promised. And if we don't get moving now, the likelihood that we will run into more trouble will increase by the second."

After finishing what was left of their water pouches, they gathered their belongings and weapons and set forth into the next passageway, with Vici continuing as their guide. The next part of the journey was a hallway, its stones reflecting a shade of dark, shadowy turquoise in the light of two meagre torches that were affixed to the walls. It was a creepy scene indeed, though not as creepy as the worshippers' chamber from within the sewers.

Once they passed through another set of connecting rooms and hallways, they came to a door, different from the rest. Its form and materials, far more elegant than the other cellar doors.

"Get your asses to the eastern defence towers! The dwarves are here! They've already destroyed our ship's fleet and they're about to infringe on the city!" The order came from a commander of superior ranking - he was not far from the other side of the door in which the party members hid.

"Move! Move! Move!" he bellowed.

Another influx of intense footsteps went thundering by, this time even closer to the travelers.

It was true.

The war really was happening.

The warnings of the wall-folk were real. The furious orders of the captain were real. The mad rushing of soldiers - real.

The mighty Dwarven Embark of the once lively Bezniel was angry. They were here for money. For land . . .

For redemption.

Had Koraivindahl's kingship stayed true to a loyal, inclusive nature, none of this would have happened. But it was the king's greed that had caused this. It was greed that had imprisoned the city in destruction and soon-to-be savage violence.

It was all about more land, more gold, more treasure. The materialistic thirsts of Varroth's royalty had gone unquenched since the beginning of their settlement from the ages of early man. An untreatable desire that, over the years and like many other legendary rulers, brought back treasures of extremely valuable opulence. Such a ruling also brought bloodshed that affected the lives of hundreds of thousands of innocent peasants, including the lives of the Gold Counter and his wife. It was the present-day king whom he cursed for this burdensome journey, for it was the emperor's reasoning that his wife be taken from him in the first place.

"Once we pass through this door, there is no turning back," Vici warned his companions. His expression, his energy - sterner than ever before, "Are you ready?" he asked.

They all nodded in agreement.

But as truth would have it, not of them were.

None of them would ever have been ready for what they were about to face, not even if they were given a thousand years to prepare for it. Sure, they had experienced the downside of violent confrontations in the past, some of them more so than others, yet not a single one of them was ready to take on the iron-clad army of the Red Hand.

··· 38 ···

Once the guards had passed, the group of warriors entered through the doorway into lengthy stretch of hallway. Seeing as the hallway was empty, it was time to move. The corridor was spacious and lined with the glow of burning torches. A handwoven carpet stretched its way up and down hallway.

"I'll go first. If there is to be a separation, you men might just be able to catch 'em in their flank - maybe even from behind," stated Vici. His knowledge was right. Though the hallway had the appearance of proper glamour, it also provided warning of impending attackers rushing through its empty, stony chambers.

Unlike their journey through Koraivindahl's awkward sewer tunnels, these hallways split off into more predictable sectors. As they approached the first corner, the travelers' senses were met with yet another frantic rush of troops making their way through the forbidding maze. The soldiers' boots stomping upon the castle's granite floor like booming war drums, each strike louder than the last as they approached.

They peered around the corner. It was apparent that the group was making headway on the soldiers.

"Get ready! Now is our chance to get the jump on them!" called out the Gold Counter, his palm wrapped around the blade of his curving sabre.

As luck would have it, just around the bend was an alcove. In it, a statue of an angel stood with a broad set of marble wings. It was the perfect hiding place for Vici.

"As soon as they pass by, I'll call out to them! Once I have their attention, it'll be up to you to strike them from behind!" he instructed.

The rest of the clan hid themselves in the alcoves just around the bend from where they had come. Statues occupied some alcoves while others remained bare.

"Get ready!"

On and on went the beating of war drums. Their malicious pounding boomed louder as the gap between the scrambling soldiers and the four-man clan closed. Finally, the king's men rounded the corner opposite and blasted through the open corridor.

The members of the party looked towards Vici, whom had glimpsed at the impending attackers. He held up a finger, signaling that whatever was about to happen, was immediate.

"Go! Go! Go!" the first solider bellowed as he tore around the corner, followed closely by the rest of his mob.

It wasn't until their final guard neared the corner that Vici stepped forth from his alcove, swinging his ball-and-chain in their direction.

"Oye! Assholes!" he called out.

The soldiers immediately halted in their tracks. Some of the king's men collided into each other sending themselves clattering to the ground. Thul jumped forward, taking advantage of their unsuspecting surprise as he brought his war hammer down through the skull of his first victim.

Before they had any chance to figure out what was happening, the Gold Counter joined the scene, sending his buccaneer-like sabre cutting through the neck of the soldiers' leader, completely removing his head from his shoulders.

"Attack! Attack!" one of them yelled as he fumbled for the side blade. It was only half unsheathed when Edgar injected him with evil magic, causing his torso to explode violently, his innards painting the entire vicinity. Within seconds, the cluster of the Red Hand had become outnumbered through way of the ongoing killings.

Before Vici had any time to react, one of the soldiers succeeded in wielding his blade before impaling the accountant's upper torso. Vici let out a howl of pain, his pitch unmatched by any other they had encountered in their journey. It was hard to believe such a noise could even come from the lips of a human. How odd?

At first, his struggle was ineffective, but he went on to kick his enemy directly in the stomach, causing him to retract his blade from Vici's upper chest. Without further delay, Vici whipped his mace around, acquiring immense momentum before bringing it down on the chest of the solider. Perhaps his strike had been offset by the rage of his flailing, but it was powerful enough to cave in the guard's chest; the sound of his ribs crunching was heard throughout the hallway.

Thul went on to grab both of the remaining foes. The surprise of the attack had left them somewhat clueless, giving the barbarian an opportune moment to utilize his strength.

He bashed their skulls directly together and let their lifeless bodies drop to the ground in a gruesome heap.

"By the Divines!" The Gold Counter shouted; his state of shock obvious. The scene was one of macabre slaughter, defiled by the ungodly, lurid mess of fresh human remains.

All but Edgar just gawked at the mess. The ghastly companion had gone on to seize their souls for himself. Gruesome, yes, but he had been so deserving of this, especially since the last of any spirit he had devoured was the one of the fish he had caught in the pond. Even then, such miniscule quintessence had barely quenched his unending thirst.

"Oye! Sick man!" Thul called out, pointing a giant finger toward Vici's shoulder wound. "How is it, ye ain't bleedin' with a gouge that size?"

It was true.

Not a single drop had spilled from his shoulder.

"Oh! I . . . uh . . ."

His loss for words was bizarre, but not nearly as off-putting as his bloodless wound.

"You should be dead right now!" the Gold Counter proclaimed.

Still, Vici had not a word to offer in the matter. His efforts to conjure forth an explanation had gone unfinished until finally, after a spell, he opened his mouth.

"I guess . . . well. I guess I've just been sick for so long."

"Bullshit!" barked Thul, his voice radiating with accusation.

It was.

No man, regardless of how sick he was or not, could withstand such an injury and not spill a single drop of blood.

He cast his view down upon Edgar who finished devouring his share of "cabbage stew." Clearly their spectral friend was ready to move on and so Vici took up the reins in furthering his distance from their conversation.

"We can't talk about it now. We must keep moving."

And with that, Vici pivoted and began sprinting down the corridor as if he were completely unharmed . . . Not a second passed before the rest of the party went bounding after him. His bloodless injury required an explanation, but that was not the time.

···39···

At long last they had reached the entrance that led them closer to their longed-for treasure room. Their expedition through the castle's groundwork had lasted much longer than expected. Albeit the distance they had made up was not large, their constant evasions from groups of guards had severely slowed their travel. Luckily, they were able to get away from their most recent scene of grotesque horror without being discovered. Such a finding would only further the influx of the Red Hand.

Upon pushing through into a much smaller corridor, guided by Vici himself, they found themselves in front of a massive, vaulted panel. Its surface had been cast in pure gold and ingrained with an eclectic abundance of beautiful gems. So beautiful in fact, it forced open the mouths of the party members.

"I . . ." Thul could barely contain himself

If a door could be this skillfully crafted, Divines only knew what was held within.

The barbarian went running up to the vault's massive handle. His efforts although, failed to open the door. Again, and again, he attempted to force the handle, but was unable to gain entry.

"Arrrgh!" he cried out, banging his fists against the door.

His love for treasure was truly admirable.

Such greed . . .

"Open this 'ere door, Vici! Open it!" he ordered the once-accountant to "magically" open the door.

To everyone's surprise, Vici went on to pull an ample-sized key from one of his boots. Had that been in there this entire time? If it had . . . that would have made for a truly uncomfortable trek. But perhaps a man's worn boot was a relatively safe place to keep such a large key.

The Gold Counter still wanted to ask Vici about his lack of blood from his injury. Since the incident, Vici had been holding the magical, apple-sized sapphire against his wound. He had done the same thing after the mountain lion attack in the rocky wasteland. Though that moment had been different. At that very time, he was not mending a set of claw marks; he was actually repairing what should have been a life-threatening injury. This was the first time they had all witnessed Vici suffer such a substantially deep wound.

With Vici's seemingly "I'm fine" status, the Gold Counter's eagerness to gain access to the kingdom's most cherished treasure room had first calling. After all, who's to say what mass amounts of fortune lay within? Anyone would be lying if they said that they weren't curious about what lay within a locked treasure room . . . right?

Vici made his way to the door, inserting the key into its intricate system of locks.

"What?" he called out. "They changed the locks!"

Thul lost it.

He threw his mighty war hammer down the hallway, sending it smashing into a corner, its steel head chipping away at one of the stones.

"You kiddin' me? You damned fool!" he shrieked.

"Okay, okay . . . I am," laughed Vici.

They went on to cackle at the barbarian who had completely lost his mind. At first, he was deeply offended. But as the laughter continued, he joined in. He then went on to retrieve his war hammer.

Perhaps the notion to let off some steam at this point was rightfully earned. For they had made it this far, and for some unexplained reason, they were all still alive. Well, almost all of them. But that was beside the point.

"Now listen," Vici's voice soon drizzled from a comical tone to one of seriousness. "Once we are within, no matter how badly you wish to touch anything, you mustn't!"

Thul howled. He was still laughing with the others; hearing Vici's warning only increased his chuckles.

"Listen to me!" Vici yelled. His voice severed the laughter of the group. "You cannot touch anything until I say. Otherwise, we all could die. The room is heavily trapped, and only those who know the correct way of passage can enter and leave. Otherwise, you might as well write your last scriptures now!"

He directed his glare specifically at the barbarian who nodded half-heartedly back. Vici went on to stare at Thul for some time before returning to the door, rotating the many cogs within the keyhole.

Finally, the inner mechanisms ended with a loud unlocking noise.

Kerchunk!

Vici gently swung the leviathan door open, revealing . . .

Nothing.

Nothing but a room of yellow brick.

All that stood in the room was a pedestal amidst its centre. Surrounding its base was a circle that looked as though it had been painted on the stone floor with a cheap coat of dye.

"What the—" Thul was cut off by the accountant abruptly shushing him, a single finger pressed to his lips.

How could this be?

This entire adventure as directed by the great Nailreign himself, led them to a simple birdbath? And why there? There were no birds. What was the meaning of this?

The Gold Counter's heart dropped in his chest. He had expected a room that was overflowing with coins, goblets of precious metals, an endless array of incredibly valuable gems, and, most importantly, the Geodes of this so-called "heal-everything" Gemsand.

"Follow me. Step only on the stone panels that I do!" instructed Vici.

Still, they failed to understand his reasoning. Yet, after some thought, the accountant ever-so carefully set forth upon the stone tiles. He placed one foot cautiously in front of the other, all the while checking back to ensure his companions did the same until they reached the middle of the painted circle.

Within the bird-bath-like pedestal was a pool of opaque metallic liquid. Its silvery viscosity implied that it was not

269

ANDREW P. WILD

the same property as water or wine, but more a sludge of some sort.

Vici went on to dab his two forefingers in the pool and press them against each member's forehead, leaving behind a trail of the sludge amongst their skin. Every time, returning his hand to the pool to get a fresh splash between companions. Even though Edgar's body wasn't physical, the liquid somehow remained on his forehead, baffling him when it did.

"Are you ready?" Vici asked, his rhetorical question conjuring feelings of concern within each of the members.

What choice did they have?

After a series of nods, Vici spoke again.

"Divines bless us in the land of the king. For is it his might, his passion and his courage that we all possess and will continue to thrive on."

It was a spell.

"Our saviour. Our lord. Our protector. Our connector to the gods. Blessed is he who serves the Red Hand, for it is the king who will outlive us all."

He motioned for the clan to bend forward and submerge their faces in the pool. As they did, he chanted:

"Long live the King.

"Long live the King.

"Long live the King."

There was a split second of unfathomable pain, and then . . .

Poof

The party vanished from existence.

···40···

Vici had purposely taken them further into the room. The pedestal was not only for decor, as it also held a magical essence, one that allowed anyone, permitting they knew the correct magical words, to be instantly teleported into another dimension.

Surrounding the clan of bewildered members, in every direction, shone an endless night sky filled with fascinating constellations. They found themselves on an ivory-tiled platform, infinitely suspended in space. From where they stood, the platform stretched across to an entirely enormous mountain of treasure. The hoard of golden riches was so grand that the Gold Counter alongside his friends could do nothing but stare in complete bafflement.

Other platforms of varying levels floated nearby. Their enigmatic suspension keeping them afloat in the perpetual night sky as they too held elevating multitudes of sparkling fortune.

It was brilliant.

It was some sort of arcane sanctuary. Its only purpose: to protect the riches within. Anyone who entered needed to know about the pedestal's proper purpose. Upon entering, one was required to summon forth the vault's key. Then, after crossing over the floor of death traps, one needed to know the spell required to undergo the teleportation.

"Scrub me' soul and call me a lemming!" their barbarian cuckooed, his sentence complete nonsense. But, before any of the other members had anytime to question him, Thul went bounding down the magical range.

"Thul! Wait!" cried the Gold Counter, turning to Vici for approval. In return, the accountant had not only chuckled, but signaled for him to join the barbarian. After a moment of hesitation, he charged off down the way. As soon as Thul reached the end of the walkway, he leapt headfirst into the king's colossal stockpile. His crash sent gold coins everywhere, some flying off the podium altogether into the endless galaxy.

Once the Gold Counter reached the base of the pile, he could do nothing but gaze up idiotically at the immense fortune. What was once a simple dream of every man within the kingdom - suddenly directly in front of him, lit with the ever-so-bright ambiance of some sort of spiritual torches that hovered nearby.

Goblets, crowns, and cutlasses were part of the display, along with gem-infused genie lamps, shimmering amulets, and perfectly rounded bangles, each crafted with flawless perfection. Pearl necklaces, platinum coated-chainmail, twinkling ritualistic articles of diverse religions, silver vases and a profusion of rare minerals in their most natural state – the list of extravagant wonders went on and on. It appeared to be a ceaseless amount of gold coins and magnificent, perfect gemstones.

"Jump in! Join me brother!" cheered Thul, attempting to swim in the deluxe heap, eventually disappearing from sight only to pop up in another part of the mountain.

"This . . . This is . . . unbelievable!" exclaimed Edgar as he floated up alongside the Gold Counter and Vici.

Such a sight was truly stunning, though it was Thul who was most affected by it all. For the Gold Counter, both the treasure and the arcane sanctuary were mind-boggling, yet for Thul it was the fortune alone.

"Take what you may, but remember that we are to journey further within the castle once we return. It would be wise to choose the most valuable items seeing as we are here, but don't weigh yourself down," warned Vici.

Thul burst through the surface at the peak of the treasure mountain, and then gleefully slid down the pile of brilliance.

"Y'all can go on without me, I'll be fine in 'ere for the rest o' me days!" he called out, throwing a handful of treasure into the abyss.

"Hah!" laughed the Gold Counter. "And just what will you do for food then, mountain man?"

"I . . ." the barbarian paused. "Well, fine. But you mark me words. You best believe I'll be back here for the rest of this here lot! She's the finest spread I've seen. The eye of gracious Seraph 'erself!"

Made sense. Seraph the Collector was god of treasury and fortune. What she lacked for in sociability, she more than made up for in her accumulation of inexhaustible wealth. It was her, among the Divines, who aided warriors and other adventurers along their quests in search of riches and mysterious plunder. Had it been her hand that touched them in their sequences of luck when it came back to the violent interactions? Only Seraph could be the one to answer those kinds questions.

"Take your time, it'll be a span before I can locate the Opal Geodes," Vici pointed out.

Right.

The astonishing sight was enough to make the Gold Counter completely forget why they had arrived there.

Just then, Vici teleported to another nearby platform. He began his search for the Geodes that encased the magical Gemsands of vitality and utmost healing. The Gold Counter made his was over to Thul and climbed halfway up the golden mountain, which rose higher than any of the other surrounding piles. After sifting through the collection, he came across a particularly interesting amulet. It captivated his interest fully.

At the end of a thinly braided gold chain was a heart. It was made entirely out one single ruby, carved into a shape of perfect curves and edges that fit uniquely within its golden casing. Four symmetrical areas surrounding the heart shaped gem were held in place by a single small, yet intricate claw-like design.

It was perfect.

He knew such a fine piece would be his only choice.

It was at that moment, after all of his planning and adventure and utmost danger, the Gold Counter realized that he would be reunited with his wife soon, most likely that evening. He had become so accustomed to searching for her, that he had only seen a distant goal. It was but an hourly venture. He stashed the amulet away in one of his pockets.

Though his intention was to greet her with a much more youthful appearance, his skin and body had been tainted with the plague that he had succumb in Crease. It had withered his body, rendering it weak and sickly. But there was hope. They were within reach of the Opal Geodes. Perchance the Gemsands could heal him and his partners of their diseases.

Soon the opals would be within their grasp. Surely, it would not take long to craft a remedy of some sort, as Vici must have had been given the recipe before leaving Crease, given the circumstances of the Gold Counter's condition. After all, Nailreign had promised him freedom from his sickness once they had retrieved the mystical stones. Still, it amazed the Gold Counter that such a refined, magical sand could heal anyone, phantasmal or not, of Crease's horrible affliction.

Vici went on to teleport from pile to pile, searching for the prized crystals in the heaps of gold. How he was able to beam from one pile to the other was a mystery. Could it have been the magic of the sanctuary itself? How could he simply disappear and then reappear without ever exhibiting the ability to teleport before? His previous occupation as gold counter for the king had no doubt aided him. Clearly, he had been in this sanctuary before, as his job would have given him such access.

"I found them!" Vici announced triumphantly, holding up two handfuls of stones, their surfaces inlaid with jet-black opals and glinting quartz. They looked like eggs that had once belonged to some ancient beast that lived far beyond the palisades of the heavenly kingdom.

Before long, he had emptied his sack of remaining clothes and receptacles and begun filling it with Geodes. He didn't stop until it was full. It was heavy when he tried to lift it over his shoulder.

"Thul!"

It took a few calls before he could grab the attention of the barbarian who was arbitrarily filling his pack with an assortment of rather gaudy treasures.

"I'm . . . uh . . . going to need you to carry this one also!"

The barbarian looked back and nodded. After all, it was his strength that the group relied on many times already throughout the course of their grand excursion. Once Vici had teleported himself back to the central pad, the others quickly finalized their choices. Upon completion, they were ready to move on. They made their way back to the beginning of the platform with the painted circle on the ivory surface.

"Is everyone ready?" the accountant questioned.

Vici signaled for the four to join hands. Once done, he began uttering the same words he had used to enter the mysterious sanctuary.

"Long live the King.

"Long live the King.

"Long live the King."

The Gold Counter took a final, brief look around the remarkable room, taking in the phenomenal totality of it before the crew vanished from its scene altogether. Upon doing so, they left behind not even a trace of their presence in the windless solitude.

The eternal torch flames went on to burn forever.

Poof

··· 41 ···

Once returned to the confines of Varroth's most tremendous fortress, they were, once again, made aware of the sound of yet more guards thundering past. It had not taken the soldiers long to come across the scene of recent violence. An alarm of some sort had surely been triggered by the soldiers. Had they known that their attackers weren't dwarves, but in fact land-goers of their own, it probably would not have made any difference in their treatment once captured.

After securing what belongings they had left, the party pivoted from the entry point of the treasure room and headed towards the nearest set of spiral stairs. Upon reaching the coiling peak, they bare witness to a heightened elegance of internal design. A hallway - its borders lined with royal-red carpets and warm torchlight from sconces that had been cast in gold.

The spaciousness of the corridors helped the travelers to prepare themselves as the echoes of the soldiers bounced off the cobalt surfaces. The companions had time to duck into alcoves behind the stone statues to conceal themselves. Perhaps such hiding places would never have worked had the castle been under regular patrol, yet at that moment the frenzied energy of it all kept the soldiers from paying close attention to any alcoves as they rushed by.

Eventually, after further navigation throughout a significant collection of hallways and spiral stairwells, the companions found themselves within the higher recesses of the castle. What may have taken a nobleman several minutes to cover such a distance, took the party only a few hasty moments in combination with a couple of stints of blessed hiding.

"By the Divines, this 'ere is bloody dangerous," whispered Thul as he poked his head up into the corridor from his position near to that of yet another stairwell's peak.

That their barbarian recognized the danger truly highlighted the significance of the situation. The Gold Counter had always admired him for his courage and his strength, yet at that point he felt as though Thul's admittance of fear had brought only worried energy amongst the party. Perchance it was the excitement of it all, especially as he neared his wife's location from within this hellish dimension of Koraivindahl's mighty keep.

"No time!" the Gold Counter exclaimed. "No time for weakness, Thul! Now is the time to run! Come on, big man!"

And with that he proceeded forth with the zeal of an entire army, almost without checking to see if any castle-dwellers were nearby. Luckily, there were not, though his actions were instantly halted with a snapping tone from Vici.

"You fool! Get back here!"

The warning came with much harshness. It instantly replaced the Gold Counter's energy of excitement with a face-reddening embarrassment.

"We travel forth as a group. You know this!"

He paused briefly, allowing the Gold Counter to recognize the seriousness of the situation. It wasn't until he nodded that Vici continued with a slightly forgiving note to his nature.

"Going forth, we can expect to be faced with individual forces that are stronger than the average man . . ." he paused before continuing, allowing the significance of the impending situation to sink in. "We will find wizards . . . those whom have been trained with the many elements of this world's existence."

Met with a sense of fatigue after their arduous climbing, the clan desperately needed to rest. Luckily, they had captured a brief moment in which to do so.

"As for you Edgar," he continued, "your powers will disappear temporarily as we near the mages' chambers. If there were any other way to reach the pinnacle, I would have chosen so, yet because we are heading directly through these quarters of enhanced magic, any who enter without being one with the castle's acolytes will lose the ability to cast spells of their own."

"But . . . I am a ghost. How can such a thing affect my sorcery?" Edgar questioned.

"It has something to do with a force field from the first king's establishment. There is no time for me to explain it now."

They nodded to show their agreement before Thul piped up again.

"So yur' tellin' me, that we're goin' up against some ol' wizards with magic fingers?"

"No . . . I am saying none of you have any preparation to deal with what lies ahead. So, we must move carefully. We must try to catch them by surprise. That way, we'll have a better chance."

A better chance?

At getting past the mages' quarter?

At . . . surviving?

Impossible. Death welcomed the party. It was by the right of the Divines that the group had made it this far, the twelfth or perhaps twentieth floor of the Royal Castle. The number of floors they had actually climbed escaped the Gold Counter's mind. Regardless, they were going to finish what they had originally set out to do.

Upon their arrival within the first corridor on the palace's topmost level, they came across two openings within the brickwork on either side of the hallway. The one on their left had been filled with an seemingly endless design of graceful tulips constructed entirely of stained glass. It was a pattern that cast a glow of iridescent beauty from beyond the other side. The opening on the right was just that: an opening of pure air that gave way to the very countryside that they had just crossed.

It was a beautiful view, capable of captivating anybody, mortal or not. The travelers pressed themselves against the ledge to drink in the awe of it all. It was a gargantuan drop below. All the floors in which they had climbed made the pond below appear as a miniscule mark upon the landscape of quintessential beauty.

The peacefully lands included rolling banks of emerald grass that glowed in the rays of the setting sun. The sky filled with a health-giving array of colours. In such a picturesque moment, it was hard to imagine the land in any other state. It was an atmosphere of holy bliss, and thoroughly contradictory to the kingdom in which the impending war had just begun. The captivating landscape was purely natural, untouched, and beautiful.

"It's moments like this that make a man wish 'e brought an extra bottle o' old monk with im," Thul announced as he licked his lips. The golden sunset reflected upon his glassy eyes beneath a hefty brow.

The openings in either side of the corridor allowed for the light to pass in through one side and out through the mosaic on the other. It was a planned detail of specialized architecture that no doubt added to the graceful styling of the Royal Castle.

For a moment longer, the party just stood there. Perhaps this was the most beautiful scene of their lives, and for that they just... looked. Each second, their faces were met with the pure simplicities of Varroth's gentle, warm breezes. Truthfully, it was a moment of procrastination, especially following Vici's heedful warning. Granted, it was still a sight that was far too grand to simply pass up.

"Ghost or not," began Edgar, "I've experienced all that life has to offer both before death and after it. Though much of it I cannot remember, I can tell you that the world does not just happen around you. But rather, that it happens for you."

Following his poetic verse, the party pondered his truthful reasoning before setting forth down the hallway, each step bringing them closer to the mages' quarters. With the task of saving the Gold Counter's wife as their only remaining goal, such a feat felt as though it might be easy – yet it was about to be quite the opposite. The mages' quarters were located within the eastern side of the palace. A side that also contained many of the king's soldiers.

Vici went first, followed by the rest of his anxious companions. When they arrived at their first corner along the castle's skyline hallway, they noticed two guards, posted on either side of a set of double doors, halfway down the corridor. The attackers moved in on the unsuspecting guards. They couldn't risk returning to a previous level within the palace as they were more likely to encounter larger groups of the watchful protectors.

A prompt advance left the oblivious guards unaware. It was the Gold Counter who went first, hacking away at one of the guard's upper torso. Luckily, his sabre struck the guard within a gap of his armour and landed a critical strike upon the Gold Counter's swing.

The second guard stood frozen in shock. Rather than retaliating in the same way the first did, he chose to come across with a submissive standing, his hands raised in efforts to prove he had no intention of drawing his weaponry. Before anyone had time to think, Thul went on to lift the solider off his feet before throwing him down against the unforgiving stone. The question of whether such action was necessary briefly touched the Gold Counter's mind. Perhaps had the guard had not been killed, he may have attacked the party from behind at a later moment.

Upon victory, Vici popped his head through the set of double doors. The room in which he peered was actually a guard's post. Inside, a single unexpecting member, gathering himself after being rudely awakened from a deep sleep. A half empty rum bottle lay next to his cot.

The hangover, though horrible for the drowsy solider, gave the party a leg up on him. It took mere seconds for Vici to move across the room, striking him upside his head with his flail, sending the solider directly to the Void.

"Apologies," he began. "The last time I was here, this particular post was empty."

Before departing, they sat for a short time around a meagre table to enjoy what was left of the bread and cheese upon it. At that point, to carry on would have been just as easy, yet to pass up a bottle of wine and some aged cheddar in the kingdom's most prominent castle, would have been a waste. Paired with a couple slices of somewhat fresh olive loaf, the party topped up their strength before continuing on into the primitive hallways of the king.

···42···
AGE: 47 ~ CURSED, SICKLY AND WEAKENED.

Since the party had risen from the sewers, the sun had reached its high point and begun a slow descent towards the opposite horizon. Beneath the cloudless azure sky, the travelers' journey was nearing its end. With bellies containing a small amount of fine wine and cheddar, (or human soul for certain individuals) they felt energized. Their weakness and fatigue were diminished and they felt more mentally alert. Every step along the corridor brought them to another opening along the palace wall, granting a view of the beautiful scenery, though what they had seen had been enough. They were more than aware that their journey was still incomplete.

Eventually, after rounding a few more corners of the seemingly endless hallway and taking on another duo of guards, the party arrived, unharmed, at a corridor leading up to the mages' quarters. The only protection between whatever powerful sorcery prevailed within and the companions was a single, circular door. One made out of a perfect piece of refined purple heart timber that had a massive display of emeralds incorporated into its surface.

The flawless brickwork leading up to the door was covered in massive ivy vines, growing from within the magical quarters. The leaves were vastly different than typical ivy as their veins were a shade of bright lilac that radiated along the hallways. It was as if the vines and leaves appeared to be breathing, pulsing with each inhale.

"What's all this?" Thul's question had certain disgust to it.

"This is it, the mages' quarters, if you haven't already guessed." Vici, though nervous, was still proud to retain his knowledge of the castle and it showed in his speech.

Something of the slightly rounding walls spoke of the fact that the inner room must have been part of one of the castle's towering, circular chambers. Whatever was inside had the attention of each of the members, a gnawing curiosity. How could vines grow through the door? What magic happens within this place? How many sorcerers are there? Of course, it was the castle's most recent gold counter who answered their questions.

"Beyond this door exists the largest tower within the castle, strictly used for sorcery. Once inside, we will have to act quickly. Though there are multiple hallways leading to rooms off the main chamber, it is the topmost doorway at the peak of the central staircase that will lead us to the bridge that connects to the alchemy laboratory.

"The staircase?"

The idea of a staircase furthered the Gold Counters's apprehensiveness over entering the room. How was one supposed to climb such a staircase whilst enemy adversaries cast beams of destructive magic their way?

"Yes, the spiral staircase leads up to the pinnacle of the tower. Once it nears the rafters, it closes off to a bridge."

What in the Void?

How was such a feat even possible?

How were they going to make it through this?

"So. What yur' sayin' here is we otta' make it past these wizards o' sorts. Climb some winding stairs. Avoid, Divines only know how many blasts o' witchcraft these bloody shit-winchers send our way, and make our way through this door you say, at the top of it all?"

Thul paused. "And come out alive? Are you nuts?"

He knew the answer. He knew exactly what kind of impossible task they were up against. Man-to-man, hand-to-hand combat is one thing, but for a man to come face to face with a wizard, his odds would diminish to pebble-sized luck. In addition, the crew only had short-range weapons.

"Listen!" Vici beckoned. Something to his voice sounded off. It had not been his anger that he had so clearly vocalized but something else.

"I got you this far, didn't I? And there is something to be said for that! And in addition to that, I told you all many times, that there is no other way! No secret path! No passage door! There is only this way - through the quarters and into the lab. That's it."

Perhaps his hostility was uncalled for. Still, the man had a point. It was this way or none at all, and seeing as they had come this far, there was no chance of return.

A single moment passed by before Vici spoke again.

"If anyone becomes injured, you must wield the sapphire. It will take only moments of pressing it against your wound before you can continue."

The Gold Counter unveiled the massive, healing sapphire from within the confines of his pack. The one stone that granted due aid to those who needed it. Its magical ability to cure the worst of injuries, as demonstrated from when Vici was attacked early that day. Given the fact that they still had it in their collection, rather than losing it to any other force that previously threatened the group, gave them a significant foot up on any opposing party.

It was time. After all they had been through, how bad could it get? They had already endured so much in their previous advances across Varroth's most violent offerings. Without further ado, the clan members choked back their feelings of apprehension and utter anxiety as they watched Vici step forward and lug open the door to the crux of their entire adventure.

···43···

The interior of the mages' quarters was beyond anything the party could ever imagine. Inside, the massive circular quarters opened into numerous areas of profound magical entities, encased within the glowing ivy. Six sorcerers, cloaked in various shades of dark grey robes, were absorbed in their own contemplations. Engrossed in thought and studies alike, they did not notice the party's presence.

Lining the chamber and the rickety winding staircase were a collection of doorways, and numerous shelves. There were bottles and vials of various potions, statuesque figurines, oddly shaped artifacts, and shelves upon shelves stocked full of spell books.

There was a perfume-like fragrance of springtime flowers in the chamber, yet its source was not obvious. Perhaps it was coming from one of the mystical flower boxes upon the tables. Each flower bed contained an array of truly bizarre plants. Their leaves and unorthodox fruits bursting with shades of deep green, amethyst, and cerulean.

Mahogany stools and tables filled the room, their surfaces piled with enchanted scrolls, unidentifiable liquids and a diverse collection of writing quills and inkwells.

Most profound, next to the winding staircase and directly in the centre of the room was a gaping opening in which all of the ivy appeared to be growing from. From within the hole, however, was some sort of blackish water. A few feet directly above the opening a giant sphere the size of a massive boulder rotated slowly, wondrously suspended in midair. There was no doubt that its hovering suspension had been conjured forth by some sort of powerful wizardry. Its glassy sides glowed a vivid colour of aquamarine as it gently spun in its floating position.

"You there!" one of the mages called out as he looked up from his table of ancient scrolls. He had noticed the group of intruders peering through the doorway.

"What business do you have here?! You are not of our kind!"

Before any of the members had a chance to respond, another mage, clad in dark robes and finely kept, long grey hair spoke:

"Their business is nothing to do with ours! Seize them!"

Just then, a third mage, clearly startled by the abrupt happenings, conjured forth an orb of swirling fusion and hurled it their way, its almighty blast missing Thul's head by only inches as he ducked out of the way just in time.

Within a split second, the barbarian raised his massive war hammer and began bounding in the direction of the closest sorcerer who had evidently been in the works of summoning forth a spell of his own. As luck would have it, Thul's weapon of brute force met with the wizard's skull, striking him down before he had a chance to finish casting whatever magic he was summoning.

"Split up! Quickly!" Vici's voice echoed around the chamber of vines and seemingly perpetual magical properties.

As they did, another wizard came forth from one of the hollowed doorways on the first landing, only to hurl another orb of dastardly shadows in their direction. This one hit Edgar dead on. Though phantasmal and immune to damage from any sort of physical weapon, his ghostly body was vulnerable to unearthly magic.

Upon impact, the orb exploded across his faded presence, sending the friendly ghost into a whirlwind of unimaginable pain as he was blown backwards from his position near the door.

"Edgar!" cried the Gold Counter as he pivoted to watch his companion fall.

"Watch out!" Edgar called as he clutched his chest with a spectral hand.

Again, another orb barreled their way, this time in the direction of the Gold Counter. With the agility of a meadow hare under the scrutiny of a famished hawk, he narrowly dodged the bolt of magic, its swirling fusion searing off a few of his neck hairs as it went thundering by. His goal, as he made his way up the swirling staircase, was to reach the wizard atop the balcony. Perhaps then he could cut down the malicious sorcerer before he was able to do any further damage.

As the Gold Counter dove forward, strategically assuming a prone position next to the wooden staircase in hopes to avoid any further blasts of magic, Vici appeared within his peripherals.

"May you seek the Void that welcomes you!" another wizard cried.

At that very moment, Vici lunged forth; his speed far greater than any mortal. A lightning-fast movement caused him to practically teleport from one end of the room to the other, striking down another wizard with his ball-and-chain mace as he flew. Blood splattered upon the nearby planter boxes as the conjurer crumbled to the floor and in a motionless mass.

Boosh

Boosh

The once quiet atmosphere, suddenly filled with wild magic. Each spell of destruction barreled through the air in the form of lightning bolts and unpredictable explosions. Although some of them smashed across the surface of the suspended sphere in the middle of the room, none of the blasts had any effect on it.

Every attempt the Gold Counter made to climb farther up the plateau was abruptly severed as the wizard atop its face had gone mad with a perpetual series of unending magical projectiles. It wasn't until Thul grabbed hold of another sorcerer and tossed him into the central well that the wizard's attention was garnered.

"You 'ere are 'bout to get a taste o' some real barbarian fightin' now, ye wizard shit!" he bellowed, charging into the shin-deep well as the sorcerer attempted to stand.

"Thul! Look out!"

He peered from his friend upon the stairs to the wizard above him, only to realize that the sorcerer had changed his direction of spell cast. Thul grabbed hold of the injured sorcerer, his gargantuan hand wrapping around the back of the wizard's head before lifting his entire being, using the wizard as a shield as he sheltered himself from the impending blast. By fluke, the orb smashed upon the wizard's torso, causing his innards to pour into the surrounding water.

That was the moment.

The Gold Counter rose from his position and began sprinting towards to the peak of the staircase. It wasn't until he was near the wizard that he finally noticed his foe was ready to meet him.

Eyes fixed upon the summoner's neck, the confidant raised his sabre, ready to bring his blade down and finally decapitate his attacker. Before he did, another fusion of black magic began forming within the wizard's clasped hands.

Just as the wizard was able to build the incantation to its fullest potential, the Gold Counter brought his sabre down with masterful force. Its blade struck the sorcerer from where his neck met his shoulder, gouging him, causing the wizard to lose all focus, his spell bursting within his hands. The explosion not only disintegrated sorcerer's own hands completely, but sent the Gold Counter flying over the banister to the floor below. His fall was lessened by the vine's thick growth yet nonetheless knocking the wind from his lungs as his body crumpled. The Gold Counter just lay there, unsure of what injuries he had suffered.

"Oye! Brother!" Thul rushed to him, after carelessly tossing the mutilated body of his foe aside.

"The stone! Use the stone!" Vici yelled frantically as he swung madly at yet another wizard next to him. For some reason, he could not land a hit upon his foe. It was as if the wizard had some sort of telekinetic power, one that somehow allowed him to see every one of the accountant's swings before actually happening. Finally, Edgar gathered himself to his fullest potential and darted over to aid his partner. Upon arrival, Edgar's ghostly body floated directly inside that of the body of the opposing wizard.

A moment later, the conjurer ceased all actions, becoming still before exploding horrendously, sending entrails of his person everywhere, coating Vici from head to toe.

A look of disgust, matched evenly with a look of astonishment, fell over the crowd as they looked at Edgar who hovered, untouched, in the exact same place that the wizard had so recently existed.

"I . . . had . . . no idea you could do that!" exclaimed Vici as he wiped the blood off his face.

"To be honest," replied Edgar, "neither did I."

··· 44 ···

Once Thul had recovered the sapphire from the Gold Counter's bag and pressed it against the wounded adventurer, the healing process began. Whatever had happened within his battered physique was far more brutal than anticipated. As he lay there, he could feel his broken ribs click back together through the quick work of the sapphire's magic.

"Owww! Oh, the Divines!"

The pain. Its presence so real, it was as if he had never experienced anything so authentic in his life. Each click and sound coming from within his being was evidence of the shattered bones repairing themselves to perfect condition.

The battle, ongoing. This time, Vici and Edgar were moving toward a series of open doorways presumably leading to yet additional mages.

"THUL! Stop this! I cannot take the pain..."

And then ...

Nothing.

After the final snap resonated from his chest, the pain suddenly vanished.

"By the Divines! The pain! It's gone!" the Gold Counter cried, jumping to his feet as if nothing had happened.

Thul shoved the stone into his pocket as he motioned for the Gold Counter to join the battle alongside their companions. With a quick nod of agreement, the Gold Counter retrieved his sabre from within magical ivy, starting towards the continuous onslaught of castle dwellers.

BWAM!

Before either of the companions could reach the bloody scene, another explosion of absolute magic erupted from the hallway, sending bodies flying into the room, Vici and Edgar's bodies included. Just then, another trio of wizards joined the scene from the same tunnel, only to be met with Thul's mighty war hammer. It struck two of them and just missed the third. They didn't perish immediately from the vicious blow, but lay disfigured near a pile of other bodies.

"Wake him . . ." he squeaked.

"Wake . . . Bilal . . ."

What?

It sounded like an order.

Bilal?

Who is Bilal?

Without a moment's hesitation, the untouched mage retreated into a tunnel, tripping as he did. Thul - hot in pursuit. Edgar rose alongside his mace-wielding comrade. Both of them seemed to be uninjured, the blast of uncontrolled magic had caught them off guard.

"Bilal?" Edgar's ghostly voice rang with echoic questioning. "Who is Bilal?"

Vici turned to the Gold Counter and then back to Edgar.

"I . . . I don't know!"

Just then, the vines that carpeted the floor of the entire chamber began glowing at a furiously rapid rate. Every vine with its violet-coloured veins started beating together in unison, as if the entire cluster had a heartbeat.

An instant later, Thul reappeared on the scene.

"Took care o' that son-of-a mongrel!" he exclaimed, his victory over yet another made clear in his voice.

Suddenly, a different voice filled the chamber, reverberating from upon highest platform, three stories up. Out stepped another mage, this one far different from the rest. Not only did he look as though he was 150 years old with a long, ancient beard, his robes and entire being had a certain transparency to them, implying that he was some sort of spirit, similar to Edgar.

"Bilal."

His voice, though calm, was strong - much stronger than anticipated. He stepped forward, passing right through the wooden banister until he cleared the platform and floated high above the confines of the stony chamber.

"What the—" Thul's questioning had been the exact thought of everyone in the group.

"Bilal!" the grand wizard called out again.

The sound of the foreign name filled the chamber, each syllable bouncing from the rubble.

"We call upon you.

I call upon you.

Bilal. The Sovereign of Shadows and Light alike!"

The ivy's beating increased, momentarily distracting the party

"We call upon your power. Your will . . .

Our saviour!"

Then, for a brief moment, he paused before resuming a final turn. This time, his jaw dropped open, allowing his gaping mouth to span a distance that nearly covered his chest in a most horrific, macabre style.

"JOIN Us-s-s-s!"

His elderly voice, suddenly hoarse with a metallic, demonic sound, filled the blood-soaked area before his entire essence detonated into a cloud of black smoke and flash of light, leaving behind only a fine powder that misted through the air, landing amongst the adventurers.

Without warning, everything began to shake with a violent rumble. Torches, books, and ornaments fell from their positions and fixings within the room, crashing upon the vibrating stonework. Chunks of staircase and brickwork from the rounding walls began to fall, causing the party to squeeze themselves together in the middle of the room near to the well and floating orb.

"Get to the stairs! Now!" Vici ordered.

Hastily, the unnerved members made their way to the crumbling wooden stairs, passing through a shower of boards and splinters as they burst downward from the ceiling.

Finally, the unidentified, floating orb amidst the center of the room burst open, sending shards of matter around the room in a chaotic, unpredictable manner.

"Look out!"

Each member of the clan searched for shelter hoping to avoid the shrapnel.

"Who awakens me?"

From within the orb appeared an abominably vulgar figure. Sitting upon an immense, crimson red pillow, hovering directly above the well, rose a ten-foot-tall figure. Everything about it, unnatural. Its head resembled a distorted bovine, with rows upon rows of pointed, razor-sharp gnashers. Branching from either side of its irregular skull were two spiraling, blood-soaked tusks. Its body blackened; the being's chest, arms, and legs looked human, though enormously swollen and deformed either through rotting cavities, oppressive scarring or an absolutely repulsive amount of bloating, extending especially from within its gut. Most horrific of all, its eyes: two hollow ovals containing irises of a sickly, yellow decay interrupted by it vertically shaped pupils of rectangular blackness.

It was an image that would forever haunt every member of the party well within the afterlife.

And perhaps even . . .
A life beyond that.

··· 45 ···

Their first attempt to reach the staircase, or what was left of it, was immediately halted by a telekinetic force. Perhaps Bilal was not a Divine of any sort, though his being contained within itself a set of extreme psychic abilities.

"*There is no departure*," the seemingly immortal bovine spoke, his demonic voice shaking the entire chamber with a metallic tone.

The Gold Counter rose and ran toward the doorway they had previously entered. It was an action of fear.

VZOMF

Before he could make his way anywhere close to the door, a massive shockwave erupted from within the centre of the room. Its source had originated from beneath Bilal. A thick, purple blast of pure energy, followed by a resonating smoke that smelled of complete and utter decay circulated around the room. It was a nova of some sort, a spell that the foul bovine had cast out amongst them.

The nova's immense power knocked the party to the floor, its energy far stronger than any mortal could possibly endure.

At that point, the party became scattered around the room, their main goal being to reach the staircase.

"*For you. There is only death.*"

The sentence came from the voice of the bovine. Suddenly, an array of stones burst forth from the wall and fell in front of the passageway, blocking the exit.

"For you there is only flame, 'cuz I like my meat cooked!" yelled Thul as he raised his weapon.

Without a moment of hesitation, he hurled his war hammer with a monstrous swing, giving it maximum momentum. It swung towards Bilal, the handle leaving his grip. Before the brute had time to realize what had happening, the iron of Thul's brutal weapon caught him upside the head, shattering his tusks and knocking him off-balance.

Vici, whom was positioned across the room, waved the Gold Counter over with the intention of escaping further into the labyrinth of the mages' quarters.

The Counter rushed around the perimeter of the room and escaped into yet another tunnel alongside Vici, leaving Edgar and Thul to continue the battle. The two ran down a short hallway and into another room containing two cots and multiple shelves that were scattered with scrolls and half empty potions.

"What are we going to do!?" he blurted out, shaking with panic.

"I have no idea!" returned Vici. "I have never encountered this 'Bilal' until now!"

Without any direction, the duo ransacked the room, searching for a solution to their impending doom.

VZOMF

Another shockwave of purple energy blasted from the main chamber, knocking the two of them to the ground. This time, cries of pain came from both Thul and Edgar.

Meanwhile, the Gold Counter picked himself up off the ground and turned to Vici for further direction. Vici too, looked back with confusion and loss.

VZOMF

Another shockwave.

It was then that the enormity of it all sunk in.

It was the end.

It had to be.

Another crashing of stone and brickwork came from the inner chamber.

"We have to destroy him!" Vici cried, picking himself up yet again.

"Destroy him? We only have hand weapons! How are we ever going to do that? We cannot even get close to him without being thrown from his blasts!"

"We have to fight!" returned the former accountant. "We have to try! Otherwise, we will go out without even putting up a battle!"

It was true. Whatever the outcome, their most promising option was to retaliate with everything they had. They grabbed what they could. Vici found some sort of a magical orb he had noticed within a nearby corner of the tiny chamber. The Gold Counter found a seemingly different kind of bubbling potion, its unbroken casing revealing a vibrant, red sludge.

VZOMF

Another shockwave. Following its dissipation, Vici and the Gold Counter made their way back into the main chamber only to find their two companions almost completely imprisoned beneath the glowing ivy. Whatever powers Bilal had, he was controlling the magical vines, instructing the ever-winding limbs to seize hold of the party members, including, somehow, that of Edgar's phantasmal being.

"What the—"

A single vine reared up, catching the Gold Counter mid-sentence. Before he had any time to react, it shot towards him and began to wrap itself around one of his arms, pulling him down into a pool of the slithering plant life. With fierce speed, Vici grabbed the Counter's sabre and began to slice away at the stems of the ivy.

"*You think you can defeat my pets?*" Bilal laughed with an utterly metallic hoarseness.

Just then, the bovine raised a hand above its head, directly atop the bases in which its tusks were smashed free. In doing so, he sent up a fury of ivy vines, almost like snakes rising from a keeper's basket. Vici cast his newly-obtained orb in the direction of Bilal in an effort to strike the unholy being across its head. His attempt proved worthless as the hovering monster simply waved it away, smashing the orb's glassy surface against the hard stone.

Before the vines had any chance to grab the Gold Counter a second time, he dashed around the perimeter of the circular room, this time heading back towards the staircase. If he could just make it to the staircase's first plateau, perhaps then he could figure out some sort of upper hand on their unholy foe.

Upon reaching the base, he brandished forth his newly found potion of fiery-red sludge just as Bilal released another chaotic nova of mass destruction.

VZOMF

The energy was enough to rattle his brain.

"Perhaps you should save your energy. You will need it to cross the Void's River"

Another series of vines reared up, wrapping themselves instantly around the Gold Counter as he feebly attempted to scale the nearly shattered staircase. This time, he drew his sabre from his side, swinging it wildly at the vines, progressively chopping each one from its base. With each disconnection, the glowing ivy squealed as its arteries spilled its lifeblood wildly.

Finally, the Gold Counter was able to free himself, allowing for a quick sprint up the staircase.

VZOMF

Each shockwave was like a nova of weakness-inducing trauma at that point. It threw him against the ledges of the staircase. That time he was able to maintain his position upon the cascading woodpile.

He peered down upon the bottled potion that had somehow remained intact despite the commotion, its crimson liquid bubbling within. Divines only hoped that it had harmful properties. Something of its shade and frothy nature suggested so, though he could not be sure. It was at that point that he wished that he'd paid more attention to his wife's work back home in the pureberry meadows.

Without further ado, the Gold Counter finished his climb up the remaining few stairs and reached the landing. He turned to Bilal which was hovering next to Vici, the accountant's body was completely encased in vines.

Suddenly, without any further thought, the Gold Counter hurled the potion directly toward the beast.

SMASH

The crimson liquid splattered all over Bilal's face as particles of the glass potion bottle rained down around him.

"*AARRUYGHAAAA!*"

For whatever reason, he failed to deflect the concoction with his rotted hand, narrowly missing it.

"*What is this?*" he cried, desperately attempting to wipe the burning sludge from his face.

The Gold Counter watched as the crimson liquid began bubbling furiously upon the bovine's ungodly features. A corrosive mixture, as luck would have it. Bilal's facial expression began to smolder, particles of rotting fleshing melting off as if they were a fine brie left too close to an open flame. Large amounts of smoke began to erupt from the massive beast as the potion sunk deeper and deeper, burning its way into the demon's epidermis.

"*DAMN YOU, FOUL HUMAN!*"

A hearty cheer rose up from the voices of his companions. They were rooting him on from beneath their prisons.

Just then, the chamber began shake as violently as if it were about to collapse entirely.

After a final massive burst of metallic screaming, an array of shockwaves exploded forth from Bilal's melting expression, sending the Gold Counter flying from his post atop the staircase's plateau. The adventurer's body was cast violently across the room. He collided into the chamber's brick wall before falling backward upon a shattered table, its broken leg piercing its way through the Gold Counter's lower back only to come protruding forth from his stomach.

VZOMF *VZOMF* *VZOMF*

"Argh!" he cried as the pain overtook him, sending him into a state of shock.

Immediately, the Gold Counter ceased moving.

His only thought and ounce of energy left was entirely consumed by the hopeless task of taking a single breath. Even that became virtually impossible, as an endless onslaught of glowing ivy began to slowly consume his broken body.

···46···

Once Bilal had regained his composure following the burning of the corrosive potion, he no longer appeared upon his hovering pillow. It had disappeared just as Bilal's patience had during his diabolical tantrum. It wasn't until the being's ravaging nova ended that the remains of the chamber were revealed. Supporting pieces of the brickwork had fallen from the chamber's ceiling, opening the entire scene up to a fresh view of the early evening sky.

As the vines continued to grow, expanding and constricting around the adventurers, each member became increasingly buried beneath the wild limbs. One by one, they ran out of strength, peering upwards from their prison of vines to the sky; to their last scene of the setting sun.

The Gold Counter peered down upon the table leg that had forced its way through his lower back, just left of his vertebrae, only to come protruding out the front side of his gut. From within the opening, a steady stream of thick blood poured upon the grasping vines. All that remained within him, were the trailing thoughts of his lifetime. The beginning of Varroth's ever-recurring perfect sunset flooded the chamber.

"Fool! Look at what you have done to me!"

Bilal went over to the Gold Counter, each step emitting a loud thundering noise, from beneath his wide set body. He clutched at his broken tusks with his rotting hands. The bovine was disintegrating from within its body of neglect and non-existent hygiene. With each movement, Bilal's dangling skin sacks and bloated belly rippled from side to side in an uncontrolled swaying motion.

It was a scene of helplessness.

Every member was in distress, as vine upon vine constricted around them. Climbing. Growing. The demonic bovine reached down across his decaying body. He towered directly over the immobile Gold Counter, brandishing forth an enormous, rust-covered dagger from somewhere within his make-shift loincloth. For any man, it was as big as a sword, yet for Bilal, it was a dagger, capable of taking any life, regardless of the size or strength of its foe. Given its elegant twisting and gem-infused handle, it was probably made for ceremonial purposes.

The confidant's heart beat with as much adrenaline as his dwindling energy would allow. From where he lay beneath the ever-growing jail of ivy, he could only see Bilal, the appearance of mass purification was about to be the very last image of his life.

"Speak now, your final words. For you will never get another chance to do so."

In attempting to speak, the Gold Counter could only cough forth a mouthful of blood, his final words stolen by the pain of his impalement.

"So be it, maggot."

And with that, Bilal reached out to thrust his blade through the confidant's skull.

Just then, another voice rasped from across the room.

Vici's.

"I'm ... sorry ..."

The demonic bovine paused mid-action, debating whether or not to carry out the end of the Gold Counter's life, or to finish off Vici's first. It was a rude interruption. He spun around to the vine-shrouded Crease citizen.

"*Ha-ha! You think that your words of sorrow have any meaning?*" Bilal coughed in a hoarse laugh.

"They were not for you," replied Vici.

He shifted his gaze from Bilal to each of his companions, "They were for all of you."

From beneath their plant shackles, each of the members of the clan stared back at Vici, no longer able to move anything beyond that of their eyes.

"I have lied to all of you."

With that, came something that no one had anticipated.

Something that could just save them from death's reaching hand.

··· 47 ···

The members of the party listened quietly to Vici. His apology was unanticipated and confusing. As hard as their journey had been, this was the strangest moment to reveal an opening of dishonesty. But for what exactly? Not only had the former counter guided them to the final chamber, but he always helped them in times of pain, times of need. Upon hearing the words of sorrow, Bilal pivoted upon his vulgar, infected legs and barreled over to Vici. When he was within a few short paces of the constricted champion, that was when the unforeseen occurred.

"It was never my idea to be deceitful to you all," murmured Vici.

A mist of wonder shrouded the arena. He continued, speaking with a sensation of confidence... of boldness.

"But I saw no other way."

Just then, as the final word left his mouth, like the splitting of a quail egg over an iron skillet, a fine, fissure-like crack emerged from the warrior's hairline, down across his face through to his neck and upper chest before vanishing behind his dilapidated armour.

"Vici!" Edgar cried; a state of shock and muddled disorder.

But the companions could only watch as a vivid, neon ray of bright light exploded forth from within his expanding gash, splitting his body in two. The growth and illumination increased as the gaping fissure continued to stretch, breaking off into smaller tangents upon the companion's winter-white skin. It was agony. Agony and a form of torture, both physical and magical. The remainder of the companions had never witnessed such a morbid deformation of a single being. Yet, their comrade remained still as his skin continued to shatter as if it were a pane of simple glass. No noise of pain came from his lips.

Suddenly, the skin upon his scalp began to tear free, falling from his being as if it were a light scarf drifting away in a mountainous breeze. His neck and exposed area of upper chest began to flake away until finally, an enormous limb burst forth, forcing its way through his decaying chest, snapping his armour of its straps and buckles, sending it clean off his body.

A metamorphosis.

The vines were unable to contain the transformation. Next came another leg, followed by a third and then a fourth, pushing their way carelessly through the overgrowth. How such a massive being could erupt from the size of a single man was beyond what the party members could comprehend. These were not the legs of a mortal. They resembled a profound, arachnid creature, crafted from within the deepest, deviancy of corruption. Yet it was something that they had once previously encountered . . .

They recognized it.

Nailreign.

⁂

One by one another leg appeared; the demonic spider lord crawled forth from what was once their most helpful companion - suddenly a simple exoskeleton of human flesh that soon collapsed to the floor, skin, bones and all. Vine after vine attempted to imprison the colossal demon during the ungodly metamorphosis, yet the actions of the sinister overgrowth proved futile. The King of Fallen Crease continued to expand until he stood, at full height, upon his eight powerful legs.

"*Where did you come from!?*" Bilal commanded, staring up at the beast as it rose to twice that of his own size.

Just as he had appeared from within the plagued city, Nailreign stared back with sockets that held swirling cores of ruby-red fusion. He leaned in, his upper torso resembling an oversized human skeleton as it branched forth form his black arthropod body.

"Why, I come from the place where you should have stayed."

A moment of silence fell between the two opposing demons.

"The Void, of course."

Bilal lunged forward, attempting to plunge his rusty dagger into the arachnid's abdomen. The blade simply bounced off the Darkened King's scales. Nailreign, on the other hand, reached down to retrieve the ball-and-chain from his former self, the once "Vici". Within seconds, he swung the mace wildly around his head, bringing it down upon his target, its various spears digging into the bovine's shoulder blade.

Bilal wheezed a cry of anguish as he clasped his injury. Perhaps the blow had not landed in the anticipated region, yet its effect had not been far off. The amount of blood that cascaded from the bovine's punctured lesion was immense...

"*Fool!*" he cried.

As Bilal remained his position, his hand covering his bloody shoulder, a cloudy fog began to form. Purple smoke filled the air, much as it did before, though this spell different from Bilal's original castings.

Not again.

The Gold Counter watched from his prison beneath the vines.

No more spells. Please . . .

Nailreign charged forth, his eight legs granting him a speed that few beasts could achieve, yet his effort to reach his foe in time failed. The bovine released a beam of thick energy directly towards the arachnid king. Within the blink of an eye, Nailreign's skeleton was struck dead centre before an explosive, cloudy exhaust erupted from his being.

His stance faltered, causing him to come crashing down upon the vines, yet Bilal's beam continued to blast. What of the corroding bovine's power that was used was beyond what he had conjured upon the other companions. It was powerful enough to bring down the King of Crease himself. The magic continued, causing the entire tower to shake. Try as he did, every attempt Nailreign made to regain his position proved impossible. He had become the proverbial hare in the hunter's trap.

"*Perhaps now, you will realize that I cannot be destroyed.*"

The beam of energy expanded in circumference, its ultimate power growing along with it. There were only moments left before Nailreign would cease to prevail, and taste the seasonings of death. It was an unimaginable task; inconceivable, even with his level of mastery and presumed "immortality."

It was then, while Bilal further approached Nailreign, that he stepped upon a sharp piece of the shattered potion bottle. Its jagged edges digging into his puss-filled hoof, causing him to lose his balance and collapse. The energy-filled hex vanished as Bilal collapsed upon the ivy-covered brickwork.

Seizing what was left of his strength, Nailreign yanked the ensnaring ivy from his body and hurled himself toward the bovine.

The timing was excellent. It was the reward for continuing on when every task felt unachievable. With no time to react, Bilal remained in a state of frigid shock caused by his misstep. It was up to Nailreign to attain victory entirely weaponless, as his ball-and-chain had disappeared amongst the surrounding wreckages.

With a final thrust, he jammed two of his skeletal fingers into the empty eye sockets of the collapsed being. His companions roared as he pushed his bones further into the bovine's decaying eye holes, penetrating deeper into the confines of his skull until his hand could go no further. Then, a brief moment of stomach-churning agony fell over the beast before his movements finally halted. He fell limp just as he let out his final, rancid breath; his soul released from within its decaying prison. What was left of their "immortal" foe – finally just a pile of rotting sludge. Its essence seeping and expanding further and further amongst the chamber floor.

They had done it.

Vici ... or rather Nailreign ...
Had done it.

Satisfied, the Dark King removed his fingers from within the insides of Bilal's brain once he was sure that the lord had been vanquished. He shook them clean of the disgusting particles that clung to them.

It was done.

The insurmountable was conclusively accomplished.

For a momentary eclipse in time, the bovine's belly began to grow as if it were being pumped full of air before rupturing in a hell storm of gory innards that splashed the chamber walls and everything within.

Just then, the vines began to squeal in anguish. They began to whip about violently as if being seared with a burning flame until suddenly wilting, their thick stalks shrivelling into lifeless, dry matter.

The Gold Counter, coated in a thick layer of blood and morbid putrefaction wiped what he could from his face with his tattered sleeve. The hold of the ivy suddenly nonexistent as he began to raise his limbs from within the crisp, flaking vines. From what the others could see, the beginnings of a genuine smile cracked his face below a set of exhausted eyes. But just before he could start his sentence, he fainted into a state of unconsciousness. Though the threat of any enemy had simply evaporated, the Gold Counter's position, impaled upon the shattered table leg, had all but thrown his body into a stifling comatose.

···48···

Just as the battle against the dark bovine had come to a close, so had the turmoil with the ivy. The glowing vines and arteries of the magical plant simply relinquished their holds among the crew members, drying instantly to a quick, flaky pile of autumn leaves and crusty stems. Thul, who was first to free himself of his prison, thrashed about, knocking the remains of the plants from himself.

"By the Divines!"

They looked to Edgar when they heard him call, "My powers! They're back!"

Thul and Nailreign could see their ghostly partner flutter in waves until a burst of bright light sent the shriveled vines blasting from his form.

They rushed to the Gold Counter's side while. One by one, Thul ripped the wilted ivy from his most cherished friend, shooting up clouds of dried leaves that whisked their way gently around the room.

"Easy! Take it easy!" beckoned their massive arachnid in a metallic voice.

The barbarian slowed his work until the last vine was carefully removed from the confidant's torso.

"It's horrible!" exclaimed Edgar, peering down at their indisposed friend.

It was.

The constant blasts of energy and dark magic had sent the Gold Counter crashing upon a trashed table, its splintering leg spraying forth from the confidant's stomach.

"Brother! Listen to me! It's Thul!"

The gargantuan man held his friend's face in his hands, being cautious not to jostle him in any way.

"Who has the stone?" Nailreign shouted.

A look of desperation came over each of the members' faces before the forgetful Thul realized that he had it within his pocket.

"I'm going to remove the table leg from his body, but as I do, you mustn't touch him," the Nailreign instructed, speaking slowly in order to get through to Thul. The barbarian hadn't always been the best when it came to reacting in times of pressure.

"Continue holding the sapphire next to him. Its healing powers should seal his wounds once the table leg is removed, but because his injuries are far too life-threatening, any contact between the stone and his actual body could send him into a state of shock, causing his heart to fail."

Thul nodded and brandished forth the stone in a readied position.

"Thul," Edgar grasped his companion's attention, causing him to pivot.

"Did you hear what Nailreign said?"

"Yes, yes! I 'eard it! Let's go already! He's dying if he's not already there yet!"

For the first time in their journey, a tear rolled from the barbarian's eye. He was one of the fiercest men in the land, yet his feelings overtook him. He just wanted his friend back.

"Here we go. Everybody ready?" Nailreign questioned, his voice anxious.

The cast looked at each another and then back to their giant arachnid as he hunched over the party members.

"One . . . two . . . three!"

Ever so slowly they lifted the Gold Counter's body, raising him from the base of the overturned table. Streams of blood began to pour from the centre of his lower back. Splinter after splinter began to tear through his stomach as the wood returned through the same hole it had once made.

"Oh shit, oh shit!" Thul exclaimed, sapphire in hand as he looked to the Dark King for guidance. Nailreign shot him a brief nod of approval. Their only choice was to do their best, just as they had done from the very beginning.

Suddenly, the Gold Counter's eyes shot open!

"ARRRRUGGHHH!" he hollered, although he was cut off mid-shout as another branch of splinters passed through his body.

"Hold him! Hold him!" Edgar screamed, reeling to help in any way possible.

A cry of torture continued until finally Nailreign succeeded in removing the obstruction. He laid the Gold Counter down upon the shrivelled ivy. The moment of anxiousness was broken by yet another scream of agony from the Counter as the barbarian held the sapphire inches from his friend's gut.

They were fully aware of the horror and chaos of it all, yet the painful crying brought a sense of hope, as well, for it meant that their friend was still alive. This was a good thing. He writhed wildly about, but was restrained by Nailreign whom held him firmly against the chamber's cold stone.

Little by little, his entrails magically stitched themselves back together. Once again, the stone shone through with its healing powers, leaving the friends bewildered. The juncture of torment went on until at last, the final opening of the wound finished its fusing, leaving behind an absolutely flaw-less image of untouched skin. All that remained were three moles, which the Gold Counter had prior to their journey.

"I . . ."

He froze, patting his gut in puzzlement. "You saved me."

He looked to Thul, to Edgar and then to Nailreign.

The pain of his injury had completely disappeared. It made him feel as youthful as a child. Even his hunger had disappeared.

"He's back!" laughed Thul, more tears bursting from his eyes as he hurled himself toward the Gold Counter. The two of them both flew backwards, landing upon another pile of broken furniture. Luckily, that time without injury.

"Hey! Easy!" Nailreign belted. "We didn't revive him only to destroy him again, you fool!"

Thul ignored the condescending order and went on to squeeze his dearest friend. Their bond was finally restored, and the two most sentimental characters were returned to their everlasting friendship. Streams of tears rolled from the Gold Counter's eyes as he peered up at his giant friend.

"I thought that was it! I thought we were dead! The end!" he cried, sniffling with pure excitement.

"Come now, ye' bastard! Ye give up to easily for ol' Thul! Why can't ye jus ave' a little ope' every now n' then?" the barbarian exclaimed as he grinded his burly fist upon the Counter's head, jostling his blood-soaked hair in a somewhat disgusting fashion.

Their excitement continued just as Edgar proceeded to pass from body to body, ingesting what was left of their souls in an effort to quench his thirst. It had been far too long since his last feast of "cabbage stew." A crude joke, yet one that made the soul-consumption process seem slightly more acceptable than it most certainly was. Still. What choice did he have?

But it wouldn't be much longer. With the crafting of the magical Gemsand, his problem of endless thirst would finally be quenched for good. Perhaps the mightiest of potions granted eternal youthfulness amongst mortals, yet it still remained as only a promise of diminishment for those already in their afterlife. For Edgar, he had accepted the fate and upon a permanent death post that of a phantasmal nature was far better than enduring such a perpetual thirst until the end of time. Besides, what's to say there wasn't a life after that one? And another after that?

Eventually, the celebration died down with the realization that the clan was still within one of the worst confines of the castle.

The Gold Counter turned to Nailreign.

"You!" he pointed.

"You have some explaining to do!"

··· 49 ···

As the crew went on to wipe themselves of Bilal's innards and collect their bags, Nailreign explained his reasoning for being disguised as Vici throughout their journey. Crossing the land of Crease, in addition to entering the kingdom of Koraivindahl had been difficult. A group of well-worn travelers would be commonly accepted in these lands of treachery, but a massive, half skeletal, half arachnid demon would definitely attract attention. Once through the open landscape, a further problem, for there was no chance his enormous size would fit within the sewers or the various castle hallways.

But above all that, he had magically shelled himself within the accountant's body as a test. For the blackened king, the only sure way to retrieve the Geodes, was for him to join the group, monitoring their progress as they neared their target.

Unfortunately, Vici had been a real man, not some fabrication of evil or of blackened descent. He was once a counter who did in fact once work within the walls of the Red Hand, counting money just as the Gold Counter had. It was because of this, that Nailreign had known the way. Contrary to their beliefs, Edgar's included, the adventurers had never known the real Vici, nor would they ever. His chapter had come to a close prior to their arrival in Crease. It was the Fallen City's king that brought his life to a close, absorbing his knowledge, his memories, and taking his form to join alongside the travelers.

"I can see how it all makes sense. But I must say, even from a ghost's point of view, the fact that you had used his body as a vessel to befriend us, and trick us into thinking that we had come to know such a great man . . . it's barbaric!" Edgar exclaimed.

He was right. How many times had they trekked alongside "Vici"? Getting to know him, understanding him, listening to his stories. His memories. His conversation and small-talk. It was all a facade of lies – or so it seemed. The epiphany came crashing down upon the party members.

"I saw no other way . . . I had to be sure we obtained the Geodes. Their sands are the only thing upon this earth that can help my people! It is the only essence that will cure my people!" Nailreign beamed as he stretched out his boney arm, a piece of blackened ribbon fluttering from it. His internal magical essence seemingly restored. Finally, the Gold Counter chimed in, his stomach back to its regular self, yet burning with its original hunger.

"Surely there could have been another way. You lied to us! You led us to—"

His words were interrupted by the sound of approaching soldiers.

"They're in here, sir! Beyond the stone!" bellowed a voice. Its source, clearly that of imperial nature.

The Gold Counter turned to the rubble that lay between them and the soldiers. It blocked the other side of the doorway.

To say how many men were on the other side was impossible, though a few small openings in the rubble revealed their increasing numbers. Just then, an arrowhead flew through the trashed brickwork, narrowly missing Thul's neck by a couple of inches.

"Tear it down! Do it now!" another voice, this one belonging to a captain. "We're going to finish them here before they get up to any more of this nonsense!"

Perhaps the guard was not aware of the devastation upon the other side of the vestibule.

"We must get to the laboratory! Hurry!" Nailreign instructed as the soldiers began dismantling the doorway's rubble that separated the opposing parties.

They made quick work of gathering their things. The Gold Counter took one look at the broken staircase, and decided to climb upon the back of his recently returned spider-king. Thul hastily grabbed his overstuffed treasure sack, accidently causing a generous sum of coins to fall from its opening. He tried to gather the coins but they fell amongst the mess of tattered vines.

"Leave them! We must get going!" the Gold Counter shouted.

Begrudgingly, he did as he was told and sealed up his sack before hopping upon the arachnid's back. There was hardly enough room for the two of them upon Nailreign's pod, yet they hung on as the king made his way past the broken staircase. Once atop, Thul smashed his way through the domain's highest threshold, sending an old, wooden door flying before crashing into a heap of tinder. He dashed through.

Another hallway.

This one different.

It had a skinny corridor, rising slightly in the middle before dipping down again, meeting another doorway.

It was a bridge.

It had to be.

The most amazing feature - its breathtaking stained glass that lined both walls. On one side, an image of a lady crouched next to a goat. She was feeding it wheat. But there was no time to appreciate her beauty as the soldiers of the Red Hand broke through the rubble that had originally blocked them from entering the lower level of the mages' quarters. The war upon Koraivindahl had only just begun earlier that day. Perhaps, given the dwarven warships, there was an advantage to a daylight invasion hence the dwarves' unexpected arrival within the city's unpredictably rocky harbour. The attack was the reason that the great majority of the castle's defenders were preoccupied with fighting off the dwarves. A problem that required beyond that of the attention needed to assess the four "simple" intruders, yet still a significant number of soldiers came pouring into the mages' quarters.

"What the—? How did they get up there? What is that foul beast with them?" one of the soldiers cried out. It was evident that the rear of Nailreign's darkened pod was within the sight of the guards.

Just then, an arrow whizzed past the party, narrowly missing Thul's head. The action of hostility was met with one of Nailreign's immense blasts of cosmic power. He cast an aura of pure energy that thundered down upon their foes, its central beam entirely frying two of the soldiers.

"Go!" He screamed, pointing a skeletal finger towards the enclosed bridge.

ANDREW P. WILD

A fresh group of soldiers came flying into the room and burst past their two fallen comrades as if they hadn't seen a thing. Again, Nailreign fired down an aura of corrosive destruction, sealing the fates of yet more soldiers and injuring the remaining nearby.

Still, another squad burst through, crashing over the bodies, each one trying to fire yet another fatal arrow into the clan of adventurers. Meanwhile, Thul attempted to smash away at yet another mighty door after passing over the bridge that connected the two towers. Perhaps the door had an iron-plated interior; the reason for such difficulty even given Thul's mountainous strength.

Edgar tried next, harnessing an orb of growing energy before firing it at door.

No use.

"Nailreign! Help us!" cried the Gold Counter.

The arachnid, exhibiting signs of adverse fatigue, turned to face them, momentarily ceasing his fight against the relentless ranks below. He decided to make his way through the enclosed bridge, not entirely knowing if he would fit. The platform was getting weaker, making it too dangerous for the companions to stand upon, except Edgar. Though for that reason, the only area they could stand upon was against the impassable door. Inch by inch, Nailreign began to work his giant abdomen through the bridge's corridor. If he were to fire any kind of magic at the door at that moment, he would surely destroy his companions within such a small space. What was his plan?

As he attempted to stuff his giant body through the modest walls of the connector bridge, the skin lining his massive pod began to split. A trail of blackened blood began dripping from his wounds as he attempted to manoeuvre his bulging physique. If he were to get stuck here, they would be done for, especially given their lack of exit.

"Get a ladder!" cried one of the soldiers from the mages' quarters.

Yet another wave of fear fell over the adventurers.

Finally, Nailreign was close enough to reach the keyhole in the doorway with his skeletal finger. Upon doing so, the lock, began to glow before exploding in a triumph of broken iron mechanisms.

With the lock broken, The Gold Counter pushed open the door. That time, there were no wizards casting spells of madness. There were no forms of dangerous magic, nor were there guards clad in iron attire. For it was at that very instant, after miles of travel, battles of bloody slaughter and what felt like a lifetime of hopelessness, he had finally reached the pinnacle of his grand quest.

Waiting for the Gold Counter...
Just beyond the door.

Alive and hiding in the corner of the small corridor.
The one they had risked everything for.
Every ounce of fear... blood... sweat and tears...

It was her.

It was the Gold Counter's wife.

$\cdots 50 \cdots$

It took but a moment for her vision to adjust, before realizing that she was no longer in any imminent danger. Perhaps she had not yet caught sight of Nailreign, the enormous being of arachnid nature. Yet the arrival of the Gold Counter and his crew was beyond that of a peaceful nature, surely far different from the king's guards that had checked on her over the years. Though she had begun to relax, she was not expecting the arrival of her husband. Not at the age that he was at that moment nor any younger. Such a task had been deemed impossible!

"Who . . . who are you?" she asked, heavy tears beading down her puzzled face. It was apparent that the woman's eyesight was poor, especially on account of her old age. "Why have you come here?"

In that moment of suddenness and surprise, the Gold Counter reacted with a similar expression of cascading tears as he fell to his knees in an incredulous demeanour.

They were . . .
Together.

Finally.

He looked at her, struggling to keep his composure. The moment of deep emotion had overwhelmed him. His attempt to speak proved futile as only the slightest squeak escaped his parched lips.

She stared blankly at the Gold Counter, attempting to make something of his reaction as she tried to gather who he was... who they were. Just as a snail would return to its peak atop the highest leaf, she gradually rose from her curled position from within the chamber's corner. Her body was old, withered with aching bones, sickness and malnourished skin. She was in an appalling state and had been for a very long period of time. The 87-year-old woman was dressed in filthy, threadbare rags. Exhausted and dirty, she could barely muster the strength to stand.

Her hair, once as vibrant as the midday sunshine, was a mop of tangled, grey strands, frizzled from years of neglect. Bruises and lacerations covered her body from head to toe, each bearing a story of woeful torture. Some of her gashes were unsettling; large in size. It was obvious that her captors had gone to great lengths to harm her, but for what reason? Her innocence and free spirit had been crushed at the hands of the king's personal guard.

"Who are you?" she repeated, this time with greater vigor.

It took the Counter only a moment more before he could gather himself. A once devastated, tattered old man, he too knew how it felt to be held captive by the king's guard. He knew what kind of pain the Red Hand had put her through. A once broken soul from the very moment his wife had been abducted, yet he was finally rewarded with the blessing of her presence once again.

"It's me!" he cried, saliva bursting from his dismally upturned mouth. His weakened bellow of agony echoed throughout the chamber. His wife, shocked by the Counter's torturous wail, just stood, staring blindly back at him. It was then, just as the morning sun sends its ever-reaching beams of hope across the meadow, that her eyes began to light up. She began to glow; her expression becoming fuller and wider as she began to comprehend . . . the impending realization of who the Gold Counter truly was.

"I . . ." She too came to a futile pause before finally speaking, "The . . . elixir . . .?"

The two paused, in fact everyone did. Waiting eagerly.

Waiting.

Hoping.

Praying.

Praying that the old woman would remember the Gold Counter, despite his younger appearance brought on by the Elixir of Youth. The party just stood, as they waited for her to recall who he was.

For it was at that very moment that she said his name.

" . . . "

Though calm, and as amiable as the day they had first met, her voice, at that very instant, touched the Counter in a way she had never done before. Never had a single word out of her mouth sent the grand adventurer into such a whirlwind of overwhelming astonishment. A single, unforgettable moment of realization, success . . . and love.

He rose from his knees, mopping the tears from his face as she ran to him without a care of age or worry of fall. As she made her way to him hastily, she did fall, but only for him to catch her just in time. The embrace of her frail body brought him the true realization that that was their reunion, at that very moment.

"I missed you so much," she sobbed. Both sadness and excitement blurted from her every pore as she continued to break down within his fortified embrace. "I missed you! I worried you would never come for me. I knew that you couldn't! It was impossible!"

The two howled uncontrollably as the remaining members of his clan gathered around, the sight of the gargantuan arachnid, eerie ghost, and monstrous barbarian proved nothing in terms of deterring the old woman as she clutched her lover in an unending embrace. She knew that the unruly members of the Gold Counter's party were of no threat.

At that moment, even if it was his very last, the Gold Counter knew, in his heart, his soul, and his core, that he had done it. He had reached his wife, just to see her . . . just to be with her once again . . .

Just then, out of an opposing corner of the room and from behind a bookshelf stepped another figure. This one of the Red Hand. Upon presenting himself, the figure appeared to be a simple yet ratty, old castle dweller clad in royal tapestry. Perhaps a mage or dignified alchemist.

"You bastards!" he proclaimed in a voice of sheer disgust and outrage. "He'll be right here you know! The king! He'll be here any moment, and he'll smite you, you damn foolish idiots!"

The dweller's blast infuriated the Gold Counter. Immediately, he waved his wife into Thul's care before abruptly charging toward the dweller, each foot slamming against the cobalt brickwork of the alchemic laboratory.

"Step back, ye bastard!" warned the jagged toothed enchanter.

His threat had no effect; not on the Gold Counter who was filled with a renewed energy and unstoppable force. The castle dweller reached around with his left hand, ungloved, and wrapped his fingers around a dagger, pulling its gnarling twist from his belt. The action in which the dweller zipped the dagger forth brought blood pouring from his own hand. With a firm movement, he held the snake-shaped dagger between the adventurer and himself. Without hesitation, the Gold Counter bashed the dweller's shaky hand and dagger to his side, only to lift the unforgiving blade of his own sabre to his foe's throat.

Struggle as he could, and through his own figure of some-what strength, the dweller squirmed as the Gold Counter caught hold of his wielding hand. Just then, with a single movement, the Gold Counter grabbed hold of the dweller's head, throwing him against the ground. Something within his head, perhaps the back of his skull, cracked as his body hit the unyielding masonry. Before the mongrel had any time to react, the Gold Counter lunged at him with his blade. Only then did his wife make her first cry of horror as he split the man of his soul by hacking his way through the guard's chest in a fit of unruly rampage.

"Stop! Please for the love of the gods!" his wife cried out.

After a moment of horror came the epiphany of his actions. He finalized the moment as he crouched over the mutilated body. Then, rising from the ground, the ashes, he turned to her. Yes, half her age, and though a world of explaining was due, and so it shall be eventually portrayed - she knew it was him. She knew that face. She knew it well; she always had over the course of her once unsullied lifetime amidst the paradise of the pureberry meadows. It took but another moment before she too had calmed her nerves of the violence. Though brutal, it held no comparison to that which Varroth's lesser characters had brought her counterpart. Perhaps though, of all the tenderness contained within their sudden reuniting, the most magical of all was when she finally spoke his name. His title. It passed from her lips, just as a butterfly emerges from its casing after the extension of a frozen winter.

Crack

The sound of a ladder being erected bounced from one chamber to the next as though it were looking for an escape in the spacing of the brickwork. That was the moment. A scene of hopelessness. Only then could the sound elude the adventurers through the shattered glass amidst the bridge. But that was all to escape. The clan, rugged and exasperated from their battle, shot only glares of anger at the brim of the ladder rungs that had been erected from within the mages' chambers on the opposite side of the bridge. At that point, it could be only moments before the influx of the Red Hand continued its closing march on the blocked captives.

For leadership, the party looked to Nailreign. There was no other exit from within the circular alchemy chamber. Even the Gold Counter's wife knew to look to him, though a goliath, spider-like monster she had never once seen nor heard of, his presence amongst the group proved worthy in her mind, at least for the time being. But just as he had once had all the answers, or at least one way of easing the tension, both in any situation or shortly after, his gaunt expression offered nothing.

"What! What now? We are trapped!" the Gold Counter called out, stating the obvious.

Still yet, Nailreign went on only to peer at the top of the ladder that was quivering back and forth. Evidently, its rungs held the weight of numerous soldiers as the ranks had begun their ascent from within the mages' quarters. Surely the blasts of Nailreign's powers, alongside that of Edgar's could hold them at bay momentarily, but it came down to a matter of time. A capsule in the waves of such a cruel condition. How much longer before the two spell casters were stripped of their energy? Before the bridge and alchemic laboratory were to be filled with legion members, hacking their way through each member of the dog-tired group?

Their first glimpse of the Red Hand atop the landing was short, as Edgar had been the first to fire a projectile of shadowy magic, sending the tarnished soul flying back into the depths of the mages' quarters. A powerful blast, though one that did not cause any sort of retreat from within the ranks of the Red Hand. Each guard, clad in a series of emblem ingrained armour and somewhat expensive clothing went bursting back, man after man.

A couple of times the adventurers' casters succeeded in bouncing the ladder free from its position against the upper landing, but a mere moment was all it took before the ladder was returned to its original placement. Following that, a second ladder was forced up against the landing, then a third, tripling the influx of soldiers.

The Gold Counter looked from Nailreign to Edgar. It was evident that since their recent battle against Bilal, the group of companions had gone far beyond the point of exhaustion. He turned next to Thul, and then to his wife. A realization that Vici was no longer amongst them, but rather his reincarnated transformation. The idea struck him with a notion of bizarreness that went alongside his growing distress.

Suddenly, an inability - a hindering fatigue fell over their giant arachnid as he attempted to cast another destructive spell. The magical failure sent him stumbling backwards into a table topped with potions and outlandish herbs. A noise of shattering glass lit up the laboratory as a series of vials and large beakers crashed to the floor around them.

"Nailreign!" The Gold Counter cried, rushing to his side.

Edgar continued to cast his own spells of destruction, avoiding any notion that could deter him from his concentration, though he too had begun to weaken to a point where his magic began to produce smaller and smaller results. His spells begun to diminish – the effect of which proved futile when it came to diminishing the ranks that suddenly appeared upon the upper platform of the mages' quarters.

"Nailreign! Get up!" The Gold Counter cried as he thrust his hands up against the king's abdomen in an effort to raise whatever energy his fallen companion had within. Suddenly, the soldiers evolved to establishing themselves a new position, one that held a somewhat structured housing of shields, walling out whatever attacks Edgar continued to conjure forth.

"March!"

The command came from the mages' quarters and had been followed by a steady movement of troops that began to step in their direction, opening up even more space for further men to take up the rear as they began to cross through the bridge's corridor.

"I . . ." Edgar, with all exertion, attempted to speak as he maintained a lesser momentum of spell casting.

"I . . . I can't . . . keep—"

"C'mon, boy! Keep fightin'!" Thul bellowed. Not even their barbarian could fathom the outcome of such a situation. Granted any other moment, he would have rushed into battle, yet his hesitation had been bestowed upon him by the fact that Edgar continued what he could to keep the infestation of soldiers at bay. To rush in meant only to become an acciden-tal target for their sapped spell caster, not that it would have done much at that point. Still, the barbarian kept on at his companion with his verses of cheer and confidence while the Gold Counter watched in horror as he held his wife.

"C'mon boy! Give it to 'em! Give these fine bastards what they deserve!"

But he could not. All of what was left of Edgar's internal vigor came crashing down, just as he did amongst the shattered vials of the alchemy chamber. Then, it took but a sliver of time before Thul lifted his mighty war hammer above his head, charging directly down the centre of the bridge's narrow mouth.

Before the castle men had any time to react they were met with the barbarian's prodigious mallet. Thul held his hammer in hand, not head-wise, but a barred hold that he had maintained across its mast, one that with the perfect horizontal force, surged the waves of soldiers back across the bridge as he collided with their wall of shields. Following the defensive surge, the sounds of men falling from their post could be heard, but then came the counterattack. A burst of the connected shields knocked the gargantuan man from his lumbersome pose.

A strong man indeed, though the force of the king's army was stronger and so he came thundering backward, landing upon his spine, flat across the bridge's arch. The blow was hardly enough to shift the bridge. Its structure vibrated ever so slightly, not so that the average eye could see, but the movement was evident as a coating of dust and fine particles fell from the ceiling above. The flecks of dust glowed in the evening moonlight that came cascading though the stained glass.

Desperately, Thul reversed himself in a frantic manner until he was back within the confines of the alchemic laboratory. Then, it became clear to the army that both Nailreign and Edgar were indisposed; weakened to the point in which they could no longer cast their spells. It left the soldiers with the perfect opportunity to approach.

The time had come for their journey to end. Even if they had planned this infiltration of the final room down to the last degree, there was no way they could have succeeded. There was no escape. Perhaps if there had been some sort of stealthy approach, yet they were far beyond that point.

No, there was no escaping.

No mercy.

Every concept of hope and existence had finally eluded them.

Bit by bit, the impending onslaught of soldiers closed the distance between themselves and the journeyers, passing over the bridge as they did. Whatever was left of Edgar's feeble powers, simply glanced off the iron shields of the Red Hand.

But just then, it was as if the Goddess of Luck and Good Fortune had decided to side with the companions once again. Without any warning at all, the bridge, its beautiful entirety of indigo brickwork and flawless stained-glass windows exploded, sending slabs of rubble and soldiers hurling into the open abyss below.

··· 51 ···

J ust as a flutter of utter confusion filled both the minds of the adventurers and soldiers alike, so did the dusk of the evening autumn sky. The eruption came as a surprise, even to Nailreign. He had always been the one everyone turned to for answers. He too remained motionless with an indication of clueless bewilderment.

Although the blast was enough to kill off the legion members that had remained central to that of the suddenly depleted bridge-way, one still remained within the crumbling alchemy tower. He turned; short sword readied to meet with a fleshy target. Only his pivoting had gone a bit too long as Thul had seized the moment to strike, smashing the head of his giant mallet into the soldier's chest plate in a single swing. The force knocked the man clear of his footing and into the mountainous cavern of endless castle peaks below.

The sight upon peering over the edge in which the bridge no long existed granted the Gold Counter with a view of the haphazard landscape that promised nothing more than a swift death following such a dastardly fall. Beneath him opened a large chasm, half of which expanding to a castle courtyard, brimming with trees that had passed their prime of mid blossom. To the other half, the unforgiving treachery of Varroth's landscape, exterior to that of the Royal Castle's wall. They were near the perimeter that surrounded Koraivindahl from the Highlands. The Gold Counter had not anticipated the Royal Castle to take up the northern border of the city. In fact, it was such that the castle had taken up the entirety of the most northern point of the city's grand wall. A feature that, especially given the heinous cliffsides, protected the castle from any intruders from the north - considering such an invasion would prove worthless, gathering that anybody chose to attempt access from that side of the wall.

Still, how had the bridge simply . . . erupted?

It wasn't as though the bridge had collapsed from the sheer weight of the ranks, but that had it just . . . exploded?

He leaned forward, hugging the broken brickwork next to him in efforts to gain some leverage as he watched the final solider fall to his death, screaming a bloodcurdling cry of fear as he did.

"Watch out!" Thul shouted as he grabbed the Gold Counter by the rear of his chest piece, yanking him back into the laboratory. Just as he did, the razor's edge of a thrown short sword from yet another one of the opposing guards amidst the mages' quarters skimmed past his face. The blade missed his cheek by barely an inch. Thul's pull brought the Gold Counter from his feet to the base of his gargantuan partner but it was there, from that angle, that he could see what had made such devastating work of the bridge.

From beyond the edge of the city to the east, past that of a few glazed buildings and roofs, each of which shrouded in a breathtaking array of amber and orchid shaded metals, floated a series of war boats amongst the harbour's edge. Each of which incredibly tremendous in size. Each boat bore flags painted with enlarged crimson conch shells, axes, anvils, and foaming stout mugs.

It was the Dwarven Army.

Many of their ships had already arrived within the city's dockyard, yet some of them still rested within the bay. The vessels were far larger than any the Gold Counter had read of within his history tomes. One boat in particular appeared to be far larger than the rest; its colossal magnitude far outweighing that of the other ships. Atop its deck a monolithic contraption of sorts stood as tall as a windmill. One that rose far differently than an average mast or other ship-like structure. A weapon of some kind?

Suddenly, another command came from the opposite side of the bridge, yet this one was newer . . . louder. Apparently, it was another captain, though his insistent order to clear his line of sight proved difficult due to the overcrowding of soldiers that continued to pile onto what of left of the tiny platform. He went on to push himself through the group, carelessly knocking a few of the guards from their post only to have them fall to their screaming deaths within the castle courtyard below. Once through, he brandished a crossbow of incredibly luxurious design; swirling patterns that matched his uniform of higher standing. The early moonlight glinted off the polished gold that made up the outer structure of the crossbow. Before the group of companions had any time to assess the newcomer, the captain went on to fire his first arrow, followed by another, then another.

With luck, the party members that stood within the opening of the alchemy chamber flashed to either side of the haphazard laboratory, taking shelter behind what was left of its cavity. Nailreign and Edgar, with what energy they had regained, hidden on one side. The Gold Counter, his wife and Thul remained on the other, each party member out of the captain's line of sight. Somehow, their King of the Fallen City was successful in manoeuvring his oversized abdomen so that it was slightly sheltered behind the protruding brickwork.

The Gold Counter peered down toward the colossal fleet within the harbour, primarily upon the ship with the enormous contraption aboard its centre. What kind of a ship was that? And what, bless the heavens, could have collapsed the bridge before them?

Granted the distance between the ongoing, peak-top battle and the harbour was large in extent, the Gold Counter was able to make out the figures of multiple moving dwarves amidst the ship deck. It was as if they were preparing the machine once again. Its massive arm-like structure, twisting back into a suspended position.

"Is that . . . a catapult?" Thul's question brought a realistic philosophy, though the machine was not quite that. They continued to watch the machine warp and bend, while two massive wheels spun upon a fixed axis on either side. It was some sort of a load-bearing machine; one that had indeed been devised to cause great damage. But why would it be within the harbour? Would the dwarves not wish it to come ashore?

Within the minds of the companions, such a collection of mysterious thoughts remained ongoing, just as the commander's arrows that ricocheted around the half-broken room once finalizing their initial impact. But just then, it came to him, clear as the night sky on a windless summer eve. That to which the Gold Counter found inconceivable to decipher, became as plain as the sea top itself.

A trebuchet.

Of course!

The rotator wheels on either side were designed to crank the machine and the arm to load the weight. It had all been linked into one system, designed to launch heavy projectiles a great deal farther than any other machine in existence.

Suddenly, its massive arm swung out wildly, snapping a load of projectiles into the air before smashing back into its "concluding" position. What could be made of the ammunition was not to say. Not only had the distance been far enough for the projectiles to appear far smaller at that point than the human eye could tell, the clan didn't have it within themselves to peek much higher than their shelters. Each member of the clan remained in hiding, barring themselves against the unpredictability of continuous savagery that fired their way from the platform across the gap. At that moment, the time was brief before the objects fired from the trebuchet came into view.

Stones?

Could it be?

Another arrow bounced off the rear of the laboratory, this one ricocheting directly into the hardened flesh of Thul's rump.

"Gawh!" he cried, before ripping the arrow free, a spatter of blood squirting from the seat of his trousers. Once affirmed that the injury was merely a minor puncture and not a life-threatening rupture, Thul went on to grab a side table nearby, covering himself as he went on to watch the flying objects approach with the rest of his cowering friends.

Whatever it was flying through the air, it was heading their way with an unvaryingly voracious speed.

Stones. It was indeed stones. A grand set of them, perhaps twenty, maybe even thirty. Each with its own size, yet some may have even been cannon balls for all they knew. None of which had the capacity of monstrous boulders, yet some . . . some appeared with the width and mass similar to that of a sow or large a pig.

Finally, the gap between the battle and the hurled stones began to close as the jagged rocks came whipping through the atmosphere, the heavier boulders diving down, smashing through the roofs and various marketplace venues. The few stones that remained in the sky rocketed straight in their general direction until finally . . .

BWAM!

The stones, cannon balls and other various projectiles collided with the castle all at once with a force that in no way resembled any notion of sympathy. While the impact amongst the towers had been of devastating measure, none of the stones had collided with the alchemy chamber but rather, the middle of the tower just below where the team of adventurers were positioned.

"Get over here you fools!" Nailreign beckoned to his partners in his demonic tone. Just then, the wall shielding the travellers from the hellfire of arrows simply fell from the building, cast into the forever-hungry abyss below.

Nervous to make the break and become possibly struck by one of the commander's arrows, the Gold Counter jumped forward, his wife and Thul dashing in his wake. The danger of another puncture ridden from existence as the entirety of the tower that rose from mages' quarters, crumbled from the impact of the other projectiles. The luck of the Red Hand was much lower than the visitors, as the soldiers along with their commanding officer fell into the abyss, mixing with the rubble of shattered brickwork as they did.

In a sense, the sadistic event added a rather satisfying energy to the collapse of the mages' chambers as the grand lot of soldiers plummeted to their death, leaving behind only a handful of non-range ranks. Still, another problem remained for the party as the idea of escaping the deteriorating tower was further becoming a hopeless matter.

Just then, another portion of the alchemy tower fell from its holdings, opposite to where the group lay still, clinging to one another out of desperation. Brick after brick of the elegant masonry began to peel away until finally, the entire tower surged in a quake of uncertainty before losing its entire leveling. Its surface began tilting toward the inner courtyard of the castle.

"It's goin' down! We ave' to jump!" the barbarian cried out.

Without any warning, Nailreign propped himself up upon his eight, massive hooves, clustering the group of his companions within the grasps of his skeletal hands.

"Hold on to me! Don't let go! It is your lives that depend on it!" he cried.

Nailreign reached down, shoveled up the rest of their bags, still well-stocked with treasure and their longed-for Geodes, before plummeting over the edge of the tower. His hold, enough to carry them all just as tower collapsed behind them the second Nailreign's final leg left its surface.

···52···

One would imagine such a massive, god-like arachnid to be powerful indeed, yet not so much to the lengths of nimble prowess. It was imagined that Nailreign, given his size and somewhat luxurious nature, would most likely not have been very agile. Given the height of the plummet from the tower's collapse, and the weight of the party members all crammed within Nailreign's cold, deathlike grip, the King of Fallen Crease proved to be quite nimble. Rather than leaping in a frenzy of hopeless measure, the arachnid king virtually sprinted down the crumbling face of the tower, placing each hoof atop the protruding pieces of the architecture, far faster than the Gold Counter's mind could possibly comprehend.

Within moments, they were atop one of the castle's many parapet walkways. Their view of the open fields, the mountains, and the gaping sea to the east, all opening up to them in a 360-degree rotation.

Of the collapse of the mages' quarters, the devastation of the fallen debris had brought serious damage to the walkway, sealing its fate with a massive gouge, close to one of the tower's bases amidst the high wall. It was only a matter of moments before the trebuchet would be fired again.

Just then, an oak door that led onto the parapet from across the stretch of the walkway in which they stood burst open, introducing an entirely new group of army combatants, each ready to charge, though the gouge in the walkway separated the two parties.

Nailreign pivoted toward the soldiers' direction, his survivors still within his hold before he went charging northbound along the parapet. Fixed planters, each complete with an abundance of beautiful shrubbery and modest trees meant nothing to the arachnid as he went blasting by them, crushing their delicate frames as he did. Once at the end of the walkway, he approached another guard's tower that segregated the next parapet before veering off at a slightly different angle to match that of the main wall's course. Bypassing that tower was barely a struggle as Nailreign leapt from the walkway to the peak of the one story tower and then back down to the walkway upon the opposite side.

Evidently, he was making his way in the direction of the Great Forest of Bane's Roth, a massive woodland that acted as Koraivindahl's outer cloister to the North. Permitting that the entirety of the Red Hand was after them from within the walls of the Royal Castle, the forest's closeness and heavy shelter would no doubt provide an opportune escape. Still, they had a grand distance; a fall of hundreds of feet from the parapet atop Koraivindahl's massive perimeter wall before they could proceed amongst the loving embrace of Varroth's emerald grasses.

Behind them, a new line of soldiers sprinting atop the wall began to grow in number. Nailreign continued, ceaselessly bounding over the ornamental gardens and occasional guard's tower. As the wall continued to bend past each outpost, circling back to form the enclosure of the castle, the gap between the companions and yet another large stone tower rising up from the fortress wall, began to close. As it did, the door that separated the soaring pillar from the parapet burst open, delivering yet another onslaught of combatants that came racing their way.

Suddenly, the Nailreign halted, his hooves abruptly scraping against the weathered brickwork.

"Here."

The angst of impending death crept up from within the Gold Counter.

"Here? Here what!?" he yelled, jammed against his wife's side from within the blackened king's embrace. "We're going to die here! Their coming at us from both angles!"

Nailreign, disregarding the Gold Counter's outburst, strode to the railing. The fall. . . the massive, vertical distance from the walkway to the open field far below was enough to make the Gold Counter nauseous. A grouping of trees amongst the plain appeared as miniatures. Varroth's landscape . . . though beautiful beneath the fading of the day's sky, was beyond a distance that any man could survive should he fall.

Below them, somewhere two-thirds up the exterior of the Grand Wall of Koraivindahl, opened a sizeable terrace, its surface thick with the elegance of ruby carpet, its trim stylized with golden scripture. Alongside it, rose a collection of planters, some having within them a multitude of blossoms, some with copious amounts small shrubs that held of fresh fruit.

"It's the King's Quarters." Nailreign announced, once the crew had a chance to examine what they could of the magnificently lavish balcony. Although they stood directly above it, gazing at it from a birds-eye view, the luxury of the veranda itself, beckoned to them. It called to them. . . inviting them down to a view that captured their imagination. The glimpse of the Royal King's terrace was enough to briefly deter the party from their time of panic. Suddenly, an arrow ended their awe-inspired trance, narrowly missing the group as it collided against the parapet.

Nailreign went on to instruct Edgar to drift down to the platform. It was a risk that was not ideal, seeing as their ghost could glide only downwards and without return. Yet it was a risk that was necessary, in order to check for guards within the king's domain.

Instantly, Edgar agreed to the order with a sufficient nod before jumping the parapet railing, his weightless spirit hovering down to the balcony a hundred or so feet below.

"It's clear!" he cried out.

Following that, there wasn't a sliver of delay before Nailreign bounded over the wall and went plummeting down toward the king's balcony. Another trebuchet fire cracked the many linings of the Royal Castle somewhere behind them. At first, the descent went on as planned. Nailreign strategically, and with the speed of a lightning bolt, went on to place one hoof in front of the other atop the various, barely protruding, bricks from within the wall. As they neared the balcony, picking up speed as their arachnid carrier shot down the length of the vertical castle surface, Nailreign misplaced one of his many hooves, crashing down upon the luxurious veranda - completely annihilating the nearby fruit trees. Luckily, his passengers remained unharmed as his massive body broke the fall.

"Nailreign!" the Counter clamored as he rose to his feet atop the rumpled carpet. "Are you okay?!"

"Yes, yes! I'm fine, just get inside!"

He was lying, or so told the action of his rising atop the veranda surface. Somehow its structure had withstood the blow and remained completely intact with the side of the fortress.

Neglecting to see if the set of double doors was locked, each with an intricate collection of glazed, French-glass panes, Thul went on to burst through the threshold, shattering the glass as he did. Once through, the immense sleeping chambers opened up to a world of polished opulence. It was a scene far beyond that of the human imagination, though similar to that of the treasure vault that existed within the confines of the secret arcane sanctuary. Perhaps it was not as impressive as floating platforms, yet the borders of the room allowed for the magnificent, three-story bookshelves to rise from floor to ceiling.

Before them, lit beneath the candle lighting of an all-crystal chandelier, and central to that of the entire room, rose a massive, duo-set sleeping mattress veiled beneath a range of immaculately white duvets and spreads. Each of the blankets appeared as though they came equipped with a densely packed weight. To the left was a carved walnut escritoire, placed next to a lounge-style resting area. Each of the table surfaces and elegant fittings came topped with a wide variety of golden artifacts, half exhausted candles and various fortunes, each inlaid with magnificent gems, that dotted their way around the domain. All of which came placed before a cavernous fireplace, capable of being stocked with the means of an entire tree, or so it seemed.

Perhaps what was most jaw-dropping was the king's massive bathing area, situated to the right side of the gargantuan hall. From beneath the floor of the quarters, central to the bathing area, was a massive hand-carved reservoir, capable of holding fifty individuals within its perfectly clear, sapphire blue water. Dotting its exterior and next to its lining of precious gems, rose the statues of women, carved entirely out of marble. Each of the women held a jug, or fancy pot of some sort, that magically poured an ongoing stream of warm water directly upon the seating areas within the pool.

"Oh ... I ..."

Thul felt as though he had died and become one with the heavens.

"Jus ..."

Still, he went on to speak, yet his words could not surface beyond the beauty of the room itself. In fact, everyone was speechless. Before them, existed the Royal King's resting chamber - the most elegant resting chamber in all of Varroth ... perhaps even that of the entire Western Chain.

Many of the walls were covered by bookshelves. Others held behemoth sets of windows above their marble surfaces. The view spanned over a great deal of Varroth's infamous golden fields, dotted with patches of shrubs and gentle ponds.

Past that came the border of the Great Forest of Bane's Roth to the north, then the snowy mountainous chain that resided behind. It was impossible to choose which view to take in, comparing the landscape to that of the interior of King's resting quarters.

Just then, Thul went hurtling off into the recesses of the domain, shoveling priceless artifacts into his pack. He stuffed away whatever gold he had lost during the battle with Bilal and the previous wizards.

"Young barbarian, there is no time!" beckoned the spider.

At first, he just went on to plunder the room, disregarding the fact that his pack was already brimming with a collection of heavy treasure. Then he then turned to Nailreign with a reply.

"Relax friend! We 'ave time before them scoundrels come a runnin' this way!"

"Oh, leave him just for now, let him have his spell. We all know it's what he lives for," laughed the Gold Counter, trying to relieve the angst of their pursuit with a little humour.

Nailreign turned to the Gold Counter, his wife, and then to Edgar.

"There's something I have not yet told you. . . "

Unbelievable.

Firstly, Nailreign had posed as Vici, whom the group of companions had come to trust, befriend and even start to love on a certain level. Only then were they all completely fooled by the rebirth of Nailreign from when he had erupted from Vici's body during the great battle. What possibly could come next?

"I have an army waiting for us . . . just beyond the mists of Bane's Roth," he proclaimed.

"An army?" questioned the Gold Counter, looking to Edgar as the thick forests of Bane's Roth came to vision within his mind. "For what reason?"

"Please, little one," started the arachnid. "Do you really think that I would have come this far without any sort of structured defence beneath me? Surely the king's men would have done away with me, regardless of the extent of my conjuring and force."

A moment of silence passed.

Well, a moment of silence given their break in conversation. The witless rampage of clattering, and over-the-shoulder ornament tossing went on in the background as Thul rifled about the king's chambers.

"Then why? Why come all this way as Vici, why not with your army from the very beginning?"

"Just as I said. Had I come as my true self, the Red Hand would have spotted us even before we crossed the field of ruinous blasting. Adding to that, there would have been no doubt that my goblins could have taken the lives of these many men, yet not so many that they would have succeeded. The war between the humans and dwarves had never been one to be caught up in. I knew from the beginning that this day would come given their mighty battle. I felt it necessary to travel with you whilst my army take their path through Bane's Roth – out of sight and out of mind."

The Gold Counter looked to his wife who just stood there, sheathed in a cloak of puzzled mystification. To her, especially given her age, the context had yet to be explained. Finally, she piped in.

"Then why the army now?" she questioned.

"My dear," he leaned in, placing a gaunt hand gently atop her shoulder as to soothe her fears. It did quite the opposite. "I have my army here to get you and your husband home safely. Once we leave this dastardly fortress that is . . . Oh, how I miss the musty, decrepit rot of Fallen Crease."

Suddenly, a violent crashing noise emitted from just beyond the entryway to the king's quarters. The guards had distinctively worked their way through the palace's main-frame, arriving at their location. Shortly after came a bold pounding upon the door combined with the yells from numerous men.

It wasn't long before the order came to open the door, or the consequences of a ramming log would come into action. At that point, Thul had finished his looting of the main chamber and had gone on to explore a further branch of chambers that sanctioned leftward to that of the grand hall. Though the threat of their ready-to-kill pursers pierced the serenity of the immaculate domain, Thul ignored them in complete disdain as he continued on with his search for the king's opulence. How could the man simply persist in searching for more wealth, even when the threat of death was literally separated from them, plainly due to a slab of fancy cherrywood that doubled as the entrance door.

"Thul! Get over here!" snapped Edgar, fearing for his friend's life.

"Oh, my sweet gods!" the barbarian yelled with ecstasy, still obviously ignoring his companions. "I've found it! I've found the royal liquor stash!"

Just then, the entry door burst from it hinges; the restless banging ceased as the door shattered and fell upon the chamber's floor, allowing for a heavy influx of the king's soldiers. The time to reconnect with Thul was all but lost as his presence beyond that of a different room became segregated as the troops stormed the chamber, flooding its confines as they did.

"Thul!" yelled the Gold Counter, desperately seeking his friend amongst the charging troops.

Except it was too late.

The moment to reconnect had closed and so there was only one option remaining.

Nailreign grabbed the Gold Counter and his wife, leaving Edgar to fight through the combatants in order to reach their barbarian. Given his phantasmal form, he wasn't likely to feel the pain of any physical damage and perhaps he could use whatever energy he had left to destroy as many of the ranks as possible. Even if it meant that he was the only one who could truly say goodbye to their barbarian for the final time.

Then, just as he had before, Nailreign plummeted over the balcony once again, his two remaining survivors in one hand, and a couple of sacks of treasure in the next. Only this time, the Gold Counter was without the companionship of his truest comrade.

His loyal partner throughout their entire journey.
His most cherished friend.

And then, just like that – just as he had first met Thul. As unforeseen and as quick as their introduction once was...

He was gone.

The barbarian with a heart of gold.

···53···

Fortunately for the remaining companions, their departure down the vertical castle wall ended in success, even though the distance that Nailreign and his partners had covered was twice that of the parapet walkway to the king's balcony. The structural form of the wall itself had just enough protrusions for the spider to make his way down its stupendous face, utilizing the occasional jut out as he did. What had usually been dotted with an array of living quarters, appeared to be rather minimal in size, provided the diminished group with even fewer holds to break their speed. It took only moments to reach their destination once they arrived atop Varroth's beautiful grassland once again. The triumph went unnoticed to the Gold Counter. With Thul behind, the thought of his giant friend, his protector, spun tales of violent hackings and a disturbing death within his thoughts. What was to be left of his cherished companion would no doubt become a macabre sight of gruesome brutality. It was unlikely that Edgar could have saved him in time.

Such a thought was far too grievous for the Counter to comprehend and so in a mindless struggle, he began to lash out at his demonic chauffeur with a notion of tear-ridden violence. He wanted only to be free of his imprisonment beneath Nailreign's skeletal hand. He wanted to climb the wall himself and free the barbarian. He had the rage to do it.

Had Thul just kept with the group, exactly as Nailreign had ordered, all would be well, presumably. The journeyers would all still be one, as a united group, Edgar included, as he too had been left to fight off what he could of the soldiers. Given their plated armours and impassible numbers, there was no way that Thul could have survived, never mind the rest of his clan.

At that point they were but a few grassy stretches from the Bane's Roth, their destination and protective haven. But it meant nothing to the Gold Counter, not at that moment. From below the cooling atmosphere, the confidant remained pressed against his wife beneath the arachnid's forceful hold as a river of tears spilled from his face.

Next came the perpetual hellfire of razor-tipped arrows. Spanning that of the parapet and protruding balconies, the king's men had begun firing with the entire force of the kingdom. What of the arrows that did not speak of incisive skewers, came coated in a sappy ball of oil-soaked rags, raging beneath a just-lit, blazing fire that stuck to whichever target it landed upon.

"Stop! Stop running! We have to save him!" The Gold Counter, riddled with lunacy, fought the grip of the arachnid, all the while knowing that such a feat was entirely inconceivable.

His sentence was ignored, and so it should have been, as Nailreign continued to gallop up the grassland towards the great forest. Being that the Gold Counter's position was frontal to Nailreign, he and his wife had been somewhat sheltered by the hellfire, though their demonic handler was not so lucky.

Thwack!

An arrow spliced its way through the Nailreign's arachnid pod, just below his bony spine, causing the beast to cry out in pain. But it was not that arrow that stopped him, nor was it the next. One after another, the steel points ripped their way through the king's body, shrouding his abdomen in a series of blood-drawing bolts.

Thwack! Thwack!

Just then, he crashed to a halt, tossing the Gold Counter and his wife as he did. At first, the Gold Counter rushed to his beloved, checking to see if her frail body had indeed landed safely. And so it had. But upon turning around, he witnessed a grueling, fair-sized rag of burning oil that had been launched into the body of his saviour.

"Get it out of me!" Nailreign shrieked, his metallic tone ripping its way over the grasslands and beyond the remote hills in the distance.

Without hesitation, the Gold Counter rushed to his side, reaching through the flame in efforts to grab hold of the blazing rod. Upon touch, the arrow shaft crumbled beneath his sizzling grip as the flame had weakened its mere thatch into to an ashy rod. Without any hold in which to grab the only other option was to peel the ball of torrid heat from the spider's body with his bare hand, and so he did, letting out a cry of inhuman torment as his hand began to corrode immediately within the blazing, oil-soaked rag.

Just down the hill was a marsh - its moldy water providing an instant saviour to the Gold Counter's burning hand. It took not a thought in the matter before he went blasting down the range, jumping into the foul pool of mustiness.

Thwack!

Another arrow, that one, landing directly within the Gold Counter's thigh.

Thwack!

Another, that one ripping through his flesh, directly above his buttocks, piercing its way out his other side.

Before he knew what was happening, it was as if Death's hand had come to him, reaching for him; beckoning to take him as the sequence of hellfire continued to rain down around him. The myriad of burning arrows lighting up the vicinity with the resemblance of a town square just as the cheers of soldiers could be heard from hundreds of feet up atop the fortress's impenetrable barrier.

Thwack! Thwack!

The shots continued, gouging their ways through the Gold Counter's body, some within his increasingly-bloodied torso, others meeting with the likes of his ragged limbs. With every ounce of stamina he had within his abolished figure, he employed a final effort to rise from his placement, half submerged inside that of the marsh's vulgarity. Nevertheless, it was a failed effort as he remained front down within the water, his head tilted to the side. The last thing he saw before the final arrow struck him between his mangled shoulder blades was a beacon of light beyond a modest hill in the backdrop.

Nothing was within its luminous beam, yet its existence was there for a reason. He knew it. He just didn't know why.

And its message, one of perplexed reasoning and promise, had inside it nothing but a luminous incandescence, just as every rose has an infinite beauty amidst its centre of bloom.

Perhaps though, the light itself had just been a figment of his shattered imagination.

··· 54 ···

Once coming to, it took the Gold Counter a moment to understand that he was, somehow, alive. Moreover, he was very-much lively with the seed of a great energy. Just as it had provided before, the miraculous sapphire of healing, the one that Nailreign proceeded to press against his wounds, had worked its inner sorcery, sealing the arrow punctures of their confidant.

At that point, the profound set of powers was to be expected of the stone, and so the Gold Counter just lay with thankfulness. How had he been lucky enough to avoid the arrows' punctures to any of his internal organs? Perhaps it would have been the removal of the arrows that would have tested his scales of pain far worse than those of the original impacts, yet favourably for him he had been unconscious during their removal.

"Are you well?" the King of the Fallen City asked.

A nod in his direction was enough. His wife on the other hand just stood there, nearly in shock as what she had just witnessed from the moment they were under siege of the hellfire to the great magic of the healing, was far beyond that of her scope of normal reality. Still, for a woman who had undergone a series of savage tortures, she still showed enough strength to adhere to the situation. Not a single chance would have been slid her way given they had to escape on their own feet, yet thanks to their arachnid king, she had been distanced from that of her horrific imprisonment.

Another moment passed before Nailreign then retreated from the Gold Counter, freeing a space for the adventurer to rise from the somewhat frost-ridden ground. Once propped upon on his elbows, the appearance of Crease's army was nearly enough to take his consciousness from him. Nailreign had snatched the adventurer from the open plains of the endless arrow fire and moved him deep within the protection of Banes Roth during his incapacitated state.

There, beneath the leviathan greenwoods of Bane Roth's, the Great Forest's most prominent, herculean woods of the frigid timberland, rose hundreds, if not a number within that of the thousands, of boil-covered, maggot-riddled goblins. Each and every single fiend stood in complete silence, resisting any opportunity even to make a peep as they listened to the conversation between their king and the Gold Counter.

Intermingled into the limitlessness of the corrupted army, came other demons and foul minions of darkened descent. Some were of phantasmal form - ghosts as they would have probably been referred to. Others were similar to goblins, yet their diverse heights set them apart. Certain other aspects such as their fiery, hue-tinted skins, and drastically pointed teeth, similar to those of a rusty saw blade, also segregated the oddly deformed minions from the rest of the fleet.

Each member, regardless of their stature, came equipped with their own array of savage weaponry; many of them discordant with sizable batching's of rust ready to cause a sickly infection upon striking. What all of the army members had in common was that they all held lengthy torches extending down to the earth as to double in purpose as adventuring pikes.

To the Gold Counter, he had expected there to be a great number of goblins awaiting their arrival, post that of Nailreign's informative telling within the King's Sleeping Quarters. He had never assumed that there were to be more in number than there were trees. Still, what had it all been in measure of?

What for, exactly?

Of course, he was with his wife, once again. The entirety of their journey complete, and for that he was eternally grateful to be reunited with his one and only true love. In addition, he had made an oath to himself - a promise to never leave her side ever again. Devastatingly, it was incredible how sickly the mind of a man can become, given his social status amongst the kingdom. How incorrect, and morally confounded must an individual become to kidnap an elderly lady from her quiet home within the meadows, sanctioning her away from her happy life in exchange for a multi-year term of torture and anguish?

Yes, the Gold Counter had achieved what he had journeyed the land for, but at what cost? Surely, not the price of his barbarian companion, but of course that had been the matter of it all at that moment. Had there not been another way? A path which he could have taken in order to prevent such a travesty? Why had he not remained with his friend as he had the other times come the moment the barbarian's internal greediness for treasure and liquor had taken over.

A tear of failure rolled from his weary eye as the confidant brought himself to his feet.

"It is always worse to know how good you've had something, once it's gone," Nailreign proclaimed, evident that his telepathic ability was capable of deciphering the Gold Counter's grief. Such a thought, however, was obvious given the Gold Counter's friend was suddenly that of the Royal Castle. Even given his substantial size and will to fight, what was the likelihood that Thul could have survived the endless ranks of soldiers, even with Edgar's help?

"This too will become a part of your memories, my friend. It is now the time for you to be happy. To rejoice with your beloved wife and to return home."

Nailreign went on to wave the Gold Counter and his wife over to an ancient redwood stump that rose central to that of the measureless goblin army. Atop its ancient surface had infused within its rings a series of symbolic emblems that was of an unfamiliar knowledge to the confidant. Each had a certain dye pasted throughout its elegantly swirling curves that began to glow a gentle aura as the couple approached.

"Firstly, your sickness," the king issued.

Long since the Gold Counter had first entered the sewers of the Royal Castle did he fail to recall that he had in fact been inflicted with the plague of Fallen Crease. The curse had riddled his body with a severe weakness and though they had succeeded in reaching the kingdom's most prominent city before his bane of hastened aging had destroyed him of old age, he had made it out, very much alive. Perhaps his body was that of a middle-aged man, yet his veins coursed with a poison that made his health that of a sick, elderly soul.

The skeletal lord reached into one of the nearby bags of treasure and newfound rewards, brandishing forth one of the long-sought after Geodes. Its opal casting glinting beneath the flame of the many surrounding torchlights. It took only a moment for Nailreign to break open the stone atop the trunk's emblem-infused surface, releasing an expanse of fine, sandy granules that gleamed of every colour within the universe's spectrum.

Once the Gold Counter had placed his hands upon the stump, covering the sand beneath his palms, Nailreign began an incantation of inhuman language. Each word that passed through his gaunt, skeletal jaw was without any meaning to the Counter or his wife, yet the goblins of his army began to chant the same language in an ominous reverberation.

Suddenly, a series of iridescent spores began to rise around the Gold Counter, beginning in a slowly spinning cycle before whipping around with nonsensical speeds. None of which actually touched him, yet it happened only for a moment longer before a blare of neon light burst from the sky, smashing down upon the Gold Counter and his entire being.

As it did, a vivacious zeal of powerful energy surged through his every vein in a single capsule of time. The powerful incantation made it feel as though every bone, every organ and every blood vessel within his body had exploded beneath his very skin, erupting into a bliss of angelic energy. The implosion of the impossible plague, decimating before the eyes of all who watched until finally . . .

Nothing.

All of the lights, the flashing spores, the psychotic flickering of rainbow designs just . . . stopped. The beam shooting from the heart of the autumn night vanished instantaneously from the scene altogether. Just then, a nova of volatile emerald light burst from the Gold Counter's chest, detonating out in every direction, abruptly extinguishing every torch that belonged to the members Nailreign's army.

Then, just as the nova continued on into the recesses of Bane's Roth, and the goblins went on to re-light their torches after gathering themselves from the unanticipated blast, the skin of the Gold Counter began to change in hue. First, from a deathly white, similar to that of the northern snows, to a pinkish-salmon hue, and finally, a healthy beige glow of regularity.

It had been done.

The unthinkability of the plague's infliction - cured with Nailreign's infamous magic.

"I feel . . ." pausing to adjust, the Gold Counter gathered himself from the blast. "I feel . . . different."

He paused to breathe the forest air.

"I feel . . . alive . . . better! Have I just been cured?"

"Yes," the demonic lord confirmed. "You need never to worry of the plague's infliction again. Even if you were to return to my city, none of its unfavourable conditions could ever break your health again. You have been cured of its affliction. And because of you, my friend, my people can be cured of it as well."

Just then a roar of crazed cheering came from the army of cursed minions as they began jumping about, throwing each other around and bouncing wildly between the frosty trees. Never had such excitement come from such a deranged collection of forgotten minions. The celebration of Nailreign's army had only just begun. Some of them reached into their moldy side satchels, pulling forth oddly shaped receptacles of liquor, which they went on to swig in celebration.

"What about you? Your people? With these Geodes capable of curing the plague, tell me that you do not plan to raid the lands of Varroth's great citizens!" pressed the Gold Counter, praying that he had not just aided the demonic king.

"You needn't worry. Though foul, these beings are my own and they all have an equal right to live. They have just as much right to live amongst these lands as you do and so, even though we were never the ones to cause the plague of Crease in the first place, we will continue on to live there. Only now can we reside in better health, longer lives, and joyous prosperity."

The mindless cheering and violently playful tossing dulled to a dim before ceasing altogether.

"We have no plans to harm the human race in any way, just as long as they keep themselves separated from our domain."

A frigid breeze blew through the forest, rustling the overhead trees of their silver needles. The sensation was enough to spike the hairs of both the Gold Counter and his wife, but nevertheless it was a breeze of freedom across their skin. Nailreign absorbed its raw iciness with a deep inhale before he continued on to speak.

"Koraivindahl is likely to fall beneath the dwarves tonight. Their members are far stronger than those of the king's, but their measure of peace is different. Once done and the army of the Red Hand has been disbanded, there can be no chance of the king's pursuit against you or your wife ever again."

He paused, allowing a moment of serenity to overcome the two.

"As for Edgar, surely he will be fine. A spectral such as himself, inflicted with the thirst of the plague, will have the promise of yet another afterlife once he returns to me in Crease. Once I have brought a peaceful end to his spirit, the one he so desires come the incantation of the gemsand, he too will be free of his cursed imprisonment of thirst."

A feeling of relief warmed the Gold Counter's soul, seeing as Edgar and his unchanging ways had forever aided him since they had first met beneath the dead poplars of Crease's badlands.

"And your friend . . . Thul," Nailreign prompted.

The confidant looked from the demonic lord to his wife, and then back to the lord once again. He prayed that the arachnid had some sort of telepathic knowledge of his barbaric friend.

He did not.

"I am truly sorry . . . I know how much he meant to you. How much he helped you, and was there for you. I wish I could speak of him to you, but alas the magic within the fortress has barred me from knowing his well-being. But you must know, that everything that could have been done - was. And so, there is no sense of self-punishment for the helplessness of your companion."

Again, more tears began to pour from the Gold Counter's eyes. But that time, with the full realization that the bond between Thul and himself had come to a close. A man of robust strength, yet an even stronger desire to simply . . . be there. Just for his friend, in the search for his wife. The Royal Castle was never meant to be a place for Thul, and so he had journeyed there anyway . . .

"Are you ready to go home?" Nailreign questioned.

Without any knowledge of what was to come next, the Gold Counter and his wife placed their palms upon the redwood stump, just as their demonic friend had motioned for them to do.

"You must now only think of where you wish to be most," he instructed for a final time.

A reflection of the Gold Counter's cottage amongst the golden, meadow hills came to him. Its rustic walls and red thatch roof, gleaming in the prosperous beauty of the midday sun. Yet of all of what had brought him the most tranquility and inner harmony was the thought of the pureberry trees. Their beautiful branches of emerald leaves gently waving in the warm breeze.

Then, following the last of Nailreign's miraculous incantations . . .

Poof

The Gold Counter, along with his wife, vanished within the blink of an eye.

EPILOGUE

A season later - come the falling snow of Mid-Winter . . .

Since their escape from the Royal Castle's boundless dungeons and continuous halls of decorative imprisonment, a passing of the autumn months into that of the midwinter had instilled upon them a blanket of fresh snow that coated the landscape of innocent meadows.

Once home, and free of his plaguing disease, the Gold Counter had become blessed with yet another influx of knowledge and healing. One that his wife had failed to mention during their escape, but conceivably for good reason. Having given her incarceration, central to that of the most well-stocked alchemic laboratory within Varroth, she continued her work on the Elixir of Youth. It was a task that had been risky in itself, as the main reason for her presence there had been to prepare concoctions of pain-relief, antidotes and other such potions designed to aid the soldiers come their time in battle. Still, when she had the chance, she would slip away beyond that of the watchful eye in order to continue the elixir until its final completion.

Granted that its complex formula had, for a while, offered nothing more than failure after a multitude of attempts, she had finally succeeded in perfecting the Elixir of Youth. No longer did it offer the problematic discovery of speedily aging, just as the Gold Counter had fallen to once drinking the previous version. At long last, the potion had been created so that any who drink its mystical nectar were to be blessed with the eternal youthfulness of blossoming adulthood. To say exactly the age to which the consumer was to be returned was impossible, yet the fortitude of the elixir's assemblage of magical herbs and intricate additives made it so that the end result was an era of one to be within their early twenties.

Not long after their arrival home, sparking to existence after Nailreign's teleportation spell, did the couple go on to drink the elixir once his wife had prepared it from inside the trivialness of her own laboratory. Luckily, she had been able to seize the remaining ingredients needed from the king's alchemy lab before their escape from within the Royal Castle, concealing the precious elements inside of her girdle.

It took a few days for them to repair the residence. Once, all that time ago, the king had realized that the Gold Counter had gone missing, as did his collection of gold coins, their amount still yet to be counted for him, he went on to send a team of reinforcements. Evidently, their goal had been to search out the Gold Counter alongside the money, and so they went on to tear up his home, tossing every piece of furniture in their wake. Nothing of significant value was severely broken except a couple of windows, their dishware and his favourite pipe. Yet the marauders had failed to recover the coins he had buried beneath the mud and floorboards of his bedroom.

Upon realizing that the lump sum of coins, some 50,000 or more was still there, the Gold Counter and his wife came to the conclusion that such an amount would sustain them for at least a hundred years if not more. Even before the couple had been blessed with the massive collection of the king's money, they had done just fine surviving off the land – rabbits, fruit, the occasional fish. But even though a weight had been lifted, the Gold Counter still felt as though he couldn't spend it. He had once drawn Thul a map to his residence, come the misfortune of his own death, so that the barbarian could return and enjoy the treasure for himself. The outcome of their journey had been a terrible parting, opposite to that which he had predicted.

The Gold Counter, youthful once again with the body of a twenty-year-old, rose from his wicker throne which had forever remained next to the warmth of their cordial hearth. He made his way to the window that overlooked the front landscape. A vision of the land, born of calmness and serenity, came beaming through the foggy glass. Fog from the tea that his wife had been making from the cookery across their cozy quarters. It had gone on to breathe a steamy condensation amongst the window's glassy surfaces, yet upon wiping it clear gave way to an atmosphere that he had been within his entire life.

Out beyond the coating of the freshly fallen snow, existed a bounty of innocent rabbits, bounding through the white powder. Perchance they had been searching for food, yet the vegetable scraps that his wife continued to toss out over the season were more than ample. The rabbits' hops and stints of dashing were merely that of pleasantry. Surrounding them, came the fantasy of the whitened, gently-rolling hills that seemed to perpetually dip in and out of the earth – at least for as far as the eye could see through the gently falling snowflakes. But that which had blessed the Gold Counter with the touching embrace of actually being home once again was the pureberry trees. Though their leafless branches bore nothing more than a series of twigs; an ever twisting of woody arms, it was their appearance that had been most desirable to the Gold Counter over the course of his journey. Not because of the wine that their berries produced (though it was the best wine since the creation of time itself) but because, to the knowledge of the Gold Counter, the trees ceased to exist anywhere else amongst the land, hence making their appearance around their homestead all the more unique.

After a moment, having taken in the beauty of the land, the Gold Counter returned to his seat and went on to stock his secondary pipe. His less favourable one, but his pipe nonetheless. Over the season, the goreath thistle he kept bundled atop the hearth had kept its flavour, and so he went on to test it within the bowl of his pipe. It took only a couple draws on the funneling stem to produce a cloud of smoke. His wife had always wished him not to do so around the main chamber, however it was winter and he had, in fact, saved her life.

Once the thistles became a sturdy root of smoldering ember, the Gold Counter went on to gaze into the fire, reflecting back on his adventure just as he had done many a time since their arrival back home. To have made it in, through, and out the other side had been a miraculous success – an unimaginable triumph, especially given the number of times death had reached its mighty hand out to him, only to be shied away in the final moments.

How different could his journey had been had he never met Thul?

Sure, the barbarian had been the cause of many disturbances along the way. Many life-threating disturbances that is, yet it was his presence alongside the Gold Counter that had kept him alive at the same time. But his entire journey could have been different. It could have been impossible if he had left on his initial quest even a moment earlier, or perhaps a moment later. For he might have never boarded that same travel caravan alongside his companion, had the timing been different.

"Would you care for some tea, my love?" his wife spoke to him from the cookery, her porcelain, untainted, youthful skin glowing beneath a flow of golden locks and sapphire eyes.

He wished rather for a glass of foxfire whiskey instead, yet it was only just the end of day's morning, a little too early to start in on something with alcohol. He accepted her offer of the herbal tea, and continued to puff away on his pipe. Shortly after, she arrived at his side, placing before him on his modest side table, his glass of tea alongside a couple home baked cookies.

Oh, how he had missed her baking.

How he had missed her cooking, her crafting, her knitting. Her companionship, her warmth, her love.

How he had missed, just simply . . . her.

Too long had he been away from her. His other half taken from him, leaving only a corpse to rot from loneliness and utter despair. But though, during that time of magic and mystical wonder, such a journey had gone on to show that anything is possible. Anything one desires strongly enough can be achieved through the greatness of persistence, strength, confidence, and pursuit.

She kissed him on the cheek before standing once again, pivoting to turn back to the cookery. Obviously, she was ready to continue on with the baking of her winter treats. But before she had finished a full turn, she paused mid stance. At first, the Gold Counter thought nothing of it, sipping the sweetness from his cupful of boiling tea. Soon after, she went dashing across the room, over to the window that overlooked the front yard.

"By the Divines . . ." she whispered.

"What? What is it?" The Gold Counter turned in his chair, attempting to find what had his wife in such a state of awe.

"Come here! Quickly!" she beckoned to him.

He joined her at her side, peering out the window at what he had anticipated to be the playfulness of a couple of bunnies. Yet what he saw was the most extraordinary sight he would ever see in his entire life.

Through the gentle falling of the prairie's gradual snowflakes, a large man appeared from beyond the whiteness of the meadow. A couple of largely stuffed bags in one hand and a bottle of Old Monk rum in the other.

It was Thul.
And at his side,

A horse named Orist.

ABOUT THE AUTHOR

Debut fantasy author Andrew P. Wild displays a sense of humour in this novel that will leave you laughing out loud even as you cringe at some of his characters' antics. His love of exploring connections in human and paranormal situations in this off-kilter universe is the stuff of movies. With true wit and superior insight, Andy has crafted an epic fantasy that will leave readers looking for more. Andy lives in Victoria, B.C., where he is working on his next novel.

Printed in Canada